A Candle in the Window

Paul R Doherty

Copyright © 2015 by Paul R Doherty

All rights reserved.

This book is a work of fiction. The names and characters are the product of the author's imagination and any resemblance to actual persons, living or dead, is entirely coincidental.

ISBN: 150600962X
ISBN-13: 978-1506009629

DEDICATION

For my children Rachael and Matthew,
and in loving memory of my parents
Brian and Yvonne Doherty.

CONTENTS

	Acknowledgments	i
1	High expectations	3
2	Homecoming	25
3	Best laid plans	45
4	Repercussions	65
5	Old friends	89
6	Beyond recall	114
7	Festivities	140
8	Settling of scores	167
9	Tragedy	191
10	Coming to terms	210

11	Lost	230
12	Reunion	250
13	Revelations	271
14	New horizons	292
15	Antipathy	313
16	Conflict	338
17	Adjusting	360
18	False hopes	380
19	Deliverance	409
	Epilogue	443

ACKNOWLEDGMENTS

There are many family, friends and colleagues of whom I owe a special debt of thanks, and I am very conscious that this brief paragraph cannot do justice to the feelings of immense gratitude I feel for you all. I would like to extend a special thanks to my wife Marcia, for her patience, motivation and for simply "being there" throughout those long nights as I burnt the midnight oil. To my sisters, Marie, Anne-Marie and Bernadette, again a huge thank you for your support and for "filling in the blanks" on those tricky parts where my memory failed me. To my friends John Moore, Kevin Beech, Tim Bailey, Bernard Lowry, and Matt Harris, I am sincerely grateful for your help in distilling my ideas, proof reading manuscripts and generally keeping me going throughout this journey. To Heidi Cherry for her patient correcting of my poor literary skills, and finally to my wider family, friends and colleagues that have taken the time to support me in so many different ways during this work, I thank you all. Enjoy.

"This above all: to thine own self be true."

William Shakespeare
Hamlet (Act I, Scene III)

1
HIGH EXPECTATIONS

"Lord, give me strength," Erin Devlin breathed despairingly. Gazing out of the small living room window, she pursed her lips as the garden gate swung closed, and a sandy haired, young boy strolled nonchalantly up her path.

At thirty-seven, Erin was still striking, with raven black hair tied tightly in a long ponytail, grey-blue eyes and pale complexion typical of many Irish women. In her youth she had been stunning, but the hard toil of rural living and the raising of four children had imposed a certain hardening to her features. Erin's demeanour, always somewhat stern, grew graver still as she eyed her visitor's approach.

"Oh Dónal O'Connor...you're a bad lad," she sighed gently under her breath. Dónal was her eldest son Thomas' best friend. Tom, as he preferred to be known, idolised Dónal and to Erin's consternation, Dónal knew this. The boys were of similar age, Dónal slightly older, and inseparable. But whereas Erin had high hopes for Tom and had fashioned what she hoped was a growing sense of responsibility; Dónal she regarded, even at ten, as a lost cause. He was a wild child and often encouraged her son to participate in one silly prank after another, exploits that invariably ended in tears for Tom at home in the evenings, especially on those rare occasions when his father was there.

The knock at the front door announced Dónal's arrival. With a slight shake of her head, Erin tucked the dusting cloth she had been holding into her apron and crossed into the small hallway.

"Hello Mrs Devlin," the boy said pleasantly when the door finally opened.

"Dónal."

"Is Tom in? Can he come out?"

For a moment the thought flashed through her mind to lie; to pretend she had sent Tom to work in their vegetable garden or attend some such errand. Yet as soon as that thought had materialised, all hope of its fruition vanished as her son's voice resounded from further back in the house. "Mam, who's at the door?"

Sighing again somewhat dramatically, Erin called back, "It's just Donny." Donny was the pet name she used for Dónal. Erin knew that only Dónal's grandmother called him that...and that he hated it. Bounding down the stairs two at a time, Tom Devlin raced to the front door. Skinny and slightly small for his age, Tom also possessed the black hair and pale complexion of his mother but, whereas Erin's features were set into an almost enduring frown, Tom's face was ever alive and joyful. Still standing in the doorway and blocking his exit, Erin fixed her son with a cold stare.

"Hello Dónal," Tom said trying to squeeze past her.

"Hi," his friend replied. "I'm going fishing at the Big Pool, do you fancy coming? The river's in spate with all the rain we had last night, and I reckon the banks will be soft enough to get some nice black-heads – "

"Black-heads?" Erin interrupted questioningly.

"Worms, Mrs Devlin. Black-headed worms; they're much better at staying on the hook than the common red-headed ones."

Erin pursed her lips once again.

Finally squirming past, Tom turned his face expectantly towards his mother. Stalling for time, Erin folded her arms across her chest. *What mischief could they get into by the river in any case*, she thought. *Aside from drowning themselves, of course.*

"Please Mam?" Tom pleaded.

Any final resistance crumbled when a loud crash, followed seconds later by a baby's intense crying, resounded from within the house.

"Mam! Mam!" A girl's voice shouted excitedly. "Wee Cianán's pulled the tea-table down on himself." 'Wee' Cianán was Erin's youngest child and at 14 months was just beginning to walk, with obvious consequences. Seeing his mother's hesitation, Tom pressed home his case.

"I'll be careful Mam, I promise, and I'll be home for tea. We can always call at Gran's for lunch if we're hungry."

"I'll look out for him, Mrs Devlin," Dónal added. That nearly scuppered Tom's chances but before Erin had a chance to change her mind and frame a suitable reply, another crash, followed by renewed howls of protest, ended all deliberations.

"Oh, away with you both," Erin said, turning from the doorway and hurrying back into the house. "And mind you are back for tea Thomas Devlin," she added over her shoulder. "Or there will be hell to pay."

"Aye Mam," Tom replied, grinning at her

retreating back. "Come on!" With a friendly punch on Dónal's arm, both boys sprinted down the path and dashed out through the open gate.

From the gateway, a narrow unmade track way with high overgrown earth banks descended steeply down to the village of Ballyfinan, a quarter of a mile or so below. The track way, known locally as Cairn Lane, also continued uphill for several hundred metres towards the summit of Croaghennan Mór before finally petering out near a small area of ancient standing stones. No other properties were situated above Tom's home, but downhill the lane dissected the only other dwelling between it and the village, that of Quigley's Farm. Like many farmsteads in Donegal during the early 1930s, Quigley's Farm was small and comprised essentially of a score of beef cattle, together with a few dozen hardy Blackface mountain sheep wandering the surrounding fields and high ground. Quigley's Farm was owned by a bad-tempered, ill-disposed character that most residents of Ballyfinan tried to avoid. Like his father and grandfather before him, Séamus Quigley allowed his sheep to roam at will on other people's land and, if unopposed, endeavoured to claim that land as his own after 12 years of "squatters' rights". Such actions had earned the Quigley family considerable land holdings over the years but, conversely, few friends in the village. Tom and Dónal had managed to establish a lucrative scheme from Séamus Quigley's exploits by charging two shillings a day for rounding up and chasing off all Quigley marked sheep from non-Quigley farmland. A fact that had, undoubtedly, added to Mr Quigley's irritability and antipathy, towards the boys in particular.

Approaching Quigley's Farm, Tom and Dónal slowed to a walk and became serious. Séamus Quigley had, on many occasions, shouted at them for running through his farmyard, and once had actually set his two dogs after them. On their right as they walked through, the main farmyard expanded towards a two storey, but rather run-down looking, farmhouse. A few chickens scratched about hungrily in the muddy yard, and lounging by the farmhouse door, Quigley's sheep dogs watched the boys intently. To the left, a small mud-churned paddock fenced in the cattle who paid the boys no attention whatsoever.

"Can you see him?" Tom asked quietly, his eyes however not leaving the dogs.

"No, just keep going," Dónal replied. "The lazy sod's probably still in bed."

"At ten in the morning, and on a Saturday?" To Tom, Saturday was an amazing day; it was *his* day. The one time in the week when he did not have to attend school, work in the garden, or carry out any one of numerous chores his mother could devise for him. Similarly, being a Saturday, there was no requirement to attend church. It was incredulous to him that anyone would want to waste a minute of such a day by staying in bed!

Dónal just shrugged.

Cairn Lane emerged directly into the central area of Ballyfinan village. Ballyfinan itself was a small rural community typical of countless others within the Innishowen peninsula of northern Donegal. With a population of just under six hundred everyone, more or less, knew everyone else; a fact much to the boys' annoyance since any misdeed was invariably witnessed by someone that knew them, and always reported back to their parents. The village had a small general store, run by a very austere widow named Mrs Brennan; a bank (which only opened on Saturday mornings); a doctor's surgery and seven bars. In the central area, known locally as 'the Square', was also a single petrol pump and behind this a blacksmiths-cum-garage. Very few in Ballyfinan owned an automobile, and other than walking, horse drawn transport was still the principal means of travel. A single main road ran more or less straight through the village, its entrance from the south straddled on either side by Ballyfinan's largest building, St Mary's Roman Catholic Church, and the village cemetery. The 'High Street' as this road was commonly known, after passing through the Square finally left Ballyfinan to continue a more tortuous route to the sea, two miles distant at Tullagh Bay. A stone bridge, high arched and covered in lichen, marked the northern end of Ballyfinan. A few hundred yards to the west of the village, a small watercourse, the Finan River, flowed generally parallel to the road, meandering in sinuous loops before diving under the bridge on its journey to Tullagh Bay. The Finan River was tidal as far upstream as the village, and offered excellent fishing for salmon, brown trout and sea trout (or white trout, as it was known locally). From the church to the Finan Bridge, Ballyfinan was less than half a mile long and along the road's length a number of small trackways, of which Cairn Lane was but one, merged from the surrounding countryside.

Stepping into the Square, the boys stopped to watch a small flock of twenty or so Blackface mountain sheep being driven ahead of them, northwards along the main road by a young fair-haired boy their own age. As the last of the sheep passed, Tom shouted, "Hey, Brendan! Where're you going?"

Turning to face them, Brendan Harkin waved and pointed vaguely in the direction of the Finan Bridge. "Down the Binnion Road to the Lower Fields, my Da wants to look them over this afternoon."

Like Cairn Lane, the Binnion Road was another trackway that led off the High Street, also snaking its way northwards in the general direction of the sea. After the Finan Bridge, the High Street itself became known as the Tullagh Road.

Leaving the flock to mill on their own, Brendan

trotted over to stand by the boys. "Is your Da back from the boats yet, Tom?" he asked cordially.

Tom shook his head. "No. Mam thinks Sunday night, or perhaps Monday. Depends on the weather, I suppose." Tom's father, Sean Devlin, like many men in the village not directly employed in farming, was a fisherman. He spent the winter months far out at sea working on the big trawlers operating out of Killybegs in West Donegal. In the late spring he would return and, along with his brother Cianán, who owned a small 25 ft open launch, would spend the summer fishing inshore for salmon, lobsters and other commercially valuable species off the Innishowen coast. Sean, along with many fathers and older brothers in Ballyfinan was expected home this weekend for the summer fishing season.

"We're going down to the river later, want to join us?" Tom continued.

Brendan glanced over to the sheep and frowned. "I'd like to but, well, my Da told me to stay with them until he comes back from Dunkeeny." Dunkeeny was fifteen miles south of Ballyfinan and the only true town of any size in the district.

"How long will that be?" Tom asked.

Brendan just shrugged. Both Tom and Dónal knew Brendan's father had a reputation for drinking heavily, and if he had gone into Dunkeeny in the morning would invariably spend the rest of the day in some bar.

"You could always leave 'em in the lower fields," Dónal suggested. "They won't wander far."

"Yeah, and get my hide tanned when Da returns and finds me gone. Sure, no thanks."

"Suit yourself. Come on Tom." Dónal turned and began walking towards the bridge. Tom glanced after his friend and then back to Brendan who was glaring after Dónal's retreating back. Brendan, like many of the other boys in the village did not like Dónal very much.

"Well, if you're sure Brendan….you know, if you change your mind we'll be down by the Big Pool. You never know, your Da may get back early?"

Brendan's sceptical face was the only reply needed. Both boys knew how likely that was.

"Well, if not I'll see you at Church tomorrow," Tom added.

"Aye." Looking over at the sheep he continued, "I'd better go. See you Tom."

"You too. Have fun!"

Brendan laughed. "Aye."

Running to catch up with Dónal, they continued

together in silence, walking casually over to the bridge. Leaning against the rough cut stonework they watched as Brendan soon disappeared from view along with the noisy flock down the narrow Binnion Road.

"I'd have left them in the fields," Dónal said finally. "Brendan worries too much."

For a moment a sudden tide of anger welled up within Tom at Dónal's insensitivity. "At least you haven't got a Da who's drunk most of the day and is happy to beat you given half a chance!" he snapped crossly.

For a second Dónal's eyes flared but then his head dropped and he remained silent, staring at the ground. Seeing his pained expression and obvious discomfort, Tom's anger instantly evaporated. Flushing, he shamefully regretted the outburst. He had never met Dónal's father and it was common, though rarely mentioned, knowledge in the village that he had left Dónal's mother, Aoife O'Connor, apparently for another woman, when the boy was only a few months old. All Erin Devlin would ever say on the subject when questioned was that Dónal's father was *"lazy, good for nothing, self-centred and selfish"* and that his friend was better off without him. Privately Erin attributed the root cause of Dónal's poor behaviour to the lack of a firm father figure in his life. Whilst, to be fair, she was prepared to admit that was hardly the boy's fault, Erin nonetheless believed Aoife O'Connor should do more to control her wayward son.

After a few moments of awkward silence, Tom eventually said gently, "I'm sorry Dónal, I didn't mean to mention your Da like that."

Dónal, still looking down at his feet, shrugged lightly. "It's okay," he replied, absently picking some encrusted lichen from the bridge stonework. Looking up Dónal's gaze passed over Tom's shoulder, focussing back towards the village centre. A slow grin stole over his face as he indicated towards Cairn Lane.

A familiar firm voice followed by a high pitched squeal instantly drew Tom's attention. Emerging from the lane, Tom's mother stole a glance left and right before striding purposely across the Square, each hand firmly held onto his younger twin sisters, Roisin and Niamh. Wee Cianán was strapped to Erin's back in a sling. As usual both girls were squabbling much to the boys' delight. As Erin half dragged, half led her daughters across the street towards Mrs Brennan's store, the baby caught sight of Tom and began yelling loudly, desperate to attract his older brother's attention.

Dónal nudged his friend. "Best make yourself scarce before your Mam sees you."

Tom nodded. "Aye....she's bound to make me help with shopping if she catches us lounging about."

As if to reinforce the point, Tom's sisters, attracted by Cianán's cries, had also seen him and were similarly trying to draw their mother's notice. Without another word, both boys scrambled over the low bridge wall and slid down the grassy embankment to the Finan River. Grinning, they ran downstream along the bank of the small river, weaving in and out of numerous, well established gorse bushes, interspersed amongst the closely cropped grass. Within moments they were out of sight from the bridge and free! The gorse, at that time of the year, was covered in bright yellow, sweet smelling flowers, and Tom breathed in deeply, relishing the simple pleasure of the honey-sweet scent. He knew Dónal would call him a girl, a sissy, or worse if he mentioned it, but he didn't care; nothing could spoil his feeling of wellbeing. Nonetheless he did keep his thoughts on the attractiveness of life generally, and the flowers in particular, to himself.

After a few minutes the boys slowed to a sedate stroll; they were approaching the Big Pool. The Big Pool was a famed fishing point on the Finan River and was located in the apex of a large meander. The fact that the dynamics of the river's flow over the years had progressively scoured away the bed at this precise location to form the pool was immaterial to the boys. All they, and indeed most of the male population of Ballyfinan, cared about was that the cool depths of the pool was a favourite location for freshly run salmon to rest on their journey upstream to spawn. Adjacent to the pool, a stunted old willow leaned out over the water, its long overhanging branches providing shade and concealment for the fish below. Not only were fish of all sizes hidden from the sight of herons and the like, but the leafy canopy also made traditional fly casting into the pool very difficult. A fact not lost on Dónal.

"Jesus, would you look at that!" Dónal exclaimed suddenly as they stepped around a particularly large gorse bush and viewed the Big Pool. At first Tom saw nothing to warrant his friend's excitement. The clear surface sparkled in the early spring sunshine and a few leaves swirled lazily in the gentle eddies formed by the current. Shaking his head Tom glanced back at his friend.

"There, you eejit," Dónal whispered, pointing towards the river's edge under the tree's shadow. "Are you blind?"

For a few moments Tom still could not see what was capturing Dónal's attention. He was about to say so when he finally registered a slight movement in the water. The unmistakable snout of a salmon's head had gently broken the surface. It remained visible for a few seconds before slowing sinking back once more a few inches under the water. With slow deliberate movements of its tail and fins the fish maintained its position in the channel, before gently rising again. This time the salmon's dorsal fin and tail broke the surface and in the crystal clear water there could be no mistake; the fish had to be nearly three feet long!

"Wow," Tom gasped. "He's huge!"

"Quiet!" Dónal snapped, but it was too late. Whether alerted by Tom's excitable cry, or pure coincidence, was now irrelevant. With a single flick of its great tail, the salmon vanished from sight into the pool's depths.

Both boys stood silently watching the spot where the great fish had been, disappointment etched on their faces. After a few moments, Tom tentatively took hold of Dónal's arm and led him gently away from the river bank. Whispering so as to avoid spooking any other fish that may be lying up he said, "That was a beauty Dónal, but we need to get the poles and dig some bait in any case. Let's get set up and come back, we may get lucky?"

Tom was guiding his friend slightly inland in the direction of a small, ruined single storey stone house, partially hidden by the ubiquitous gorse. The thatched roof and supporting timbers of this once neat farmer's cottage had long since fallen in, and the ravages of time and weather had now only left three of the walls standing. The ruins themselves provided a convenient shelter for the numerous sheep that grazed the lowland plain of the Finan River, as well as providing the perfect hideout, and secret den, for Tom and Dónal. With the arrival of spring and the steady improvement to the weather, both boys had managed over the preceding weeks to store a variety of odds and ends at their den, including two stout ash fishing poles, together with lines, hooks and lead weights. Their treasures also included a variety of tins, a small trowel, a couple of rough hewn wooden catapults, and a sharp, if rusty, fillet knife. Dónal's prize item, however, was a box of matches stolen from his mother's kitchen.

Arriving at the old cottage, Tom stepped carefully over the jumbled heap of moss and lichen encrusted stones that had once formed the south wall. Inside, the stone floor was filthy with the accumulated mud and dirt of many years' exposure to the elements and animal habitation. The boys, however, had previously cleared a space against the, more or less intact, west wall. It was here that they had hidden their possessions, protecting them from the weather by an old sheet of corrugated iron and a number of hessian farm sacks.

"Give us a hand," Tom said, bending down to grasp the corrugated sheet. When no reply resounded, Tom glanced round, puzzled. Dónal was still outside the ruins, staring back towards the river. "Are you okay? What's wrong?"

Dónal turned to regard Tom and just smiled. "We won't be needing the poles. Come back out, but bring that cloth you got from your Mam the other day."

Frowning, Tom nonetheless obeyed, grabbing the now not so clean tea towel Erin had used previously to wrap his lunch in. The fact that he had 'forgotten to bring it home' had not been lost on her, and Tom had gone to bed without supper that night, and Erin's scathing words ringing in his ears.

"Why do you want it?" Tom asked, returning to stand beside Dónal.

His friend just winked. "I'll show you."

Walking cautiously back to the river, Dónal pulled a curled length of thin wire from his pocket. Carefully unravelling it, Tom saw that one end of the wire comprised a long, free sliding loop, and the other end had been bent over and twisted on itself to form a grip handle.

"That looks like – "

"A rabbit snare?" Dónal interrupted. "Aye. Give us that rag would you." Taking it, Dónal wrapped the cloth tightly around his hand and grasped the grip end of the snare. "I twisted this handle so I could hold it," he explained. "See?"

Tom shook his head, still confused. "But what do you want it for?"

"Watch," Dónal smiled in return.

As they heard the river, Dónal signalled silently

for them both to crouch down low. Creeping slowly forward, they edged towards the bank of the Big Pool.

"There!" Dónal exclaimed hardly above a whisper. "He's back." Tom was smiling too now. The salmon they had seen earlier had returned to the same spot; its tail and dorsal fins clearly visible breaking the surface. "I'm gonna try and snare him," he continued quietly. "Don't move Tom, we don't want to scare him again."

Lying on his stomach, Dónal inched forward, his eyes never leaving the beautiful fish just a few feet before him. For Tom, watching behind, time seemed to stand still. At one point the salmon moved slightly within the channel and Dónal froze for several minutes, until he was happy that the fish had settled once more. Hardly daring to breathe, Dónal finally reached the water's edge. The salmon was less than a foot away. With infinite slowness, Dónal stretched out his arm, the snare inches from the fish's tail.

After remaining tense and still for so long, the sudden explosion of movement and Dónal's excited cries made Tom jump. Quick as a flash Dónal had slipped the snare over the salmon's tail; in that instant the fish had finally recognised the danger and dived, but it was a fraction too late. The swipe of its powerful tail coupled with the effect of Dónal jerking the snare upwards and away, had pulled the loop tight trapping it. Unfortunately for Dónal, he had underestimated the strength of the huge salmon. His cries of delight quickly changed to dismay as the fish thrashed violently and fought to get away. Trying to stand, his arm was wrenched violently from side to side, and with a final wail, he plunged head-first into the river.

"Dónal!" Tom screamed. Sprinting to the bank he watched, panic-stricken, as his friend was twisted round and round under the water. Within moments, however, Dónal broke the surface, gasping for air. For what seemed liked minutes to Tom but was in reality only a few seconds, Dónal thrashed and struggled before finally being able to plant his feet on the bottom. Fortunately, this near to the sea, the Finan River widened and as such was comparatively shallow, though nonetheless the water still reached the boy's chest. Tom stood mesmerised; fascinated as the huge fish frantically beat the water, trying to escape, and steadily dragging Dónal along with it.

Dónal's excited cries suddenly stirred Tom from his pseudo-trance. "Tom!" he called, his own voice shrill, "Get something to hit this thing with."

When Tom hesitated Dónal swore at him to move. Looking wildly around, Tom shook his head in disbelief. "There's nothing here!"

"Well, bloody find something! Hurry up, I can't hold on much longer."

Spurred into action, Tom scrambled along the

riverbank, frantically searching for something to use. Skidding to a halt by a few moss-covered boulders and rock slabs poking through the grass, he desperately tried to lift one after another, but they were far too heavy to move.

"Come on!" Dónal urged from behind. Cursing, and feeling panic rising again, Tom scanned left and right, his gaze finally falling on a thick piece of driftwood, washed up onto the bank by some forgotten flood. Grabbing the wood, Tom sprinted back to the river.

"Here, I found this," he cried in triumph. "What shall I do?" Dónal looked near exhausted; the salmon was still struggling as vigorously as ever.

"Get in here!" he shouted.

"But I'll get soaked, and Mam will..."

"Jesus, Tom! Just do it! Sod what your Mam'll say for once, this fish is pulling my bloody arm off!"

Somewhat reluctantly, Tom slid gingerly down the bank and into the flowing current. The water was icy cold. Wading carefully across towards his friend, he bit his lip to prevent gasping aloud.

Dónal's face was covered in water, mud and weed. Through clenched teeth he said, "I'll try and pull his head up; when I do, hit it as hard as you can."

With both hands wrapped round the cloth-covered snare, Dónal heaved backwards, dragging the salmon to the surface. Closing his eyes, Tom smashed the stick down hard onto the water. "Careful!" Dónal swore, glaring at him. "That just missed me."

Although Tom's strike had missed the fish, the force of the impact had spurred the salmon into an increased frenzy.

"Hit him again, Tom!" Dónal shouted. Raising the stick high over his head, Tom, pausing to aim this time, again slammed the branch down. Within seconds he was raining repeated blows, water and small, rotten splinters of wood flying in all directions. More by luck than judgement, one blow struck the salmon squarely on the head, momentarily stunning it.

Feeling the salmon's struggles falter Dónal began to step backwards towards the bank. Smiling at Tom, he said, "Help me get him on the bank. Quickly now, before he starts off again."

Still holding the branch, Tom followed after Dónal. With his free hand he grasped the snare below the makeshift handle and pulled. Working together, the boys soon hauled the subdued fish through the water to the bank. As its body scraped the shallowing gravels of the river bed, the salmon awoke to the danger and began to writhe once more. However, weakened by its fight, it was too late and with one final heave they dragged the fish free of the water, and collapsed in a muddy heap on the bank. Flinging himself across the salmon's flanks, Dónal managed to restrain its thrashing. "Once more, Tom" he said breathlessly. "That ought to do it."

Doing as he was told, Tom struck the fish's head once more, and with a final quiver the great salmon finally lay still. Looking from one to another and then back at the fish, for a moment both boys stared in silence. Then in spontaneous delight, peals of resounding laughter echoed over the now still waters.

2
HOMECOMING

"Well?" said Tom, as Dónal emerged back onto the street.

"I told him to stuff it," his friend replied in disgust. "The mean old sod only offered me a penny a pound. For that money I'd told him we might as well feed it to the cats!"

Somewhat despondently the boys slouched against the outside wall of Kearney's Bar, and silently considered their next move. Since mid-morning they had carried their huge prize to all the bars in the village, but after having it weighed, no one would buy their twenty six pound fish. Well, not for the price they thought it was worth. Kearney's Bar was the last in Ballyfinan where they hoped to sell the salmon. It was now well past lunchtime and hunger, plus fatigue from the effort in carrying the heavy fish, was beginning to take the edge off their enthusiasm. The warm spring sunshine was also taking its toll, particularly on Dónal's temper.

Suddenly Tom's face brightened. "We could try Father Aidan, he might give us something?"

"And why in God's name would he do that?" Dónal replied incredulously.

"Well, er, he might buy it and give it to some poor family."

Dónal shook his head. "He'll more likely make us donate it, and then give it away."

Again they fell silent. Lost in their own thoughts, neither noticed Séamus Quigley's slow, ponderous approach towards Kearney's Bar. Whilst only in his early forties and still relatively young, Quigley had nonetheless let himself go. Naturally a big man, he was nevertheless a good two stone overweight. A mass of dark curls, greasy from lack of washing, hung limply down his fleshy jowls which, together with a heavy stubble growth, did little to enhance his appearance. Despite his looks, the mind behind Séamus Quigley's somewhat bloodshot eyes was sharp, and calculating.

"I see you lads have been poaching salmon again, then?" Quigley said, stopping in front of the boys. He nudged the fish at their feet with his boot. "Not a bad size, too."

"Ah no, Mr Quigley," Tom said politely. "We caught him this morning."

"Hmm...I'd like to see the rod you two owned that'd pull a fish this big from the river." Quigley replied dubiously.

"We borrowed Tom's Da's rod," Dónal answered, a

little too quickly Tom thought.

Quigley turned, looking hard at Tom. "I didn't think your Da was back yet?"

"He's not," Dónal answered before Tom could say anything. "But he said Tom could use his gear whilst he was away, so long as he looked after it." Dónal's face was a picture of sincerity whilst Tom, remaining silent, squirmed uncomfortably. Unlike Dónal, lying did not come easily to him. Seeing the younger boy's discomfort, Quigley's eyes narrowed suspiciously.

"Well, to be sure now, perhaps I should take this fish to the Garda to see what he has to say." Stooping towards the salmon he continued, "I wouldn't want you boys to get into any further trouble now."

Despite his bulk, Séamus Quigley could move quickly when he had a mind to. Before either boy could react, he had reached down, and with a grunt, hoisted the salmon onto his shoulders.

"No, Mr Quigley!" Tom cried. "That's our fish!"

Ignoring the protests, Quigley began walking slowly back towards the village centre. Ballyfinan had no formal police station but the local Garda, Pat Doherty, lived in the house next to Mrs Brennan's general store, the ground floor given over to an office. Whilst on duty, if not cycling the countryside, he could almost always be found at his station house.

Cries of anguish, coupled with the spectacle of Séamus Quigley holding aloft a huge salmon from two distraught boys, soon began to draw attention from passers by. A number of puzzled looks and a few comments were directed towards them but, undeterred, Quigley marched on towards the Garda's house. Unfortunately for Tom and Dónal one of those attracted to the commotion was most unwelcome.

"Thomas Devlin!" Erin shouted from the doorway of a house they had just passed. "What in the Lord's name is going on?"

Erin had been visiting a friend for lunch when she had heard the disturbance as the trio had passed by the open window. Tom, Dónal and Séamus Quigley all froze and then slowly turned to face her. Despite the almost comical spectacle, Erin's eyes flared as she took in her son's dishevelled, wet and mud-stained appearance. Her anger was clearly only just being kept in check as she snapped, "Look at your clothes, they're filthy! What have you been up to?" Tom opened his mouth to speak then thought better off it. "And where are your shoes!" Erin continued in exasperation. Dónal, along with many boys at that time, did not own a pair of shoes. In consideration of his friend's situation, Tom often refrained from wearing his own as much as possible when they were together. His mother did not share his sensitivities and insisted that he wear his shoes at all times when out of the house.

Tom swallowed nervously; he had kicked them off that morning after sprinting through the open gate into Cairn Lane, and in all likelihood they were lying discarded under a bush somewhere.

"Mam, I...we were..."

"And what have you to say for yourself, Mr

Quigley?" Erin interrupted, as if noticing the farmer for the first time.

"Well now, Mrs Devlin, it's like this," Quigley smiled pleasantly. "The boys have been helping me down by the river. I'd caught this grand fish here, but slipped on the muddy bank trying to bring him in; the lads helped out and we all got a wee bit wet and dirty like. It's my fault, now, and you mustn't go blaming the boys. Isn't that right lads?" Quigley glanced down at them, still smiling. Inwardly fuming, neither Tom nor Dónal said anything.

"So what was all the shouting about?" Erin enquired quietly.

"Why, I am sorry about that too, Mrs Devlin, but you know what boys are like. They wanted to carry the fish again but as you can see it's a fair weight now, and after dropping it twice already I said no. It is, after all, my fish and I didn't want it damaged."

Privately, Erin Devlin didn't believe a word Quigley had said. Everyone in the village knew he had no interest in fishing and the thought of him spending a Saturday afternoon by the river instead of drinking in one of the village bars was absurd. Still frowning she looked back at her son and slightly raised an eyebrow, her meaning clear.

Tom's mind was racing. The salmon was theirs. They hadn't poached it, just caught it, arguably, in an unscrupulous manner. Quigley had no right to say otherwise or, as was plainly evident, to try and steal it and keep it for himself. However to admit the truth would, likely as not, simply invoke his mother's wrath further. In all likelihood she would drag them both down to the Garda for using a snare, and they would still lose their catch. She would, at the very least, also ban him from playing with Dónal for ages, seeing him once again as the cause of this trouble.

Glancing at his friend, the resigned barely perceptible nod confirmed to Tom that Dónal had reached the same, inevitable conclusion.

"I'm sorry Mam," he said quietly. It was all he could manage to say. Erin paused for a moment before replying. "And so you should be, carrying on so. Now wait for me here whilst I collect the twins and wee Cianán from Mrs Comisky." Turning to Dónal she added, "Best you go home straight away too, my lad, and get cleaned up. I can't imagine what your mother will say."

Dónal just nodded; he knew better than to argue with Tom's mother, especially in her present mood.

"And I'll be away too then," Quigley said, still smiling amiably. "Good day to you, Mrs Devlin. Bye lads, and thanks again for all your help." The last was said with a sly wink, unseen by Erin. Neither Tom nor Dónal answered; both simply stared after him. It was no surprise to either that he walked passed Mrs Brennan's store and Pat Doherty's house without stopping. Crossing the main street, Séamus Quigley turned right into Cairn Lane and disappeared. From the doorway of Mrs Comisky's house Erin Devlin appeared, Tom's younger sisters and brother in tow.

Seeing the two of them still standing together Erin

growled, "Away with you now Dónal O'Connor...Tommy, home now." The boys shared a quick look; nothing further needed to be said. Dónal silently walked away towards his mother's house on the opposite side of the village, in the direction of St Mary's Church. Watching his friend depart, Tom felt like crying. *Why was life so unfair? How dare Quigley steal their fish!* Despair, however, was soon replaced by anger. He would get even with Séamus Quigley somehow! But his thoughts for vengeance were suddenly curtailed by a new and more impending concern. With his mother by his side, how was he going to retrieve his shoes before she saw them?

*

Sunday morning dawned bright, if rather chilly. The wind had backed somewhat northerly during the night and freshened considerably, sending the few wispy clouds racing across an otherwise unbroken blue sky.

Despite the apparent promise of a fine spring morning, an open turf fire burned briskly in the living room of the Devlin household. Tom had long since finished breakfast and was sitting quietly by the hearth, trying his best to keep out of everyone's, and particularly his mother's, way. There was only one priority, from Erin Devlin's perspective, on Sunday mornings and that was church. Sunday Mass at St Mary's started at ten thirty, which meant leaving the house by ten at the latest in order for the family to walk the mile or so, and arrive with enough time to get a good seat. Being late was not an option and even Tom's twin sisters knew better than to play up on a Sunday morning. Wee Cianán, however, was a law unto himself.

Tom glanced up at the old clock over the mantelpiece. It was already five past ten and no one else was downstairs yet. This didn't bode well.

As usual he was dressed in his Sunday best; a freshly starched white shirt, green jumper, black trousers and, of course, clean shoes. He had felt quite pleased with himself the previous afternoon, having managed to surreptitiously distract his mother with a pretend sighting of a bird's nest in the undergrowth. As Erin had, somewhat dubiously, scanned the hedgerow, Tom had secretly retrieved his shoes from under an adjacent bush. If Erin had been aware of his subterfuge, she had given no sign.

Fidgeting uncomfortably, Tom ran his finger around the inside of his shirt collar. Despite pinching his neck and numerous protests in the past, his mother always insisted that the top button was done up. *"Jesus suffered on the cross for you Thomas Devlin, the least you can do is look presentable for Him on Sundays,"* was one of her favourite sayings whenever he brought the matter up.

Sighing, Tom stood and tried once more to stretch his neck. At that precise moment, Erin suddenly appeared at the living room doorway. "Are you ready, Tommy?" she asked.

"Aye Mam."

"Good boy. Run upstairs now and tell your sisters that if they're not down here with coats and shoes on in one minute, they'll feel the back of my hand."

Erin's threat proved unwarranted since Roisin and Niamh were already coming down the stairs as Tom went to fetch them.

"Hurry up, Mam's wanting to go," he said. Roisin ignored him as she skipped past to the front door; Niamh simply poked her tongue out. In moments Erin joined them, Cianán nestled in his carry pack on her back, still snivelling following his recent howls of protest at having been forcibly made to get ready for church. Giving her three older children a final look, Erin nodded in satisfaction, and opened the front door.

St Mary's Roman Catholic Church was the focal point for religious worship in Ballyfinan; virtually the entire village was Catholic and, more to the point, practising. In such a small, tightly knit community, few could afford to offend their neighbours, or Father Aidan, by so blatant an act as refusing to attend Sunday Mass. Among those few that did, however, were Aoife O'Connor, and her son Dónal.

Having arrived impeccably, with a minute to spare, Tom and his family sat in their normal seats towards the back of the church. Cianán remained uncommonly quiet during what was an unusually short, and to Tom's mind, uninspiring service. As Ballyfinan's Parish Priest, Father Aidan was famed for his blunt, no nonsense manner. Rarely did he protract a service and today, to Tom's, and if truth were told, most of the congregation's approval, he fairly sped through the prayers and restricted the customary hymns to only three verses each. As a result, Mass was over by a little after eleven o'clock.

Outside the church, Tom and his sisters waited around as Erin chatted cordially with numerous women from the village. Bored, Tom began to walk down the church path towards the boundary wall and entrance gates. Either side of the path small children ran in and out of the gravestones, chasing each other with screams of laughter, earning shouts of disapproval from irate parents. Deep in thought, he didn't notice a young girl running to catch up with him.

"Hello Tommy," the girl said reaching his side.

Starting slightly, Tom turned and smiled. "Oh, hi Cathleen. How are you?"

"Grand. And yourself?"

Tom shrugged. "Okay, I guess."

Cathleen Kearney was nearly a year older than Tom, like him slightly built, but at least two inches taller. She was also very pretty. Like Tom, Cathleen was wearing her Sunday best, a red flowery dress the colour of which matched her long auburn hair and pale blue eyes perfectly. The Kearneys and the Devlins, as well as being related, were also close friends. Tom and Cathleen's grandmothers were sisters, and from his earliest memory, such was the closeness of their relationship, he and Cathleen, officially second cousins, had regarded each other as brother and sister.

Walking by his side, Cathleen said, "I overheard my Mam talking with Mrs Comisky earlier, you know, before Mass." When Tom did not answer, she carried on, "Mrs Comisky said you and Dónal had tried to steal Mr Quigley's salmon. Is it true?"

Tom stopped and stared at his friend. The bitter memory of yesterday resurfaced and, frowning, he shook his head. "No, it's not. Dónal and I caught the fish ourselves and Quigley took it from us. We were trying to get it back when my Mam saw us."

"Oh, but that's awful! Why would he do such a thing?"

Again, Tom shrugged. "Who knows, but Da's always said he's a bad piece of work." Pausing for a moment he stared into space. "But I'm going to get even with him though."

The expression on Cathleen's young face grew serious. "Be careful Tom, Mr Quigley scares me. My Mam doesn't like him either, but has always warned me to keep out of his way."

Tom only nodded.

The arrival of Erin Devlin and the rest of Tom's family forestalled any further conversation on the subject.

"Hello Cathleen, your Mam's looking for you up by the church," Erin said pleasantly. Taking the hint, Cathleen smiled and after saying her goodbyes ran back up the path.

"Well Tommy," Erin said drawing him back to the present. "Shall we go to Gran's?"

"Aye Mam," he replied quietly. Unusually for him, he reached for her hand as they walked out of the churchyard gates. With his sisters skipping along infront, and wee Cianán looking round contentedly from the backpack carrier, Tom and Erin walked in silence for a few minutes. Eventually he said softly, "Mam, I heard that Mrs Comisky said that Dónal and I tried to steal Mr Quigley's fish." Erin looked down at her son but said nothing. After a few moments he glanced up at her, "We didn't you know," he whispered.

Erin Devlin smiled slightly and gave his hand a gentle squeeze. "I know, Tommy."

Erin's mother, Eileen O'Brien, lived alone in a small, neat whitewashed bungalow half way up Binnion Hill, a rugged windswept highland overlooking the Atlantic coast at Tullagh Bay. A widow for nearly six years since the death of her husband Charlie, Eileen had lived in the house all her adult life and both Erin and her older sister Keira had been born there. At sixty-eight she was stIll fit, and in good health, as well as being fiercely independent. Eileen adamantly refused to let Erin do her shopping for her (Keira now lived in London after marrying an Englishman), insisting that she walk the two miles to Ballyfinan every other day to buy her fresh milk and other necessities. She did, however, greatly look forward to her daughter's regular Sunday lunchtime visits with the family, and as was her want, would spoil the children shamelessly. For their part, all Erin's children loved their 'Granny' dearly, and enjoyed their weekly visits as much as she.

Well fed and content, Tom sat quietly on the open doorstep of Eileen's cottage, gazing out over the large, horseshoe-shaped, sandy beach that was Tullagh Bay. Dressed once again in everyday clothes, (Eileen always kept a spare set in the house knowing how much he disliked wearing Sunday best), Tom watched absently in the distance as a number of herring gulls soared effortlessly over the waves.

"It's a lovely day, isn't it?" Eileen said quietly, coming to stand behind him in the doorway.

Looking up, Tom smiled and nodded, "Aye, Granny." Thinking she might have an errand for him, he climbed to his feet. "Do you want me for anything, Gran?"

"No love. I just wanted to see if you were alright? You seem a little quiet today."

Tom shrugged. "I'm fine Gran, really, but thanks for asking."

"Well, that's grand then." Eileen smiled in return, but inwardly unconvinced. Behind those pale grey-green eyes she knew something was troubling her eldest grandchild.

For a while they silently looked out together over Tullagh Bay. "You know, Tommy," Eileen said after a few minutes, "your mother's putting wee Cianán down for a sleep and your sisters want to do some embroidery with me. Now, I don't suppose you'd like to join us in the sewing circle, would you?"

Tom laughed, "No Gran."

"I didn't think so. Well, in that case why don't you go down to the beach, and while you're there get some nice mussels for my tea; the tide should be far enough out in half an hour or so."

The boy's face lit up. "Thanks, I will!"

He had only taken two hurried steps before a firm, strong hand clasped his shoulder. Turning him round Eileen fixed him with one of her infamous stares. "Now, listen young man, you be careful and mind you are back before your brother wakes up, say an hour or so, or your mother will have both our guts for garters!"

"Aye, I promise."

"Grand. Take that wee pail by the gate and don't forget my mussels."

Tom shook his head. "I won't, Gran," and with that, sped off down the little path through the garden.

"Tommy!" Eileen O'Brien shouted suddenly as he was about to step through the gate.

"Aye?"

"Best leave your shoes off here, rather than on some seaweed covered rock!"

Grinning, Tom kicked them off with apparent disregard, and with a final wave disappeared from view. Chuckling, Eileen went back into the house where her two granddaughters were waiting, almost patiently.

From Eileen O'Brien's cottage a single, unmade track way ran left and right from directly outside the garden gate. The left path steadily declined in a gentle gradient back to join the Binnion Road and hence to Ballyfinan itself. The right hand track continued to rise for a further hundred yards before descending through the craggy, gorse-covered hillside. Snaking downwards in long lazy loops, the path finally dwindled out at the marram-dominated dunes that ringed Tullagh beach. Half-running, Tom hurried along the twisting path, every so often surprising and scattering a few isolated Blackface sheep, grazing on the lush, springtime vegetation boarding the track. Rounding the penultimate turn before the dunes he slowed to a walk as he approached the only other inhabited dwelling within three hundred yards of his grandmother's bungalow. Like Eileen's cottage it was also a small, single story dwelling facing the sea. There, however, the similarity ended. Unlike his grandmother's clean whitewashed walls and tidy, well kept garden, the bungalow was shabby and clearly neglected. Years of grime and salt spray encrusted dirt covered the walls. The gate to the small front garden was missing and the vegetation within wild and overgrown. Litter and rubbish lay strewn about the house and the whole ambience portrayed a grey, forlorn, virtually derelict air. Despite appearances to the contrary, Tom knew the cottage was not deserted. Mrs Monaghan, a widow like Eileen O'Brien for many years, still lived within its neglected, run-down walls.

Through the dirt of a small, grime-encrusted window, the light from a single candle burned brightly. Tom had not seen Mrs Monaghan for many months, and indeed only twice could he recall her in the village since the Service of Remembrance. Nonetheless he knew that Father Aidan, his grandmother and many others from the community visited her regularly. His mother would often spend half an hour or so with Mrs

Monaghan, during their Sunday visits, but neither Tom, nor his sisters or brother were ever allowed to accompany her.

Unconsciously, he stopped in front of the cottage, staring at the flickering candle within. It had been nearly a year since the accident. Mrs Monaghan's three adult sons had left early one bright, sunny June morning to check the salmon nets laid a mile offshore. They never returned. Their empty, partially submerged boat was subsequently found adrift in the current after a frantic day's searching, but no bodies were ever recovered. From that day, Mrs Monaghan had kept a candle burning on her windowsill overlooking the sea, day and night. Months later, Tom had asked her why she lit the candle. Mrs Monaghan had smiled kindly at him and replied that it was a light for her sons; a light to guide them back home from the sea. Puzzled, he had later questioned his mother on this. Erin had explained that the light was symbolic; a guiding beacon for the souls of the departed to the light of heaven. Although he kept his opinions to himself, Tom privately felt Mrs Monaghan's explanation was more literal, and that she truly believed that her sons would return to her one day.

The mournful cry of a sea gull flying over head brought Tom back to the present. Turning away from the cottage he ran the rest of the way down the path before scrambling over the tall sand dunes onto Tullagh Beach. For the next hour or so Tom was quite content. He searched the high tide line, sifting through the flotsam and jetsam for potential treasures thrown up by the sea; he found nothing of particular interest other than a dead dogfish. He fought imaginary battles against sea invaders with a sword-shaped piece of driftwood, and built an impressive castle complex in the wet sand, decorating the battlements with razor shells and sea bird feathers.

It was as he was admiring the castle that he remembered the mussels.

Whilst Tullagh was essentially a sandy beach, at the far end of the bay from Binnion Hill an impressive rocky outcrop area, known as Tullagh Point, was revealed at low tide. As the sea retreated, these rocks formed innumerable rock pools, and represented the perfect habitat for many sea creatures, including significant clusters of tightly packed mussels. By the time Tom reached the rocks, the falling tide was beginning to reveal the larger beds, towards the low water mark.

Walking gingerly over the barnacle encrusted rocks, Tom first spent several minutes peering into the various pools, searching for crabs, small fish and shrimps. Eventually he reached the larger mussel beds and skilfully dodging the surging waves, quickly collected a dozen or so good size specimens. Filling the pail with sea water to keep them fresh, Tom made his way cautiously back onto the beach. Looking up across the bay and towards Binnion Hill in the distance, his grandmother's whitewashed cottage was still clearly visible. A number of tiny figures could just be made out in the garden. Judging his free time to be up, Tom wisely decided to return.

Daydreaming happily, he had almost reached the foot of the track way leading back up Binnion Hill, before he noticed the man, sitting within the dunes, watching him quietly. Slightly startled, Tom stopped and stared; he was a stranger. Nodding a greeting, the unfamiliar figure stood and smiled. He was of average height, clean-shaven with short fair hair, and well dressed in a fawn-coloured jacket, dark trousers and black shoes. A plain, blue checked shirt completed his overall casual, but smart, appearance.

"Hello," he said pleasantly, descending to the beach and walking to stand beside Tom. "I hope I didn't frighten you just then?"

Tom shook his head. "No, just made me jump a bit, that's all."

"Well, that's alright then," he replied, still smiling slightly. "I've been watching you out on the rocks for a while now. What were you after, crabs? Shrimps?"

Tom held up the pail.

"Ah mussels, and fine ones at that," he continued, nodding approvingly. "I used to collect them too from those same rocks, when I was your age. They make good eating, are you having them for your tea?

"No, I don't like them. They're for my Gran." Even though the man was unknown to him, Tom found his voice and overall manner reassuring. For a few moments they stood together in silence, admiring Tom's catch.

"Do you live around here? I've not seen you in the

village before," Tom asked after a while.

Running his fingers through his hair, the man again nodded. "Well, I was born in Ballyfinan and grew up here, but I left some years ago, for Dublin." He paused for a second before continuing. "I missed the village though, and my friends I grew up with. City life is grand in its own way, but now I know it wasn't for me. So, I decided to come home."

"Why did you move away?"

He laughed. "Now that would be a tale, but your Granny wouldn't be best pleased with me if I kept you here all afternoon in the telling of it." Tom laughed too. Whoever he was, he certainly seemed okay. On impulse, a new idea came to mind.

"Would you like to meet my Gran, you could have tea with us? She won't mind and only lives up there in that white cottage. I visit her every Sunday, with my Mam, sisters and brother." Following Tom's outstretched arm, he looked first in the direction of Eileen O'Brien's bungalow, and then back at the boy. For a moment the stranger's face was unreadable.

"Your Gran's Mrs O'Brien?" he ventured quietly.

Tom nodded, saying nothing, suddenly apprehensive that he may have said something wrong. Seeing the boy's discomfort, the man smiled kindly again. "Thanks for the offer, but I'd best be heading back home myself. I've a big day tomorrow. I start my new job and still haven't unpacked from the move yet." Holding out his hand, he shook Tom's in farewell. "It was nice meeting you, Thomas. Give my regards to your Gran...and your

Mam." With a slight laugh he continued, "And make sure you're on time for school tomorrow."

When Tom did not answer, a puzzled expression on his face, the stranger's smile only broadened. With a mischievous wink, he said, "I'm your new School Master, Thomas, Mr Kennedy."

It was only when Tom reached the gate leading to his grandmother's cottage that he finally understood the troubling thought that had niggled at him since his encounter on the beach. How had Mr Kennedy known that this was his Gran's cottage...and that his name was Thomas?

3
BEST LAID PLANS

On waking, the initial disappointment Tom experienced after learning that his father had not returned home the night before was quickly forgotten in the regimented chaos that heralded the start of a new school day. Effectively a single parent for much of the year, Erin Devlin would stand no nonsense in the mornings with three children to be up, dressed, breakfasted and out of the door for school by ten past eight; addressing wee Cianán's particularly demanding needs was just another complication. All three of her older children were expected to obey their mother's requests or, as Tom deemed them to be, orders, without question. Even the twins had learned the hard lessons that resulted from slovenliness and inattention to the tasks at hand.

On this particular Monday morning, to Tom's mind, operation 'out the door' as he liked to think of it, had gone, more or less, to plan. Indeed, he and, quite amazingly, the twins were ready to leave a good five minutes earlier than was necessary. Since the start of the summer term, his mother had judged Tom old enough and, more to the point, sensible enough to walk himself and his sisters to the village school unaccompanied. At first Tom had felt thrilled at the independence and responsibility bestowed upon him, but as the days, then weeks, went by the novelty of escorting his invariably bickering sisters on his own had worn off. Today was no exception and Tom, as was his now usual custom, walked a few yards ahead of the girls, trying his best to ignore them.

The Ballyfinan village school was not actually in the village at all but a good mile and a half on from the Finan Bridge, along the main Tullagh Road. A large, two storey red-bricked building, the school had nearly sixty pupils and served the children aged six to fourteen from the village, isolated dwellings and small hamlets, up to ten miles distant. Since the retirement of the old School Master eight weeks previously, the principal teaching role now fell to the three elderly Nuns left at the school. The most senior of whom, Sister Madeleine, had taught at the school for nearly thirty years. It was commonly thought by pupils, parents and the community at large that it was simply a matter of time before Sister

Madeleine would be appointed as the next Headteacher.

As they neared the school, Tom's pensive mood deepened further. Thoughts of his father's absence, together with his strange encounter with Mr Kennedy the evening before, preoccupied him. For reasons he couldn't explain, he had decided not to mention his conversation with Mr Kennedy to either his mother or grandmother. Somehow he felt they would not have approved.

Outside the gate, a small group of boys lounged casually against the school wall, chatting amiably. Approaching the entrance, he spotted Brendan Harkin amongst the gathering, who, seeing Tom, waved and beckoned him over.

"Hi," Brendan said to Tom as he drew near. "Hello girls," he added as Tom's sisters ran on past and into the school yard without saying a word.

"Charming as ever I see?" Brendan continued, nodding towards the departing girls.

Tom just smiled. "Aye."

Bending down, Tom removed his shoes and put them into his school bag. None of the other boys standing beside him wore anything on their feet. A short, dark haired boy called James Dooley, grinned and said, "Good job your Mam's not here to see you do that, you'd get a beating for sure."

Tom pretended to nod sagely. "Well, what she doesn't know can't hurt her...or me!" All but one of the boys laughed at Tom's joke. The silent individual was taller and stockier than the rest and had untidy flame-red hair. He had a chubby, unattractive face, not helped by a plethora of pre-adolescent spots, and the fact that his demeanour was almost constantly moulded into a belligerent scowl. His name was Dennis Quigley, and he was Séamus Quigley's nephew.

Pushing past a couple of the others to stand in front of Tom, Dennis Quigley poked a finger somewhat forcefully into Tom's chest. "My uncle said you and that loser O'Connor tried to steal his salmon on Saturday."

"Well, your uncle's a liar then. It was our fish…he took it from us!"

Glaring, Quigley's hands balled into fists but before he could say or do anything, he was roughly barged out of the way by Brendan. "Lay off him Dennis, we've all heard the story and I know who I believe."

James Dooley and another boy stepped up to join him, blocking Quigley's path to Tom. Like his uncle before him, Dennis Quigley was a bully, and like most others, when the odds were no longer in their favour, backed down. Muttering under his breath, Quigley stomped off into the school yard.

"Thanks." Tom said quietly.

"That's okay." Brendan replied. "But you'd better watch yourself, though. Dennis seems to have got it in for you."

Tom smiled ruefully. "So what's new? The Quigleys have got it in for just about everybody."

"Well now, who do you suppose that is?" the boy standing beside James and Brendan asked, pointing into the school yard. Turning, they all saw a tall, well-dressed man walking alongside Sister Madeleine. The pair crossed the playground and headed towards the main entrance. Several mothers and other children standing outside the gates also stopped and stared.

Brendan shrugged. "Who knows, could be anybody. He looks tight in with Sister Madeleine though."

Whilst the boys could not hear their conversation, both the nun and the newcomer could be clearly seen smiling and sharing some form of joke as they disappeared into the building.

Tom said nothing.

Frowning thoughtfully, James Dooley said, "I don't know who he is but I did see him yesterday."

"Where was that?" Brendan asked. All eyes turned to regard James.

"He came into the Bar last night. My Da seemed very pleased to see him, like they were old friends or something?" James's father, Cormac Dooley, owned Dooley's Bar in the Square.

Further discussion, however, was precluded by the appearance from the main entrance of Moira O'Mahoney, the school prefect. Within seconds, the sound of the school bell echoed loudly around the playground, heralding the start of a new school day.

"Come on," Tom said, grateful for the opportunity to change the subject. "We'd best go."

Following the last of the stragglers in through the gate, the boys walked across the yard and up the stone steps to the building. As they passed Moira, still enthusiastically ringing the bell, Brendan turned to Tom and asked, "Where's Dónal?"

Tom's only answer was a shrug.

For Tom, the remainder of the school day passed in a blur. After morning prayers Sister Madeleine visited each of the school's three classes, formally introducing Mr Kennedy as the new School Master. When it was the turn of Tom's class Mr Kennedy gave no outward sign that they had met the previous day. He appeared friendly and genuinely pleased to be part of the school. Sister Madeleine also informed everyone that in addition to being the new School Master, Mr Kennedy would be teaching all classes in Arithmetic and Geography, an announcement that earned a good humoured groan from all. Dónal O'Connor was noted as being absent from school all day.

At the end of school, Tom collected Roisin and Niamh and joined the mass exodus through the gates. Passing through the waiting mothers and younger children he heard scraps of conversation, much of it relating to the new School Master. For once, he felt no inclination to linger and eavesdrop on what was being said.

A few hundred yards past the school, on the left-hand side of the road, stood the shell of the small, ruined church of St Mary Magdalene. The wooden roof had long since fallen in and the building itself, along with the adjacent tiny graveyard, was overgrown with weeds and tall grasses. Never rebuilt following the fire that had destroyed the church in the early 1920s, Tom and his friends had explored the ruins many times in the past. There were only three standing gravestones in the cemetery and Tom always felt strangely sad when he thought about them. The graves were of three young British soldiers, all aged seventeen, who had been killed in a training accident in 1917. During the First World War a military training base had existed on the coast, a few miles past Tullagh Bay. The British Government had abandoned the base after the war but these recruits would remain here forever. To Tom's knowledge, having once asked Father Aidan about the burials, no one had ever visited the graves, and it was likely that no one ever would. Tom often imagined that three lonely ghosts wandered the confines of the tiny graveyard, yearning for someone to come and pray for them at their eternal graveside.

As he walked past St Mary Magdalene's, his sisters a few yards behind, a voice called out from within the graveyard. Over the low, half-demolished stone wall surrounding the church, Dónal O'Connor grinned at him. Hands behind his head, and back resting comfortably against one of the solder's gravestones, Dónal was a picture of contentment.

"Why weren't you at school today?" Tom asked, slightly startled by his friend's sudden appearance. It was not unusual for Dónal to miss school on a fairly regular basis, often without an acceptable excuse and much to the annoyance of Sister Madeleine.

Still smiling, Dónal jumped up and scrambled over the wall to join him. "Well, I felt a bit funny this morning; must've swallowed some river water on Saturday. Mam said I'd better stay off, and so here I am!"

Tom's eyes narrowed suspiciously. How honest Dónal was being with him remained to be seen.

"Anyway," the older boy continued happily, "I'm feeling much better now."

"So I can see."

"Oh, come on Tom, don't be like that."

Tom knew from past experience that there was little point in staying annoyed with Dónal and he let it drop. In any case Roisin was tugging on his sleeve. "Mammy said we were to come straight home," she said.

Tom nodded. "Aye, let's go."

Walking alongside them along the Tullagh Road Dónal said, "Is your Da home yet?"

Tom shook his head. "No, not yet...well not since this morning that is."

"Good, I want to borrow his fly rod this afternoon."

"Why?" Tom asked, slightly surprised.

"Fishing of course, you dolt." Dónal replied, slyly.

Tom stared at his friend for a few moments unsure what to do. "Well, I'm not sure now Dónal," he finally said hesitantly. "Besides I've had enough of fishing for a while, what with Quigley and all."

Dónal only smiled again. "It's not what you think, Tom. I've a plan to get back at that fat sod, and I need your Da's rod to do it. We can get even and Quigley will never know it was us."

"What do you mean?"

Dónal inclined his head slightly, indicating Tom's two sisters a step or so behind. "Not here, and besides it'll spoil the fun if I tell you now."

Tom just cursed quietly under his breath.

*

Dónal O'Connor waited silently outside the back door to Tom's house, partially obscured from view behind a small fuel shed. Whilst not exactly hiding from Erin Devlin, he nonetheless did not really want to see her, or more to the point, her to see him. He liked to keep Tom's mother at a respectful distance as much as possible. After a few minutes Tom emerged from the back door and walked across to him, his face slightly downcast.

"Mam said I must be back within an hour for dinner. I can't see how will we have time to go fishing? She's in a foul mood as it is and I'll be murdered if I'm late."

Dónal grinned. "Don't be such a baby, we'll have plenty of time! Come on, you'll see."

Sighing, Tom knew it was pointless protesting further.

Adjacent to his house, and separated by a few yards of shingle driveway, was a single storey wooden outbuilding. Until a few years ago Tom's father had owned a horse, and the building had been partly used as a stable in the winter months. His parents had been forced to sell the horse after the twins were born and the building was now a dumping ground. Sean Devlin adamantly refused to throw anything away and the 'Barn,' as the family referred to it, was an Aladdin's Cave of odds and ends, most of which Erin Devlin regarded as just junk. However, amongst those few items of genuine worth stored in the Barn was their old gig, now kept under a dusty canvas sheet, and Sean Devlin's prized split-cane fly fishing rod.

From under a flat stone next to the Barn's double doors, Tom retrieved a large key and unlocked the doors. Replacing the key, the boys pushed open the doors, the rusty hinges creaking alarmingly in protest. Tom glanced over his shoulder nervously, half expecting to see his mother come running across from the back of the house. When he turned back, Dónal had already disappeared inside.

"Tom!" his friend whispered from within. "Where is it?"

Still unhappy, but resigning himself to the inevitable, Tom followed Dónal into the Barn.

The air inside was musty and stale, and for several seconds he let his eyes grow accustomed to the gloom. Dónal was already clambering over various boxes and prying into dark corners, searching for Tom's father's fishing equipment. Stretching up from a rickety chair, Dónal's foot suddenly slipped. With a cry, the boy lost his balance, arms cart-wheeling he tipped backwards knocking a number of paint tins from an adjacent shelf, the resulting crash sounding deafening to Tom's ears.

Like rabbits caught in a hunter's light, both boys

froze. After a minute, when it appeared by some miracle that they had not been heard, Tom sighed heavily in relief.

"Are you alright?" he asked, helping his friend to his feet.

"Aye, just about."

"You eejit. I'll get my Da's rod. You stay by the door and keep watch. I can't believe Mam's not heard us with the racket you've made."

Dónal simply grinned wolfishly at him, but for once, did as he was asked. Keeping a close eye on the house, he heard Tom moving around in the Barn behind him. After a few moments the younger boy appeared at his side, a small canvas bag and a ten foot rod in his hands. It was already fully tackled with a battered, much used reel and dark green fly line. From the tip of the fly line, three feet of clear leader ended with a bushy sea-trout fly, held securely in place through a small wire loop on a cork handle.

"Yes!" Dónal exclaimed, playfully punching Tom on the arm. "Well done, let's go."

"Help me shut the doors first."

"Sure."

As Tom replaced the key under the stone, Dónal held and admired Sean Devlin's beautifully crafted rod. Although old, it was professionally made and obviously expensive.

"Okay, I'm ready," Tom said, and began to walk cautiously down the sloping gravel driveway between the two buildings towards Cairn Lane.

"Not that way," Dónal replied with a mischievous smile. Turning he walked quickly back up the driveway towards the end of the Barn. Passing the backdoor to Tom's house on the right, Dónal reached the end of the Barn and disappeared left, following the perimeter of the building. Frowning, Tom had no choice but to follow.

Behind the Barn, the boulder-strewn slopes of Croaghennan Mór, a gorse and bracken dominated hillside, rose steeply to a height of over 300m. A patchwork of fields, enclosed by low, often crumbling, dry-stone walls ringed the hill, its whole appearance wild and barren. Tom's family owned a number of the fields, mainly on the southern slope and towards the summit.

Much of what remained belonged to Séamus Quigley.

A sturdy iron gate, and beside it a stone stile, provided the only access point to Croaghennan Mór from the Devlin's property. By the time Tom rounded the Barn, Dónal had already scaled the stile and was beckoning him to hurry up. Muttering quietly under his breath, Tom vaulted the stile easily and ran to catch up.

Tentatively grasping Dónal's arm and stopping him, Tom said, "I don't understand, why are you going this way? The river's over there," pointing back towards Cairn Lane.

"Aye, that's true enough, but I've something else planned."

"What?"

"You'll see!"

Grinning infuriatingly again, Dónal hurried on around the perimeter of the field, angling west and slightly downhill towards a patch of newly emerging bracken. At that time of the year the fronds were only just visible. Tom almost swore in frustration, but nonetheless tagged along behind. The area of bracken eventually ended in a four foot high stone wall running north-south. The wall, encrusted with lichen and moss, marked the western boundary between the Devlin's land and that of Quigley's Farm. As Tom approached he could see Dónal was already studying the wall intently, looking for best hand and foot holes for climbing over.

"Wait Dónal!" Tom cried. "That's Quigley's land! I don't think we should –"

"I know," his friend interrupted dismissively, still gazing at the wall. Unseen, Tom shook his head; this time Dónal was going too far. Following him on some scam or other was one thing; trespassing onto Quigley's land, especially without a reason, was something completely different. If they were caught, not only would Quigley beat them, but his mother would also box his ears for sure for deliberately disobeying her. Tom had been expressly forbidden to go onto any land owned by Séamus Quigley.

"Dónal, I'm not going onto Quigley's land," he finally said, hoping to sound as resolute as possible.

"Hold this," his friend replied, ignoring the comment and passing the rod and fishing bag back to him. "Toss it over to me once I'm across."

"Dónal! Didn't you hear me? I *mean* it. My Mam will skin me alive if she finds out we've been on his land and besides, you know what Quigley said last time…he'd set the dogs on us again he if catches us – "

"Well, we'd better make sure your Mam doesn't catch us then, and for sure Quigley won't see us if we're careful. He's probably not in anyway."

"But what if he is?" Tom insisted. "We don't need to go across his farm to the river, we can go back by my house."

"We're not going to the river."

"Huh? But you said we're going fishing? Why did you want my Da's rod and all this stuff then?"

Scrambling up to the top of the wall, Dónal continued to smile back tiresomely.

"We're going fishing, Tom, just not at the river." Seeing his friend's annoyed frown Dónal's face grew more serious. "Listen, you want to get back at Quigley as much as me, right?"

Tom nodded. "Aye."

"Well, to be sure we can. I grant you this plan of mine is a wee bit risky an' all, but it'll be worth it."

Tom continued to look up at the older boy, but now was obviously hesitating.

"Alright, how's this. If we find Quigley's in, or see his dogs in the yard, I'll call it off. I can't say fairer than that now, can I?"

Tom regarded him dubiously. "Your word, now?"

"Aye."

Sighing, Tom added nodded slowly. "You still haven't

told me what your plan is?" he added somewhat sullenly.

Dónal just laughed. "All good things come to those who wait! Come on, hand me the rod and bag."

Still feeling anxious, Tom did as asked and watched as Dónal jumped down over the other side of the wall. A low curse and a tirade of expletives indicated he had evidently landed in some mud-like, but far more unpleasant, substance. Smiling to himself in perverse satisfaction, Tom climbed slowly over the wall and dropped more carefully to the ground. Wiping his bare feet on the tussocky grass, the look Dónal gave him was obvious; the younger boy's smile simply broadened.

Walking slowly and carefully westwards, not just to avoid the bovine deposits on the ground, the boys crossed the field, the topography continuing to gently dip down towards Quigley's Farm, a hundred or so yards in the distance. A few shaggy beef cattle calmly watched their progress but gave no other outward sign of interest. At the end of the field another dry stone wall, in significant need of repair and interspersed with low shrubs and blackthorn bushes, blocked their path. Crossing over into another field they moved stealthily on, the ground becoming increasingly boggy and heavily pockmarked by the presence of livestock. Juncus rushes, sedges and other rough grasses dominated the poor grassland vegetation. The periphery of this field marked the northern boundary to Séamus Quigley's farmyard.

Dónal, with Tom a step behind, crept through the

mud-churned gateway into the farmyard. Looking cautiously around there was no sign of Quigley, or his dogs. The windows to the large farmhouse were all closed and Quigley's small, battered Morris truck was nowhere in sight. Only a dozen or so chickens were evident, scratching around the open area searching for seeds, bugs and other scraps of food.

"What are we doing here?" Tom whispered nervously, his eyes darting left and right.

"There," Dónal answered quietly, pointing into the yard. Tom shook his head, confused.

"What am I looking at?"

"There!" Dónal repeated more earnestly. "Chickens."

"Chickens?"

"Aye, we're going fishing for chickens."

Tom exhaled deeply, exasperated. "Are you mad? You can't catch a chicken with a fishing rod, you eejit."

"I know that!" Dónal shot back. "I'm not daft, but I can use the fly to lure one of 'em towards us...and then you can jump out and grab it."

"Me! I'm not chasing after – "

Dónal cut him off abruptly. "Listen, old Harry Boyce, you know that mad old hermit that lives out behind the Market House – "

"I know who he is Dónal!"

"Grand then, anyway he says he'll give me, give us I mean, sixpence each for any chicken we can find *wandering around*, lost like."

"But these aren't lost," Tom protested.

"So?"

"But that's stealing!"

"Like the way that fat git stole my fish!" Dónal retorted angrily. Tom saw little point in reminding his friend that it was their salmon Séamus Quigley had taken, not just his.

"Besides," Dónal continued, "he won't even notice; he's got lots of them and they're always wandering about. And even if he does, the lazy sod will probably think it's got lost, or a fox has had it, or whatever."

Seeing Tom turning these arguments over in his mind, Dónal quickly unhooked the fly from the rod-handle and began to pull out a few feet of line, the drag clutch causing the old reel to squeal alarmingly as the line was freed. After a few moments, Dónal flicked his arm back and then rapidly brought it forward attempting to cast the line out. A clear snap resounded in the air above them and the line fell in a tangled heap a few yards in front of them.

"Not like that!" Tom exclaimed suddenly, and louder than he had meant to. "You're trying to cast too fast. You've got to give the line time to pay out behind you. Give it here, before you break something."

Taking the rod from Dónal he continued, "You have to hold the line in your left hand and wait for it to level out on the back cast before you whip it forward." Effortlessly practising a couple of false casts, Tom then released the line on the final forward cast, propelling the artificial fly twenty five feet directly in front of them. "See?"

Tom was still looking at his friend when all hell broke

loose. Within seconds the tranquil farmyard scene was transformed into utter chaos. A hen, seeing the artificial fly land a few feet to the side, instantly pounced, seizing the apparent succulent morsel in her beak. Feeling the sudden resistance from the near invisible leader, she sharply tried to pull her head away, setting the hook painfully into the side of her mouth. In panic the hen leapt into the air, flapping her wings and shrieking noisily. The panicky attempts at flight only served to further entangle the bird in the fly line, adding to her distress. The commotion terrified the other chickens in the yard and in seconds all the birds were running in all directions, squawking in alarm. At that exact moment, from behind the farmhouse, Quigley's two sheep dogs appeared. Barking excitedly they ran wildly into the yard, their sudden appearance adding to the birds' distress. The nightmare, from Dónal and Tom's perspective, was completed when a second later the door to the farmhouse was flung open, and a red-faced Séamus Quigley emerged, a look of absolute thunder upon his face.

Surveying the chaotic scene before him Quigley roared. "What the bloody hell is going on? Jess! Mac! Heel! Come 'ere, damn it or you'll feel my boot!"

"Oh sweet Jesus," Tom whispered from the gateway, his face ashen.

"Run!" Dónal cried, and grabbing Tom's arm dragged his friend half-stumbling out into the field. Sprinting across the sodden, waterlogged ground, the boys reached the comparative safety of the first partially ruined boundary wall within moments. Behind them, barking and Quigley's own angry shouts could clearly be heard. Risking a glance behind, Tom murmured a quick prayer of thanks; there was no sign of pursuit evident as yet. Clambering desperately over the wall, ignoring the scrapes and scratches from the weathered stones, they ran on, not slowing until they neared the second wall, and the boundary to Tom's own land. Near exhausted, they climbed wearily over this wall and dropped down onto the other side, breathing heavily. Feeling relatively safe Tom sank to the ground, his back resting against the stone wall and legs spread out before him. Dónal collapsed besides him, head bowed, hugging his knees tightly.

For a number of minutes neither spoke, their breathing continuing to come in loud, heaving gasps. Tom stared straight ahead, his mind racing. After a short time, he looked down at his hands; they were still shaking. Dónal's eyes were closed.

It was sometime before Tom eventually said, "Do you think he saw us?"

Dónal shook his head. "I don't think so. To be sure he would have set the dogs after us if he had."

"Jesus, Dónal! I near wet myself when Quigley came out of his front door."

Dónal half-smiled, his eyes still shut. "Aye, me too."

Laughing quietly, they enjoyed a few moments welcome relief from the tension. Suddenly, Tom's euphoria evaporated; a cold stab of panic constricting his chest. Tears welled up in his eyes as he looked across at his friend. "My Da's rod, Dónal, we left it behind."

Dónal opened his eyes and slowly looked across at Tom. For a while they stared at each other and then Dónal leaned back against the wall once more. His eyes closed. Nothing further needed to be said.

4
REPERCUSSIONS

Erin Devlin was many things, but heedless of the general atmosphere within the family home, and the particular needs of her children, was not one of them. As she served dinner that evening, despite the distractions of her three youngest children, it was obvious that something was unsettling her elder son. Always a quiet, thoughtful boy, it was nonetheless rare that Tom would not engage in conversation with her. She had already tried to promote a discussion about his school day to no avail. Indeed, after mentioning the latest village gossip concerning the appointment of a new School Master, he had become, if anything, more withdrawn. Watching him closely over the table as he played disinterestedly with his food, Erin frowned, her thoughts increasingly troubled.

After dinner her concerns over Tom's unusual behaviour were, by necessity, put to one side as the daily routine of bathing and preparing his younger siblings for bed ensued. Wisely, Tom made himself scarce.

For Tom, the inevitable knock on the front door came shortly after his mother had finally settled wee Cianán and the twins. Lying on his bed, fully clothed and staring up at the ceiling, he contemplated what his mother would say and, more to the point, what his father might do, when they found out. Downstairs he heard his mother's voice, short and brusque but not raised, obviously making an effort not to disturb the children. Trying to listen he struggled to make out any of the words. For several minutes Tom continued to lie still, puzzled why the anticipated summons had not materialised. Unable to contain himself, he finally sat up and crept out onto the landing. Through the wooden banisters he saw his mother in the hallway, speaking in curt whispers with a tall figure, partly obscured in the twilight on the doorstep.

"I said no and I mean it. Now please go!" he heard Erin say tersely. "You can't just turn up at my door like this – "

"Erin please, just five minutes" came the quiet, but equally resolute reply. "I wanted to tell you in person that I've come home. I didn't want you to find out from... well you know, the village gossipers of this world. I know how you must feel –"

"Like hell you do."

"Erin, will you just listen to me, please?"

"Damn you Declan, you can't just appear back into my life like this. You haven't written in years; God knows what Sean will say when he hears..." She left the sentence hanging.

"I'm not trying to," the partially concealed figure replied softly, stepping into the hallway. "I just wanted to talk. You owe me *that* much at least." Tom gasped. Standing there, framed in the lamp light was Mr Kennedy.

Hearing the noise Erin turned round and looked up. "Tommy! Away with you to bed now! Put your pyjamas on. I'm coming straight up."

Declan Kennedy glanced up at Tom and inclined his head slightly in greeting but said nothing. Shocked, Tom couldn't move.

"I mean it now, Thomas, into your bedroom." Facing Declan once more Erin glared angrily. "Please leave," she said firmly. "I can't deal with this now."

Declan nodded. "I'm sorry Erin, I never meant to cause any trouble. Goodnight."

Closing the door behind him Erin sighed heavily. "Damn you, Declan," she murmured under her breath. As if suddenly released, Tom scampered back along the landing into his room.

Hearing his mother slowly climb the stairs he began to undress and get ready for bed. There was no sense in annoying her unduly tonight. Erin had just reached the top of the stairs when a heavy and persistent hammering on the front door resounded, followed moments later by Séamus Quigley's booming voice demanding to be let in.

Tom did not attempt to eavesdrop on his mother's conversation with Mr Quigley, as even lying in his bed with the door closed, the farmer's angry shouting and remonstrations could clearly be heard. Burying his head under the pillow only served to partly block out the sounds. After what seemed like hours, the shouting stopped and quiet descended upon the house. For a long time Tom did not dare move, enjoying the comforting solace of the protecting pillow and blankets. When he eventually emerged he was not surprised to see his mother kneeling beside the bed, a small chimney-glass oil lamp glowing brightly in her hand.

"Is he gone?"

Erin nodded silently. Tears began to well up in Tom's eyes. "I'm so sorry, Mammy."

Stroking her son's forehead Erin said quietly "We'll discuss it tomorrow, try and get some sleep now." Sniffing heavily, Tom nodded back in agreement.

"Here, take this and dry your eyes." Handing him a handkerchief she leant over and kissed his head gently. Tired but his mind still reeling, Tom knew sleep would be far off.

"Close your eyes now, my love," his mother said gently. Obediently he did as asked and heard her whispering to him to relax, but the images of the day still flashed through his mind. Why had he been so stupid to go along with Dónal's scheme?

Suddenly a new thought sprang to mind. "Da's rod!" he exclaimed sitting up in panic.

"Shush now," Erin admonished. "Mr Quigley's brought it back."

Pushing him gently but firmly back down into bed Erin tucked him in, and continued to caress his cheek. For a long while after Tom had quietened and eventually fallen asleep, she sat beside his bed, silently watching him.

*

A grey, overcast sky heralded the start of a new day. Heavy rain had fallen during the night and low clouds and freshening winds brought the promise of further squally showers to come. Looking out from the window of his small bedroom, Tom reflected on the sombre appearance to the sky. The depressing gloom matched his mood perfectly.

The house was strangely quiet. From downstairs only faint sounds arose; a chair being dragged across the stone kitchen floor, together with the gentle chinking of crockery and other tableware, but no voices. For a few moments Tom wondered whether he had awoken too early and everyone, apart from his mother, was still asleep. Quickly he dismissed such thoughts. It was Tuesday and a school day and as such it would be Erin's routine to wake the family while it was still dark. Despite the greyness of the day it was obvious the sun had already risen, albeit hidden by the clouds. Too depressed to consider the issue further, Tom decided to get up. Quickly throwing on his clothes, he ran his fingers a couple of times through his unruly dark hair and crept out onto the landing, heading for the small bathroom. The unmistakable and mouth-watering smell of fried bacon unexpectedly greeted him from downstairs. Something strange was happening; his mother would never ordinarily cook bacon for breakfast, such treats were strictly reserved for birthdays and highdays. Passing his sisters' bedroom he stole a glance inside. The twins were still sleeping peacefully. Frowning, Tom relieved himself and then splashed cold water onto his face, spluttering a little against the chill. Drying his face on a rough towel he looked up to see his mother standing in the doorway. Tom could not help his start of surprise; Erin looked dreadful. Her normally immaculate hair was lank and lifeless, her eyes puffy and red-rimmed. It was obvious that she had been crying and probably, Tom thought, not slept much either. A wave of guilt swept over him.

"I'm glad you're up and dressed," Erin said tiredly. "Have you finished washing yet?"

Tom shook his head. "Nearly. I just need to clean my teeth."

"Well when you have, go downstairs and help yourself to breakfast, I'll be getting the girls up now."

"Aye, Mam." Hesitating for a moment, and misconstruing the origins of her distress, he added quietly, "Mam, I'm sorry about last night...I didn't mean for Mr Quigley to upset you so much."

For a second Erin just stared at him, her face unreadable. Slowly a thin, kind smile appeared. "Don't you be concerning yourself with such things now. Hurry up and finish getting ready."

She turned to go.

"Mam?"

Looking back, Erin stared at him, waiting patiently.

Uncertain of what he really wanted to say, Tom simply smiled in return.

"Come on Tommy, get along now."

Sighing, he turned back to the basin and reached for the toothbrush.

Descending the stairs, the sounds of his sisters being bullied from their beds behind him, Tom swung round the banister and headed for the kitchen. Stepping through the doorway he suddenly froze. Sitting at the table, a half-eaten fried breakfast of bacon, eggs and sausage before him, was a thick set, dark haired man.

"Da!" Tom exclaimed, utterly amazed.

Sean Devlin looked up and, wiping his hand across his mouth, nodded. "Hello Tom."

"Da," Tom repeated, still stunned by his father's presence. "When did you get home?"

"Late last night, your mother felt it best not to wake you all." Pushing the chair away from the table, he stood and walked across to his son. A tall, powerfully built man, Sean stroked the two-day stubble growth on his chin thoughtfully. Grasping Tom's shoulders in each hand he stared down at him. "You've grown lad," he said out loud after a few moments, though privately he thought his elder son still looked small and thin. Whilst not particularly close to his father, Tom nonetheless beamed at the apparent praise. On impulse he threw his arms around Sean Devlin's thick waist; the familiar stale smell of dried sweat and fish strangely comforting.

"I'm glad you're home, Da."

Ill at ease with such emotional displays, Sean gently prized Tom free.

Holding him at arms length on the pretence of looking him over again he said, "Aye, me too. Now then, have you been good for your Mam whilst I've been away?"

Tom nodded, not trusting himself to speak. *Hadn't his mother told him about the incident at Quigley's Farm?*

"Well, that's grand then." Turning back to the kitchen table, Sean sat down heavlly, the chair groaning under his weight, and set about finishing his breakfast.

Hesitating for a moment, Tom followed his father to the table, and sat facing him. "Did you catch many fish this trip Da?"

"Aye."

"Any sharks?"

Sean laughed. "No lad, nothing so grand, just cod." When Sean did not proffer anything further an uncomfortable silence developed between them. Watching his father eat, Tom's stomach inadvertently growled loudly. Realising his own hunger, Tom got up and helped himself to bread, butter and a glass of milk from the larder. As he busied himself toasting the bread on the hotplate of the old pot-oven, Sean glanced towards him.

"Put a slice on for me boy," he said, his mouth still full.

Silently Tom obeyed. A sudden squeal of delight from the doorway made them both turn round. "Da!" Roisin and Niamh cried out together. Running across the room, they were enveloped in a huge bear hug from their father. Standing behind them, Erin Devlin held Cianán in her arms.

"So, how are my bonnie lasses then?"

"Grand Da," Roisin replied excitedly.

Niamh nodded enthusiastically in agreement. "Are you home for good now, Da?"

"Aye, a good while at least."

"Did you bring us anything?"

"Niamh!" Erin scolded from the doorway. "Don't be so bold."

Looking up Sean saw his wife and younger son had not yet entered the kitchen. "And how's my wee Man?"

Walking slowly over, Erin tried to pass the baby across. Burying his head in her shoulder Cianán stubbornly refused to release his grip from around her neck.

"Come on now, let's have a cuddle." Sean said, trying to pull his son free; the act only resulted in the boy crying out in alarm.

"Let him be Sean, he's not seen you for months. It's going to take him a wee while to get used to you being around again, is all."

As we all will. Tom thought privately.

Sean shrugged. "Whatever." Looking back at his daughters he inclined his head towards a large, dark blue canvas holdall lying under the kitchen window. "See my dunnage bag in the corner?" Nodding, the girls looked up at him expectantly.

"Well then, let's go see what we can find in it."

Distracted by events, and slightly aggrieved that his father had not asked him to help look for, presumably, presents, a sharp shout from Erin brought Tom's wandering thoughts back to the present. From the neglected hob, clouds of black smoke spiralled serenely to the ceiling from the burning toast.

After breakfast, Erin surprised everyone by announcing that she, along with Cianán, would be accompanying all three older children to school that morning. Tom held his mother's hand all the way down Cairn Lane, subconsciously squeezing it tightly as they passed through Séamus Quigley's farmstead. Tom's fear at the thought of an irate Mr Quigley chasing him down the lane, armed with a broom handle, his two dogs biting at his heels, was nonetheless unfounded. Indeed, there was no sign of Quigley at all. The dogs, however, were present, lying in the yard silently watching the small procession. The chickens gave no sign of recognition.

After crossing the Finan Bridge and leaving the village, Tom knew it was time for him to broach the subject of the night before. His sisters were walking ahead, out of earshot, and whilst his mother had not mentioned anything of the events surrounding Mr Quigley's visit, Tom was sure she was expecting him to make the first move.

"Mammy" he began quietly, resigned to the inevitable.

"Aye, love?"

"What did Mr Quigley say last night?"

Erin looked down at him for a while before replying. "I think you know, Tommy." When Tom made no further comment she continued. "He said that two boys had tried to steal some of his hens. He accused you of being responsible, since he found your Da's rod in the yard, with a poor wee bird snared on the line."

Greatly daring, Tom tried a small dodge. "How did Mr Quigley know it was Da's rod?

Erin's eyes narrowed ominously. "Your Da has his initials carved on the handle, it being such a valuable rod and all. As well you know!" Despite his mother's opinion, Tom actually hadn't known this.

"Oh," was all he said meekly.

Head bowed Tom walked on in silence, Erin patiently waiting for him to continue. A few heavy drops of rain began to fall from the dark, overcast sky, the precursor for an imminent deluge from the heavens.

"We didn't mean to hurt Mr Quigley hens," he said eventually, genuinely remorseful. "We just wanted to catch one, you know, to get even with him for stealing our salmon the other day."

"And you think taking something from Mr Quigley is

acceptable after what he did to you?"

Tom nodded, though less certain than he had been.

"And I suppose Dónal was the other boy with you?"

Again, another nod.

Erin snorted. "I might have known he'd be at the bottom of all this."

"No Mam, you can't just blame Dónal. It was both our idea," Tom protested, feeling strangely protective towards his friend even though, as usual, it was him that ultimately ended up in trouble and punished.

Erin inhaled dramatically and raised her eyes skyward as if to emphasis her despair. In the carrier on her back Cianán yawned, and began playing with her hair. Reaching behind, Erin prized free his grasping fingers and looked back to Tom.

"Just because somebody, and it doesn't matter who, does something to you that's wrong – "

"Even stealing?"

"Aye, even stealing...and don't interrupt. That doesn't give you the right, no matter how you feel, to do the same back to them. Stealing is a sin, it's dishonest...and you know better than that."

Tom stared at his feet again. "So, you believe me now, about the fish and all?"

"Tommy, I've always believed you, but that's not the point. Don't you understand?"

"Aye Mam." Looking up he continued barely above a whisper, "I *do* know what you mean, and I am sorry."

Erin nodded, apparently satisfied. "Cianán! Will you stop that! Anyway, it's not me you need to be sorry to, even though I was very angry with you Tommy. It's Mr Quigley that you need to apologise to, and I've a mind to take you there tonight."

"Mam no!" Tom exclaimed, his face stricken. "Please don't make me."

"Give me one good reason why I shouldn't," she snapped crossly. "You've shamed me, and yourself, and this will teach you a lesson!"

Hearing their mother's raised voice the twins stopped and turned to see what was happening. Seeing the girls regarding her, Erin waved them on. "Keep going, this doesn't concern you."

Tears welled up in Tom's eyes as he reached for her hand once more. "Mammy, please don't make me go to Mr Quigley's. I know stealing is wrong, but he *did* steal our fish and he *laughed* at us Mam, he laughed because we couldn't do anything about it. I'm sorry for upsetting you, truly I am, but not him. He's a bad man."

Considering his words carefully Erin eventually nodded. "Very well, I won't force you to admit what you did and apologise to Mr Quigley – "

"Not admit to?" Tom interrupted. "So he doesn't know it was us then?"

Damn. Erin swore inwardly, chastising herself mentally for forgetting how quick her son was at reading a situation. After a moment's pause, she sighed and said out loud, "Aye, when he came round raving last night he suspected it was you, having found your Da's rod and all, and having seen two wee boys running away back towards our house. But, when I questioned him as to your involvement, he begrudgingly had to admit he couldn't be sure it was you. If he had, mind you, Mr Quigley said he'd have gone straight to the Garda, and you can be sure of that!"

Outwardly Tom tried to keep his face grave and contrite, but privately was delighted. Séamus Quigley hadn't seen them last night! He couldn't identify them. The faint hints of a smile threatened to steal across his mouth. All he and Dónal needed to do was –

As if reading his thoughts, Erin interrupted coolly. "Now, Thomas Devlin, don't you go thinking that just because Mr Quigley didn't see you, doesn't mean that I'm not going to punish you for what you did." Tom's smile faded.

They walked on together in silence. Approaching the ruins of St Mary Magdalene's, numbers of children, many accompanied by their mothers, began to appear, all making their way towards the school. Ahead, Tom spotted Cathleen Kearney talking with James Dooley, but felt no inclination to join them.

"What'll you do, Mam?" he asked quietly as the school gates came into view.

Erin glanced at him momentarily. "I don't know, Tom...I need to think. Part of me wants to teach you a real lesson."

"Will you tell Da"?

Erin had already considered this and, equally as quickly, dismissed the idea. If Sean knew Tom had taken his prized rod he would, without doubt, fly into a wild rage. The inevitable outcome would be a beating for

Tom, which didn't seem the most positive start to his return to the family home.

"No, love, I won't be telling your Da. I put his rod back last night before he came home so he doesn't have to know, but you must swear to me *never* again to take it without asking."

Tom nodded, "I promise."

"But I am going to speak to Mr Kennedy."

"About his visit last night?"

Erin blinked. "No Tommy!" she exclaimed, her voice more passionate than she would have liked. "You must forget you saw him at our house."

Seeing his slightly confused and hurt look, Erin continued more kindly. "People talk, Tommy, and some like to gossip – "

"Like Mrs Comisky?"

"Well, let's just say I wouldn't want your father to hear about it, and for him to get the wrong idea."

"So why did Mr Kennedy call round then?"

Erin gave her son one of her *that's enough looks*. "Never you mind! I'll hear no more about it now."

They reached the school gates as she finished speaking, and the press of women and children outside the entrance, chatting amiably, curtailed further conversation. A group of young mothers eagerly engaged Erin with greetings and expressions of surprise at her unaccustomed presence. Forcing herself to smile and make small talk, she did not notice her son silently walk away into the schoolyard.

For the first hour of the school day, Tom sat attentively in his usual desk at the back of Sister Frances Mary's history lesson. It was not that he was particularly interested in history, indeed the beginnings of Christianity in Ireland in the fifth and sixth Centuries and the struggles of St Patrick, were, dare he think it, uninspiring to the ten year old boy. However, the reason for his and, if truth be told, all the class's vigilance, was Sister Frances Mary was by far the most strict of the school's three nuns. As she read from her text book she would regularly walk between the aisles of the neat rows of single desks, a wooden ruler in one hand to wield on unsuspecting knuckles of any she deemed to be lacking concentration. Tom was convinced she possessed some form of sixth sense; Sister Frances Mary would always know when he or someone else was misbehaving, even if her back was turned. Thus, despite having Dónal sitting beside him, Tom dared not say anything, other than a quick whispered greeting, since the lesson had begun. Desperate for the break-time bell in order to talk to Dónal, it took all of his self control to sit still and not fidget, thereby attracting the wrath of Sister Frances Mary.

The clock on the front wall of the classroom had nearly reached ten when the door opened and Mr Kennedy entered, accompanied by Sister Madeleine and Moira O'Mahoney, the school prefect. As one the class rose to their feet.

"Good morning Mr Kennedy. Good morning Sister

Madeleine," the children proclaimed with a harmonic dirge. They all ignored Moira O'Mahoney.

"Good morning class," Mr Kennedy replied without smiling. "Please sit down."

Crossing to address Sister Frances Mary he continued, "I am sorry to disturb your class, Sister."

"Not at all School Master. How may I help you?"

"May Sister Madeleine and I trouble you for a moment outside please? I've asked Miss O'Mahoney to supervise your class while you are absent."

"Of course, School Master!" Sweeping an icy gaze over the class, Sister Frances Mary raised a single warning finger. "I will be back shortly, and I expect to hear from Miss O'Mahoney that you have all sat quietly and that there's been no misbehaviour," she said firmly. Satisfied by the collective nods from around the room, she followed Mr Kennedy and Sister Madeleine out into the corridor, closing the door behind her.

In less than a minute, Moira O'Mahoney's cries of protest as chaos ensued were completely ignored.

Turning to Dónal and shouting above the noise, Tom said "Do you think this is about us?"

"Don't be stupid, why should it?"

Wincing slightly at the rebuke, Tom replied, "My Mam came with me to school today. She said she was going to see Mr Kennedy about last night."

Dónal's expression darkened and he remained silently thoughtful for a while. Finally he said, "Well, we just say it wasn't us. To be sure Quigley couldn't have seen our faces and all."

Tom shook his head and sighed in resignation. "Dónal, My Mam knows. We dropped my Da's rod in Quigley's yard and he came round later yelling and screaming. Da came home last night and Mam said she won't tell him, but she got me to admit it was us."

Dónal swore. "What in God's name did you do that for? You're too soft, Tom. You didn't have to tell your Mam, we could have –"

Dónal's conversation was suddenly interrupted as a rubber thrown from across the class room struck him squarely on the side of the head. Yelping more in shock than actual pain, he looked round to see a grinning Brendan Harkin and another ginger-haired boy, Patrick Hogan, waving at him from across the room.

"Sorry Dónal," Brendan hollered. "I was aiming at Tom!"

"Sure you were," Dónal muttered under his breath.

Suddenly, if not totally unexpectedly, the door to the classroom flew open. "Class!" Sister Frances Mary exclaimed in the entranceway. "What's going on in here? John Kelly, Liam O'Neill, get down off those desks and the rest of you return to your seats immediately!" Hands on hips, she stepped into the room and glowered. "I leave you for two minutes and this is how you conduct yourselves. You should all be ashamed."

"Sister," Moira O'Mahoney protested quietly, "I told them to behave but they wouldn't listen to me. James Dooley and Rachael Duffy, for instances, started to –"

"Thank you, Miss O'Mahoney, that will be all. You may return to your own class now."

By the time Sister Frances Mary had walked to her desk, and the door had closed behind the clearly aggrieved Miss O'Mahoney, order had been restored to the classroom. All eyes watched her expectantly. Lowering herself with deliberate slowness into her chair Sister Frances Mary looked up and said, "Mr Devlin, Mr O'Connor." Instantly both boys stood. Tom's stomach contracted inwardly and he felt like he had been punched. "Please report to Mr Kennedy's office at once."

Without uttering a word, the boys left the classroom and walked apprehensively towards the School Master's office. In the corridor, their footsteps echoed loudly on the solid wooden flooring and neither was inclined to speculate on what awaited them. Tom felt sick.

Outside the office, Sister Madeleine was waiting for them, her demeanour stern and unfriendly. "Dónal, go straight in now. Thomas, sit over there until you are called," she said, pointing to a small bench against the wall. "And for the love of God don't move from that seat, if you know what's good for you."

Without a second glance or word to him, Sister Madeleine closed the door behind Dónal and strode back down the corridor. Staring at the School Master's closed door, Tom bit his lower lip, trying to forestall the tears that were already threatening to overwhelm him. What was Mr Kennedy saying inside? What had his mother said to him earlier? Would Dónal try and deny their stupid scheme to get even with Séamus Quigley? What should he say himself? He could hardly lie now, after admitting everything to his mother that morning. All these thoughts and more passed rapidly through Tom's mind. He could hear Mr Kennedy's voice but given the thickness of the walls and door, could not make out any of the words. Time dragged on. The break-time bell rang but Tom hardly noticed. He barely acknowledged the looks he received from fellow pupils as they passed by, some sympathetic, some smug in the way of children when they knew someone else was in trouble. Continuing to stare into space he only just realised the office door had again opened before Mr Kennedy and Dónal were standing before him. Jumping up Tom tried to catch his friend's eye, but Dónal's head was bowed. In his hands he held a white envelope. Stealing a quick glance he just managed to make out the hand-written text on the front: "*For the attention of Ms Aoife O'Connor*" – Dónal's mother.

"On your way now Dónal," Mr Kennedy said coolly. "And remember I'll be calling on your mother in the next couple of days, and if she's not seen the letter..." he left whatever previously stated threat unsaid. Turning to Tom, Mr Kennedy inclined his head towards the office door. "Inside, Thomas."

The interior of the School Master's office was sparse and rather dim; the only natural light emanating from one small window opening onto the schoolyard. An old oak desk, the wood riddled with years of woodworm, and a worn leather-backed chair were the principal furniture. In front of the desk were two further metal framed chairs for visitors. A few small, but rather uninspiring, seascape paintings hung from the walls. Tom sniffed subconsciously; the office smelt damp and musty. Even with the window ajar, the faint, sweet, aroma of years of burnt turf from the small fireplace in the corner clung to the fixtures like a shroud.

Rather than sit behind his desk, Declan Kennedy sat in one of the two visitor chairs and invited Tom to take the other. For what seemed to Tom an eternity he simply regarded him closely, his face unreadable. Squirming uncomfortably, Tom silently endured the scrutiny, terrified of what was to come.

"Do you know why you are here, Thomas?" Mr Kennedy finally asked, his eyes never leaving Tom's. In that instant, Tom knew he had no choice but to speak the truth.

"Aye Sir. My Mam said she was coming to speak to you about, about me and Dónal –"

"*Dónal* and I," he corrected with a faint smile.

"Sorry Sir, Dónal and I. We got into trouble with Mr Quigley."

"Again, from what I've heard?"

Tom nodded. "It's a long story, you see last Saturday –"

Declan held up his hand, stopping Tom in mid sentence. "Thomas, I've heard all of this from your Mother earlier. What Mr Quigley did, or did not do, and what you subsequently did in terms of retribution, is *not* why you're here. The real issue, as your Mother sees it, is the influence that Dónal O'Connor is having on you, and more to the point on your behaviour. I know

I've only been at school a very short time, but I've had some very disturbing reports from the Sisters concerning Dónal's attitude and behaviour. If you're not careful and you continue to let Dónal influence you the way he is doing, you run the risk of getting yourself into some very serious trouble someday."

Whilst he had been speaking, Tom's gaze had progressively sunk, until now he was looking downcast at his feet. Leaning forward Declan put his hand under Tom's chin and gently raised his head until their eyes met again. "You're not a bad lad, Thomas, and neither your Mother nor I want to see you become one. Do you understand what I'm saying?"

Tom nodded, but felt no inclination to speak.

Sighing deeply, Declan stood and returned to the far side of his desk. Sitting and leaning back in his chair thoughtfully; in that one gesture he became the School Master once more.

"Well, Thomas, it's an unfortunate business. I said earlier that I'd not called you here to discuss your feud with Séamus Quigley, but notwithstanding Dónal's role in your exploits, what you did was wrong, and your Mother wants you suitably punished."

Tom steeled himself, simply whispering, "Aye Sir."

"This isn't to my liking but your Mother wants you punished here at school rather than at home. Furthermore she and I want you to reflect on your relationship with Dónal O'Connor."

Again, Tom nodded. "I will, Sir."

"I hope you do," Declan added meaningfully.

Standing, he crossed to the window and gazed out, hands clasped behind his back, considering carefully what he was about to say. Break-time was finishing and the children were beginning to file back to their classes. Tom remained sitting, awaiting whatever judgement, fate and Mr Kennedy were about to bestow upon him.

Turning back to face him, Declan Kennedy paused for a moment before saying, "Starting tomorrow you'll stay for an extra hour after school for the rest of this week, and all next. In addition, and until I tell you otherwise, you and Dónal O'Connor will not sit together in class nor, whilst you are on the school premises, talk to one another unless directed to do so by me, or one of the good Sisters." Removing his fob watch from his waistcoat pocket Declan glanced at it before continuing slowly, "I understand if you think I'm treating you harshly, Thomas, but you need to understand everything I have said this morning and understand why you are being punished in this way."

Tom nodded. "Aye Sir."

"Do you understand Thomas?"

Again the slight nod. "I think so, Sir." Whilst a little naïve at times, Thomas Devlin was far from stupid. He had always known that his mother did not like him associating with Dónal; by being kept behind at the end of the day and forced not to speak at school, the opportunities for he and Dónal to meet and converse were greatly reduced.

Well, Tom thought silently, *they'd just have to see about that wouldn't they.*

"I do hope so," Declan concluded, studying him carefully. Stepping briskly to the door he opened it for Tom. "Please return to your class now. Tell your Mother what I've decided, and be sure she knows you'll be home late for the next two weeks."

"Aye Sir."

As Tom walked out of the office a sudden thought occurred to him. "Sir, what did you say to Dónal?"

For a moment Declan considered not saying anything, it was, after all, none of the boy's business. Debating in his mind whether the truth would help the situation, Declan quickly concluded it might. By knowing what had happened to his friend, Tom would hopefully begin to appreciate both his and Erin's resolve to address the issue.

"I'm sure you're aware that Dónal has been warned many times in the past about his behaviour at school and outside. The incident with Mr Quigley, I'm afraid, was the final straw. He's been suspended for the remainder of the week and I've sent a letter home for his mother, explaining the situation, and my judgement."

Tom's eyes widened in surprise. Before he could say anything, Mr Kennedy continued, "I've also told Dónal that if he does not show significant signs of improvement in behaviour, or if an incident such as yesterday is repeated, then I'll have no alternative other than to permanently expel him from this school."

5
OLD FRIENDS

For Tom, the next two weeks passed surprisingly quickly. In a strange way he quite enjoyed his extra hour's detention after school. Rather than, as he had expected, being forced to sit in silence in front of Sister Madeleine's desk writing lines or solving maths problems, he had spent much of the time reading quietly in Mr Kennedy's office. On a number of occasions Mr Kennedy had spoken at length with him, and on a variety of topics. Together they had discussed such diverse subjects as the life cycles of honey bees, to the impact on the farming community from the 'economic war' currently raging between Britain and the Irish Free State. The quiet, unaccompanied walk back from school each evening also gave him time to think, and the late arrival home had the added bonus that he avoided many of the post school jobs, such as helping his mother prepare dinner.

One issue that did concern Tom, and was increasingly occupying much of his thoughts, was his father. With Sean Devlin's return a perceivable tension was progressively growing within the family home. It had taken a little under a week for Sean to grow irritated at being around the house. Wee Cianán's demands for attention and corresponding howls of frustration when these were invariably denied, together with the twin's almost constant bickering had taken their toll on his generally short temper. Arguments between Erin and Sean were increasingly becoming commonplace. Unsurprisingly, Tom's father had soon joined his older brother Cianán, and had returned to the sea in the latter's twenty-five foot open launch. The summer salmon and lobster fishing season had begun, and Sean now spent the best part of the day at sea or on the beach, mending the fine gill nets or wicker lobster pots. He would return home only after dusk when the failing light made shore work too difficult, or being at sea in such a small boat too dangerous. More disturbing, particularly for his mother, was the fact that his Da was also spending more and more time in the evenings drinking in the local village bars.

The only other matter that troubled Tom during those weeks was Dónal's standoffish behaviour towards him. True to his word, Tom had studiously avoided his friend during class lessons. The boys were made to sit at opposite ends of the long, narrow classroom; Dónal at the front on a desk by himself and Tom at the back, sharing one with Cathleen Kearney. A true friend to him since as long as he could remember, Cathleen was delighted to sit beside him, and would frequently whisper jokes during the Sister's lessons. Fearing further reprisals if caught talking, Tom tried his best to ignore her, but Cathleen's sharp wit and dry sense of humour more than once had him on the verge of laughing out loud.

During lunch or other break-times, Tom similarly avoided direct contact with Dónal. They were both well aware that they were being watched, not only by the particular Nun on playground duty, but by Mr Kennedy, and also a good number of children. The likes of Moira O'Mahoney, Dennis Quigley and others of that ilk, would have liked nothing better than to run to the School Master or Sister Madeleine to tell on them for a clandestine meeting. Tom did, on a few occasions, try to catch his friend's eye across the school yard, but if Dónal saw him, he gave no outward sign. What truly puzzled Tom, however, was throughout those two weeks when he had to serve detention, not once did Dónal endeavour to wait and / or meet him outside the school grounds. Virtually everyday Tom expected to see his friend sitting atop the crumbling church wall of St Mary Magdalene's waiting for him, but never once did he appear. Even at the weekend Dónal obviously kept to himself, this despite Tom's best efforts in surreptitiously searching the village and all their favourite haunts for him. The worrying thought began to form in Tom's mind that Dónal was truly aggrieved with him.

*

In a dimly lit corner of Kearney's Bar, Sean Devlin toyed absently with his empty pint glass, contemplating whether to have another. Glancing at the gilt-framed clock over the bar Sean smiled ruefully. It wasn't late after all, only just past nine and this was also only his third. Erin would probably complain that it was late in her eyes but then again, Erin would invariably nag him whatever he decided. Sure she had four children to look after but she was at home all day, not working like him. He was the breadwinner in the family and worked hard all day to provide for her and the family. Why couldn't she accept that he *needed* to relax in the evenings, and have some time to himself?

Feeling sorry for himself at the apparent injustice of it all, Sean looked up from his table, gazing through the smoke-filled haze at the other dozen or so patrons around the bar. He knew them all by name and whilst most were chatting amiably in twos or threes, other than a brief nod in his direction, none had volunteered to approach and engage him in conversation. Not an unpleasant man, Sean Devlin was nonetheless not a very popular one either.

Sighing, he dug his hand into his pockets searching for more change. Concentrating on sorting through the coins, he did not notice a figure stand up from his seat in a darkened corner and cross to stand in front of the table.

"Can I get you another, Sean?" Declan Kennedy asked quietly. Staring up at the tall teacher, Sean at first said nothing. Then with a slight shrug he nodded his agreement.

"Do you mind?" Declan said, glancing at the vacant chair opposite.

Sean shrugged again. "Suit yourself."

Taking the seat, Declan leaned round and called to the landlord. "Joe, two pints when you're ready – what are you having Sean?"

"Guinness."

"Another Guinness Joe please, and a Best."

The landlord, Joe Kearney, a middle-aged, stocky man with a pleasant demeanour, waved an acknowledgement. Declan turned back to face Sean. For a while the two men sat in silence, cautiously watching each other.

Finally, Sean pushed his empty glass away and sat back. "So, you're back then."

Declan simply nodded.

"I heard you'd taken the new Master's post, so I take it you're here to stay then, and this isn't some token visit?" The words, whilst spoken softly were said with an obvious hint of resentment. If Declan took offence by the slightly bitter tone, he didn't show it.

"Aye, I've had my fill of Dublin now. I'd heard the old Master had finally retired, so when his job came up, well, I felt it was the right time to apply. Ten years is a long time to be away from your home."

"So Ballyfinan's to be your home then?" Sean replied rather tersely.

Declan shifted slightly in his seat before answering. "I always thought it was, Sean."

"As maybe." Sean sniffed loudly and rubbed the stubble on his chin. "So, you'll be buying some place?"

Again Declan nodded. "Aye, eventually. I've seen a nice wee cottage for sale in Tullagh but I'm not in any particular hurry. I'm happy enough staying with my sister and her family in the village for now."

Further conversation was halted by the arrival of the drinks. Joe Kearney was no fool, and like most of the older community of Ballyfinan, knew that bad blood had, and probably still did, exist between the two men. What the origin of that ill feeling was, Joe did not know, nor did he particularly want to. He did, however, know that as boys growing up in the village, Sean Devlin and Declan Kennedy had been inseparable. But that friendship had suddenly and dramatically ended in a huge and very public fight on a stormy, rain-soaked night in the Square, ten or eleven years ago. Shortly after, Declan had left and had not been seen or heard of in the village again, until this spring.

Placing the drinks on the table Joe noted the palpable tension and withdrew to regard the pair from the shadows. A patron at the bar caught Joe's eye and, nodding in the direction of the table, smiled knowingly. "Trouble?" he said quietly.

Joe frowned. "Perhaps – Devlin's a fiery temper on

him, but at least he's not drunk."

"Not yet at least."

"Hmm."

"Thanks," Sean murmured, sipping from the glass and waiting for Declan to speak.

Declan smiled slightly. "How've you been, Sean?"

"Fair, I suppose; a little more money would be nice. Times could be better...but I've known worse."

Declan nodded in understanding and hoped the gesture would not appear condescending. With no qualifications to speak of, he knew Sean earned his living from the sea. For much of the year Sean served as a deckhand on Killybegs' deep-sea trawlers, and Declan could only surmise at how physically hard and demanding such work was. Reliance on fishing for income was also capricious.

"And the family?"

Sean's eyes narrowed fractionally. "Fine," he allowed guardedly. Another period of prolonged silence developed. Throughout the bar the low, background hum of conversation died away as the regulars surreptitiously strained to hear, whilst outwardly appearing to ignore the two men.

Closing his eyes for a moment and unconsciously rubbing the bridge of his nose, Declan tried to gather his thoughts. From the moment he had decided to return to Ballyfinan, and had accepted the position of new School Master, he had known meeting Sean Devlin again would not be easy. Declan had hoped that after all these years his one time best friend would have put the past behind him. Obviously he had not.

"What is it you want, Declan?" Sean said sharply, cutting into his thoughts.

"I want to talk."

"About what?"

"About us for one thing. About the fact that I'll be living around here again, and well, if I'm honest with you, I'd like us to be friends."

Sean's stare hardened. "'Honesty' is an interesting word coming from you."

Pausing, Declan breathed deeply before replying. "It doesn't have to be like this, Sean. I regret what happened – "

"You regret?" Sean jeered.

"Aye, I do...you know that, I've said it a hundred times in the past." Staring at each other, for a moment neither man said anything further. Allowing his gaze to fall to the table, Sean took solace in his drink, waiting for Declan to continue. Behind them, Joe Kearney edged nearer, conscious of the heightened atmosphere.

After a minute, Declan leant forwards, "Listen Sean," he began quietly. "As I said, I want us to be, well if not friends, then at least – "

"I don't give a damn what you want!" Sean spat back, his voice suddenly trembling with rage. "And there is no us, okay! Not after what you did!" Angrily he drained his glass and stood up aggressively to leave, tipping the chair over in his haste.

"Take it easy now, Sean," Joe warned from a few

feet away, retrieving the overturned chair. "I'll have no trouble in my bar tonight." Ignoring the landlord, Declan eased back in his seat, thoughtful. "I've moved on, Sean; Erin's moved on...and so must you."

"Don't tell me what I must do, you arrogant bastard."

"Right, that's enough," Joe said laying a firm hand on Sean's shoulder. "I think it's time you left."

Shrugging the landlord's grip off, Sean continued to glare coldly at Declan.

"I'm sorry, I didn't mean it to sound the way it did, but Sean, please, for all our sakes, at least consider what I'm trying to say. The past is past. I cannot, will not, walk on eggshells around you or your family. I have professional responsibilities, as far as your children are concerned and – "

"Listen Kennedy," Sean interrupted in a dangerously sober voice. "I'm warning you, stay away from me, and stay away from my wife."

Declan shook his head. "I can't. Erin's already come to see me, at school. She's worried about Thomas and wants me to –"

Banging the glass down hard, Sean Devlin leant across the table, fists clenched and resting on the wooden surface. "What did you say?" he said quietly, his face inches from the School Master's.

Joe made to seize Sean again, but Declan waved him off.

"I'm waiting," he continued menacingly, his voice barely above a whisper.

"Sit down," Declan said calmly, "Stop making a fool out of yourself before Kearney throws you out."

For a moment he remained standing, glaring. Sipping his pint, Declan calmly waited. Finally Sean lowered himself slowly back into his seat, but continued to stare with obvious hostility across the table.

"As I said, Erin has already come to see me. She's concerned for Thomas."

"When did she come to see you?"

Declan sighed. "A couple of weeks ago, but that's not important, what is, are her concerns for your son."

"Such as?"

"Such as the trouble Thomas has been getting into recently. Erin's worried about the influence some of his friends have been having on him. You must've noticed that I've been keeping him back after school for the last two weeks?"

Sean nodded. "He prefers Tom, not Thomas, and of course I have." He hadn't, but wasn't about to let Declan know that.

"Well, the reason I've detained him was to try and stop him associating with one boy in particular, Dónal O'Connor. I've also arranged that they no longer sit together in class. Dónal's not a bad lad on the whole, but he does have a disruptive attitude. The issue, Sean, is that there is only so much that *I*, as Thomas' School Master can do."

"And?"

"And," Declan said, taking another sip, "I think the boy needs some greater direction from his father."

*

Yawning somewhat excessively, Tom watched sleepily as the half dozen or so fishermen readied themselves for the days' work at sea. Even in mid May the immediate post-dawn temperature was cool and the boy shivered despite the extra layers of warm clothing that his mother had insisted he wear. Not that he minded the chill in the slightest. Tom still couldn't quite believe his good fortune. Today was Friday, and a school day after all! He had gone to bed the night before, expecting to be woken by his mother at seven o'clock as usual the next day, and endure the ensuing manic rush to get ready for school. However it was Sean Devlin that had roughly shaken him awake well before sunrise and brusquely informed him that he was to help on the boat today. Half asleep Tom had nonetheless obeyed his father's curt commands to get dressed quickly, and go downstairs to have breakfast. In the kitchen he could still hear his mother nearby arguing fervently, but quietly, so as not to wake the rest of the household. Erin's anger at her husband's sudden and unilateral decision to take her son fishing was clear. Sean, however, was adamant; the boy was going to sea, school or no school, and that was that. No one had asked Tom's opinion, not that either of his parents would have considered it in anycase.

"Tom!" Sean called crossly. "Stop day dreaming and take this bag down to Cianán.

"Aye Da. Sorry," the boy added quickly. Grasping the

heavy canvas holdall containing their lunch, drinks and wet-weather gear, Tom walked as fast as he could towards Lenan Pier and the awaiting boats. Lenan Pier itself was a simply designed but solid, concrete breakwater, stretching a hundred yards or so directly out into Lenan Bay. Along the lee side a number of evenly spaced, rusty metal ladders dropped down to the sea, where less than a dozen small wooden fishing boats were moored. On the seaward side and running the length of the open walkway on top of the pier was another, much narrower, raised wall that offered some shelter to the fishermen from the elements.

As Tom walked along the pier, careful to avoid tripping over the various ropes, ring-bolts, lobster pots and other similar hazards strewn about, a number of the fishermen nodded pleasantly in greeting. None however stopped in their work to talk; the tide was on the ebb and no one could afford the time for idle conversation. At the very end of Lenan Pier, Cianán Devlin's twenty five foot long open launch rocked gently in the sheltered lee. The smell of the sea was strong, and Tom could not help beaming as he looked down the ten feet or so to where his uncle was stowing coils of rope and other equipment neatly out of harm's way.

Glancing up, Cianán raised a hand in greeting. "Well, good morning to you Tom. Are you ready for your first day at sea?"

Tom nodded enthusiastically.

Cianán smiled. Like his brother he was a tall, well-built man, but unlike Sean's dark almost black hair,

Cianán's was much lighter, a mousy brown that was only now starting to show the first signs of grey. His eyes were pale blue and alive with merriment. He could have been described as quite handsome, if it were not for his heavily pockmarked face, the scarring a result of a severe pox illness suffered as a child. The two brothers were equally unalike in temperament. Whereas Sean was much inclined to brood and suffer prolonged spells of deep sullenness, Cianán was invariably happy and cheerful. Although a popular man in the village, Cianán was not married; his generally positive, optimistic outlook on life, however, put that down to simply a matter of time. He made no secret of the fact that he dearly wanted to marry and have children, but in the meantime he cherished his nephews and nieces as if they were his own. Erin Devlin always thought her elder son's personality had been inherited more from his uncle than his father, and privately was very thankful for it.

Stepping from the launch onto the corroded metal ladder, Cianán Devlin effortlessly climbed the rungs to stand beside Tom on the pier wall. Dressed in heavy jeans and a thick red checked shirt under yellow oilskin dungarees and boots, he smiled kindly down at his elder nephew.

"I've been telling your Da for weeks now that you should come and give a hand on the boat. I'm glad he's finally seen sense and asked you."

Tom did not think it appropriate to say that his father had not exactly asked him. Instead he simply smiled back and said, "Aye Uncle Cianán, I'm really looking forward to it." Glancing down at the launch he continued, "Do you think we'll catch many fish today?"

Cianán chuckled. "Well, God willing and seals notwithstanding." Seeing Tom's slightly puzzled look he roughed the boy's hair with his large hand. "Never mind, perhaps you'll see later."

Inclining his head slightly towards the bag at Tom's feet, Cianán added, "Is that from your Mam?"

"Aye, lunch and drinks and such."

"Well, we'd better get it stowed aboard then before your Da gets here."

Lifting the bag easily over his shoulder, Cianán climbed back down into the boat. Tom watched as he slid it carefully under the stern seats. Turning back, Cianán beckoned for him to join him. After a second's slight hesitation Tom obeyed, carefully stepping onto the ladder and slowly climbing down.

"Now lad, sit yourself up front, in the bow, whilst I check a few things. Your Da will be here shortly when he's finished talking to Mr Callaghan."

Tom's gaze followed his uncle's outstretched arm. At the far end of Lenan Pier a single dirt track meandered gently back to a dozen or so single storey cottages that comprised the hamlet of Lenan. At the end of the track, a single black Ford B pickup was parked, beside which Sean Devlin and another man were talking.

"Uncle Cianán, who's Mr Callaghan?" Tom asked.

Not looking up from his tasks Cianán replied "He is our agent, for the catch – do you know what an agent is?"

Tom shook his head, but seeing his uncle was not watching added, "No sir."

"Well, when we get back with the catch, Mr Callaghan buys our fish from us. He'll then sell them on the bars and hotels in Dunkeeny and the like. Your Da's negotiating with him now to get the best price for our fish."

As Tom watched he saw his father shake Mr Callaghan's hand and stride purposefully back towards the pier.

"Why don't we sell our fish to the hotels ourselves?"

Cianán stood up and smiled inwardly, admiring his nephew's insight. "You're a bright lad Tom, don't let anyone ever tell you otherwise." Rubbing his chin thoughtfully he continued, "Unfortunately we need Mr Callaghan's help. You see, he's got all the contacts, and besides neither your Da nor I have a truck, or a horse. It's a long walk to Dunkeeny and how would we carry all the fish!"

Tom grinned back up at his uncle's smiling face.

Already a couple of boats had cast off from the pier, their two-man crews raising a hand cheerfully to Cianán and Tom as they slowly motored passed. Fascinated, Tom watched them depart until a voice from the embankment wall above drew him back to the present.

"Ready?" Sean Devlin called down without preamble.

Cianán nodded, "Aye, Sean."

"Well, let's be away then."

Taking up a heavy looking iron starting handle, Cianán cranked the lever sharply and on the third attempt the solid, diesel engine spluttered into life. Simultaneously Sean untied the fore and aft moorings, tossing the thick ropes into the boat. Swiftly climbing down to the foot of the sea wall ladder he helped shove off the launch from the pier before jumping across the widening gap onto the decking. Cianán gently adjusted the throttle and the small craft got underway.

"What did Callaghan agree to?" Cianán asked quietly after a minute or so.

Sean did not look up from carefully coiling the mooring ropes safely away on deck. "Five pence per pound in the end" was the curt reply. "The bastard will sell them for ten."

Unseen by his brother, Cianán simply shrugged in resignation. That was life.

The natural entrance to Lenan Bay, with its sheltered anchorage and small fishing community, was at best only four hundred yards wide. After rounding the pier's head it was not long before the full force of Lough Swilly, and the Atlantic swell beyond, had the small launch pitching and rolling as she struggled out to sea. The wind, from the North West, a fresh force four or five, raced across the surface whipping minute droplets of sea spray constantly from the wave tops. Tom, leaning out over the prow, was soon soaked but nonetheless exhilarated as the boat relentlessly plunged into the troughs before rising once more to crest each wave. Wiping salty spray and wet hair from his eyes he could not help grinning. Enthralled, he watched half a mile ahead as the two earlier departed boats similarly laboured in the choppy seas.

Aside the tiller, Cianán initially maintained their westerly course for a few moments before steering north towards Lenan Head, a craggy headland of ancient Precambrian rock, marking the northerly boundary of the bay. Passing Lenan Head they continued to hug the coastline, two hundred yards or so offshore, for a further four miles, before rounding Dunaff Head, another ancient granite promontory rising almost vertically over seven hundred feet above the waves. Cruising parallel to the promontory, Tom watched a flight of small sea birds returning from the open sea, flying directly towards the steep, rocky cliffs.

"What are those?" he asked to no one in particular and pointing at the birds. Sean shrugged, clearly not interested, and continued busying himself about the boat, preparing for the day's fishing.

Shading his eyes with one hand from the low early morning sun, Cianán stared after the birds for a few moments. "They're kittiwakes Tom," he said with a slight disapproving glance towards his brother.

"They look like sea gulls to me."

"Well, in truth they are. Prettier than your normal gull mind, and quite common here abouts, out at sea that is. You don't often see them inland though."

Tom continued to regard the flight, frowning

thoughtfully. "Are there lots of gulls out at sea then Uncle Cianán? How do you tell them apart, they all look the same to me."

Cianán chuckled. "Aye, there are – but there's gulls and there's gulls, as we say. You're probably thinking about the Common Gull or the Herring Gull. Kittiwakes are similar but you can always tell them apart, when they fly their black wing tips don't show any white, unlike the other gulls. See, it looks like they've been dipped in ink."

Tom was genuinely impressed. He would never think of sea gulls in such a simple way again. "How do you know these things, Uncle Cianán?"

"'cause he spends too much time gazing out to sea when there is work to be done," Sean growled sullenly. Silence descended once more upon the boat.

From Dunaff Head Cianán steered the launch gradually more to the North East, still following the coastline but bearing progressively further out to sea. Before them, two to three miles distant lay Tullagh Bay, its entrance marked by yet another jagged headland, Tullagh Point, thrusting out like an angry finger from the land. Intending to navigate the boat well to the north of Tullagh Point with its hazardous, partially submerged outlying rocks, Cianán aimed to arrive at their fishing grounds within the Bay, a half mile or so offshore. As they passed Tullagh Point and headed across the bay towards Binnion Hill on the far side, Tom turned his attention from watching the shore to regard his father.

Sean Devlin, standing in the centre of the boat, was calmly gazing out over the surrounding sea, swaying with practised ease with each roll of the waves. Watching him, Tom's confused feelings began to rise once more. He wanted to be closer to his father, to be accepted and make him feel proud, but somehow Sean Devlin always seemed to erect a barrier between them. Deep down Tom hoped his father loved him, and wanted him, but unlike his mother's love, he could never be sure it was there.

A noticeable change in the steady tone of the boat's engine ended Tom's reflections.

Easing back on the throttle, Cianán gently slowed the launch, its reduced forward momentum still allowing steerage towards a prominent yellow buoy directly ahead. The buoy marked one end of the brothers' submerged salmon net. Unseen below the waves, the fine gill mesh hung vertically to a depth of nearly five fathoms, held upright by a line of smaller white buoys bobbing serenely on the surface. Tom gazed at the line, stretching in a gentle arc for over a hundred yards, before ending in another of the larger yellow marker buoys.

Seeing his apparent interest, Cianán waved, indicating Tom should join him.

"Would you like to know how all this works lad?" he asked pleasantly.

Tom stepped tentatively along the deck to stand beside him at the stern. "Aye, please."

"Well, the net yonder hangs in the water, like a wall.

Those floats on the top and a few wee weights along the bottom help keep its shape. Your Da and I use a mesh of five inches, that way only the biggest fish get caught. Any wee salmon can swim through free."

Tom nodded in understanding. He had seen men working before mending and preparing nets on the foreshore. A sudden thought occurred to him. "But Uncle Cianán, how do you know there'll be fish here? The sea's so big."

Cianán chuckled and tapped a thick forefinger against his nose. "Old fisherman's trick. Look, where are we? What can you see?"

Tom looked around as bidden. "Well," he said slowly after a few moments. "We're obviously in Tullagh Bay...and that's Binnion Hill over there."

"And?"

Frowning slightly, Tom struggled to grasp what his uncle was inferring. Sean looked across, watching the exchange with unexpected interest, but saying nothing.

Inclining his head slightly, Cianán indicated in the direction of Binnion Hill. "What else can you see?"

Tom chewed his lower lip, concentrating. "There's the mouth of the river, and next to that the dunes."

Raising an eyebrow, Cianán waited to see if the boy could bring it all together. Evidently he could.

"And the salmon swim into the river!" he exclaimed.

"Aye, well done lad. That's why we're here. The ones we're after swim back and forth a few hundred yards offshore, sometimes for days on end, waiting for the right conditions to make their run upriver."

"Like at high tide."

Cianán nodded. "Aye, that and the cover of night and the smell of a wee bit of freshwater flowing to the sea make it very appealing to them. The Finan's in spate with all the rains we've had this week, and –"

"And yesterday's full moon means a Spring tide," Sean Devlin said suddenly, strangely feeling left out of the conversation and not liking it. "A very high tide."

"Aye, all this means conditions are about as ideal as they get. Your Da and I have had the nets out all night...and now we shall see what we shall see."

Tom listened, fascinated. He had no idea how complex salmon gill netting could be.

As they approached the nearest yellow buoy, Sean leaned out over the side, a small gaff in hand to capture the marker. Cianán eased the throttle back further and the launch virtually stopped.

"Got it?" he asked after a few seconds' pause.

"Aye, kill the engine."

As Sean pulled the buoy in over the side, Cianán cut the engine and joined his brother in the centre of the boat. With the loss of headway the small craft pitched and rolled more excessively in the heavy swell and Tom lurched dramatically from side to side trying to keep his feet.

"What shall I do Da?" he asked, staggering but managing at least not to fall over. Both men turned to face him, pausing momentarily in their work. For a moment an awkward silence developed. Finally Sean pointed to a large wooden crate lying towards the stern.

"When we free the fish from the nets, drag them over there. Okay?"

Tom nodded eagerly.

"And for God's sake don't drop any overboard. Everyone ready?" Cianán and Tom both grinned in anticipation.

"Right then, let's go."

Trying to keep out of the way, Tom watched as his father and uncle slowly dragged the net in. Working together, Sean slightly in front of his brother, they hauled it over the side, skilfully coiling it onto the deck behind them. Their efforts, combined with the heavy swell, caused the small launch to rock even more, and Tom was forced to grasp hold of the boat's side rail to steady himself.

A feeling of panic was instantly banished by his father's excited shout. "'ere they come!"

Tom stretched to see past them, but before he could establish a better vantage point, the first silvery salmon was on deck.

"Not a bad size," Cianán said to no one in particular. Smiling, he expertly freed the thrashing fish from the net and slid it across the decking towards Tom. "About ten pounds I reckon. There lad, get it in the crate now, quick as you can."

Dragging the struggling, slippery salmon to the crate, Tom quickly manhandled it into the box. Before he had a chance to consider what to do next, his uncle had already freed another, similar sized fish, and with a shout, slid it towards him.

After nearly an hour, and with three quarters of the netting stowed on board, Sean called for a short break. Twelve glistening salmon, none of which, Cianán had assured Tom, was smaller than eight pounds, lay quivering within the wooden crate. A few minor tears in the net had made Sean frown, but other than that he seemed pleased with their catch so far. Tom was soaked and cold, but nonetheless thrilled.

Stretching his back to ease stiffness, Sean Devlin said, "Tom, go and see what your Mam has packed for us to eat."

Rummaging in their canvas bag Tom eventually replied, "There are some sandwiches Da, slabs of cheese, a few apples and a flask."

Walking over to him, Sean helped himself to a sandwich and the flask. "You want one Cianán?" he asked without looking up.

"Aye, and I expect young Tom could do with a bit too, eh?" Cianán answered, offering a friendly smile to the boy.

Tom grinned back. "Aye, please. Fishing's hungry work!" Sean made a dismissive humph sound, but nonetheless handed out the food.

The break was soon over. Standing behind his father, Tom waited absently for the next fish to be delivered. Suddenly, Sean swore angrily, startling him. Unsure what was happening, Tom glanced towards his uncle, who was intently watching the incoming net rise from the water. As the two men heaved the net behind them onto the deck, Tom saw Cianán shake his head and purse his lips. There in the netting, neatly trapped at the gills was the head of another large salmon; its body however, other than a few attached entrails, was nowhere to be seen.

"Bloody, bloody seals!" Sean continued to rave. Ripping the head violently from the net he tossed it angrily over the side. Cianán looked back at Tom and simply shrugged.

By the time the last of the net was safely on board they had only managed to land three more live salmon. Another four heads with partly devoured bodies had been discovered tangled in the netting. Worse, the mesh around each of these fish had been torn and damaged, in some cases quite dramatically, as the seal or seals had struggled to dislodge the trapped salmon. They would have to take the net back to shore for repair, a long and time-consuming process and Sean was furious that they would now miss tonight's run.

As the brothers prepared the boat for the return trip, Sean continued to curse and mutter darkly. Wisely, Cianán and Tom tried, as far as possible, to keep out of his way. When all was ready, Cianán restarted the engine and, throwing the tiller over, steered the launch back towards Lenan Bay. Sitting quietly next to his uncle, Tom let his gaze sweep casually over the sea, his thoughts drifting. For a second he did not register the small round head watching them closely, fifty yards astern. With a rueful smile, Tom stared at the grey seal as it floated on the surface for perhaps half a minute before disappearing, without a splash, beneath the waves. Sensibly, he decided not to mention his latest wildlife sighting to anyone.

6
BEYOND RECALL

After breakfast the next day, Tom was surprised when his mother made no demands for his time and informed him she needed no errands run that morning. Erin Devlin was unusually quiet and even a noisy squabble between the twins did not invoke her customary wrath. Slightly perturbed but nonetheless not wanting to tempt fate, it being a Saturday and all, Tom fled the house as soon as he was excused.

Descending Cairn Lane Tom casually passed through Quigley's Farm. There was no chance that Séamus Quigley himself would be up this early, and taking his time continued on, considering what to do. Without conscious effort he found himself heading towards the river and the Finan Bridge. As he approached the bridge a new thought occurred to him; *he hadn't visited his and Dónal's secret hideout since the day they had caught the salmon. Perhaps Dónal would be there?* Having genuinely missed his friend over the last few weeks, more than he liked to admit, Tom was still confused and a little hurt that Dónal hadn't made any effort to contact him. Picking up his pace, he hurried across to the bridge. Clambering over the low wall he dropped down onto the grassy bank below and headed across the gorse field to their den.

Sometime later Tom sat thoughtfully on the high sand dunes at the foot of Binnion Hill. Below, the golden expanse of Tullagh Bay stretched out for over a mile. Alone, he watched the breaking waves relentlessly crash onto the sandy beach, the brisk onshore wind whipping a constant mist of spume, that hung suspended like a thin fog, above the surf. Dónal had not been at the hideout. Further, there had been no evidence that he had visited it in recent days. Disappointed, Tom had wandered aimlessly downstream, following the course of the River Finan to its confluence with the sea, adjacent to Binnion Hill. After throwing a few stones into the brown, peat-rich waters, he had climbed the marram covered dunes and stared out unhappily over the sea.

Without a watch Tom had no way of telling how long he had sat watching the waves' ceaseless assault on the foreshore. A sudden grumbling of his stomach coupled with a realisation of a prolonged stiffness in his backside paid testament to the fact that time had not stood still. Glancing up at the sun, which was almost directly overhead, Tom deemed it to be near enough lunchtime. Standing, he dusted himself down and for a few seconds considered his options. He had no intention of going home for lunch, his mother was more than likely to have changed her mind since the morning and would undoubtedly find jobs for him to do. He contemplated visiting Cathleen Kearney but quickly dismissed the idea. Cathleen's house was on the far side of the village, near St Mary's Church, and Tom was beginning to feel too hungry to wait. Besides, Cathleen's mother, Mary Kearney, whilst a lovely lady, tended to fuss over him too much. No, with a flash of inspiration Tom skipped down the bank of the sand dunes until they petered out, merging with the low lying sandy grassland bordering the edge of Binnion Hill. Racing around the perimeter of the hill, he eventually stopped on reaching a narrow, familiar track leading up. Starting to feel hot after his exertions, Tom pulled off his jumper and wrapped it around his waist. Grinning in anticipation of the surprise his visit would bring, he began the slow, steady climb towards his grandmother's cottage.

In the summer months Eileen O'Brien often left the front door, and the windows, to her small cottage open; with the fine weather, today was no exception. Tom stole quietly up the garden path, crouching low to avoid being seen. Nearing the open doorway, he paused. Voices could be heard from within, one obviously his grandmother's, the other a man's, but indistinct. Intrigued, Tom crept closer, conscious he was eavesdropping but nevertheless unable to help himself. Approaching to within a few feet, the conversation became discernible.

" – surely he has the right to know?" the man's voice said.

There was a slight pause and then Eileen answered. "But you inferred before that you don't know? Not for sure in any case?"

"No, not for sure."

"And can you honestly say then, that it's *he* that has the right…or is it *you* that wants it?"

Again there was a pause before Tom heard the man reply quietly, "Aye, you're right, I do want to know…but is that so wrong?" His voice was familiar though Tom couldn't quite identify it. It didn't help that he was speaking softly. Heart pounding Tom tiptoed closer to try and hear better.

"It is," he heard his grandmother say in return. "If by striving to fulfil your own desires you cause suffering and anguish to everyone else concerned. Erin's having a hard enough time at the moment as it is. I can't believe you, of all people, would want to inflict this upon her now." Eileen O'Brien's voice became slightly raised, but the reply was as calm and measured as before.

"Mrs O'Brien, you know – "

"Eileen, please."

"Eileen, you know, I've no intention of hurting anyone, least of all your daughter. God knows I know what her husband's like. But I left, remember, and at Erin's request. I've spent ten years away from Ballyfinan, and if Erin's marriage is under strain, it's not on my account."

Outside the open doorway, Tom unconsciously held his breath; they were discussing his mother!

Shock had replaced the feelings of unease and guilt. He knew he should leave but his feet wouldn't move.

A few seconds passed before Tom realised his grandmother and her visitor had stopped talking again. Only the faint sounds of chinking teacups carried across to him. Slowly he tried to calm his racing thoughts...the sensible thing to do would be to quietly slip away. Listening in was no longer the fun Tom had anticipated it to be. He had known something was wrong at home, but having it confirmed like this was more than unsettling.

"So then, Declan. What is it you want from me?" he overheard Eileen say abruptly.

Declan! The penny dropped. Declan Kennedy was his grandmother's visitor! Unwittingly Tom gasped.

"Hello? Who's there?" Eileen said, the sound of a chair being pushed back resounding audibly.

Instinctively Tom rapped loudly on the wooden door. "Gran, it's me!" he exclaimed, a little too excitedly. "Surprise!" Stepping into the cottage he strode quickly into the living room. Eileen O'Brien was already standing, the look on her lined, weathered face unreadable. Declan Kennedy sprang to his feet, almost upsetting the small tea table at his side. His shocked expression, Tom thought, would have been highly amusing if the situation had not been so serious. Standing before them Tom grinned, trying to look pleased with himself that his 'surprise visit' had worked as innocently as he'd wanted them to think it had.

"Hello Tommy," Eileen said evenly, her eyes never leaving his. "This is a surprise. Are you on your own?"

"Oh, aye, Mam's at home and I've been playing on the beach." Glancing at Mr Kennedy, Tom thought he perceived a flicker of relief in his eyes. "I'm hungry Gran, can I have some lunch please?" he continued, trying to steer the conversation on to safer grounds.

"Of course, dear. Go into the kitchen and help yourself; I'll join you in a wee while. Mr Kennedy and I are just talking. Would you like to join us for lunch, Mr Kennedy?"

Declan looked up from rearranging the tea table. "That's fine Mrs O'Brien, but I really should be going."

"Are you sure, now?"

"Aye, thank you all the same, and for your time. Good afternoon." With a slight nod to Tom, he walked to the front door, Eileen following to see him out. Tom decided it was best to do as he was told and headed for the kitchen.

At the door Declan offered his hand. "I'm sorry if my visit may cause any difficulties."

"Not at all. I'm only sorry you feel you have to leave. Tom is a good boy, I'm sure he's not heard anything he shouldn't have."

"I'm sure too, but I think it's for the best, for now at

least. His father and I had a bit of a...disagreement the other night, and I wouldn't want Sean to get the wrong idea."

Eileen nodded understandingly. "Aye, you're probably right. I'll speak to Tom, to put your mind at rest at least."

The School Master smiled appreciatively. "Thank you, Eileen."

He was half way down the neat garden path before Eileen called after him. "Mr Kennedy – "

Stopping, Declan turned to face her.

"You're always welcome here, please remember that. Come and visit me again, if you feel the need to talk. I'll try and help in any way I can."

Nodding in gratitude, Declan Kennedy simply waved, but said nothing. Eileen watched him disappear through the gate, lost in thought.

*

Crossing the Square, Tom cast a tentative glance across to Cairn Lane. For a moment he considered returning home, then quickly dismissed the idea. Despite feeling slightly disturbed by the overheard conversation he nonetheless did not feel inclined to see his mother just yet. Erin Devlin was a very shrewd woman and Tom knew from past experience that she was bound to notice his distracted mood, no matter how hard he tried to hide it. Like a terrier Erin would persistently worry him until he revealed what the trouble was. He needed time to think this through.

Recalling every aspect of the conversation in his

mind, Tom passed Mrs Brennan's shop, oblivious to the tempting sweets and pastries on display. Two small children, their noses pressed hard up against the window, gazed longingly at the liquorice laces, brandy balls and icing sugar birds' eggs in meringue nests visible through the glass. As he walked slowly by, their mother proffered a passing greeting but, if he heard, Tom gave no outward sign. A little further on three old men relaxed on a wooden bench outside Kearney's Bar, chatting amiably and enjoying the pleasant sunshine. They too tried to engage Tom in conversation but again to no avail as he passed, head bowed. A raucous shout and roar of laughter from within did however make him look up. Registering the bar, a sudden flash of inspiration occurred to him. *Kearney's Bar... Cathleen Kearney!* Cathleen would know what to do. Decision made and sighing inwardly in relief at finding direction, Tom increased his pace, striding briskly towards Cathleen's house, on the far side of the village. The attack, when it came, took him completely by surprise.

A sudden sharp crack, rebounding head-height off the wall to his right made him jump; his head turning instinctively towards the sound. The flight of the small projectile ricocheted behind him unseen. A second later Tom cried out, his hand instantly grasping at a sharp pain below his left ear. Spinning round, his peripheral vision registered the small pebble bounce off the pavement, before rolling harmlessly to a stop in the gutter. A harsh cry from across the street further drew his gaze.

Two shabbily dressed boys holding makeshift catapults laughed cruelly at Tom's obviously shocked expression. The larger of the two raised his weapon once more and purposefully took aim. The smaller boy followed suit, but then swore angrily as his stone fell from the catapult's cap onto the ground. Stunned, Tom could only stare, his legs refusing to move despite the danger. The larger boy shouted something as he lined up his sights, but Tom didn't hear what was said. Firing the catapult, Dennis Quigley's gleeful expression changed instantly, and he cursed as his small stone rebounded harmlessly off the wall to Tom's right. Quigley's companion, recovering his own projectile, also took aim and fired. This time Tom didn't see or hear where it landed; the spell was broken and he ran, racing away from Kearney's Bar towards the far end of the village, and St Mary's Church. Another stone struck his back, but either the increasing distance or adrenaline coursing through his veins, dulled any pain. Head down, arms pumping at his sides, Tom fled. Not even the unmistakable sound of breaking glass behind caused him to stop or look back.

Running as fast as he could, Tom didn't finally stop until, near exhausted, he had reached the last outlying houses before the Village Hall, adjacent to the church. As such he didn't see Dennis Quigley and the other boy flee also into one of the back lanes leading away from the Square. Neither did he see a very irate Deirdre Comisky emerge from her house and tirade passers by about her broken window. One such apparently sympathetic individual was Séamus Quigley.

On a low, moss covered stone wall overlooking the two acre enclosed playing field, known locally as "the Park," Tom absently rubbed the back of his neck, and watched a group of boys playing football. Attracted by the shouts and cries from the game, he had sat quietly observing the match for ten minutes or so before being seen. Ordinarily he would have eagerly joined in, indeed two of his friends, Brendan Harkin and James Dooley, were playing and had already waved him over. Not in the mood, Tom had declined, feigning a headache, which was not far from the truth.

Unusually for a Saturday afternoon no one had been at home at the Kearney's large, if somewhat rundown looking, old farmhouse. Disappointed, Tom had continued to wander, passing the church before arriving at the Park, also the official village green, where amongst others, the annual summer Sheep Festival was held. When not given over to the Festival and other communal village events, the Park was the favoured retreat for the youth of Ballyfinan.

The shock from the unprovoked attack had worn off, replaced now by feelings of confusion and anger. Tom had recognised the fat unkempt figure of Dennis Quigley instantly, and had a reasonable idea of his companion. Why Dennis had attacked him, though, was a mystery. To be sure, Tom admitted to himself, he and Dennis were not the best of friends but he couldn't think of anything he had done to alienate him to such a degree. Unless, of course, it was out of pure spite, a feat certainly not beyond any of the Quigley Clan.

It was not long before the warm sun, coupled with fatigue from his escape, began to take effect. Head gently nodding, Tom's chin gradually sank towards his chest and he dozed. Flight filled images raced through his mind and then from a distance it seemed someone was calling his name...

"Tom! Tom! Wake up, silly." Tom's eyes flew open. Standing directly before him and smiling, obviously amused, was Cathleen Kearney.

"I've been calling you for ages. I thought you were going to fall off the wall. Anyway, why were you asleep?

"I wasn't," Tom protested feebly.

"Liar!"

Tom sighed, but decided against arguing the point. "Alright, but – ", he hesitated slightly before continuing, "Cathleen, where have you been? I need to talk to you."

A mischievous twinkle entered the older girl's beautiful blue eyes and, without asking, she climbed swiftly up onto the wall to sit beside him. Placing her arm through his, Cathleen pulled him slightly closer and smiled. "Why, Mr Devlin," she said playfully, "whatever is it that you need to speak to me so urgently about? I do hope your intentions are honourable?"

Tom stammered something unintelligible and blushed scarlet.

Laughing, she flicked her long auburn hair from her shoulders, a gesture that did nothing to ease Tom's awkwardness.

"I'm sorry Tom, I shouldn't tease you."

To Tom's mind Cathleen sounded anything but sorry. Glancing down at his arm, uncomfortably aware that her hand still rested affectionately on it, he simply shrugged and said, "That's okay."

At his shy response, Cathleen's smile softened. Slightly more seriously she said, "Now, what do you want to talk about?"

How long they sat together that summer's afternoon, quietly talking, neither of them could afterwards properly recall. The football match on the Park finished, the participants departing unnoticed. The shadows lengthened as the setting sun descended towards the rugged mountain backdrop and still they remained together, sometimes speaking, often just sitting in silence, taking simple comfort in each other's company. For the first time Tom spoke openly about the fears and concerns that had been plaguing him over the last few weeks. He recalled not only the troubling events of earlier, but also the worrying changes in his mother's behaviour since his father's return. Cathleen listened attentively to accounts of conversations Tom had had with Mr Kennedy, and the growing closeness he felt for the School Master, paradoxically at the expense of his cooling relationship with his father. Tom spoke of Dónal, and his uncertainty with respect to their friendship. On this subject only, Cathleen smiled knowingly and told him not to worry. Despite being pressed she would, however, not elucidate further. The matter of Dónal notwithstanding, Cathleen listened to

Tom and offered advice and encouragement, where needed, with skill and tact far beyond her years. In those hours Tom's respect and fondness for his lifelong friend grew and developed in a way he couldn't quite explain.

Eventually, as the first of the flocks of starlings began to gather for their evening roost, they agreed it was time to go. Walking Cathleen home, her arm still linked with his, Tom felt at peace. He was not quite sure what had happened that afternoon, but something had changed, for the better, between them.

The front door to Cathleen's home was pulled briskly open as they were still crossing the muddy yard to the old farmhouse. Cathleen's mother, Mary, stood in the doorway, hands on hips, a look of annoyance deeply ingrained on her face. Normally a very pleasant, benevolent woman, her irate demeanour stopped both children in their tracks.

"Cathleen! Where have you been? I expected you home hours ago. Your father's still out looking for you and is furious that he's missing his skittles match."

Taken aback, the girl lowered her head and apologised, explaining she had been with Tom all afternoon.

Looking at Tom, Mary Kearney rubbed her hands on her apron and regarded him intently. Under those piercing blue eyes, Tom squirmed uncomfortably, and also looked down.

"Well, best go straight home now Tom, I know your

mother wants to see you." Something in Mary Kearney's tone made Tom glance up. Her slightly flushed face betrayed more than she was obviously willing to divulge. Something wasn't quite right.

*

The sky had turned a vivid scarlet by the time Tom turned into the small garden and trudged slowly towards the front door. He half expected the door to fly open and his mother rush out to envelop him in her arms. Tom had convinced himself in the time taken to walk from Cathleen Kearney's house, that the only possible explanation for Mary's behaviour was that his mother must also be worried about him. Following the expected slight scolding, a humble apology and suitably contrite manner would see everything right again.

As usual the front door was not locked. Entering, the house was strangely quiet. In the hallway, Tom removed his shoes (at least his mother couldn't chastise him for not wearing them today) and stepped into the small living room on the right. Despite the small turf fire burning in the hearth, no one was present.

"Hello?" he called out quietly, retreating back into the hall. "Is anyone in?"

An immediate stampede of footsteps overhead was followed by first his sister Niamh, then Roisin appearing at the top of the stairs. Niamh raced half way down before stopping and grinning gleefully at him. "You're in *big* trouble!" she said excitedly. "Mamma's going to kill you!"

Stunned, Tom could only stare up at her. At the top

of the stairs, Roisin jubilantly joined in with the taunting, "Mamma's going to kill you!" Mamma's going to kill you!" Tom poked his tongue out at them.

The disturbance brought Erin Devlin, her face like thunder, from the kitchen at the back of the house.

"Niamh! Roisin! Be still the pair of you! Get back upstairs to your rooms and don't dare come out again until I call you." Giggling, the two girls scampered away only to reappear seconds later out of sight of their mother, faces pressed eagerly between the landing rails.

Erin turned her fierce gaze towards her son. "And what have you to say for yourself?" she said coldly.

Tom shook his head stupidly. "What do you mean?"

Misreading Tom's confusion for insolence Erin stepped swiftly forward, grasping his arm and steering him forcefully into the living room. "I've no time for such foolishness Thomas Devlin. Get in here!" Upstairs his sisters nudged one another and again tried to stifle a laugh.

Releasing him to close the door, Tom backed away, nearly tripping over a small side table in the process.

"Well?" Erin reiterated, her curt tone in no mood for argument.

Tom's mind was racing. Rarely had he seen his mother this angry. For the life of him he couldn't think what he had done to warrant such wrath. Again he shook his head. "Mam, I really don't know what you're talking about. What've I done?"

"Don't lie to me, Tom...not over this."

"I'm not. I swear it!"

Erin raised her eyes dramatically heavenward. "Jesus and all the Saints, Tommy! Do you think I'm daft? You were seen! Don't you understand? You were seen throwing those stones at Mrs Comisky's window."

"What?"

"You broke her window you stupid boy! Why did you do it? Did Dónal put you up to it? By God, if he did I'll have his hide too. Mrs Comisky's been here most of the afternoon and it's taken hours for your father and I to calm her down, and persuade her not to go to the Garda. As it is your Da's there now, trying to make amends by installing a new window."

Tom rocked back and forth on his heels. This was madness.

"The shame you have put this family through," Erin continued, still incensed. "We'll be the talk of the village!"

"Mam," Tom finally said, trying to sound calm and composed. "I did not throw any stones at Mrs Comisky's window! Someone was throwing stones at me! I know who it was but don't know – "

The slap across his face brought instant, stinging tears to his eyes, more from shock than actual pain.

"I told you not to lie to me Tommy," Erin shouted angrily.

"I'm not!" he yelled back, obstinately stamping his foot. "Who saw me then? Who said I broke her bloody window?"

"Don't you *dare* use such language in this house!"

Erin raged, unconsciously raising her hand once more.

Flinching, Tom looked down, his expression sufficiently abashed to forestall further punishment.

"I'm sorry," he allowed somewhat grudgingly. "But I *didn't* do it and you still haven't said who saw me."

"It doesn't matter. What does matter is –"

"Yes it does. If Dennis Quigley said it was me, then he's lying. It was Dennis who –"

"Dennis Quigley?" Erin interrupted in turn, the anger leaving her voice and the first trace of doubt evident.

"Aye, Dennis Quigley. He and some other boy had catapults and started firing stones at me as I walked through the Square. They hit me on the back of the neck, here." Tom twisted round and indicated where the stone had struck him. There was no mark but Erin was not looking in anycase. Distracted, she gazed past her son lost in thought.

Turning to face her once again Tom said, "So, was it Dennis then?"

Looking back to him Erin answered quietly, "No Tommy. It wasn't. Deirdre – Mrs Comisky said Séamus Quigley told her he'd seen you throwing stones at her window."

Quigley! Séamus *bloody* Quigley! Tom shook his head in disbelief. Opening his mouth he considered voicing more colourful opinions of that horrible man, but then thought better of it. Remaining silent, he glared at the floor, angry and frustrated at the injustice of it all.

The forceful slamming of the front door made both

of them jump.

"Dear Lord," Erin breathed. "Your father's home."

"*Where is he?*" Sean Devlin roared from the hallway. "You girls, get to your beds or I'll take my belt to you!"

Instinctively Tom shrank behind his mother as the living room door was almost pulled off its hinges. Framed in the doorway, Tom's father, his face purple with rage, glanced first at his wife before stepping inside the room.

"Sean," Erin said quickly. "I think there's been a misunderstanding – "

"Where is he?" Sean repeated menacingly, ignoring Erin completely. The small oil lamps in the living room had not been lit yet, but even in the dusky gloom Tom knew it was just a matter of time before he was spotted. Holding his breath, his eyes tightly closed, he prayed, but to no avail. Swinging his head from side to side like a bull, Sean searched the room, his own eyes gradually growing accustomed to the dim interior. Within seconds he saw Tom's hiding place, and with a beast-like growl, strode forward.

"Sean, no!" Erin cried, standing protectively before her son.

"Get out of my way, woman."

"No. Please listen –"

Erin Devlin staggered across the room, her grasp on Tom's arm torn free by the force of the blow.

"Mam!" Tom screamed, bursting into tears. For a few seconds Erin could do no more than hold her own hand to her face, and watch in shocked silence as her husband towered over the cowering boy.

"Be damned if I will. Four shillings and sixpence you cost me, you little bastard," Sean Devlin spat, his fists opening and closing at his sides. "Not counting the bus fare to Dunkeeny and back to get the glass. Four shillings and sixpence!"

Tom sniffed heavily and wiped his nose across his sleeve. "Da, I didn't – "

Quick as lightening, Sean reached out and grabbed the front of Tom's jumper and shook him violently. "And all the men in Kearney's Bar laughing at me as I fixed that damn window!"

The sight of her husband aggressively shaking Tom jolted Erin into action. Stepping back she grabbed Sean's arm and tried to pull him away, screaming at him to stop. She might as well have been striving to move a rock. Shrugging Erin off, Sean simultaneously held her at bay with one hand, whilst stubbornly not releasing his hold on Tom.

"Be still woman," he threatened menacingly. "Or I'll take my belt to you too!"

Writhing, Tom desperately punched and kicked his father, trying to get free. Finally and unthinkingly, he bit deeply into Sean's hand. Crying out in pain, Sean instinctively released him but then instantly stuck Tom with a back handed slap, hard across the face. The impact lifted the boy clean of his feet and propelled him backward across the room. Tom heard his mother scream again as he crashed headfirst into the iron grating astride the hearth; then blackness took him.

*

Shafts of sunlight stealing through the curtains and the unmistakable melody of a blackbird's song slowly roused Tom from the depths of sleep to wakefulness. He knew without having to open his eyes that he was in his own bed; the feel of the mattress and the familiar, comforting smell of the woollen blankets told him as much. For a few minutes he lay perfectly still. His head hurt terribly and as his consciousness crystallised, memories of the night before gradually began to coalesce. He remembered arguing with his father, but little else. A vague memory of laying in bed and a dark, shadowy figure bending over him flickered across his mind. Suddenly a grinning image of Séamus Quigley leapt unbidden into his thoughts and Tom's eyes flew open. Staring at the ceiling, the magnitude of what Quigley had done fully dawned on him. The man was despicable; not only had he spitefully tried to frame a ten year old boy but his actions had resulted in his own mother being beaten. Struggling to sit up, Tom winced in pain and held a hand to his forehead. A cloth bandage was wrapped around his head, and tentatively his fingers probed the extent of the dressing before withdrawing.

"How are you feeling?" a soft voice asked from across the room.

Looking round Tom saw his mother sitting in a low chair, opposite the bed. Smiling and stifling a yawn behind her hand, Erin slowly rose and walked over to sit on the edge of the bed. Gently she eased him back into the pillows. "Lie still, my love. The Doctor said you must rest today and stay in bed."

"The Doctor?"

"Aye, you gave us all quite a start. Doctor Kerrigan has been here most of the night, in fact he's only just left. He bandaged your head, and he and I have sat with you all this time. He'll be calling in again to see you later on this morning."

Tom's hand reached again for the dressing, but Erin intercepted it and placed it tenderly, but firmly, back onto the sheets.

"It hurts Mam," he said quietly but nonetheless remained still.

Erin gently stroked his forehead. "I know sweetheart."

"What happened? I can't remember much."

Again Erin smiled kindly. "Don't worry about it now, Tommy. We'll talk later. Now try and get some sleep. Do you want any water?"

Tom shook his head slightly, but instantly regretted it as shooting pains stabbed him between the eyes. Seeing him grimace, Erin's concerned frown generated a rueful smile from Tom. "No thanks Mam, I'm fine." Nodding, she started to rise from the bed.

"Don't go Mam, please. Stay here with me a wee while longer."

"Of course, my love. I'm not going anywhere, just stretching my back is all. Do you want me to carry on stroking your head?"

"Aye, please. I don't feel sleepy though" he said

untruthfully, trying to stifle a yawn.

Sitting beside him once more, Erin continued to caress him affectionately. "Just try Tommy. Close your eyes now and try to relax."

Closing his eyes, Tom did as he was bidden. Within two minutes he had drifted back off to sleep.

He awoke briefly sometime later to see his mother talking quietly in the corner with a tall, grey haired man with a smartly trimmed beard. Well dressed in a tweed jacket and fawn trousers, Tom recognised Doctor Kerrigan immediately. Lying still and unnoticed by either of them, he simply closed his eyes again, not feeling inclined to talk. Within minutes he was asleep again.

The next time Tom awoke the room was empty. The curtains had been opened and his bedroom was bathed in dappled sunlight. From the half opened window the sounds of cattle being driven down Cairn Lane filtered through. Struggling to sit up, Tom looked around. A glass of water and a thickly cut sandwich lay beside him on the bedside table. Seeing the food Tom's stomach gave an involuntary grumble; he had not eaten anything since he was at his grandmother's yesterday lunchtime, and he was famished. Learning across, and wincing slightly at the pain, Tom reached first for the water and then the food. Concentrating on his meal he did not see the door slowly open, and his mother enter.

"I see you've not lost your appetite," Erin said pleasantly, the traces of a faint smile hovering on her lips.

"No Mamma," Tom replied, his voice and mouth full.

"Don't bolt it down too fast, young man. Would you like another sandwich?"

"Aye."

"Aye, *please*."

"Sorry, please." As she closed the door gently behind her, Tom relaxed. Leaning back into his pillows he chewed slowly on the last of the sandwich, his thoughts drifting. Without warning a vivid memory surfaced, his face falling in consternation.

"Mam!" he cried out in alarm.

Running back up the wooden stairs Erin rushed into the bedroom and anxiously regarded her son. "What is it, Tommy. Are you alright?"

"Da hit you Mam! I remember now, he hit you when he was holding me."

Unconsciously Erin's hand reached up to touch her cheek. Seeing the gesture Tom stared at his mother's face. The bruising on her left cheek was clearly apparent, despite the generous application of blusher. Embarrassed under his intense gaze, Erin turned her head away.

"Are you okay Mam?" Tom persisted, his tone clearly worried.

Erin nodded. "Aye love, I'm fine. Don't go getting yourself —"

"But where's Da?" he interrupted.

"Hush now, Tom. Your father's not here." Seeing him open his mouth to ask the obvious question Erin leant across the bed and gently placed a finger against his lips. "That's enough for now. We'll speak later, I promise." Standing, she straightened her dress and continued, "Be good now, and I'll be back shortly with that sandwich."

It was not long before Tom heard the telltale sound of approaching footsteps on the stairway. As the door opened, he glanced across; the surprise on his face unmistakable. Grinning wolfishly, a tray with two plates of sandwiches and thickly buttered fruitcake in his hands, Dónal O'Connor laughed out loud at his friend's shocked expression.

"Dónal!"

"At your service, my man. Where do you want this?"

"How? But...where have you been?" Tom managed to stammer.

Continuing to grin, Dónal carefully put the tray down on the end of the bed. "Your Mam let me in just now," he said, dodging the question. "Cathleen told me what happened at church this morning. I thought I'd better wait until this afternoon, you know, before coming over...your Mam might – "

Tom frowned in confusion. "At church? Since when have you gone to Sunday Mass? And besides, how does Cathleen know what's been going on?"

"Tom," Dónal said suddenly serious. "Everybody knows."

A potential, awkward silence was averted by the appearance of Erin at the doorway, two steaming mugs in her hands. "I've brought you boys some hot chocolate. Tom, I said Dónal can stay and have supper with you, for a while at least. But remember Dónal, Tommy still needs his rest, so don't tire him out."

"Aye, Mrs Devlin. Thanks." Nodding in satisfaction, she departed, quietly closing the door behind her.

"Your Mam seems a wee bit more friendly towards me nowadays." Dónal said conversationally.

Tom ignored the comment. Gathering his wits he stared hard at his friend. "Dónal, where have you been?" he repeated. "I've not seen or spoken to you for weeks. I'm not stupid, I know you've been deliberately ignoring me. I was beginning to think you didn't like me anymore." Inwardly Tom cringed as the last comment come out, expecting a sarcastic retort or at best to be laughed at. To his surprise, Dónal only smiled and nodded in understanding.

"Aye Tom, I have been avoiding you, but not for the reasons you think. You are, and always will be, my best friend. But after that day at school I knew Mr Kennedy, your Mam, that little telltale Moira O'Mahoney, and probably everyone else in the village would be watching me like a hawk. I needed to throw them off the scent; make them think I was truly sorry, and had changed my wicked ways! And the best way to do that was...?"

He left the question hanging for Tom to answer. Silently, Tom just shrugged.

"To do as I was told of course! Be good; leave you alone; do my homework; go to Mass, etc, etc. Now I'm a reformed character, and see the results of my endeavours...your Mam invites me in with open arms, and gives me hot chocolate and buttered fruit cake to eat!"

Despite the obvious deviousness of Dónal's plan, Tom couldn't help but laugh at his friend's outrageousness.

"You really are an evil man you know," he said happily.

"Oh, aye," was the proud reply.

7
FESTIVITIES

With the arrival of the heady days of summer, life for Tom settled down into a semblance of normality. In the weeks following the incident at home, he and Dónal continued to observe the restrictions placed upon their relationship at school, but progressively allowed their friendship to be publicly seen around the village. Dónal also became increasingly genial with many of Tom's other friends, and in particular he and Tom were often seen playing football and other games together with the likes of Brendan Harkin and James Dooley. On many occasions Cathleen Kearney also joined the boys in their antics. To Tom's mind he and Cathleen continued to enjoy what he thought of as a 'special' friendship.

However, the physical closeness that had occurred on that fateful day had, as yet, not been repeated – much to his disappointment.

When Tom finally had returned to school any qualms he had felt about seeing Dennis Quigley again proved unfounded. The larger boy's heavily bruised face and thick split lip, combined with the knowing grins from Dónal, Brendan and James, were testaments enough to how his friends had reacted to Dennis' part in Tom's misfortunes. Tom decided there and then to let the matter be; he wasn't vindictive, and besides didn't want to make another enemy within the Quigley clan. But if Tom had seen the vicious looks Dennis Quigley directed at him behind his back, he would have been in no doubt as to the other boy's feelings towards him.

Erin Devlin also began to increasingly spend more time with her elder son, especially after the summer term finally ended, and the school holidays began. On Sundays in particular, it became a regular routine for them, following lunch at Granny O'Brien's, to walk together along the beach at Tullagh. Often wee Cianán would accompany them, strapped to his mother's back; the twins invariably stayed behind with their grandmother. Tom enjoyed and valued immensely this 'special time' as he thought of it, with his mother. They talked of many things, some trivial, some serious. More often than not they simply strolled side by side in silence, each taking solace in their own thoughts, and valuing the other's company. Only once did they discuss the incident at home. After some initial reluctance, to

Tom's surprise his mother had been remarkably open and willing to listen. As they had walked bare-footed across the sands in the shallows of the advancing waves, Séamus Quigley's mischief-making was eventually acknowledged, and Tom's innocence finally accepted. Despite this admission, Erin made Tom promise not to take matters into his own hands and seek revenge. His mother's clearly evident concern that he would escalate the entire episode with potentially dire and unforeseen consequences, troubled Tom sufficiently that he agreed to let the matter lie. Erin did promise to have a quiet word with Mrs Comisky though.

Tom learnt his mother had been terribly worried following his injury, and had on more than one occasion tried to speak to his father about his violent temper. Sean Devlin adamantly refused to discuss the matter. Tom wasn't surprised. For weeks now his father had been avoiding not only him, but the family as a whole. Whenever he was in the house, which ironically, following the striking of his wife and son, was increasingly more often, Sean rarely said a word to anyone. He certainly had not been, and appeared to have no intention of, engaging Tom in anything like a meaningful conversation. Sean avoided the village bars and clubs in the evening now, preferring to drink alone at home. Although never publicly spoken of, it was obvious to Tom and Erin that Sean's drinking was progressively starting earlier each day. Moreover, he was often semi-drunk by mid-afternoon and increasingly cried off going to sea to fish with his brother. Although Sean had not hit either of them again, his temper most of the time was only barely kept in check. All Tom's family, even the twins, adopted a certain watchful wariness in his presence.

*

"You're quiet Tommy," Erin said softly, leaning across the Kearneys' large kitchen table to squeeze his hand. It was the first Sunday in August, and Mary Kearney had invited Tom and his family back for lunch, after Mass, to celebrate the traditional Celtic harvest festival of *Lughnasa*.

Tom did not look up, but absently pushed the half eaten, customary meal of Colcannon (mashed potatoes, onions, cabbage and milk) and bacon around his plate.

"What's wrong love? Are you feeling alright?"

Tom shrugged. "I'm fine."

"There must be something. You've hardly touched your dinner, and it's one of your favourites."

Eyes still downcast he whispered, "You'll only laugh if I tell you."

More puzzled than concerned, Erin lifted his chin up to face her. "I won't...I promise. Now, what is it?"

Sighing, Tom regarded his mother guardedly for a few moments. "Cathleen's asked me to take her to Magheramore Hill this afternoon...to collect bilberries."

Erin blinked hard, then burst out laughing.

The festival of *Lughnasa* was known by a variety of names but probably the best known being *Bilberry Sunday*. On this day, it was traditional for young people to climb the mountainsides, for the first time in the year, to collect bilberries. These small, dark blue berries, were the first summer fruits to mature and finding them hidden within the dense heather bushes of their highland, bog habitat, could take all day. With young men and women spending long hours together searching for bilberries, *Bilberry Sunday* had also become associated as a time for courting. It was often said that many a lad had met his wife on *Bilberry Sunday*. As a teenager, Erin herself had celebrated many a memorable *Lughnasa* on the high slopes of Magheramore Hill, one of the best bilberry / heathland habitats close to Ballyfinan.

"You said you wouldn't laugh!" Tom protested crossly.

"Oh, I'm sorry Tommy," Erin replied, still chuckling. "It's just, well...you know, very sweet and I'm happy for you." Tom continued to glare at her.

"What's so funny?" Mary Kearney said, coming over from the sink and wiping her hands on a towel. Glancing at his unfinished meal she added, "Didn't you like my Colcannon, Tom?"

"It's fine" he replied sullenly.

"Tom," his mother warned. "Mind your manners now." Turning to her cousin Erin grinned. "Cathleen and Tom are going to Magheramore Hill this afternoon, Mary."

"Are they now?" Cathleen's mother answered with a smile of her own. "Well now, I'm sure you'll both have a grand time of it."

Tom glanced away again, muttering darkly, his ears

already burning.

As they neared St Mary's Church, Tom grew increasingly nervous. Sensing his mood, Cathleen had teased him mercilessly, deliberately relating romantic tales of how wonderful *Bilberry Sunday* had become. The church was the long-established after lunch meeting area for the festival's outdoor excursions, and already a large gathering of teenagers and young people were present. Various groups of girls huddled together in small groups, chatting excitedly and giggling; the boys stood detached, pretending disinterest, but nonetheless talking overly loudly. Many of the girls had flowers in their hair, another time-honoured tradition. *Bilberry Sunday* was also a family day out and although many younger children were there, running around, laughing and chasing each other, it was an unwritten convention that the collecting of bilberries on the higher slopes of Magheramore Hill was strictly out-of-bounds to all but courting couples.

"There's Siobhan!" Cathleen exclaimed, pointing to her older sister. Nearly eighteen, Siobhan was tall and attractive with long, auburn hair and bright blue eyes. For years she had been pursued by many potential suitors from the village but, as far as Tom was aware, none had been successful. As they approached he saw she was standing next to a similarly tall, fair-haired young man, smiling and laughing at some remark or other.

"Who's she with?" he asked casually. "I don't

recognise him."

"Oh, that's Paul Geraghty, her fiancé...they've only just got engaged, isn't it amazing!"

Tom made a noncommittal sound from his throat but wisely said nothing further.

"I think he lives near Dunkeeny. He's really nice, and Mam and Da like him, which says something, don't you think?"

"Aye, I suppose..."

Tom was only half listening as Cathleen continued. "Paul's here for the Sheep Festival, the week after next. He's one of those special workers, you know, shearers or clippers or whatever they're called, that all the farmers want to hire. He travels around, looking for work and Da hired him earlier on this year. That's when he and Siobhan met. He's been sending his wages to her, and what with the bar work she's been doing, Siobhan thinks that, with the money he'll earn this summer, they ought to have saved enough to get married next spring. Come on, let's go and say hello!"

Before Tom had time to react, Cathleen had grabbed his hand and, half dragging, led him through the milling assembly to where the couple were talking.

Along the Dunkeeny Road, a few hundred yards past the last house in Ballyfinan, an unmade high-banked trackway branched off to the east, snaking its way upwards to finally end in a rusting, metal gate. Beyond, the heather-dominated boggy slopes of Magheramore Hill stretched away into the distance. Close to the gateway, on the lower ground, a number of large, rectangular stacks of freshly cut turf lay drying in the summer sun. Each stack had literally hundreds of small, individually cut 'bricks' piled end on end. Not one of these storage heaps was less than twenty feet long and all were well over eight feet high. A great number of straight cut ditches, some extending for over fifty yards, criss-crossed the lower slopes, testimony to this extensive peat extraction industry.

As Tom and Cathleen scaled the gate, they could already see many children and their parents scrambling over the wet heathland, searching the slightly less waterlogged hummocks for the elusive bilberry shrubs amongst the heather. Ascending to the higher slopes, many couples, often hand in hand, were disappearing from view. Tom was fully content to search the blanket bogland near to the gate, but Cathleen was having none of it. On the pretext that the best berries were to be found towards the top of the hill, she marched purposely on, seemingly oblivious to his anxieties. Trudging along behind, Tom had already endured a number of wry grins, and the occasional wink, from parents of younger children on the heath, much to his distress, and their amusement.

After perhaps half an hour of hard walking, Cathleen called a halt. It was hot, with little breeze and only a few wispy clouds to break up the sun's intense glare. The exertion of the climb and the radiant weather had made her face glow.

"Here," she said, taking a water bottle from her

shoulder bag and offering it to Tom.

"Thanks." Drinking thirstily he passed it back, and after they both had had their fill, they turned to survey the landscape.

They were over three-quarters of the way to the summit. In the far distance, innumerable ant-like figures could be seen below searching the lower slopes, whilst around and before them, only a few couples were still evident, most having dispersed throughout the hillside seeking seclusion.

"So, what do you think?" Cathleen asked quietly. Tom shot her a quick, hesitant look.

"Ah, it's very nice," he replied cautiously.

Cathleen laughed. "No, silly! About this spot I mean...for collecting the berries."

"Oh...aye, it looks grand." She flashed him a dazzling smile and Tom's heart almost skipped a beat. He could feel his face glowing but hoped she would put it down to the warm sun and the climb.

"Well, come on then let's get started!"

Despite his preconceived anxieties about spending time alone together on Magheramore Hill, and his obvious nervousness, Tom thoroughly enjoyed the afternoon. Sometimes sitting together, talking quietly or occasionally remaining silent, gazing out over the dramatic scenery, absorbing the peace and tranquillity. Other times they hunted enthusiastically for bilberries or fought mock battles, throwing the fruits at each other and rolling in the heather, trying to force one another to eat them. But, as the sun waned and increasing numbers of couples began to appear, descending hand-in-hand from the heights, thoughts reluctantly turned towards home.

"Perhaps we should head back soon?" Tom repeated the suggestion he had made a few minutes earlier.

Cathleen sighed. "Aye, but I don't want to; the afternoon's gone too quick and I don't want it to end."

Tom nodded. "Me either." Smiling wryly he continued, "It's been fun…well, much more than I'd thought – " Seeing her frown slightly he added quickly, "I mean, I never realised how spending time with you, alone like this could, ah, make me feel so happy. You mean a lot to me Cathleen…"

"Really?"

"Aye, really."

Beaming, she suddenly stepped forward and kissed him squarely on the mouth. Spinning around, her long auburn hair momentarily whipping his face she marched purposely down the hillside. "Well, that's grand then," she called over her shoulder. "Perhaps we can do it again next year?"

Stunned, but grinning stupidly, Tom could only nod readily.

*

Even before the side of the launch had bumped up against Lenan Pier, Tom had grasped a rusty metal rung, and began to deftly scale the sea ladder, a sodden mooring rope clasped tightly in one hand. Within seconds of reaching the breakwater he skilfully secured the bow mooring to an encrusted, heavy iron ring, one of a number interspersed evenly along the concrete causeway. Walking back, Brendan cast the aft mooring up to him and that too was quickly tied off. With the boat safely moored, Cianán Devlin cut the engine, his cheerful countenance clearly reflecting the end of a good day's fishing. As he busied himself battening down the engine's canopy for the night, Dónal and Brendan began to haul the heavy crate containing their catch towards the jetty ladder. Although Tom had accompanied his uncle a couple of times on trips since the end of school, always when Sean was absent, this was the first time Cianán had allowed his two friends to join them. The boys had all worked hard and unknown to them, Cianán was pleased with their efforts. Indeed, given Sean's increasingly erratic behaviour, he was considering asking if they might want to join him on a regular basis.

After checking the overnight salmon nets first thing, which had been unusually poor (only three fish), Cianán had steered a course further out to sea, and they had spent the entire day pirking for bass. There were innumerable wrecks off the wild Atlantic coastline, and all of them made excellent habitats, not just for bass but many other deep sea species. Like any good fisherman, Cianán was well aware of the locations of many such wrecks. A particular favourite was eight miles or so north of Tullagh Point, and here they had spent the afternoon drifting repeatedly over the sunken vessel in search of their quarry. The boys had quickly grasped the technique of keeping the 'pirk,' a slim but heavy metal lure ending with a razor-sharp triple hook, continually moving up and down, a few feet above the wreck. The trick was to use the movement of the pirk to entice any large fish sheltering in the body of the wreck itself. The pirk had to be close enough (and its movement lively enough) for a bass to see it and be enticed to quickly strike out for it. Too close to the sunken wreck risked entanglement, but too far above it would not draw the fish from the safety of their chosen refuge. Pirking was a skill that even experienced fishermen could not easily take for granted. Cianán was immensely satisfied with Tom and his friends' dedication, with only three pirks lost and nine prime bass, all over six pounds apiece, plus a dozen good-sized pollock to show for their efforts. The pollock were kept, despite their low monetary value, as fresh bait for lobster pots.

Seeing Dónal and Brendan struggle to lift the heavy crate containing the bass and salmon at the foot of the ladder, Cianán called out for them to wait. Crossing over he heaved the box onto the breakwater, Tom helping to drag it away from the edge.

"A grand day's work lads," he said with a smile. "Even if I do say so myself."

All three of them grinned back and nodded in agreement. Cianán had said those or similar words at least half a dozen times before, but none of them minded in the slightest.

Dónal, with Brendan following, climbed the slippery ladder to join Tom. From the launch Cianán called up to them, "Can you lads manage the catch from there?"

"Aye," Tom replied. "We'll be fine. What do you want us to do?"

"Take it to Mr Callaghan; can you see him on the track way Tom?"

Staring to where his uncle was indicating, Tom recognised the catch agent immediately. "Aye, he's talking to some other fishermen though."

"That's alright. You and your friends take the fish to him and say I'll be there shortly."

Tom nodded. Dónal and Brendan had already grasped the rope handles tied at either end of the wooden crate, and lending support on Brendan's side, all three began to slowly stagger along the concrete walkway. Hands on hips, Cianán watched them struggle on their way for a few moments. Chuckling, he shook his head and smiled before returning to the task of securing the boat for the night.

Dónal yawned dramatically. "Fishing's hard work, I feel I could sleep for a week."

"You wouldn't know hard work if it bit you on the arse," Brendan retorted but with a grin. The three friends were sitting on some upturned lobster pots watching Cianán and the agent discussing the catch. Eventually agreement was reached and the two men shook hands. From his jacket pocket Callaghan produced a wallet, and a number of notes and some coins were handed over.

"And you would?"

"Aye. You try driving sheep off the hills before breakfast each morning and see what that's like."

Dónal made a noncommittal 'grunt' but said nothing further.

Tom climbed slowly to his feet. "Come on, my uncle's finished. Best we say goodbye and head back. It's well after teatime and I'm starved."

As his friends reluctantly stood, Cianán Devlin strolled purposely over to meet them.

"Here lads, take this," he said with a smile. Into each of their hands he deposited two shillings. "Fair payment for a fair days work?"

"Wow! Aye, thanks Mr Devlin," Dónal and Brendan exclaimed together.

"Thank you, Uncle Cianán!" Tom repeated a second later. Neither he nor the others had expected any money for their efforts. Each had regarded their day's fishing, quite simply, as a fun adventure.

"No, thank you lads for all your help, you did a grand job." All three of them grinned back at him. "Now, best be on your way; I don't want you getting into trouble being late home and all. And tell your parents from me that I was pleased with you."

The boys nodded enthusiastically that they would.

"Can we come out with you again, Mr Devlin?" Dónal asked the question all three were independently thinking.

Cianán frowned, rubbed his chin and pretended to consider the matter thoughtfully. Trying not to smile as the boys squirmed before him, he finally nodded. "Aye, we can be shipmates again lads, whenever." A chorus of shouts and exclamations greeted this announcement. Laughing, Cianán sent them on their way before returning, somewhat reluctantly, to his boat; one of the troubles with fishing was the jobs didn't end even when the catch was landed.

The boys had not gone far down the track, just past the last of the small thatched cottages making up the hamlet of Lenan, before they heard the sound of Mr Callaghan's black pickup rumbling behind. Stepping onto the verge to let him pass, they waved pleasantly as he drove by. The battered and mud splattered Ford had barely travelled another fifty yards before it stopped, and the agent's head appeared out of the driver's side window.

"Do you boys want a lift back to Ballyfinan? I can drop you off on my way through to Dunkeeny if you like?"

"Thanks!" Dónal shouted back, sprinting towards the automobile. Tom and Brendan glanced quickly at one another; they didn't need to be asked twice and ran to catch up with Dónal.

"Park yourself in the back with the fish," Mr Callaghan said ducking back inside the cab. "And mind you don't sit on any of them!" Climbing eagerly over the tailgate, they jostled for the best seating amongst the wooden crates.

Dónal slapped his hand on the metal panel behind Mr Callaghan's seat and shouted, "Let's go!"

"None of your cheek, now" was the good-humoured

reply. "I can still make you lot walk back!"

Content in their good fortune, Tom and his friends chatted amiably as they were thrown and pitched mercilessly along the rough, potholed trackway. The vehicle's erratic motion lessened considerably when they eventually reached the Dunaff Road, and improved further still when they finally merged with the Tullagh Road leading back to Ballyfinan. Legs hanging over the tailgate, they watched the stonewalled fields and overgrown hedgerows recede behind them. Overhead swallows banked and dived in impressive aerial displays, screaming shrilly in the early evening sunshine.

They were perhaps halfway home when the Mr Callaghan's pickup unexpectedly slowed to a stop. Turning around the boys soon saw the reason. Like water forced round a large boulder in mid channel, alongside either side of the truck streams of Blackface mountain sheep desperately sought to run past. Ewes, and their half-grown lambs, bleated loudly in an effort to keep together. Occasionally one would leap up the steep vegetated bank, trying to avoid the crush, only to invariably slide back into the heaving melee. As the sheep filed by only Brendan, unsurprisingly, was indifferent to their presence; Tom watched with interest while Dónal fell silent, unexpectedly thoughtful. As the last of the stragglers ran alongside, the driver, a tall teenage lad, crook in hand and two border collies at his side, walked past with a nod and a word of thanks to Mr Callaghan. As they began to move once more, Dónal continued to stare after the back of the young man, and the retreating flock.

"Who's that?" he asked to no one in particular. "I've not seen him around before."

Tom shrugged. Brendan looked up and said, "I have. Not sure of his name though but he obviously works for Finn McGonagle. Presumably McGonagle hired him to help with the sheep fair next week."

"How do you know that, he could work for anyone?"

"Not with those markings. Their Finn's sheep, so he must work for Finn."

All the boys knew Finn McGonagle; a larger than life, charismatic individual, known throughout the village and the surrounding district. The McGonagle family owned by far the greatest extent of local farmland and had farmed the land, predominantly with sheep but also significant numbers of dairy cattle, for generations.

Noticing Dónal's interest, Brendan explained further. "You see the red dye on each sheep's left shoulder, well that's Finn's mark. No one else has a mark of that colour –"

"But you're Da's sheep have red markings," Dónal interrupted.

"Aye," Brendan nodded patiently. "But not on the shoulder. We mark our sheep on the rump. No one else has red on the left shoulder."

A sly smile spread across Dónal's face. "Do you know everyone's markings then?"

"Of course. I wouldn't be much of a sheep farmer if I didn't."

Tom had only been half listening to the exchange.

Not interested in sheep farming particularly, he was simply content to observe the green countryside passing by. The Tullagh Road continued to twist and turn on its route to Ballyfinan and long after the sheep were lost from view his friends continued to remain engrossed in their conversation.

As the truck turned out of a particularly sharp bend, the outer buildings of Ballyfinan Village School came into view. At this time of year the school was obviously closed; Sister Madeleine and her colleagues having long since returned for the summer to their convent in Letterkenny. In the few moments it took for them to drive past, Tom absently regarded the deserted playground and empty classroom buildings. Feeling a tug on his arm, he started to turn away. Just as he did so, and for a fraction of a second only, Tom's eyes met those of Mr Kennedy staring out from a ground floor window. Neither had time to register shock or surprise before their gaze was swept apart by the automobile's onward progress.

"I said, what do you think Tom?" he heard Dónal say in a somewhat exasperated tone.

"What?"

"Haven't you been listening to anything we've been saying?"

"Well, no actually – "

"Jesus!" Dónal swore out loud. "You tell him Brendan."

Struggling to pay attention with distracting thoughts of Mr Kennedy flashing through his mind, Tom's disquiet was plain to see.

Grinning, Brendan said, "It's quite straightforward really. Most of us will have already brought the sheep down from the hills by now; my Da and I certainly have. The wee lambs are pretty much weaned by early August anyhow, and that makes it easier to separate the flock out, you know into those that we'll keep for next year's breeding and those to be sold on, or culled."

"Culled?" Tom asked.

"Aye, culled, killed. You don't farm sheep for fun you know. Once a beastie is past her best, well, she's gotta go." Tom looked slightly shocked.

"Besides," Brendan continued. "That only happens on the last day of the Festival, after the grand sheep market in the Park."

Tom nodded, but still puzzled why his friends, and in particular Dónal, were so interested in this.

"And it's *after* the market sales that the flocks are shorn, marked and prepared for breeding before being released back into the hills," Dónal added passionately. "It's the perfect opportunity."

"For what?" Tom asked, now thoroughly confused. Dónal just grinned back at him.

"Hey, Tom, isn't that your Mam?" Brendan suddenly exclaimed, pointing back behind them and inadvertently changing the subject. Glancing round, Tom saw a tall, lithe woman wrapped in a dark green shawl, walking hurriedly back along the road. Despite having her back to them, the long dark hair, distinctive clothing and purposeful stride were obvious to him.

"Aye" he murmured thoughtfully. "It is."

As Mr Callaghan's battered pickup continued on, it was clear that Erin Devlin had not seen them. Ordinarily Tom would have been secretly pleased to have avoided his mother's attention, but again that strange feeling of unease stole over him.

"Where's she going, Tom?" Brendan asked. "And where's the rest of your family? There's not much out here, not this far from the village."

"Other than school," Dónal added.

"Aye, but that's closed," Brendan countered. "Besides, who wants to go to school, especially when it's shut?" That got a general laugh but Tom's was slightly forced. Beginning to feel uncomfortable with the way the conversation was heading, he endeavoured to change the subject back to safer ground.

"Who knows?" he shrugged, in what he hoped was a disinterested manner. "And besides, who cares. So, why are you two so suddenly interested in sheep? I can understand Brendan's sad obsession," Tom ducked beneath a friendly cuff, "But not yours Dónal. Come on, what's going on, you still haven't told me."

Brendan looked across at Dónal and eyed him slightly suspiciously. "Aye, why do you want to know all this stuff?"

"No reason," Dónal lied, unconvincingly.

"Come on, you're planning something, I know you are. What is it?"

Dónal studied his two friends as the pickup bumped over the Finan Bridge before emerging into the Square.

Slowing to a halt, Mr Callaghan banged his hand on the outside of the door.

"Out you get now lads."

Scrambling out they thanked him and watched silently as he drove off towards the far side of the village, and the outward road to Dunkeeny. As the truck passed Dooley's Bar a familiar, stocky figure stepped out onto the High Street, yawning excessively.

"That's why," Dónal said darkly. Tom directed a worried glance at Brendan but said nothing. If Séamus Quigley had noticed them watching him, he gave no outward sign.

*

The annual Ballyfinan Summer Sheep Festival traditionally started on the third Saturday in August and lasted for seven days. The event was the highlight of the village year and each day attracted hundreds of visitors from the neighbouring hamlets, and surrounding district. For children and adults alike it was a time of games, sports, entertainment and above all feasting. For that one week in the year the inhabitants of Ballyfinan put aside life's daily toil and perpetual struggle. Parents' customary iron-grip on their children was relaxed and the children in turn embraced their new found freedom, running and playing unsupervised throughout the village, and often staying up late, well into the night.

In the days prior to the opening ceremony the whole community of Ballyfinan, but particularly the children, participated in the 'Tidy Village Effort' and by the Friday evening not a scrap of litter, debris or horse manure could be seen on the streets. The High Street through the village was criss-crossed with bunting and coloured flags, and many houses were similarly decked out in garlands and other decorations. Fresh flowers were planted in many window boxes and in the centre of the Park a raised wooden bandstand was erected, covered by an old but serviceable marquee. Several other tents for serving drinks and food were also put up nearby.

To many of the inhabitants of Ballyfinan, the origins of the Festival were lost in the mists of time. It was generally known that for generations an annual sheep market had been held in the village and that the Festival had developed over time to coincide with this historic event. The sheep sales themselves were now held on the morning of the second Saturday, and aside from this time, each day of the Festival hosted a variety of events. An opening pageant, with children's fancy dress, heralded the start to the Festival and throughout the week activities such as seven-a-side football tournaments, horseshoe throwing games, tug-of-war and running races of various descriptions were held. Sheep dog trials were another popular event, as were the sea fishing competitions undertaken from both Lenan Pier and also offshore in various boats. Evenings were given over to eating and for many, more importantly, drinking. Local musicians and singers would entertain the revellers each night, performing from the bandstand in the Park. On the final Saturday, after the sheep sales and the sports prize giving awards, a traditional céilidh was held, and the music and dance would continue well into the early hours of Sunday morning. Not that Father Aidan allowed any concessions for non-attendance at Mass the next day.

For Tom, the annual Festival had always been a time of great excitement and fun; but not this year. He had worried continually ever since Dónal had first outlined his latest plan for getting even with Séamus Quigley, his growing concern overshadowing his enjoyment of the carnival atmosphere. Initially Dónal's plan had sounded farfetched, and to Tom's mind frankly unrealistic. Whilst he had not said anything openly, privately he was convinced that his friend's grand scheme was nothing more than a pipedream, and as such would inevitably amount to nothing. It was simply a wonderful sounding idea that was fun to fantasise about pulling off.

Tom, however, had significantly underestimated Dónal's determination to succeed.

In the days leading up to the start of the Festival, Dónal had thoroughly researched his plan, and continually refined its details. He had spent hours discussing the finer points with Brendan Harkin, as well as surreptitiously questioning a number of adult sheep farmers and Festival organisers. Unbeknown to Tom he had also kept a watch on Quigley's Farm, lying hidden in the bracken covered fields, quietly observing the farmer's dealings. With great daring he had even crept into the main farm outbuilding one afternoon, a bold but certainly profitable endeavour from the point of view of progressing his ideas. But for all Dónal's efforts, his plan would still have failed to come to fruition had it not been for the timely intervention of Cathleen Kearney.

On the first afternoon of the Festival, Tom, Dónal and a group of their friends including Cathleen sat watching the opening rounds of the men's 'tossing the wellington boot' contest. There was a great, but sporting, rivalry between Cathleen's father, Danny Kearney, and his brother Joe, and Cathleen was shouting herself hoarse supporting each man in turn. After the contest (both men having made it through to the next round) the group broke up, and Tom found himself wandering across the playing field towards one of the food pavilions with Dónal, Cathleen, Brendan Harkin and James Dooley. James had recently been brought into their conspiracy and as usual Dónal was outlining his latest ideas, seemingly oblivious to the fact that Cathleen was with them and listening to all that was said.

Tom himself was only vaguely paying attention, his thoughts distracted, if truth were told, by the closeness of the girl at his side. Cathleen was again holding his arm, unmindful of the presence of the other boys. Half-heartedly, Tom registered that Dónal was growing increasingly animated in his apparent failure to resolve a problem in his overall plan. Concentrating more on the conversation, the thought materialised that without a solution, Dónal's whole scheme was seemingly doomed. When Cathleen unexpectedly suggested that she ask her older sister's fiancé, Paul Geraghty, who was in an ideal position to help, Dónal was beside himself with glee. Cathleen's confidence in Paul's unequivocal support, once the idea had been put to him, made Tom feel sick.

With all the components of the plan in place and the enthusiastic support of Tom's friends, Dónal surged ahead. The time of execution was set, immediately after the sheep sales, and throughout the Festival week Dónal drilled the participants in their roles. As the weekend approached, Tom's apprehension and sense of dread grew. He had never known a time when he had least enjoyed the Festival, or a time where it appeared that he bumped into Séamus Quigley at every opportunity.

*

Unable to sleep, Tom lay in his bed on Friday night, restlessly tossing and turning. It was warm and, with his window ajar, the sounds of merriment and music filtered through to him despite the lateness of the hour. Staring up at the ceiling through the darkness Tom wished, for what seemed the thousandth time, that tomorrow would never come. He recalled the disagreement he'd had with Dónal, and surprisingly Cathleen, earlier that afternoon, arguing that they should forget the whole idea. Dónal's obvious reluctance to do so was understandable, but Cathleen's unwillingness to stop had genuinely surprised him. Séamus Quigley hadn't, as far as he was aware, ever done anything to make Cathleen feel particularly aggrieved, but nonetheless Tom had been caught unawares by her determination to see the plan through.

A heavy crash, followed by a barked laugh and hushed cursing resounded from somewhere outside Tom's window. Startled, for a second he continued to lie still, listening intently. Another crash, and more laughing ensued. Climbing out of bed, Tom crept softly across to the window and peered out. Directly below, past the small garden and out into Cairn Lane, three teenage boys were struggling to lift a large, and obviously heavy, oval-shaped object. As he watched it was clear the youths had been drinking, judging by the way one in particular swayed as he stood berating his companions. Inevitably they dropped what they were trying to carry again, and Tom smiled in amusement as the unopened steel beer barrel rolled a few yards down the lane.

Swearing and shouting more loudly than they probably realised, the boys staggered after the wayward barrel, eventually catching up with it before it careered into the roadside ditch. As they renewed the efforts to retrieve the cask, the door to Tom's house opened and a swathe of light illuminated the scene. Stepping out and marching down the garden, Sean Devlin, bare-chested and dressed only in pyjama bottoms, roared at the boys. For a moment they held their ground, but the sight of the angry man, fists clenched striding purposefully towards them was soon too much. As one they fled, falling over themselves in their efforts to run back towards the village. From his window, Tom shrank back slightly but continued to watch, hidden by the dark interior of the room and the thick curtains.

Sean smiled grimly. Silently he waited until all three teenagers disappeared from view, his bare foot absently resting on the barrel rim. After a few minutes he glanced around furtively, his head slightly inclined as if listening. Somewhere in the darkness an owl screeched. Tom's heart was beating faster despite the fact that his father clearly was unaware of his presence. Sean looked back at the house and then once more up and down the lane. Satisfied that no one was observing he grasped the barrel with both hands and with a grunt lifted it up. Staggering slightly under the weight, he frog-walked carefully back inside the house. Hearing his father walking heavily around downstairs, and fearful that his mother would get up and potentially find him out of bed, Tom quickly returned and dived under the covers. From the kitchen the sounds of drawers being noisily opened and closed, followed by loud hammering resounded. Despite burying his head under the pillow, Tom heard his mother leave her bedroom and walk downstairs. The ensuing argument was short and terse, but as Erin returned to bed the hammering continued.

A few moments later wee Cianán started crying.

8
SETTLING OF SCORES

Nervously Tom toyed with the remains of his lunch, pushing the half-eaten meat pie around the plate. Sitting next to him on a low bench beside one of the food tents, Brendan Harkin sighed heavily before nudging him in the ribs. "You going to eat that?"

Tom shook his head. "No, you have it if you want."

"Grand. Give it here then." Shovelling the pie into his mouth Brendan nodded his head in front of them. "Not long now, I reckon. The sales'll be finished soon."

Tom didn't answer, his mind preoccupied with the events to come. Before them the playing field had been transformed into a vast network of sheep pens and holding areas. For the last few hours, farmers with serious expressions had wandered between the pens, appraising the flocks and occasionally stepping in amongst them to physically inspect individual sheep. Owners and buyers had haggled, often vocally, over prices and many a handshake agreement reached. On the periphery, aged members of the farming community and hired hands watched the proceedings with interest, drinking beer and offering sage advice to any that would listen. Women generally did not attend the actual sales, other than to provide refreshments. This year, however, was slightly different. Tom knew his mother, together with many other wives from the village, had set up a number of stalls in one corner of the Park, selling local crafts. As such there were also an unusually large number of small children running around the field, generally getting in the way and making a nuisance of themselves. As if to emphasis the point, Tom smiled wryly as he watched a group of small boys chase an escaped sheep across the field, much to the annoyance of the farmer trying to herd it back to its pen.

"Tom," Brendan said quietly, his tone clearly serious.

Looking up, Tom caught his friend's eye.

"Tom," Brendan repeated. "I have to go soon. I can see my Da's finished his business and he'll want me to drive them back home and get ready for shearing; you know how he is."

"Aye...I know."

"Listen. I really hope everything goes alright today. I

wish I could help more, but with my Da and all – " he left the sentence hanging.

Again Tom nodded in understanding. The irony was not lost on him that Brendan *really did* want to participate further in Dónal's grand plan but was physically unable to do so.

"Anyway, I'd best go but I'll catch up with you tonight at the *céilidh*. We can celebrate then!"

Tom smiled weakly. "Perhaps we can pinch a glass of beer and really enjoy ourselves?"

Brendan laughed, standing to leave. "That I'd like to see, you downing a pint!"

Tom's smile slowly faded, his mind wandering and distracted by resurfacing thoughts of the previous night. He didn't know when he had finally fallen asleep, but it must have been very late. Despite sleeping in, he had still been very tired that morning, and Erin had had to eventually wake him. At breakfast, his father had been absent but the ale barrel, forcibly prised open and half-empty, was a poignant reminder of the troubles facing the Devlin home.

Watching Brendan walk away towards the pens, Tom felt like crying. Holding his head in

his hands as tears welled up from within, he didn't notice the quiet approach of a tall, fair-haired young man. Standing over Tom and dressed in plain, worn clothing with a large canvas bag slung over his shoulders, Paul Geraghty smiled sympathetically at Tom's apparent distress.

"Having second thoughts, Tom?" he asked gently.

"Huh?" Tom exclaimed, startled. Sniffing loudly, he rubbed his eyes with the back of his hand. "No. Well, yes! God, I don't know anymore."

Nodding understandingly, Paul dropped the bag and sat down besides him. "I can appreciate what you're going through", he began kindly, putting a reassuring arm around the younger boy's shoulder. "If you don't want to go through with this, you just have to say so. No one will think any the less of you."

Dónal will...and Cathleen too probably, Tom thought inwardly. Aside from their first, brief introduction on *Bilberry Sunday*, it was only two days previously that Tom had met Paul again, having called round to visit Cathleen at her farmhouse. Despite the relatively short time they had known each other, the young man's pleasant, friendly manner and dry sense of humour had made a marked impression on him. No friend of Séamus Quigley, Paul Geraghty had not hesitated to help after Dónal had outlined his plan to him. They had all, and Tom in particular, been impressed by his reasoned appraisal of the risks involved, and Paul's subsequent suggestions to modify Dónal's ideas, thereby reducing the danger and improving the chances of success, were universally well received.

"If you like, I can do this on my own?" Paul offered, watching Tom closely.

Looking up, Tom shook his head. "No, I'll help. I'm just a bit scared, that's all. Quigley's not someone you want to take on lightly."

"And neither are we!" Paul replied with a grin.

Despite his anxiety Tom couldn't help but smile back; there was something in his manner that conveyed reassurance.

Together they sat in silence for a further few minutes, before Paul slowly rose.

"Come on then, let's get on with it." Holding out his hand he pulled Tom to his feet, and flashed once again his infectious smile. Tom struggled to return it.

Strolling calmly around the sheep pen area, Paul nodded and exchanged greetings with a number of farmers and other labourers. Tom walked cautiously behind him, trying to remain inconspicuous and saying nothing. After what seemed an eternity they finally spotted Séamus Quigley leaning against the rail of a pen and arguing animatedly with a small group of farmers.

"Ah, good day to you, Mr Quigley," Paul said rather loudly to attract the man's attention. "There you are now, I've been looking all over for you."

"Where the bloody hell have you been Geraghty!" Quigley shot back angrily. "You're late, I said to be 'ere nearly an hour ago."

"Well Sir, I'm sorry about that, but you see there's been a slight problem...that's why I was a wee bit late – "

"What do you mean, a *problem*?" Quigley muttered suspiciously, a frown deepening across his red face. At the same time he noticed Tom, standing like a statue behind the older boy. "And what the bloody hell is he doing here!"

Tom shrank visibly before the fierce gaze of the irate

farmer, desperately wanting to turn and flee, but equally knowing he couldn't do so.

"Now, don't be taking on so, Mr Quigley. Tom here has agreed to help me out."

"What! I'm not –"

"As I was saying," Paul interrupted, continuing on easily. "We've had a wee bit of bad luck. My mate Danny is sick…a bit too much of the drink last night, if you ask me. I was just over there and the lad can't get his head off the pillow, the stupid eejit. Been throwing up all night and best part of the morning, so he has."

Quigley opened his mouth to reply but Paul Geraghty simply carried on regardless. "And as you know Mr Quigley, it takes two of us to drive and clip your sheep. I can't do it on my own, especially since Danny owns Beth and she won't come to me – "

"Beth?" Quigley finally managed to ask, confused by the rapid turn of events; as Paul knew he would be.

"Beth. That's Danny's sheep dog Mr Quigley. Without a dog there's no way I'll be able to control your sheep on my own."

"Aye, the lad's right you know Séamus," one of the farmers standing beside them added. Scowling, Quigley tried to ignore him.

"Then get someone else, but not him," Quigley said pointing a thick, stubby finger at Tom. "I'll have no Devlin near my sheep, or on my land."

Paul spread his hands dramatically. "Well, I would if I could Mr Quigley but you won't find another driver now, not after the sales and all the work to be done."

Again several of the farmers listening to the exchange nodded sagely in agreement. The simple fact of the matter was that following the sheep market, all the sheep needed to be driven back to their respective fields and then clipped, inspected and marked before being released back to the surrounding hills. It was skilled, demanding work and experienced drivers and clippers came from miles around to offer their services. Skilled sheep labourers were always in demand, and at this late hour, all would be committed to one farmer or another. Quigley knew this, and Paul Geraghty knew that he knew this.

"Young Tom's the only help available," he continued pleasantly.

Séamus Quigley shook his head stubbornly. "Not him! Anyone else, aye, but not him!"

Paul Geraghty feigned annoyance. "Tom's a good lad Mr Quigley, he may be small but he's hard working. He knows how –"

"I said no, damn it!" Quigley shouted, his anger surfacing once more.

For a few seconds the two men stared at each other. Finally, his face expressionless, Paul shrugged. "Suit yourself, there are plenty of others that will need us this day. Come on, Tom." Turning his back on the group Paul started to walk away, gently pushing Tom along before him. Glancing up Tom saw that the older boy was grinning wolfishly. "Any second now," he whispered under his breath.

"Here, wait up a minute!" they heard Séamus

Quigley call out from behind.

"Ah." Winking at Tom, Paul turned round, his face once more expressionless. "Aye, Mr Quigley?"

Furious, but obviously striving to keep his temper in check, Séamus Quigley inhaled deeply, his eyes never leaving Paul's. The farmers beside him grinned openly, heedless to his discomfort.

"I'll hold you fully responsible for him," he growled darkly.

"Of course."

"And I'll tolerate no delays or pay extra if it takes you twice as long to finish."

"Fair enough. But as my mate, I expect you to pay Tom Danny's wage."

Quigley nearly exploded. "Bollocks! He's never clipped a sheep in his life, or driven a flock."

"Perhaps not, but it'll be a hard day's work nonetheless. I need the boy's help and he's entitled to payment, and I'll not have it from my money."

Stubbornly, Quigley shook his head. "I'll not pay a full wage, he isn't skilled, and besides he's half your mate's size."

"Fine then, he's entitled to half the wage!"

Opening his mouth to protest further Quigley froze, suddenly unable to think of a counter argument.

"Seems fair to me Séamus," one of the farmers ventured. Several others nodded their agreement.

"Time's getting on Mr Quigley," Paul pressed, deliberately looking around the field and clearly inferring he was considering other employment options.

Already large numbers of sheep were being driven from their pens and being shepherded away.

"Will you shut up and let me think!" Waiting patiently Paul stole a glance at Tom, the corners of his mouth turned up in slight smile.

"Alright. Half then. One and a half pence a sheep for the boy."

"Sounds reasonable. Is that okay with you, Tom?" Paul asked. Tom simply nodded, not trusting himself to speak. Not only was their plan seemingly working but he was now going to get paid for his part!

"Done then." Paul grinned, spitting onto his hand and holding it out. Reluctantly the farmer shook the proffered hand; with a number of independent witnesses there could be no going back now.

"That's grand Mr Quigley. We'll make a start then. Are you already ready for us back at the farm?"

"Aye, there's a penned area in the lower field, the boy can show you where, I'm sure." With his head down, Tom didn't see Quigley's eyes boring into him. "I've a few things to settle here first, but you can drive the sheep to the field. Come with me and I'll show you which ones."

Leaving the other farmers, they followed Quigley to the market area and were quickly shown the pen containing his flock. Tom estimated that there were perhaps forty or fifty sheep crammed into the enclosure, perhaps half identified by Quigley's own blue, left shoulder mark; the remainder having other dye and mark positions, testament to purchases made during the morning's sales. After giving them some last minute instructions (and scarcely veiled threats) Quigley left, agreeing to see them back at his farm in an hour.

"Thinking about how much money you're going to earn today?" Paul asked quietly, misreading Tom's thoughtful expression as the younger boy gazed into the pen. "There's forty eight sheep in there. At one and a half pence a sheep, Quigley's going to owe you, ah let me see now, that's six shillings! Provided we get to finish that is," he added with a slight laugh.

Tom shook his head. "No, it's not that, I was wondering how we're going to get them back to the farm. I told you and the others I've never driven before. Once we open the gate they'll just run and we'll never catch them. I don't know what to do –"

Seeing the growing panic in his eyes Paul held up his hand, indicating he should stop. "Listen Tom," he said kindly. "Before Cathleen talked to me, I was going to have to drive and clip Quigley's sheep by myself anyway. So, any help from you is a bonus. You'll be fine."

Tom frowned, confused. "But, what about Danny...and his dog? You told Mr Quigley you couldn't do this by yourself."

Paul laughed again. "Aye, that I did and for good reason. Danny's my dog –"

"Your dog? I don't understand. What do you mean?"

"Well, if you let me finish? Danny isn't a *person*, he's my sheep dog. I'd already persuaded Quigley that this was a two man job, which, to be fair, it is. My original plan was to turn up today, spring the play on him about my *friend's* sickness, and demand double the wages. At such short notice I would've had him over a barrel, and he'd have to pay up."

"That's dishonest."

"And?"

Tom shook his head in disbelief. The day's events were progressing far too quickly for him. "So where is this dog of yours then?" he asked finally.

Pointing to the far side of the field, Tom's gaze followed his outstretched arm. For a second Tom saw nothing obvious. He was just about to shake his head again when he spotted a small figure, sitting very still, alongside the boundary wall. It took him only a moment to recognise Cathleen Kearney. At her feet a black and white collie lay waiting patiently. Paul waved, and from an unseen signal from Cathleen, the collie leapt up and streaked across the field towards them. Within seconds the dog came skidding to a halt before them, its tail wagging excitedly.

"Good boy!" Paul exclaimed, kneeling to cup the collie's head in both hands. Enthusiastically Danny began to lick his face.

Tom grimaced. "That's disgusting!"

"Aye, it is." Paul feigned annoyance and pushed Danny's head from him. "Away with you now, that's enough." Standing, he wiped his sleeve across his face and smiled back a Tom. Unexpectedly rejected, Danny stepped across to Tom and sought renewed attention, rubbing up against his leg. Looking down, Tom tentatively stroked behind the collie's ears.

"So what will you say when Quigley finds us with a dog you said you didn't have?" he asked after a moment. Suddenly, another thought stuck him. "And you said Danny's dog was called *Beth*...Quigley's not a complete fool, he'll notice she's a he, I mean he's a —"

"Oh, I'll make something up," Paul interrupted. "And besides I think Quigley's going to have more on his mind than any concerns over some stray dog don't you?"

The truth of that statement brought everything back to Tom. Seeing his face fall, Paul frowned slightly. "Come on," he said quietly, laying a reassuring hand on Tom's shoulder. "Let's go."

Tom nodded, but didn't reply. Looking across to where he had last seen Cathleen, he half raised an arm to wave goodbye, but his friend had already gone.

Their journey from the playing fields through the main street of Ballyfinan, up Cairn Lane and finally to Quigley's Farm truly impressed Tom. Paul Geraghty had, through a series of commands and whistles to Danny, expertly controlled the skittish flock. Tom had watched in awe as he had repeatedly directed the seemingly tireless collie back and forth, never once allowing the sheep to panic, scatter or run off. They had herded Quigley's sheep past rowdy bars, with raucous patrons spilling out onto the pavement, around backfiring automobiles and on one occasion a poorly driven horse and cart. Tom had led the procession, his main job to prevent any sheep from running past, but in reality it was really Paul and Danny that had driven the large flock, skilfully managing their steady progress.

In little over an hour the sheep had been driven to Quigley's Farm, and once again forced into a wicker holding pen in the lower field.

Resting from their endeavours Paul and Tom sat together in silence, each content with their own thoughts. Behind, the boulder-strewn, bracken-covered slopes of Croaghennan Mór towered over them, casting a lengthening shadow as the afternoon progressed. Overhead a pair of crows rode the updrafts, cawing raucously in their pursuit of a passing buzzard.

Distracted by the aerial display, Tom watched absently until a low growl from Danny drew his attention; Séamus Quigley's slow, ponderous approach evidently apparent. Scrambling to their feet Tom forced himself to appear calm. Despite butterflies churning through his stomach, he prayed his nervousness wasn't too obvious. Struggling with a heavy looking wooden clipping stool, plus a large hessian sack, Quigley's progress across the field was painfully laboured.

"Should we help him," Tom murmured quietly?

"Nah," Paul whispered back, half smiling and clearly amused.

"Give us a bloody hand then!" Quigley eventually shouted drawing close, his breathing, heavy and gasping.

"Of course, Mr Quigley," Paul replied pleasantly, stepping forward and removing the strange looking stool from him. "You only had to ask."

The clipping stool was elongated, narrower at one end and supported by stout wooden slats. Its primary function when used properly, being to help prevent back strains during the clipping operation.

"I already did but you two don't sodding hear well."

"Ah, I'm sorry about that now – "

"Forget it," Quigley snapped, clearly irritated but in no mood to engage in prolonged conversation. "I'm 'ere now, so just get on with it. I want the entire flock clipped and marked before dusk. The dye's in the sack, if you need more I'll be in the house. And don't damage my stool either."

At the mention of dye, Tom's already jittery stomach constricted markedly.

"Absolutely, Mr Quigley, we'll be finished long before then – " but Quigley had already turned to leave. Walking away, he seemingly noticed Danny for the first time, lying quietly at his master's feet. Pausing, he glanced back at Paul, a puzzled expression upon his face. Paul Geraghty simply smiled back at him but said nothing. Tom held his breath. After a second, Quigley turned away once more, muttering something inaudibly as he trudged back towards the farm buildings. The grin Paul threw Tom couldn't have been bigger.

"Right then Tom, best we get started," Paul said positioning the clipping stool to his liking, firmly on the ground and a few feet from the penned area. Rummaging in his own bag, and then through Quigley's, he retrieved an old stained leather apron, and placed it over his clothes. From it Paul hung a pair of sharp-looking metal clippers, and on the ground within easy reach placed a stained, wooden dye marker, a short knife and beside these a large steel-grey tin. On the new unopened lid, a white manufactures label clearly said: *"McCready's Premiere Sheep Dye – Dark Blue."*

As if anticipating what was about to happen, the sheep in the pen were becoming increasingly agitated and bleating noisily. Paul had already explained to Tom how the clipping operation was to proceed. They would both climb into the pen and he would firmly grasp a sheep and drag it to the hinged exit gate. Tom's job was to open the gate just enough to allow Paul to drag the selected sheep out, but prevent any others escaping at the same time. Danny sat opposite the gate, lying on the ground and panting eagerly; his presence an added deterrent to any sheep considering a bid for freedom.

Scaling the pen, the sheep instinctively shied from Tom and Paul's presence, bunching together into an even tighter knot, as far away from them as possible. In such close proximity, Tom was struck by smell and noise emanating from the frightened animals.

Paul strode purposefully forward; the flock tried to scatter but hemmed in by their own numbers and the confines of the holding area, he easily managed to grab an individual. The remaining sheep fled either side of him along the edge of the pen, as he dragged the ewe towards the gate. Fascinated, Tom didn't move until a shout from Paul drew him back to his senses. Blocking the exit with his body he opened the gate a fraction, and at the last second, widened it enough to allow Paul to pass. His earlier concern that the entire flock would suddenly bolt towards him never materialised; with the capture of one of their fellows, the flock were content to watch once again from the far side of the enclosure.

Half carrying, half dragging the first sheep to the stool, Paul sat down on the narrow end and positioned the ewe at the broader, in such a way that the animal was brought up to his level and held firmly between his legs. Leaning over he set to work, expertly clipping the wool in short, deliberate snips. Climbing out of the pen, Tom stood to one side and watched, mesmerised by the young man's skill.

"He's very good," a voice said quietly at his side.

"Jesus Dónal!" Tom exclaimed. "I near wet myself, you sneaking up on me like that! Where have you been?"

"Over there by the boundary wall," his friend replied, thumbing his fist behind him. "Well, to be fair, hiding behind it actually. I had to wait until Quigley had left before I could come over."

Tom didn't reply but simply frowned, seemingly annoyed.

"Made you jump though?" Dónal continued, grinning evilly.

Despite his anxiety, Dónal's smile was infectious. "Aye...but I prefer to think of it as cat-like reflexes."

Dónal shook his head and sighed in mock disbelief. "Sure."

Together they continued to watch in silence for a

few more minutes before Dónal finally nudged Tom to gain his attention. "Come on, he's nearly finished."

Knelling down Dónal fumbled with the drawstrings of a small sack he had been carrying. Tom hadn't noticed it before, but knew instinctively what it contained.

"You got it then?" he ventured quietly.

Dónal didn't look up. "Aye. Brendan stole it from his Da's shed last night. He reckons he was so drunk yesterday afternoon after his trip to Dunkeeny, that he'll probably not remember buying it. Bugger these strings! Anyway, Brendan said he'd deny seeing it, even though his Da gave it to him to put away...before he collapsed that is. Ah, finally!" Grinning, Dónal finally opened the bag and, reaching inside triumphantly removed a similar looking grey tin. Tom's eyes were drawn to the label: "*McCready's Premiere Sheep Dye – Cherry Red.*"

In a surprisingly short time the sheep was clipped. Looking up, but still firmly holding the ewe, Paul Geraghty regarded the two boys staring at the tins of dye.

"Last chance to call this off," he said seriously.

"No," Tom replied after a moments hesitation, his apparent firmness surprising himself. "We've come too far now to turn back." Dónal nodded in agreement but said nothing.

"Right then," Paul said with a final glance back towards Séamus Quigley's farmhouse. "Get the lids off those tins." Spurred into action, Dónal retrieved the knife and prised off each lid. Conscious of not wanting to spill any, Tom carefully selected the tin containing the red dye and carried it over to Paul. The lid from this tin Dónal then replaced back onto Quigley's original containing the blue dye. With the blue dye tin resealed, Dónal quickly placed it into his own small sack.

"Left shoulder mark?" Paul enquired, even though all knew it to be correct.

"Aye, left shoulder," Tom agreed.

Bending down Paul grasped the wooden dye marker and, dipping it in the tin, deposited a generous red mark high on the ewe's left shoulder. That done he leant backwards and simultaneously released his hold on the animal. For a second the ewe struggled to rise but, quickly finding her feet, sprinted towards the hillside and freedom. After thirty yards she stopped, staring back at them and the remaining penned sheep, torn between the desire to be free and the comfort of being once more within the flock.

Standing up, Paul reached down to pick up the ragged fleece. Rolling it inside out, edges to the middle then tail to head, he quickly tied it round with a piece of wool coarsely twisted from the neck area. The rolled fleece, neatly packaged, would hence keep together for subsequent transport.

"One down, forty seven to go," he said cheerfully. The first sheep had been marked and the tension seemed to melt away.

"We did it!" Dónal suddenly cried out. "We really

have. That sheep has Finn McGonagle's mark and Quigley will *never* be able to prove otherwise."

"Not unless he catches you still here with that tin," Paul added earnestly.

"God! Aye, you're right. I'd better go. Tom, I'll see you later at the *céilidh*."

"Whereabouts?"

"I don't know, wherever."

"And what you going to do with that dye?"

Dónal shrugged. "Dump it somewhere I suppose? Does it matter?" Already he had gathered his bag and turned to leave, heading in the direction of Tom's fields.

"Just don't leave it on my land is all."

Dónal grinned. "Since when did you own any land?" With a final wave he was gone, running over the field towards the low boundary wall. "Don't work too hard," he shouted back as he scaled the wall and disappeared from view.

"Cheeky sod," Paul murmured but with a smile nonetheless. "Well, these sheep aren't going to get clipped by themselves; best we get on, eh?"

It was exhausting work that warm summer's afternoon and despite an ever freshening breeze Paul and Tom were quickly dripping with sweat. Twenty-two rolled fleeces lay off to one side before Séamus Quigley reappeared. Seeing the fat farmer's slow and arduous approach, Paul beckoned Tom closer to him. Handing him the fleece he had just rolled he whispered quietly, "Alright Tom, just as we planned now." Tom nodded and scurried away dragging the neatly bound fleece to join the others.

"Ah, Mr Quigley, Sir." Paul said smiling, rising to his feet, stretching to ease his back and pretending to see the farmer for the first time. "I would shake your hand, but I'm a wee bit messy."

"How many have you done?" Quigley growled, without preamble and again breathing heavily.

"That's twenty three now, I think. Tom! How many fleeces have you there?"

Tom made pretence of counting the rolled fleeces, more to avoid Quigley's eye than for any other reason. Before he had a chance to reply Quigley spotted the opened dye tin, its red contents plainly exposed. For a second he said nothing, simply staring, then visibly shaking his face turned a blotchy purple colour.

"Are you alright Mr Quigley?" Paul asked, sounding suitably concerned. "You don't look too well. Would you like to sit down? Here take this – "

"*What is that!*" Quigley finally roared, pointing a stubby finger at the tin.

"Ah, that's your dye, Mr Quigley, you gave it to – "

"It's *red!*" he shouted, interrupting again.

"Aye, I noticed that, and to be fair, did think it a wee bit strange, you normally using blue and all, but – "

"I don't use *red* you eejit! I use *blue*. I've always used blue."

"Well now, Mr Quigley, there's no reason to be rude. But it's hardly my fault if you changed your mind, and now want to use another colour – "

"Listen, you half-wit! I *haven't* changed my mind. I gave you a brand new tin of blue dye earlier." Quigley was still shouting and waving his arms in exasperation. Paul was standing before him, an expression of mock hurt and defiance upon his face. Tom tried to blend in with the fleeces as the two men argued, cursing and accusing each other of various wrongdoings. Finally Quigley stomped around the clipping area, eventually spotting the dye tin's discarded lid.

"Look!" he spat, stooping to pick it up and stabbing a finger at the label. "Look, right here! It says *blue* not *red*. Didn't you stop to think something was wrong when you opened the lid! Jesus, Mary and Joseph, what's wrong with you man?"

This was the moment Paul Geraghty had been waiting for. With a subtle lowering of his voice he simply said, "But I can't read Mr Quigley. How was I to know there was anything wrong?"

For perhaps twenty seconds Séamus Quigley just stared. His mouth opened and closed several times but no words came out. His anger evaporated and he visibly deflated before their eyes. Glancing up he scanned the slopes of Croaghennan Mór behind them, his red marked flock already disappearing from view, scattering amongst the gorse, bracken and lichen encrusted rocks. There would be no getting them back off the hillside now, not without having a major round-up. Even then Finn McGonagle's own recently clipped and marked sheep would be interspersed in their midst, and Quigley knew McGonagle would swear blind that they were all his. For a moment a new suspicion surfaced, that Geraghty and McGonagle had somehow colluded to swindle him; they must have swapped the dye tins and –

"Time's getting on Mr Quigley," Paul said, disturbing his thoughts. "Do you want me to carry on clipping?"

"What? No, go, get off my land. I'll get someone else to finish the work properly."

"Well if that's how you feel about it, we'll be off. Good luck finding someone now though," he continued glancing up meaningfully at the waning sun. Tom followed his gesture. Already it must be late afternoon and even Tom knew there would be no free hands available for Quigley to employ. Following the morning sales, every other skilled labourer in the district would be hard at work with other farmers, eager to finish the tasks of clipping and marking, before the start of the night's festivities.

"Come on Tom, pick up that bag for me there's a good lad. I'll just wait for you by the farmhouse then, Mr Quigley, for our wages"

The mention of money instantly rekindled Séamus Quigley's temper. "You'll get no payment from me, damn you, not after the trouble you've caused me!"

Tom watched impassively as another furious argument ensued. At one point Tom thought they might actually come to blows, but eventually Quigley backed down. He had no proof of any foul play, and to all intents and purposes it was his mistake; albeit he could argue that the manufactures of the dye were ultimately to blame for 'mistakenly' placing the wrong descriptive lid on the tin. Quigley had also publicly agreed a price for the work with Paul, and if he subsequently reneged on that agreement, all in the sheep farming community would know of it. His chances of employing skilled labourers again would be virtually non-existent. Finally, he still needed to have his remaining sheep clipped, marked and released. They could not remain in the pen overnight. Whatever else, Séamus Quigley was no fool. He knew all this, and Paul Geraghty knew that he knew.

It was well after seven in the evening before Tom and Paul finally left Quigley's Farm. The sun was beginning to dip towards the distant mountains as they walked slowly back together, through the village towards the playing fields. After begrudgingly agreeing to clip and mark the remainder of Séamus Quigley's flock (Paul had insisted on an apology first) they had worked hard all afternoon. Quigley had found an old, half empty tin of blue dye in the farmhouse and on handing it over had resolutely refused to leave. He had stood over them, arms folded and obviously still furious as they completed their tasks. The angry farmer's presence had taken the edge off any joy Tom felt at finally getting his own back, but it did, nonetheless, spur them on to finish as fast as possible.

At the gates to the Park, they shook hands and parted company. Smiling, Tom watched Paul join the mass of other partygoers entering the field, eager to celebrate the end of the Ballyfinan Sheep Festival. A local band was already playing loudly, though as far as he could tell the *céilidh* had not as yet started. Hands in pockets, Tom absently toyed with the six shillings he had received from Séamus Quigley. It was more money than he had ever had in his life, and its ironic acquisition turned his smile into a broad grin. Within seconds he was laughing out loud, oblivious to the slightly puzzled glances from passers by. Sprinting through the entrance, Tom weaved through the crowds looking for his friends.

9
TRAGEDY

Twilight was deepening and the first of the evening stars were beginning to appear in the eastern sky as Sean Devlin stared in drunken annoyance at the now empty stoneware jug. Muttering in disdain, he tossed it away, the ensuing crash on the concrete breakwater of Lenan Pier shattering the serene atmosphere. Suddenly concerned about being observed, he glanced around quickly. Cursing as his rapid movement almost caused him to fall, Sean swayed for a few seconds, gradually regaining his balance. Listening to the tranquil sounds of small waves lapping over the sandy foreshore and faint music carrying across the still night from the distant *céilidh*, he simply smiled.

"No one here but us, 'eh, big brother?" Sean said out loud, and then belched raucously. Again he looked round, this time rather guiltily, before giggling stupidly. Face down and lying unconscious at his feet, Cianán Devlin was in no position to reply.

Glancing at the prone figure Sean's laughter quickly faded, replaced by hoarse, uncontrollable sobs.

Why do things have to end like this? he cried inwardly.

Within a minute his composure returned, and he wiped his hand angrily across his eyes.

"Damn you Cianán," Sean whispered softy, blinking back the tears. "Why couldn't you just let me be?"

After a moment and as if engaged in a conversation, he continued, "You shouldn't have tried to stop me...I did warn you."

Somewhere in the hamlet of Lenan a dog barked. Fearful of discovery, Sean stepped over his brother and staggered along the breakwater towards the far end and the moored boats. He only managed a few yards before he tripped, his trailing foot catching on a large ringbolt on the pier's surface. Falling heavily, Sean cursed and felt tears well up again from within. Lying on the damp, salt encrusted jetty, images washed over him in waves and Sean's mind drifted sleepily.

The day, or rather the afternoon by the time he had risen from bed, had started well enough. The house was quiet, Erin was gone, presumably somewhere with the children. His head was thumping from the night before but the peace and tranquillity was wonderful. Lounging in their small living room, he had enjoyed the solitude.

By mid-afternoon Erin had returned along with the twins and wee Cianán. Within minutes she had gone on at him again, nagging about the drinking. Sure he'd had a few the night before and okay, another one or two already earlier on, but that was just to ease his headache. The argument had escalated. Sean couldn't quite remember about what, probably money, work or suchlike, but the shouting and screaming had driven him mad. In a fit of temper, he had finally left the house, slamming the front door with such force that the hinges cracked. Angry and aggrieved, Sean Devlin felt unfairly persecuted. Why did Erin always irritate him like this? Why couldn't she leave him be? He was his own man after all and if he wanted a drink now and then, that was his business, not hers.

As he stormed down the path, swearing in bitter resentment, Erin had collapsed in floods of tears in the tiny hallway, the twins looking fearfully on from the kitchen.

For the remainder of the afternoon and early evening, Sean had drunk steadily in Kearney's Bar, generally feeling sorry for himself. He had pointedly avoided all attempts at conversation from the patrons, and even Joe Kearney, the normally jovial landlord, wisely left him alone. Over the preceding weeks he had progressively been banned from all the bars in the village, except Kearney's. The fact that Joe only tolerated him since, to all intents and purposes, he was family, did little to improve his temperament; Joe's sister-in-law, Mary Kearney, was Erin's first cousin.

Sean's drink-fuddled thoughts couldn't recall leaving Keaney's Bar; he had in fact been thrown out, finally running out of money and becoming abusive when refused service. Wandering purposelessly first through the village and then the surrounding countryside, he finally ended up at Lenan. Why the sudden impulse to go fishing had occurred, he had no idea, but Sean had smiled smugly, imagining catching huge numbers of salmon and presenting them in triumph back home. That would show Erin what sort of man he was!

On the pier Sean was still smiling as similar, pleasant thoughts drifted in and out of his consciousness, and sleep began to claim him. An urgent need to relieve himself made him start. He had nearly fallen asleep! A low groan from behind further focused his attention on the present. Willing his limbs to respond, Sean climbed slowly to his feet and brushed himself down. Looking back towards his brother, Cianán still hadn't moved, and was now silent again. Watching him, Sean tried to recall when he had met his brother; his confused mind remembering little of their previous conversation. Unbeknown to him, Cianán had visited Erin earlier that evening and on hearing of the argument had gone looking for him, finally finding him stumbling out along Lenan Pier. At first Cianán had tried to persuade Sean to come home and talk things through. When that failed, and learning of his brother's intentions to go fishing, he'd tried to prevent Sean from taking the boat. Their disagreement had become violent, and in the ensuing fight Cianán had fallen to the ground, his head hitting the concrete breakwater, and was struck senseless.

Staring at his brother, feelings of guilt and remorse began to resurface. *Perhaps he should go and get help?* Sean almost took a step back when Cianán groaned again, louder than before, and shuddered slightly. The urge to flee became too strong and, with remarkable dexterity, Sean turned on his heels and ran to his brother's boat. For several seconds he fumbled with the moorings on the quayside before finally freeing them, and practically sliding down the metal ladder, virtually fell into the launch. The small boat rocked dangerously and, arms outstretched, Sean swayed along its length, veering from side to side. Pitching almost head first into the tiller seat, he rested for a minute before searching the bottom of the boat for the starter handle. For once the noisy diesel engine fired first time and, smiling, Sean finally began to relax.

It was fully dark by the time Cianán Devlin eventually regained consciousness. For several minutes he could do nothing but lie perfectly still on the breakwater, his head pounding. Blinking repeatedly, his vision swam, and waves of sickness threatened to overwhelm him. Raising a shaking hand Cianán tentatively touched the congealing wound on his temple; his fingers coming away stained with drying blood. Despite the pain and nausea, his recollection of the recent events was clear.

Grunting with the effort, Cianán slowly climbed to his feet, closing his eyes in an effort to stem the feelings of dizziness. Mastering the urge to vomit, he turned to look out to sea, the fading phosphorescent trail of an erratically handled boat zigzagging into the blackness. Cianán closed his eyes once more, but this time in despair.

Tom had no idea what time it was other than very late. The band were still playing, although by now most of the festival-goers had given up participating in the *céilidh*, and were instead concentrating on eating and drinking. Propped against the side of an abandoned trailer, decorated in colourful garlands and carnival bunting, Tom and his friends sat and relaxed in sated fulfilment. Cathleen Kearney had already fallen asleep and, consciously or otherwise, had snuggled into him, resting peacefully on his left arm. Despite the beginnings of cramp, Tom dared not move for fear of disturbing her; besides, he admitted to himself, the warmth of her closeness was curiously appealing. On his right Dónal, Brendan and James Dooley pretended not to notice, but Tom was well aware of the sly grins continuously passing between them.

Despite their protests, Tom had generously divided the money he had received from Séamus Quigley amongst his friends and, in spite of gorging themselves on sweets, cakes and home-made lemonade, they all had significant amounts left. This, together with the immensely satisfying memories of Quigley's humiliation, combined to induce an almost euphoric sense of wellbeing. Paul Geraghty had wasted no time in conveying the news of the sheep dye 'mix-up' to the other farmers at the end of festival party. By the time Quigley himself made an appearance it seemed not a soul in the Park hadn't heard the news. Quigley had tried to put a brave face on events, but the constant comments and knowing smiles from passers by soon tried his already stretched patience to breaking point. Even the band stopped pretending to play and, like everyone else, watched the inevitable confrontation with Finn McGonagle in the middle of the playing field. But, and as Dónal had originally planned, without any evidence to the contrary, Séamus Quigley could not prove anything. Tom and his friends watched happily as he was eventually escorted off the Park by Pat Doherty, shouting and swearing in anger and frustration.

Nudging Tom in the ribs, Dónal inclined his head slightly, indicating Paul Geraghty passionately embracing Cathleen's older sister Siobhan at the edge of the bandstand.

"That'll be you two next," he smirked wickedly.

"Be still, you eejit," Tom shot back, but grinning nonetheless. Looking down at her auburn hair, a sudden desire to tenderly stroke Cathleen's head came over him. "Do you really think so?" he murmured quietly, almost to himself. Dónal burst out laughing.

Blushing furiously, Tom cursed himself inwardly for being such a fool in front of his friend. Disturbed by the laughter Cathleen awoke and, sitting up sleepily, enquired what was so funny. Unseen behind her back Tom's eyes pleaded with a grinning Dónal not to say anything.

Toying with the idea of teasing him further, Dónal rubbed his chin meaningfully, pretending to be deep in thought.

"Come on Dónal, what's going on?" Cathleen asked again, a slight edge to her voice, thinking she was being made fun of.

"Ah now, Cathleen, I'm not sure that I...." Dónal's voice trailed off as out of the darkness a tall figure loomed. Tom's smile and half-spoken greeting died on his lips at Declan Kennedy's solemn, troubled disposition. An uncomfortable silence developed as the School Master continued to stare down at them, his face unreadable. Nervously, Tom and his friends glanced at one another; something was obviously very wrong.

After what seemed an eternity, Declan finally seemed to collect his thoughts.

"Thomas," he said somewhat hesitantly, clearly uncomfortable.

"Sir?" Tom replied, climbing slowly to his feet. The others followed a second later.

"Thomas," Declan repeated, steeling himself. "You need to come with me."

Tom nodded obediently, but said nothing.

"Where's Tom going, Sir?" Dónal asked, as respectfully and calmly as possible, despite the fear that somehow their role in Séamus Quigley's misfortunes had been discovered foremost in his mind.

"That is none of your concern, Mr O'Connor," the School Master's tone now clearly evident. Pausing for a moment he continued, but in a softer, sadder voice. "I suggest you all go home now – it's very late. I know for a fact, Cathleen, that your mother is looking for you."

"I will Sir," Cathleen promised but made no move to leave.

"Mr Kennedy?" Tom said quietly, drawing his attention back. "What's happened?" Instinctively Tom knew that whatever was going on it had nothing to do with Séamus Quigley.

Declan felt compelled to kneel. Gravely he regarded the young boy level with his own eyes. "I'm not sure, not for certain anyhow, but I think there's been an accident...at home." Standing, he sighed heavily and added, "Involving your father." Glancing briefly at his friends, and then back to Tom, Declan nodded gravely. "Come on Tom, let's get you home."

For much of the journey they walked in silence. At some stage Tom's hand unconsciously crept into Declan's, and the tall School Master, without outwardly acknowledging it, gave him a reassuring squeeze. Approaching the dimly lit turning to Cairn Lane, Tom shivered involuntarily; whether from the night's chill or the myriad of troubling thoughts cascading through his mind, he was unsure. The temperature had indeed dropped noticeably and the wind increased markedly.

Turning to him Declan said, "Are you cold Tom? Do you want my jacket?"

Tom shook his head. "No, I'm fine."

Looking up at the building cloud cover Declan mused quietly, "I think there's a storm coming." Tom didn't reply.

Starting the steep climb, light filtering behind from the gas lamps in the High Street softly illuminated their path, throwing lengthening shadows flickering before them. Within fifty yards this dim radiance had waned considerably and in near blackness they cautiously approached Quigley's Farm. The entire yard was still, with no lights or sounds evident from the farmhouse.

Passing across the silent farmyard, Tom finally steeled himself to ask the inevitable question. "Sir, do you know what's happened to my Da?

Mentally, Declan had rehearsed his answer many times. In truth, he didn't know exactly but nonetheless suspected the worse. Sean Devlin's propensity to drink and behave recklessly was well known.

"Thomas," he began, continuing to walk past the farm. "I'm not altogether sure, but what I do know came from Father Aidan, and then only very quickly." Calmly he recalled how Father Aidan, with Mrs Comisky in tow, had stopped him outside Kearney's Bar, the pair themselves on route to Tom's house, and had spoken briefly of the need to find Tom. "They didn't say much, Tom," Declan finally finished, "only that your father had decided to go fishing tonight, and may have got into difficulty. Apparently your father's brother was also – "

"Uncle Cianán?" Tom interrupted unnecessarily.

"Aye, your Uncle Cianán. As I was saying, it seems he was with your father and raised the alarm. Whether Cianán had met Father Aidan or – "

"I don't understand" Tom interrupted again frowning, the gesture barely noticeably in the darkness. "That would mean Da went off by himself. Uncle Cianán would never let him do that, especially at night."

Declan had no answer; together they continued to walk side by side in silence. *The boy's no fool*, Declan reminded himself; Tom had already drawn the same conclusion he himself had made. There must have been some altercation between the two brothers. Knowing Sean as he obviously did, Cianán wouldn't have allowed his brother, presumably drunk, to take the boat out on his own.

"Why would Da want to go fishing now, Mr Kennedy...it's so late?" Tom asked quietly, disturbing his thoughts.

They had reached the wooden gate leading through the small well-managed garden to Tom's front door. Lights shone brightly out into the darkness from the downstairs windows, despite the half drawn curtains, every now and then a shadow passed fleetingly from within. Looking directly at Tom, Declan laid a hand gently on Tom's shoulder. Already tears were welling up in the boy's eyes.

"I don't know Tom, I really don't," he said softly. "But I think we need to go in now."

Rubbing his eyes, Tom simply nodded. Following

Declan along the path, the thought suddenly occurred that tonight was the first time Declan had called him *Tom* not *Thomas*. Curiously, the thought was pleasantly reassuring.

The front door, as usual, was unlocked and Tom entered quietly, squinting as his eyes adjusted to the brightness. Hesitating in the hallway, a gentle steer behind from Declan directed him towards the living room. For a few moments he remained unnoticed. On the far side of the room his mother sat in the worn armchair, silently cradling his brother. Wee Cianán was evidently asleep, and Erin gently stoked his fair, blonde hair, staring absently into the distance. A well stoked turf fire burned in the hearth and, kneeling before it, Father Aidan led Mrs Comisky in prayer. Tom's grandmother sat in the only other chair in the room, her eyes closed but lips moving soundlessly as she recited the rosary, the simple wooden beads clasped tightly between her fingers. On the windowsill the bright flame from a single candle burned poignantly, and as Tom's eyes were drawn to it, a cold shiver ran down his back as its significance dawned.

Behind him Declan discreetly cleared his throat. All but Erin turned towards them.

Eileen, first to react, struggled out of the chair and outstretching her arms, embraced Tom tightly. "Oh my boy" she whispered, her voice trembling. "Are you alright?"

"Aye, Granny, I think so?" Tom replied, unsure if he

was or not.

"Grand." Looking at him closely Eileen tried with difficulty to smile. "Okay now, come and sit with your mother, she needs you." Taking his hand, Eileen led him to Erin's chair and slowly knelt besides her daughter.

"Erin" she whispered gently, "Tommy's here. Let me take the wee baby to bed now, there's a good lass." Without replying or even looking up, Erin Devlin allowed her mother to carefully take the sleeping Cianán from her.

"Mammy?" Tom said softly, sitting on the floor at her feet. "I'm here."

Looking down at him Erin seemed to smile very slightly but said nothing. Laying his head on her lap, Tom closed his eyes and welcomed the comforting touch of her hand as she tenderly began to stroke his head.

Mrs Comisky followed Eileen out of the living room, ostensibly at the latter's request to make some tea, leaving Father Aidan and Declan to converse in hushed tones in the doorway.

"Any news?" Declan asked quietly, shaking hands with the priest.

"No, not for the last hour or so. Pat Doherty came by here, not long after I'd met you, and said only a few boats had gone out to look for him. With the festivities and all, there aren't many fishermen sober enough to put to sea."

Declan nodded understandingly, but said nothing.

"Dr Kerrigan has examined Cianán and taken him to

the Kearney's place. He's got a slight concussion, and Mary's been told to make sure he stays in bed."

"Well, Mary will do that sure enough," Declan replied ruefully. Mary Kearney, like her cousin Erin, was not a woman to be argued with.

For a minute or so the two men stood together in silence, each contemplating privately the night's events. Eileen came slowly down the stairs, wee Cianán apparently content in his room, and joined Mrs Comisky in the kitchen. Their subsequent subdued conversation, in deference to the sleeping children, was barely audible.

"How's Erin doing?" Declan asked, glancing back into the living room.

Father Aidan combed his fingers through his thinning silver hair and sighed. "To be honest Declan, I'm not sure, but not well I think. She's not said a word since we arrived. I know Eileen's tried to talk with her a number of times but, well, it's probably the shock and all." The old priest absently undid the top button of his black shirt; the white dog-collar long since removed given the warmth of the room. "I can't believe her husband could be so foolish!" he continued animatedly. "God's gift of life is too precious to risk on prideful shenanigans."

"What do you mean?"

The priest gave him a meaningful look. "Well, it's clear from Sean's behaviour over the last few weeks that he's a troubled man. There are obviously problems at home; I think he feels the world's turned against him."

"That seems a wee bit dramatic, Father."

"Is it? I heard about your, how shall I say it, *discussion* with him at Kearney's a while back. He's a proud man Declan and, well, let's just say I don't think he took kindly to your advice."

"So you're inferring it's my fault then?" Declan replied somewhat defensively.

"No, I'm not, and keep your voice down. All I'm saying is that there are some things that are best left within the family to address, and for a man like Sean Devlin, the raising of his son is one of them."

Declan nearly laughed. "I'm sorry Father, but I can't accept that. Not only am I the School Master of this village with a duty to ensure that the children under my tutelage are cared for, but I'm also a *conscientious* member of this community. If anyone comes to me for help, either in my professional role or personally, I will do my utmost to facilitate such help as I may. And if the outcome of that makes others, like Sean for example, uncomfortable because of their own failings or shortcomings, then surely that just reinforces the message that others should be doing more."

Eileen and Mrs Comisky returning with the tea curtailed further conversation. Thanking them, Declan endeavoured to steer the topic back to safer ground. "So, what exactly has happened tonight? The boy asked me, but I could tell him little other than there's been some fishing mishap..."

Mrs Comisky, accustomed to taking centre stage instantly replied, "Well Mr Kennedy, 'tis a shocking thing that's occurred. I was getting myself ready for bed when Helen Kerrigan, that's the Doctor's wife you know, came hammering at my door. Well, I knew then that something must be wrong, given the time and all, so I – "

"Deidre," Father Aidan interrupted, a little exasperated, "I think what Mr Kennedy really wants to know is what happened to Sean."

Flushing slightly at the obvious rebuke, Mrs Comisky wrung her plump hands together. A short, stocky woman in her mid-fifties, the heat of the room was already making her perspire heavily. The grave, intense scrutiny of her audience for once began to make her feel uncomfortable. Even her lifelong friend Eileen's demeanour was grim and humourless. Tonight was not the time for grand embellishment.

Retrieving a handkerchief from her sleeve, she wiped her brow and gathered her thoughts. In uncharacteristically short sentences she explained how Cianán Devlin had raised the alarm, staggering on the verge of collapse to Dr Kerrigan's door. After ascertaining what had occurred, the Doctor reacted quickly, first sending his son to find Pat Doherty, and then on to inform Danny Kearney. Whilst he treated Cianán, Helen Kerrigan had gone to Mrs Comisky's and en route had met Father Aidan who, taking charge, had sent Mrs Kerrigan back home with the message that he and Mrs Comisky were going to the Devlins' house. Arriving they discovered Erin awake but distraught with a crying baby; wee Cianán was teething and wouldn't settle. Mrs Comisky had stayed with Erin whilst Father Aidan had left to fetch Eileen O'Brien. Pat Doherty had called round not long after they had returned to say that a number of boats had left in search for Sean. The Garda had then subsequently left for Lenan Bay.

"Thank you Deidre," Father Aidan said when she had finished speaking. "I'm sorry if I appeared short with you earlier."

"Not at all, Father." Still somewhat flustered she looked away, for once glad to be free of the attention. Noticing the untouched (and now undoubtedly cold) tea cups, she made some pretence of getting fresh drinks, and quickly fled back to the kitchen.

Declan briefly removed his pocket watch and frowned slightly. "So, we've heard nothing now for, what, two hours?"

The priest nodded gravely. "Aye, not since Pat was here. But it's a fair walk to Lenan and back; we mustn't lose sight of that."

*

Tom awoke to the sounds of heavy rain hammering on the exterior window. Blinking the sleep from his eyes, he gradually registered the storm-force winds howling incessantly around the house. It was obviously morning, judging by the now opened curtains, but what little light shone through the small window was significantly reduced by the dark, overcast sky outside. Every few seconds, savage gusts rattled the glass panes and Tom watched transfixed as the candle on the narrow sill flickered alarmingly, despite the window being firmly closed. *The candle!* In that instant everything came back to him. He slowly sat up, stiff with cramp from having spent the night curled up on the living room chair. A grey woollen blanket that someone had covered him with slipped unheeded to the floor. Alone in the room Tom considered what to do. The house was strangely quiet. For a long time he sat still, silently recalling the night's events and listening subconsciously to the sounds of the raging gale.

A heavy sob from the direction of the kitchen eventually stirred him into motion. Walking barefoot from the living room and through the hallway he cautiously peered into the kitchen. Across the table his mother sat gently cradling Niamh in her arms. Eileen O'Brien stood behind her, Roisin similarly held lovingly in an embrace. Both girls were still in their nightgowns and both were crying softly. Leaning against the far wall Father Aidan looked on, an expression of profound sorrow upon his face. Tears formed unbidden in Tom's eyes. Deep down, he knew what he was about to be told.

"Mam?" he ventured quietly. Five pairs of eyes looked up at him.

"Oh Tom," Eileen answered, her voice thick with emotion. "Come in child." Slowly extracting herself from her granddaughter's entwining arms, she stepped towards him. Roisin tried to follow but was quickly intercepted by Father Aidan, and gently guided to her mother's side.

"Tom," his grandmother repeated softly, kneeling to

face him and cupping his face in her hands. "I need you to be brave now – there's bad news, very bad I'm afraid…"

Tom nodded slightly but didn't speak. Tears began to flow freely now, but oddly due to the emotionally charged atmosphere, rather than any heart felt sense of loss.

"There's been an accident, on your Da's boat…he's…oh Tommy…he's gone." The final words came out in a rush and Eileen choked back a cry.

"You mean he's dead?" Tom said, almost carelessly.

Eileen blinked hard at the seemingly curt reply and simply nodded. "Aye love, I think so. The men found his boat. It was just drifting way out at sea…and your Da wasn't in it. They searched for hours but it was dark and then the storm came and they were forced to return. This morning they tried to go out and search again, but the waves were too high; the gale's made it too dangerous to put to sea."

Tom wiped his sleeve across his eyes. "I understand Granny – "

Before he could say anything further, Eileen drew him in close. "There, there, my love. I'm so sorry. Don't be afraid to cry…we'll work out everything, in the end."

What did she mean by that? Tom thought inwardly. For reasons he couldn't explain, he no longer felt like crying.

10
COMING TO TERMS

Sean Devlin's body was never found. Within Ballyfinan and the surrounding scattered communities it was the commonly held belief that, being incredibly foolish and moreover blind drunk, he had either passed out or tripped in the boat, and either way fallen overboard. Obviously incapable of saving himself he had simply drowned and his body swept out to into the Atlantic by the ensuing storm. No blame was ever laid at Cianán Devlin's door and undoubtedly tragic though the accident was, few tears were shed at his younger brother's sad demise.

For three days and nights following the tragedy, the

storm that had suddenly struck the North Western Donegal coast continued to rage unabated. In all that time Tom had been confined to the house, frustrated in his endeavours to escape by the ravages of the weather. Not that despite the torrential rain and wind he and his family had been left in peace. Every day a more or less constant stream of visitors had called upon them, all contrite and sympathetic to their loss. Eileen, having decided to stay temporarily, took it upon herself to receive and primarily entertain their, if not exactly unwelcome, certainly unasked for guests. Under his grandmother's direction Tom found himself kept busy enough making innumerable cups of tea and fetching slices of fruitcake or biscuits. Not that the latter were ever in short supply since virtually every caller to the house invariably arrived with a bestowed food gift. Erin, though often present in the living room during these visits, rarely engaged in the predictably common, sad-themed conversations. She was more often than not simply content to cuddle her younger son and allow her mother to take charge of events.

If truth were told, Tom was beginning to feel uneasy with his mother's general lack of interest in life around her. Erin Devlin's apparent indifference was growing daily and to Tom's mind she was becoming increasingly distant and withdrawn. Only once had he actually heard her cry since the accident and that was only after his uncle, Cianán Devlin, had arrived similarly unannounced. Cianán had called round the evening before, his face still heavily bruised and bandaged, and begged forgiveness for not having stopped Sean, sobbing uncontrollably in Erin's arms. From the landing, Tom had watched his mother gently stroke the big man's hair and whisper comforting words, as if he were a child. For seemingly hours that night Tom had lain awake, staring up at the ceiling. Lying on a mattress on the floor of his mother's bedroom (his grandmother having moved into his own room), he had listened silently to her softly crying, unable to think of anything comforting to say.

*

Cathleen Kearney nervously walked up the narrow garden path to the Devlin's front door. Before her, clutched tightly in both hands, was a wicker basket full of freshly baked bread from Mrs Brennan's store. Mary Kearney had given her daughter four pence to buy the bread but on hearing of her errand, Mrs Brennan had refused payment and insisted she take the loaf for free. What was more, she also filled the basket with jam, butter and various sweets for the children. At any other time Cathleen would have been exceedingly pleased at such good fortune, but not today. The reality of having to see Erin and face her grief had taken the edge off any excitement she would have felt. It had been exactly a week since the fishing accident and although Mary Kearney had visited her cousin everyday, today was the first time that the severe weather had relented sufficiently for her to be happy sending Cathleen instead. It was not that Cathleen didn't want to see her 'Auntie Erin', far from it. The girl was very close to her, and had been deeply upset by the news of Sean Devlin's death. It was more that Erin, from what Cathleen had managed to glean, eavesdropping on late night conversations between her own mother and father, was behaving strangely. Apparently she was not 'grieving as a wife should', according to Cathleen's mother. Erin spent virtually the entire day in her bedroom or kitchen, hardly speaking and avoiding contact with all except her immediate family. Mary Kearney was also worried that Erin wasn't eating properly, despite the food gifts and donations from well wishers.

Cathleen knew the front door would be unlocked and ordinarily would have walked straight in, calling a greeting on entering. Today, she simply knocked and waited, nervously jiggling from one foot to another. It seemed like ages before the door finally opened; the relief on her face at seeing Tom's grandmother rather than his mother, plainly obvious.

"Why Cathleen, how nice to see you," Eileen said genuinely. "Please, come in, come in." Standing aside to let her pass, she smiled pleasantly, trying to put the girl at ease. "I've just sat down for a cup of tea. Would you like one? Or a glass of milk, perhaps?"

"No thank you, Mrs O'Brien, I'm fine. My Mam just asked me to call round and deliver these," she said, holding up the basket. "I shouldn't stay long, Mam wants me straight back." She hoped the lie wasn't as obvious as it sounded, and felt terrible for it.

"Well, that's probably for the best. Tommy's Mam is having a wee sleep at the moment and it's probably best we don't disturb her."

"Oh?"

"She'll be sorry to have missed you though." Taking the basket she made pretence of looking through it, smiling inwardly. Like her own grandson she could read this child like a book. "Be sure and thank your Mam for me, this looks grand – and the bread smells delicious. I'm sure Tommy will love it for his lunch. I don't suppose you could find him for me? If you've time that is?"

"Of course!" Cathleen exclaimed. "I'd love to. Where is he?"

Smiling openly now, Eileen did have to think for a moment. "Well, now that the rain's finally stopped, I'm sure he said he was going to the back fields. He knows I want him home for supper and not to go far. Aye, try our fields first." As an afterthought she added, "If he's not there you better come back and let me know. I don't want you wandering about and not knowing where you are, not with your mother expecting you back and all?" The knowing look levelled at Cathleen made the girl blush and look down.

Eager to find Tom, Cathleen skipped briskly down the path running alongside the house. Passing round the back of the Barn she stepped smartly over the low stile and entered the lowest of the Devlins' fields. With the recent torrential rain the ground was sodden, sticky and heavy going. As she began the steep climb, numerous rivulets of water cascaded past her, meandering through the rough grassland, like tiny river channels. Despite wearing stout boots, the long wet grass quickly soaked through to her socks and feet.

After about five minutes Cathleen stopped, hands on hips and breathing heavily. Looking round she was impressed how far up Croaghennan Mór she had already come. Far below she watched attentively as tiny figures moved slowly through the main High Street of Ballyfinan. Even this high it was fascinating how faint traces of conversations and other sounds, including that of an unseen dog barking, could be heard.

The chilly breeze, unnoticed during her steady climb, suddenly made Cathleen shiver. Pulling her duffel coat tighter around her slim frame, she continued upwards. The Devlins owned much of the rough grazing on Croaghennan Mór and Cathleen knew from experience that if Tom was on the hill, he would be found on their highest field, near the summit. As she ascended, first heather and then bracken began to dominate the slope's vegetation. Progress, difficult enough due the steepening gradient, became even harder going. It was not long before Cathleen was sweating heavily, despite the fresh wind.

Scrambling up onto the last field boundary wall before the "Top Field" (as it was known), she was confronted by a virtual wall of bracken. By late summer the hillside bracken was over five feet high, and from the top of the wall the dense green thicket stretched towards the rock-strewn summit like a miniature forest canopy.

"Tom!" Cathleen shouted. "Are you up here?" Her

sudden cry startled a pair of crows that had been foraging in the undergrowth, screaming alarmingly into the sky. A hundred yards away a head appeared within the sea of jade coloured fronds.

"Cathleen? Is that you?"

"Aye, who else do you think it is, you eejit! How do I get down to you? It looks like a jungle from here."

Tom smiled, genuinely pleased to see her. "It's easy, just walk along the top of the wall until you get to that large gorse bush...there'll be a path right in front of you."

Puzzled by what he meant, Cathleen nonetheless obeyed, carefully stepping along the loose stones until she reached the gorse. Glancing back, Tom was nowhere in sight. She was about to call out to him again when she noticed, below the wall, an area of bracken had been trampled down. From this area a narrow pathway was obvious, leading into the depths of the ferns. Sitting down first on the wall, she carefully lowered herself to the ground and studied the path. Smiling, though shaking her head slowly, Cathleen entered but after a few yards stopped; the beaten down bracken track way branched left and right!

"Tom! Whereabouts are you?"

"In here," came the distant reply.

"I know that! But which way, there's two paths?"

"Go right...I'm coming to meet you."

"Mine or yours?"

For a few seconds there was silence. "Ah, your left, sorry." Tom's somewhat mumbled apologetic reply was evidently getting nearer.

Muttering under her breath, Cathleen took the left path.

"Don't take any other turns Cathleen," Tom cried more forcefully. "I'll be with you in a second."

Resisting the temptation to make a sarcastic retort she carried on, dutifully ignoring two subsequent tracks off to the left from the main pathway. After a few more yards the path curved round a large boulder and Cathleen came face to face with a grinning Tom.

"Sorry about the left – right thing," he said sheepishly.

Cathleen tried to level what she thought of as one of her mother's best frosty glares, but it was no use; in moments she was grinning openly also.

"Tom, this is great! How did you do it? It must've taken you ages to cut your way through all this."

Shrugging, his natural shyness and awkwardness at being praised began to resurface. "Aye, it did take a wee while, but it's not been that hard," he said untruthfully. "Besides, Dónal and the others helped."

"And you never asked me to?" Cathleen teased, her face a picture of mock hurt and rejection.

"Ah, well, the lads wanted it as, well, as our den...you know, a sort of boys' hideout – "

"Tom!"

"Look, come on, let me show you around," he added quickly, wisely trying to steer the conversation back to a safer topic. Impulsively grabbing her hand, which on later reflection Tom thought was very self assured of himself, he led his friend through a virtual labyrinth of trampled bracken pathways. Laughing, they ran together through the tracks, Tom occasionally taking sudden turns and diving down branching paths. Now and again a path would open out into a larger, circular area of beaten down fronds, before leading off again into the thicket. A game of chase soon developed but Tom always managed to keep just ahead of Cathleen. In truth he had doubled back on himself a few times but even accounting for this, the scale of the hidden camp was truly inspiring.

"I really can't believe this place, Tom." Cathleen said finally, stopping to rest and breathing hard. "It's huge! You've got paths and camps everywhere."

"Well, to be fair, if you stamp on the stems when they're young and small it's pretty easy really; you just have to redo it every few weeks to make sure that they don't grow back."

"Well, I still think it's very impressive – even if you didn't tell me about it!" Playfully she poked his chest in mock indignation.

Tom smiled. "Thanks." Inclining his head for her to follow he continued, "This way, we're nearly there."

Frowning slightly Cathleen did as he asked, walking slowing along the crushed fern path until it emerged into the largest open area she had seen so far. Roughly circular in shape the clearing was easily ten yards across. Three half-rotten tree stumps had been placed strategically around the area, presumably serving as seating. In the centre much of the bracken had been completely removed to reveal bare ground. Within this a small ring of stones had been built up and a shallow campfire burned gently.

"Wow!" was all Cathleen could say, completely taken aback.

"Come and sit down," Tom said quietly, guiding her to one of the log seats near the fire. "What do you think then? Surprised?"

"Aye, very – I still can't quite believe this place, you have seats and everything."

Tom grinned. "Well as I said, the others helped, it wasn't all my doing." Secretly he hoped his apparent show of modesty would be misconstrued to appear that, in reality, he'd done most of the work. Again he had that strange feeling of wanting to impress Cathleen and gain her approval.

"You shouldn't have left fire burning unattended you know," she said holding her hands out grateful for the warmth.

Tom nodded, a little taken aback by the slight reproach. "Aye, you're right...it's probably okay though, given that it's been so wet lately; all the fronds are still dripping."

"I suppose," Cathleen conceded, thinking it through. Then another thought occurred. "So where did the dry wood come from?"

"Ah, by being prepared," Tom replied with a flourish. Stepping round the fire to an adjacent wood stump, he retrieved a dirty looking cloth sack that had lain hitherto unnoticed. Returning to kneel beside Cathleen, he opened the sack and tossed a number of split logs onto the fire. "Took them from the kitchen store this morning," he added, still smiling. "Along with this!" From out of the bag emerged a small, dark frying pan and half a dozen thick sausages, wrapped in a tea towel.

"Dinner?" Tom enquired graciously.

"Why certainly, sir," Cathleen laughed in return.

Sucking her slightly burnt, sticky fingers, Cathleen watched Tom closely as he wiped the pan clean with wet, bracken fronds. The last of the dry wood had been thrown onto the fire and as the flames took hold it spat and cracked loudly, noisily interrupting the peaceful silence that had developed since lunch. Not once since they had met that afternoon had Tom mentioned the accident or how, (or if Cathleen considered inwardly on reflection) he was coping. Neither had the topic of his mother been raised. Knowing him as she did, Cathleen knew he would want to talk about it; it was just a matter of how to get him to open up.

"It is lovely up here," she said at last. "So quiet."

Tom looked across at her. "Aye, I like it. I know it's a bit of a hike and it's great to come up and mess around with Dónal and the others...but sometimes I just want to be by myself and enjoy the peace. I like to think when I'm here. It helps to clear my head."

Staring directly back at him Cathleen patted the log beside her, indicating he should join her. Waiting for him to do so, she said, "Tom, you can tell me to mind my own business if you like, but, I've been worried about you since...since your Da's accident." Hesitating slightly, she added softly, "I'm here...if you want to talk about it?"

For a while Tom said nothing, staring thoughtfully into the flames. He had suspected that at some point Cathleen would ask how he was feeling. In truth he was almost grateful she had, since he did want to talk; if he was honest he *needed* to talk. But now she had finally raised the subject, he unexpectedly felt uneasy. *Where did he begin? How did he truly feel about his father's death? He hardly felt saddened, much less dismayed. Why did guilt assail him for this? And what was happening to his mother?*

"I'm sorry Tom," Cathleen said a little abashed, misreading his continued silence. "I didn't mean to pry."

Glancing up at her he smiled kindly. "It's alright Cathleen, I don't mind you asking."

"Really?"

"Aye." Picking up a twig he poked absently at the fire before continuing slowly, "After all, who else have I got to talk to?"

Cathleen frowned. "What do you mean? Haven't you spoken to your Mam?"

Tom's face fell noticeably and he shook his head sadly. "That's part of the problem, Mammy doesn't listen, it's like she doesn't want to hear at all. She just sits there all day and hardly speaks...it's like she's in a world of her own." After a slight pause he continued, "I know Gran's worried, I can see it in her eyes; not that she would ever say anything to me though. I heard her talking to Dr Kerrigan, a few days back, and he said Mam was *traumatised with grief* or something like that."

Cathleen gently laid her hand over his and squeezed reassuringly. "Have you tried talking to your Gran about this?"

Again Tom shook his head. "She's always far too busy looking after all of us. Besides, as I said I'm sure she already knows...she's not stupid and it's pretty obvious to anyone coming round that Mam's not right. I'm surprised your Mam's not said anything to you, she's been over more than anyone else has."

Cathleen felt her cheeks burning and quickly looked away, pretending to be deep in thought.

"The thing is," Tom continued, unknowingly saving his friend's blushes. "I don't believe Mam is grief stricken, not like Dr Kerrigan or everyone else thinks."

Looking up Cathleen said nothing but simply waited for him to go on.

"She's never cried, well, only once and that was in bed when she thought I was asleep. Mam doesn't even look sad when anyone asks her about Da; she just smiles back or stares into space and ignores them."

"My Mam says people grieve in different ways," Cathleen offered.

Tom shrugged. "Maybe, but I think Mam's more worried about what's going to happen next."

"What do you mean?"

"Well, now Da's...gone, how is she going to provide for us? She hasn't got a job."

Cathleen blinked hard. That thought had never occurred to her, but Tom was right, with Sean Devlin's death and Erin not working there would be no future income. Moreover, with four children to care for, Tom's mother would not even have the time to work.

"We'll help," she replied instinctively. "And your Gran and I'm sure the Dooleys and all will – "

"Aye, I know," Tom interrupted. "But Cathleen, we can't live on charity forever. Gran's pretty old, as well you know."

I wouldn't let her hear you say that if I were you she thought, but instead said aloud, "I'm sure it'll be alright Tom, things always have a way of working themselves out." She tried to smile encouragingly, but even in her own mind the words sounded hollow.

A few heavy drops of rain began to fall. Glancing up at the sky, Tom smiled ruefully at the dark, ominous looking clouds. "I think we're in for a soaking," he said quietly.

Cathleen nodded. Sheltered in their camp from the full force of the wind, they could nonetheless hear its growing intensity around them. "Do you think we'd better go?" she asked reluctantly.

"Aye, probably. Come on now." Standing, Tom held out his hand to help her up.

"What about the fire? We can't just leave it."

Tom considered for a moment; even with the impending cloudburst his natural good sense would not allow him to abandon the blaze to chance. Stepping over to the edge of the cleared ground he collected a handful of wet, trampled ferns and used them to smother the flames. The burning wood hissed and spat angrily, but the fire was quickly extinguished.

"That'll be fine now, at least until it rains properly," he said finally.

Leading the way, Tom guided Cathleen through the maze of pathways to the edge of the bracken thicket. Clambering over the dry stone wall they rapidly descended through the enclosed fields of Croaghennan Mór, twice startling a few isolated mountain sheep in the process. An observation from Cathleen that all the animals bore Finn McGonagle's red shoulder mark drew an ironic half-smile from Tom.

They were perhaps halfway down the hill before the full force of the squally shower hit. Within minutes they were completely drenched and the driving wind chilled them to the core. In spite of the cold, they couldn't help laughing hysterically. For Tom, on later reflection, it was the first time he had laughed in a week.

From the kitchen window Eileen O'Brien watched as Tom and Cathleen scrambled over the stile and sprinted through the rain towards the house. Breathing a silent prayer of thanks at their safe return, she crossed the room and opened the back door.

"Come in now, quick, before you catch your death," she said, gesturing for them to hurry. "Jesus and all the Saints! You look like a pair of drowned rats."

Standing in the doorway Tom grinned and began to strip off his wet clothes.

"Not here!" Eileen scolded. "Up into the bathroom…and mind you don't make a mess, I've just cleared up!" Behind her, wee Cianán, firmly strapped into his small wooden highchair, squealed with delight as his brother entered the kitchen.

"Aye Gran," Tom said, heading off and ruffling Cianán's hair in passing.

"And whilst you're there, bring a towel for Cathleen from the cupboard…and some spare clothes too." Glancing down at the girl she continued, "I don't know what your mother will say, young lady, but I'll not have you going home in those wet things."

Cathleen looked horrified and shook her head adamantly. "I'll not be wearing boys clothes Mrs O'Brien, everyone will laugh – "

"And who do you think will be out to see you on a day like this?"

"But –"

"No arguments now, you'll do as you're told."

An abrupt crash and a giggle from behind ended further conversation. From his highchair, Cianán had rejected his supper, deliberately tipping his bowl and its contents onto the stone floor.

"Oh, you wee Devil!" Eileen exclaimed, "I can't leave you for a minute. Cathleen, quickly now, fetch me that cloth from the sink."

On hands and knees they worked together, clearing up Cianán's mess. Tom returned from upstairs, a towel and some of his spare clothes in his hands.

"Having fun?" he said, grinning openly.

"None of your cheek now," Eileen replied, slowly climbing to her feet. "Go and make yourself useful and put the kettle on, the tea in the pot is stewed to tar." Still smiling, Tom tossed the towel at Cathleen's head and walked across to the Aga.

"Where're the twins Gran?" he asked, wrapping a cloth round the handle of the iron wrought kettle and carrying it over to the sink pump.

"Oh, I took them down to Mrs Dooley's. Geraldine kindly offered to have them for a while. They're happy playing with wee Brenna and it gives me a bit of a break and all."

"Where can I change?" Cathleen interrupted, towelling her hair and looking disparagingly at Tom's offerings.

"What? Ah, use the downstairs toilet dear, or if you like go upstairs and use the bathroom."

"Has Mam gone to the Dooleys as well then?" Tom added.

"Sorry?" Eileen replied, a little distracted.

"I said has Mam also gone with the girls, to Mrs Dooley's house?"

Eileen shook her head, frowning slightly. "No, she's in bed, asleep."

Tom stopped what he was doing and looked directly at his grandmother. "She's not Gran. I checked Mam's room when I went upstairs; she's not there."

For a second Eileen hesitated, uncertain what to say. She had left her daughter asleep in her room less than half an hour ago to take the girls to Geraldine Dooley's.

She had assumed, on returning, that Erin was still upstairs resting. It took all Eileen's willpower not to rush out of the kitchen to search the house; such action would certainly unnerve the children.

"Well now," she finally said, trying to smile reassuringly. "I'm sure your Mam's just popped out for a wee walk, to get some fresh air or such like. What with this dreadful weather we've had lately, that wee clear spell was just what we all needed."

"But Gran, it's tipping down again – "

"I know Tom, but don't you go worrying about that now, your Mammy's not daft; she won't want to get caught in this rain. I'm sure she'll have gone to visit Mrs Brennan, or Mrs Comisky."

Tom's eyes narrowed. "I think I should go and look for her."

Eileen shook her head. "No, love. There's no sense in you getting wet again – "

"But we can't just do nothing!" he interrupted angrily.

At first she did not answer. Walking to the kitchen window, Eileen gazed out and considered her options. Although still windy, the intense cloud burst was obviously passing, but judging by the look of the dark, threatening sky, it was also clear that more heavy rain was on its way. Despite her reassurances to Tom, Eileen knew that in her current state, Erin was unlikely to be simply visiting friends. It was impossible for her to go and search, not with having wee Cianán to look after. She also needed to get Cathleen home. Thinking quickly, Eileen came to a decision. Turning, she fixed her grandson with one of her "no-nonsense" stares; Cathleen was still out of the room getting changed.

"Tom," she began, "when Cathleen's ready and before it starts raining again, I want you to take her home. If your Mam's there, all well and good, but if not can you ask Mary to come over, if she's free? I'll also write you a note, you can drop it off at Geraldine Dooley's on the way – "

"What are you going to say?" he said tersely and interrupting again.

"Well, for one, I would like her to keep the twins for a wee while longer."

Cathleen came back into the kitchen, looking sceptically at her borrowed fawn trousers and baggy grey jumper. "Don't laugh," she said, but seeing the serious expressions, quickly fell silent.

"Cathleen, I've asked Tom to walk you home, before the weather takes another turn for the worse."

"But for sure, Mrs O'Brien, I'll be fine going home on my own."

"I know child, but it's getting dark early now, what with this storm coming, and in anycase, I want Tom to ask your Mam something for me." Without waiting for a reply, she looked back to her grandson. "Where does your mother keep her writing paper, Tom? I need to see about that note."

"I think there's some in her dresser, beside the bed. Do you want me to see?"

Eileen hesitated for a moment. "No, that's alright

love, I'll go." As an afterthought she added, again trying to smile, "At my age you need the exercise." It was an obvious lie but Tom and Cathleen both had the good sense not to let it show.

Tom waited for a few minutes, listening intently, until Eileen could clearly be heard moving around upstairs. Sprinting out of the kitchen, he disappeared for perhaps thirty seconds before returning to join his friend at the back door.

"Where did you go?" Cathleen inquired, slightly perplexed.

"Just needed to check something. I'll tell you later, but Gran's anxious you know, about Mam I mean."

"Aye," Cathleen agreed. "She's not very good at hiding it though. Where do you suppose your Mam's gone?"

Tom frowned. "I don't know, but wherever it is, it's certainly not Mrs Comisky's."

Further conversation was cut short by Eileen's return. "Here now Tom," she said crossing over to them and handing him a white envelope. "Drop this off on your way at Mrs Dooley's please." Glancing at it he nodded and put the envelope in his pocket.

"Don't forget my message to Cathleen's Mam now?"

"No Gran."

"Grand. And come straight back. No detours Tom, not today, okay?" The last was said almost as a plea, rather than a strict order.

11
LOST

"See," Tom said out loud, having just read the note to himself. "I told you she's worried. Listen to this:"

"Dear Geraldine,
Erin's gone from the house, I've no idea where. She's still not herself and I'm dreadfully worried that she might do something silly. I'm sending Tom to fetch Mary Kearney, but please can you keep the twins for me a wee while longer. I'll get word to you if Erin's at the Kearneys' place (doubtful?) but if Cormac's free, I would be grateful if he could check at Mrs Brennan's and Mrs Comisky's. Anywhere else you can think of?

Thanks and God bless,
Eileen.

Ps. please don't show any concern in front of the boy."

Standing together at the bottom of Cairn Lane, Tom looked at his friend and passed the note across. The sky was growing blacker by the minute. Waiting patiently, he watched as Cathleen squinted in the deepening gloom, her lips silently moving as she read the letter for herself. Tom had noticed in his grandmother's haste to write the message that she had forgotten to seal the envelope. He knew reading private mail was wrong, but as Cathleen finished, he strangely didn't feel guilty about doing so.

"What are you going to do?" she asked after a few moments, handing the note back to him.

"I'm not sure," he answered, a little despondently. Replacing and then sealing the paper in the envelope, he inclined his head, indicating that they should continue walking. "Perhaps I should try looking for her? Mam's not got her coat with her, I checked in the hall while Gran was upstairs. It was still hanging up, along with her shawl, and if she gets caught in this storm..." his voice trailing away as the implications of his own words sank in.

Cathleen placed her hand through his arm and drew him closer in. "Tom, I think we'd best do as your Gran says," she said softly. "Let's take the letter to Mrs

Dooley and then go and see my Mam...I think you need to tell her everything though, including what your Gran has written." Studying her face closely, Tom simply nodded.

Crossing the Square, they arrived at the Dooleys' single storey, thatched cottage just as the first spots of rain began to return. Geraldine Dooley answered the door herself and quickly ushered them into the hallway. Like her son James, she was short and dark haired, with a warm, pleasant nature. Reading the note expressionlessly, which in itself impressed Tom, she immediately agreed to look after his sisters as long as necessary. Tom was told to tell his granny that they could stay overnight if that would help. As they said their goodbyes, Tom genuinely wanting to be away as soon as possible to avoid another soaking, Mrs Dooley causally remarked that she would send James' father, Cormac, over to see Eileen shortly.

By unspoken consent, Tom and Cathleen hurried along the High Street in silence, heads bowed in the face of the strengthening wind. They passed only a handful of other pedestrians, none of whom looked up, or gave any outward sign of acknowledgement. Everyone it seemed was eager to be indoors before the storm hit. By the time they finally reached Cathleen's home, the heavens had opened again. Unlike the earlier torrential shower, the steady, persistent nature of this latest downpour inferred that the rain was here to stay.

Mary Kearney had just finished lighting the oil lamps

throughout the old farmhouse, when they arrived. Her disapproving glare at her youngest daughter's late arrival for dinner and obvious change of clothes quickly faded as she saw Tom and Cathleen's expressions. On hearing the news, Cathleen having urged Tom to report it in full, including the truth concerning the contents of Eileen's letter, she immediately took charge. Calling Siobhan down from upstairs, she sent Cathleen's sister to fetch her father back from Kearney's Bar. Siobhan was then to go and stay with Eileen, reassuring her that help was in hand.

Whilst waiting for her husband to return, Mary sat them both down at the end of her large kitchen table, serving each with a steaming bowl of stew and freshly baked bread. Danny Kearney appeared within minutes, a large man with dark, grey-shot, closely cropped hair and ruddy complexion. Mary wasted no time in instructing him where to begin searching for Erin. Eating his meal in silence, Tom kept his head down and tried to remain as unobtrusive as possible. He was conscious that both adults were casting occasional glances in his direction. After she had finished speaking, Cathleen's father nodded soberly and, crossing the room, knelt before Tom, vowing to find his mother. Seeing him to the front door, Mary whispered something out of earshot and firmly shut the door behind him.

Turning, she walked slowly back to the table. "We'll find your Mam, Tom, I promise." Again, Tom said nothing and just nodded in reply.

Outside the wind continued to howl in fury.

News of Erin's disappearance quickly spread. Within the hour a number of people had called at the Kearneys' farmhouse, asking what they could do to help. Mary dispatched them on one task or another. Sitting quietly in the kitchen with Cathleen, Tom had received many sympathetic looks, but thankfully had avoided having to talk with most of the visitors, other than the Garda, Pat Doherty, who had questioned him incessantly before leaving. Already, from reports delivered back to Mary Kearney, it was clear that Erin wasn't visiting any of her many friends in the village. Neither was she praying in the church, nor in any of the local bars (not that anyone had expected her to be in the latter). As time wore on, Tom's pessimism deepened.

It was fully dark by the time Danny Kearney returned, cold and weary. Framed in the doorway, the wind and rain whipping around him into the room, he scanned the expectant, upturned faces. Meeting his wife's eyes, the slight shake of his head portrayed all that needed to be said. Tom looked away, downcast. Glancing over his shoulder, Danny gestured to a tall figure partly hidden in the shadows to follow. Stepping into the kitchen, Declan Kennedy, dripping rainwater from a shabby, full length riding coat, cautiously entered. Standing, Mary guided both men towards the open hearth, ignoring their wet, muddy trail across her stone floor.

"Sorry about the mess Mrs Kearney," Declan said, wiping water from his eyes and looking back.

"It's fine. I'll clear it up later."

Danny rubbed his large hands together before the turf fire. "Just needed to warm up for a wee bit, Mary," he said quietly. "It's bitter out there. I take it you've heard nothing?"

"No, Pat's been here – "

"Aye, I met him earlier. He's got everyone he can think of out looking." As if suddenly remembering Tom was in the room he continued softly, "How's the boy doing?"

Mary raised her eyebrow slightly and shrugged.

Sighing, he turned and walked across to him. "Tom lad, listen to me," he began. "Your Mammy's not daft, she knows how to look after herself. Being caught out by the storm, I'm sure she's just sheltering in some croft or outbuilding somewhere. I know we've not found her yet but we will. There's a lot of people looking for your Mam and we'll spend all night if we have to."

Having helped himself to a mug of tea, Declan joined them, sitting next to Tom at the table. Mary also came across and pulled up a chair. "Tom, I know you have been asked this," he began, "but can you think of anywhere your Mam – "

A sudden hammering on the front door stopped him cold. Within seconds Mary had run across the room and violently wrenched the door open. To everyone's surprise Tom's friend James Dooley stood there, panting heavily.

"James?" Tom asked curiously, once the boy had been ushered inside. "What are you doing here?"

Small and naturally shy, James was evidently nervous with so many eyes upon him. Smiling kindly, Mary tried to make him feel at ease. She showed him to a seat and while he caught his breath, Cathleen was sent to find the biscuit barrel and a glass of milk.

"Now, what can we do for you, James?" Mary finally asked, when she deemed him settled.

"Ah, well, my Mam sent me to tell you something." Mary nodded, encouraging him to continue. "Mam, you see, said she had just overheard Tom's sisters talking."

"Oh?" Sounding slightly mystified, Mary nonetheless indicated he should go on.

"The girls were playing with my wee sister Brenna, Mrs Kearney, and Brenna apparently asked when it was that their Mammy was coming to take them home. My Mam overheard Roisin, I think it was, then say 'After she's visited my Da.' Mammy then asked Roisin what she meant by this and following their conversation, she's pretty convinced that Tom's Mam has spoken to the girls about needing to say 'goodbye to their Da.'"

For a few moments nobody said anything, each silently considering the implications of these words.

"Gone to say goodbye..." Declan murmured, his eyes staring off into space. Without warning he suddenly leapt up. "Jesus! I think I know where she is."

"Where?" Mary cried, also standing and knocking over her chair.

"Lenan Pier! Erin's gone to Lenan Pier. It makes

perfect sense. Danny, have you got a bike?"

"What? Aye, out the back....but wait man, why Lenan? Why there – "

"Think about it!" The School Master exclaimed, clearly animated. "Where else would she go to say 'goodbye' to Sean?"

Danny nodded thoughtfully. "Okay, sounds reasonable to me, but by bike will take too long. Come on, we'll get Joe to drive us in his truck."

"I'm coming too!" Tom cried, standing.

Danny Kearney shook his head. "No son, stay here. Help Mary and Cathleen get blankets and hot water ready." Before Tom had a chance to argue he turned and followed Declan who was already opening the front door.

"Be careful – " Mary called as the door slammed shut behind them.

*

"I can hear them!" Cathleen shouted excitedly, her face pushed up against the glass of the kitchen window. Sure enough, as her mother rushed to join her, the headlights of Joe Kearney's dark pickup swept up the short drive up to the family home. Tom remained where he was at the table, head bowed, staring at the half-eaten plate of biscuits and cups of cold tea. Cathleen gasped.

"Saints and Our Lady preserve us," Mary Kearney breathed. "Tom, they've found her!" Scrambling to his feet, he was virtually at the door as it opened.

"Mind now, Tom." Declan said, staggering in, Erin

Devlin in his arms and wrapped in his old stained riding coat. Danny, and his brother Joe, followed a step behind.

"Easy!" Mary commanded. "Bring her over to the fire. Cathleen get me those towels and blankets – quickly now."

Gently, Declan lowered Erin into a chair set before the hearth, and stepped back. Removing his coat, Mary bit her lip to prevent herself crying out at her cousin's frightful appearance. Erin's lips were tinged blue, and her closed eyes sunken and dark rimmed. Under the coat she was still only wearing her long, white night gown which, sodden, clung to her thin frame like a pale shroud. All colour had drained from her legs and arms and she was shivering uncontrollably.

"Oh Erin," Mary whispered sadly, rubbing her arms and legs vigorously with the towel, trying to get the blood circulating. "You men now, out you go," she said more forcefully over her shoulder. "I need to get Erin out of these wet things. Danny, tell Dr Kerrigan I need him straight away, and someone needs to let Eileen know she's safe. Tell her also that Tom will be staying the night with us. Oh, and let the Garda know she's been found, and the Dooleys'."

The men in the house did not need to be told twice, not when Mary was in this frame of mind. Within seconds she heard movement behind her and the front door opening and closing. Tom came to stand beside her and his mother. Looking up, Mary regarded him kindly. "Your Mam's safe now, Tom." With a reassuring smile she added, "Everything will be alright –"

"Mary?" Erin breathed, her eyes still closed.

"I'm here Erin."

"I...I'm..."

"Shush now...You're safe now...try not to talk, you need to save your strength."

"Oh Mary...*I'm...so...sorry!*" Forcing the words out, Erin Devlin burst into hacking, uncontrollable sobs.

*

Tom awoke the next morning surprisingly refreshed; he had obviously slept well. With the trauma of the previous evening, he had gone to bed in Cathleen's small room (Cathleen having had to share with Siobhan), fully expecting to lie awake for hours, unable to sleep. The house was quiet, though he could just hear subdued voices talking downstairs. Listening for a few minutes, he tried without success to make out what was being said. For a while he considered staying in bed, but as always curiosity got the better of him. Swinging his legs out of bed, he tiptoed across the narrow landing to peer round the door of the guestroom. It was clear that his mother was still sleeping; Erin looked peaceful, if still very pale. Conscious of Dr Kerrigan's instructions from the night before regarding the need for undisturbed rest, Tom silently retreated and headed for the bathroom.

In the kitchen Mary and Danny Kearney looked up from their conversation over the breakfast table as Tom walked down the stairs.

"Good morning, Tom." Mary said pleasantly. "You're

up early. I hope you slept well?" Danny nodded a simple greeting.

"Aye, I did thanks. Mam's still asleep though."

"Well, best we leave her be. She's had a tough time of it of late, and sleep's the best thing for her." Pushing back her chair, Mary stood and crossed to the larder. "What would you like for breakfast now? We have fresh bread, or toast...or I can do you some porridge, or would you like a boiled egg? I'm sorry there's no bacon left, mind, not after that gannet of a husband of mine ate the last of it!"

Sitting down opposite Cathleen's father, Tom just smiled. "Toast will be grand thanks. I don't tend to eat much in the mornings anyway."

"You should eat well first thing Tom, it sets you up for the day," Danny said, wiping a chunk of bread round the edge of his half finished plate of bacon, beans and fried eggs. Like his brother Joe, Danny was a big man and certainly used to a hearty breakfast each day.

Nodding, Tom answered, "That's what Mam and Gran always say."

"Well, they're right lad." Pausing for a moment, Danny took a bite of his bread and with his mouth still full continued, "Talking of your Gran, you were in bed by the time I got back with Siobhan last night, she's coming round for lunch with your brother and sisters after Mass this morning."

"There you are love," Mary interrupted, reaching from behind to deposit a plate of thickly cut toast on the table. "Help yourself to milk and there's honey or blueberry jam in that cupboard if you want it. Just make sure that wicked man in front of you keeps his hands to himself!"

Thanking her again, Tom was thoughtful for a moment. "What's going to happen now, with Mam I mean?"

Concentrating on his breakfast he did not see the Kearneys share a quick, meaningful look. With a slight nod, Danny indicated his wife should take the empty seat besides him.

"Tom," Mary began after sitting down, staring directly into his eyes and deciding there and then that he should know the whole truth. "Your Mam's very weak. You must've noticed that for the last few weeks she hasn't been looking after herself." Tom nodded but said nothing. Choosing her words carefully, Mary continued, "She's lost a lot of weight, and if I'm honest, since your Da passed away, I don't think your Mam's hardly touched her food. You know Dr Kerrigan examined her last night and, well, after you and Cathleen went to bed, the three of us had a serious talk."

Tom stopped eating; those familiar feelings of panic were beginning to surface once more.

"Mary, I'm sorry, but I need to be away." Danny cut in, wiping his mouth and rising from the table. "I'll see you later."

Sighing in slight resignation, Mary accepted a kiss, and with a passing nod to Tom, Danny left. Watching him depart through the front door, Tom absently

241

noticed that, although still breezy, the rain at least had stopped.

"I haven't discussed this with your Gran yet, but I, well we that is, think it's best if your Mam stays here for a wee while. She needs caring for and your Gran can't do that and look after all of you. I won't lie to you Tom and say I'm not worried, because I am. Without rest, and someone on hand to look after your Mam, I'm concerned she will become very ill."

As implications of his aunt's words began to sink in, Tom knew she was right. His mother did need caring for and no matter how much he wished it, that wasn't going to happen at home. Tomorrow was the start of the last full week of the summer holidays, and after that there would be additional stresses of getting everyone, other than wee Cianán, ready for school each day.

"You'll be able to come and visit every day, Tom," Mary added, hoping that would ease his worries. "And to be sure, it won't be for very long."

Resigned, Tom nodded his agreement.

"There's a good lad. Now, have you had a wash yet, or done your teeth?"

"No," he confessed, disappointed that he had not already avoided that particular morning ritual.

"Well, best you do now...you'll want to be in that bathroom before my two girls get in there. Saints preserve us but they take all day! There's a towel on the wee chair in your room, and beside it are some clothes that your Gran sent up last night."

Back in the bedroom, Tom picked up the towel and

stared at his Sunday Best, neatly laid out, waiting for him. His highly polished shoes, in particular, drew a wry smile.

Arm in arm, Declan Kennedy escorted Eileen O'Brien slowly down the gravel path, meandering skilfully through the end of Mass congregation, outside the main entrance of St Mary's Church. In front of them, Siobhan Kearney was cradling wee Cianán, the boy squealing with delight as she playfully rubbed her long, reddish-blonde hair into his face. The twins had already run on ahead and were obediently waiting by the churchyard gate, for once doing as they were told and not having disappeared unaccompanied. Tom and Cathleen were nowhere in sight, but had already been given permission to go straight home by themselves.

As they walked past the milling parishioners, Eileen smiled and nodded greetings, but studiously avoided any attempts to enter into conversation. It was obvious from the many knowing looks that Erin's latest misfortune was already the subject of much debate and speculation. Even Mrs Comisky was politely, but firmly, rebuffed, Eileen informing her that she did not have time to chat this morning, which was, more or less, true. The only family that Eileen deliberately sought out were the Dooleys, to thank them personally for their help the previous night.

"Nice service," Declan murmured as they moved on, trying to appear relaxed, and smiling at a waved greeting from a girl at school.

"Aye, it was. Kind of Father to mention Erin in his prayers." At the gate, Eileen waved Siobhan and the children on. "Off you go now, Siobhan take them straight home...we'll be following on. Tell your mother to put the kettle on." Considering further and, casting a stern eye at the twins, she added, "And girls, you'd better keep those dresses clean, if you know what's good for you."

Crossing the main road, Eileen and Declan walked silently together, each content with their own thoughts. They passed the Park, now cleared of festival bunting and structures, and continued on slowly for a few minutes before Eileen finally asked the question that had been troubling her all morning. It was a question Declan had, nonetheless, been expecting.

"I need to know, Declan," she began quietly, "what happened last night, when you found Erin."

Nodding in understanding he replied, "Aye, I know."

"When Danny came round last night, to collect Siobhan, he only told me briefly what had happened...he said you found Erin at the end of Lenan Pier and that...that she was about to jump into the sea?" The fear in Eileen's eyes was very real.

Declan did not answer immediately but considered carefully how he should reply.

"Declan, please, I must know...was Erin trying to –"

"No Eileen, she wasn't," he finally replied, turning to face her. After a moment he continued, "When we got to Lenan, we couldn't see Erin at first. The storm was terrible and in the dark and driving rain it was hard to see anything past a few feet. Joe and Danny shouted that they were going to search in the village and I headed towards the harbour. It was then that I spotted her, standing alone at the end of the breakwater. I called, but she didn't respond. I assumed at first that she simply couldn't hear me, so I ran out to the pier..."

Eileen waited patiently for him to continue. "Please go on."

"Aye...as I approached I had to slow down, the footing was treacherous and the waves kept crashing over the wall. I never stopped calling Erin's name, but, Eileen, it was like I wasn't even there. Even when I touched her arm she didn't acknowledge me at all. Her skin was like ice and she simply continued to stare out to sea." His voice was becoming thick with emotion and Eileen squeezed his arm reassuringly. "Anyway, I picked Erin up and carried her back to Joe's truck; he drove us back to Mary's house and, well, you know the rest."

They were nearing the Kearneys' farmhouse. Entering the start of the short lane that led to the open yard area, various family members were in evidence, milling around outside the house and chatting amiably. Hanging back, Declan suddenly felt uneasy.

"Eileen, I'm not really sure about coming to lunch," he said, a little apprehensively.

"What? Don't be daft."

"I'll be putting Mary out, turning up unannounced like this."

"Not at all. And since when has Mary ever turned anyone away? There'll be plenty to eat, and one more mouth won't make any difference," she added, continuing to dodge the question.

"That's not what I meant, and you know it. This is a family day...and I don't want to intrude. Erin's been through enough lately, and I'm sure she – "

"Now listen here Declan Kennedy," Eileen said more forcefully and regarding him keenly. "My daughter, likely as not, would not be here today if it hadn't been for you. Erin needs you now, more than ever, even if she can't admit that to herself. I know you love her – now don't look at me like that – you just need to give her time. And besides," she added, pointing a finger at his chest, "as far as I'm concerned, you're already family."

Speechless, Declan allowed himself to be led to the Kearneys' front door.

For Tom, that afternoon at the Kearneys, would always stay in his memory as one of the most pleasurable ever. Despite his fears, Declan was welcomed with open arms, as were the other invited guests, not least of which, at Mary's insistence, included Cianán Devlin. The big man, his fading bruises still clearly evident, was understandably self-conscious and reserved at first, but was quickly put at ease and made to feel at home. Mary was in a typical, commanding mood. She lay on a huge feast, the centrepiece being a whole leg of lamb and a side of roast pork, complete with mountains of roast potatoes, red cabbage, mashed carrots and parsnips. Twelve, plus wee Cianán, eventually sat round the large kitchen table and the meal was loud and boisterous, with quick-witted banter flowing freely back and forth. But for Tom, nothing brought him greater joy than the fact that his mother was with them. Although quiet, Erin nonetheless sat at the table nearest to the hearth, wrapped in a thick dressing gown. For the first time in weeks she smiled and appeared genuinely happy, periodically joining in with the various conversations and jokes flowing around her. It seemed to all that a dark cloud was finally lifting.

After dinner, Declan helped Erin to a more comfortable chair, as Mary bullied some of the adults and Tom and Cathleen into clearing up. Eileen watched them surreptitiously as she lent a hand to Siobhan and Paul Geraghty, in getting the younger children to put their coats on for a late afternoon walk.

"I've not had a chance to thank you, for everything," Erin said quietly, as she lowered herself tentatively into an armchair.

Declan simply smiled. "There's no need, Erin, I'm just glad you're okay." Kneeling at her feet, he added. "You did scare me for a while though."

Erin shook her head. "I've been such a fool."

"Hush now, no one thinks that – "

"But I do! God, what was I thinking of, going off like that?"

Declan did not reply, but continued to regard her closely.

After a moment she said, softly "All last week...it

seems like a daze. I couldn't get Sean out of my head."

"It was a terrible loss," Declan agreed, sympathetically.

"No, but that's just it. I didn't feel his loss. All I kept thinking was why don't I, why am I not crying and screaming in despair and, God help me, what am I to do now? Have I been such a poor wife?"

Before he could reply a sudden fit of coughing possessed her and for several seconds Erin fought for breath. Glancing round nervously she was relieved that no one appeared to have noticed. Unbeknown to her however, Eileen had.

"Are you alright?" Declan asked frowning, the concern clearly apparent in his voice.

Erin nodded but did not speak at first.

"Do you want me to get you anything? Should I fetch Mary?"

"No, I'm fine. Just feel a little shaky. I've probably overdone it today. Don't look so worried, I'm not dying yet you know."

Despite her smile and attempted humour, Declan remained straight-faced.

For the remainder of the day, Erin appeared well and made great show of joining in with various family games and story telling. There was no repeat of the coughing fit and for much of the time Tom was blissfully content, sitting at her feet, his head gently being stroked. Around teatime, Erin made her apologies and retired to bed, claiming a slight headache, probably due to tiredness from the day's activities. Kissing her goodnight, (Eileen having agreed to Mary's suggestion that Erin stay with her for the foreseeable future), Tom promised to visit first thing in the morning.

Later that night as he lay in his own bed reflecting happily on the day, Tom had no idea that Dr Kerrigan had again been called out to the Kearneys' farmhouse.

12
REUNION

The following Tuesday heralded the start of September and with it the arrival of the first family visitors from outside Ballyfinan for Sean Devlin's forthcoming memorial service. Father Aidan had, not long following the tragic accident, scheduled the service for Thursday the 3rd. With travel arrangements already made, it would be impractical to change the date now, despite Erin Devlin's sudden and unexpected decline. Whilst never the most popular member of the family, nor the village community generally, Sean had nevertheless married into the O'Brien and Kearney Clan. As such it was expected that all close relatives and family friends attend the service. Members of Tom's family from Letterkenny, Donegal Town and as far away as London were all due to arrive in Ballyfinan over the next few days.

In the centre of the Square, Tom sat on the low kerb adjacent to the garage with its single petrol-filling pump. Behind him, the steady ringing from the blacksmith's forge of hammer striking metal was starting to give him a headache. Sighing, he looked for what seemed the hundredth time back down the High Street towards the church; there was still no sign of the Dunkeeny bus. Standing, Tom stretched his legs and, yawning, considered going home. Frowning, he quickly dismissed the idea. The bus was bound to arrive the moment he left and his grandmother would certainly be cross, having given him explicit instructions to wait for it. Eileen had told Tom and his sisters the evening before that their Aunt Keira and her husband, Derek McDonagh, were expected today. She had said they would have been travelling since the weekend from London, with the final stage dependent upon catching one of only two bus services per day from Dunkeeny to Ballyfinan. Tom knew from experience that the published bus timetable rarely agreed with the actual arrival time and that the bus generally turned up anytime mid morning, and then again late afternoon. Officially due in at ten o'clock, Tom considered that he must have already waited well over half an hour extra.

From the direction of Finan Bridge he heard his name being called. Turning, he saw Dónal and Aoife

O'Connor striding purposely towards him.

"Hello Tom," Dónal's mother said as they drew near. "How are you?"

"Fine, thank you."

Standing next to him, Aoife nodded and then looked away, shading her eyes from the sun with her hand to scan the High Street. She was a thin woman, with sharp, finely defined features and short, reddish-brown hair. Whilst she had never been unpleasant to him, Tom always felt slightly uneasy in her presence. Aoife had a hard reputation in the village and was never particularly welcoming to anyone.

Tom glanced at his friend's feet. "New shoes?" he inquired, half smiling.

Dónal grimaced. "Aye, and they hurt like buggery."

"Dónal! Mind your language," his mother snapped, without looking round.

"Sorry, Mam."

Tom grinned behind her back. "So, what's the occasion? With the shoes I mean?"

Rolling his eyes dramatically Dónal said, "Mam wants to go shopping in Dunkeeny." Leaning closer he whispered, "Not that I'd much choice mind...I've got to go and there's no way she'll take me into town without them."

Inclining his head slightly, Dónal indicated that they should walk a few feet out of earshot. Regarding his friend intently, his face suddenly serious, Dónal asked quietly, "How's your Mam?"

Tom's grin slowly faded. "I'm not sure," he began

"She's not good, but no one will tell me anything. Mam's still staying at the Kearneys', and when I called round this morning she was still in bed. Dr Kerrigan was with her again, but my aunt wouldn't let me go up and told me to come back later on." Blinking back tears, Tom continued, "I could hear Mam coughing though, it sounded horrible."

"Do you know what's wrong?"

Tom shook his head. "No. But I did hear Gran talking to Mrs Dooley yesterday evening though. She said she thinks Mam caught a chill, from being out in the storm and all."

"Well, she could be right you know," Dónal nodded sagely. "Maybe it's just a bad cold, or something."

Tom looked sceptical. "I don't know, Mam's cough is pretty awful…"

"Come on Tom," Dónal smiled, trying to sound cheerful, "You've got to think positively, I'm sure – "

"At last!" Aoife cried, disturbing them. Gesturing she continued, "Dónal, the bus is here. Say goodbye and come on now."

Glancing down the High Street, the boys watched as the single-decker, Leyland Lion bus, with its distinctive grey, green and black livery of the Lough Swilly Bus Company, slowly approached.

"Here we go," Tom murmured under his breath.

Dónal frowned, "What do you mean?"

"My Aunt Keira and her husband should be on it," he replied, still staring at the advancing bus. "Or the one this afternoon. Not sure really, but they're due to arrive from London today. Gran sent me to meet them."

"Ah, I see. So when's the last time you saw them?"

Tom simply shrugged. "It's been a while, a few years at least. I've only ever met him once before, just after they were married. They got married over there and came over after to meet the family."

"What's he like?"

Another shrug.

"Listen, are you doing anything tomorrow?" Tom asked quickly.

"Don't think so. Why?"

"I just need to...I don't know, do something. Go fishing or whatever."

Dónal nodded, "Aye, sure. How about if I – "

"Dónal! Will you hurry up! Aoife shouted. "I'll not be telling you a third time."

The bus pulled into the Square and in a squeal of breaks, slowed to a stop, the engine idling. A number of people within were already standing, preparing to disembark.

"Look, I'll see you later," he said, jogging over to stand beside his mother. "Are you in tonight?"

"What? Aye, but it's probably not a good idea to come round, not with my aunt having just arrived...how about we meet tomorrow, say after lunch, by the river...assuming the weather's okay?"

Dónal could only nod briefly before being forcibly made to stand in front of the bus door, as the first of the passengers stepped off. The third person to get off was Keira McDonagh.

Tom watched as she gazed around, surveying the Square, an enigmatic smile upon her lips. Dressed well, in a long, dark blue coat, Erin's older sister was a tall woman, with a tanned, slightly round face. Her dark hair, styled and cut shorter than Tom last remembered, added to her youthful appearance, and although nearly forty she could easily pass for someone in her late twenties. Behind her, Derek McDonagh struggled off the bus with a large suitcase and shoulder bag. Not a particularly large man, he too was of a similar age but, unlike his wife, looked older. His face was lined and weathered, and thin, receding brown hair covered barely a quarter of his scalp. A rather rotund waist also paid testament to Derek McDonagh's rather indulgent lifestyle.

Stepping onto the bus, Aoife O'Connor cast a backward glance at Keira, but said nothing. Leaning causally against the garage wall Tom watched as his aunt and her husband conversed together. It was obvious neither of them had seen him as yet. Resigning himself to the inevitable, he reluctantly pushed himself off the wall and walked towards them.

"Auntie Keira," he said quietly, smiling shyly. Behind them the thirty-two seater, Lough Swilly bus swung ponderously round the Square and headed back down the High Street in a cloud of exhaust smoke, towards Dunkeeny.

"Tom!" Keira exclaimed, turning at hearing her name. "How lovely for you to meet us. What a surprise!" Embracing him, she bent and lightly kissed his cheek. "You remember Derek?" she added, beckoning her husband forward.

Derek also smiled and held out his hand. "Hello Tom. It's good to see you again. You've grown a lot since we last met."

"Thanks," Tom answered, shaking the proffered hand and smiling inwardly... Derek's English accent always sounded so funny.

"Your aunt and I were very sorry to hear about your Father's accident," he continued soberly. "I can appreciate what a great loss it must be to you." Tom fell silent.

Keira nodded sympathetically. "I know there's nothing we can really say, Tom, that will help, but we want you to know that we're here for you. You understand that, don't you?"

Unexpectedly, Tom felt tears welling up again. "Aye...I know – "

"Keira O'Brien!" A voice cried across the street. "Welcome home!" Looking up they all saw Mrs Comisky waving frantically.

"Thank you Mrs Comisky," Keira replied, forcing a smile. "It's nice to be back." Pretending to be distracted with adjusting Tom's collar she whispered, "You'd think she could get my name right by now. Quick, let's go, before she comes over and we're stuck here for a month of Sundays."

Sniffing loudly, Tom wiped his eyes and nodded, trying to smile in turn. In moments they had fled, leaving a slightly flustered Deidre Comisky gazing after them.

Holding his hand firmly, Keira hurried towards Cairn Lane, practically forcing Tom to run in order to keep pace with her. She talked incessantly and Tom was soon lost in her excitable and confusing tales of life in London. He learnt that Keira had recently changed jobs, now a school secretary after years spent in retail (whatever that meant) and worked in a large primary school in Manor Park, somewhere in the East End of London. Names and places became a blur and, as it often did in such circumstances, Tom's mind began to wander. Marching steadily behind them and breathing heavily, Derek McDonagh surveyed his surroundings, contentedly indifferent to his wife's discourse.

As they approached the small garden gate to Tom's home, Keira suddenly stopped and looked closely at him. "I'm sorry Tom, I've been prattling on haven't I?"

"Not at all." A grin. "Well, a bit maybe."

Keira laughed lightly. "Such a diplomat! But listen, before we go in, please tell me, how is your mother? The last letter from your Gran said she hasn't been herself, and not eating very well? Is that right? Sure it's understandable and all, after everything that's happened, but...Tom what's wrong? Are you alright?"

Tom had already looked away, his smile gone.

"What is it?" Keira persisted quietly, the concern clear in her voice.

Without looking back he simply said, "I think you better speak to Gran."

"And so, your journey was fine then?" Eileen enquired pleasantly, taking a sip of her tea. They were all seated in the kitchen, Tom, his grandmother, Keira and Derek. Wee Cianán was asleep upstairs and the twins, after the initial excitement of seeing their aunt, had disappeared to play elsewhere within the house. Periodic cries and the occasional banging was evidence to the fact that Eileen's instructions to be quiet and *not* wake their brother were being ignored.

"Aye, no problems at all really, other than the time it takes."

"Well, 'tis an awful long way." Eileen agreed. "My Charlie, God rest his soul, took me to London once, years ago now it was. I'll not forget it; never seen so many people in my life! What with the noise and the hustle and bustle, well…" she rolled her eyes heavenwards, her meaning, as to the foolishness of living in such a place, clear.

"London's not all that bad, Mrs O'Brien" Derek disagreed, albeit in good humour.

"Call me Eileen, please."

Derek nodded, "Eileen." Reaching for his tea he carried on, "There are many lovely parks and gardens, and some of the buildings are truly beautiful. Take St Paul's for example."

"Well, that's as it maybe, but it's not for the likes of me." Smiling, Derek was sensible enough not to push the point further.

"Anyway Mam," Keira cut in, changing the

conversation, "we managed to spend a couple of nights in Edinburgh on the way over."

"Edinburgh?" Eileen asked incredulously. "Why in God's name did you go there? My geography's not that good but even I know it's on the wrong side of the country."

With a light laugh her daughter continued, "Oh Mam, it was quite convenient really! You see, there's actually a passenger service, by ship I mean, from Wapping, non-stop to Leith, in Edinburgh. It takes all day but it's a delightful voyage and the company that operate the sailing...the London Ship... something or other – "

"The London and Edinburgh Shipping Company" Derek assisted.

"Well, whoever, they certainly know how to look after you. The ship we were on...what was it called again Derek?"

"*The Royal Archer.*"

"Aye, the Royal Archer, it was lovely. Anyhow, we've been meaning to go to Edinburgh for ages, and when we heard the news last week, well, we thought it would be a nice way to break up the journey. Edinburgh is such a lovely city; the views from the Castle are breathtaking."

Tom listened expressionlessly as his aunt went on to describe the delights of their brief stay in Scotland's capital. Glancing at his grandmother he wondered whether she was having similar, slightly resentful thoughts as he; clearly they had used the opportunity of his father's forthcoming service for a short holiday. From Eileen's somewhat grim demeanour, he suspected he might be right.

From Edinburgh, Keira explained how yesterday they had taken the train to Glasgow, before a short evening crossing to Belfast. Spending the night in Belfast they had caught an early morning train to Dunkeeny, arriving in time for the first bus service to Ballyfinan. As Keira finished speaking, Roisin Devlin bounded loudly down the stairs, and re-entering the kitchen announced that wee Cianán was awake. Muttering under her breath, Eileen slowly stood and left to see to the baby. Behind her back Tom's sister grabbed a handful of biscuits from the table, and stuffing them into her pocket, followed her out.

For a few moments nobody spoke in the kitchen. Tom glanced towards the window. The sun was shining through the net curtains and after the depressing, sombre weather of late, he longed to enjoy the warm, late summer day. Sighing, he knew he would not be able to escape for sometime yet. He also wanted to go and see his mother again.

"Penny for them, Tom?" Derek McDonagh mused.

"Sorry?"

"Penny for them, your thoughts I mean. You looked far away?"

"No, not really...just thinking about Mam is all." Keira and Derek shared a look as Tom absently toyed with a teaspoon.

"Tom," his aunt said softly. "Where's your Mam?

What's happened?" Looking up, Tom stared at them, hesitating. "Would you prefer if I spoke to Gran?"

"No, that's not it...it's just...it's just I really *don't* know what's going on. One day Mam seemed okay, and the next..."

Keira made as if to reply but, with a slight shake of his head, Derek indicated she should wait for Tom to continue.

After a few moments he said, "Mam's at the Kearneys'. Mary's kept her in bed since Sunday. She told me Mam's caught a bad cough and cold but I'm not stupid; I've seen the way she looks when she thinks I'm not watching. And if it's just a cold why is Dr Kerrigan always round there?"

"No one's ever thought you're stupid, Tom," Eileen said in the doorway, wee Cianán half-asleep in her arms. "But equally no one wants to upset you or the girls unduly." Stepping into the room Eileen added, "But, I'll tell you all I know, if that's what you really want?"

"It is," he replied, a little defiantly.

Keira stood and held her arms out to cuddle Cianán, but the boy drew back, burrowing his head into his grandmother's shoulder. Smiling ruefully, she sat back down and made room for Eileen. Everybody waited for her to speak.

Gazing round the table, but directing her words to her older grandson, Eileen finally said, "Mary was telling you the truth, Tom, your Mam has a caught a chill, or a fever. No doubt as a result of Sunday's shenanigans."

Seeing Keira's confused frown she added, "I'll explain about that later. But, from what Dr Kerrigan has said, it's gone to her chest, and...it's not getting better."

*

It was not until late afternoon the next day that Tom, finally, was able to slip away. His entire day had been a whirlwind of activity, principally running various errands demanded by both his grandmother and Mary Kearney. With Sean Devlin's memorial service scheduled the following day, the remaining family members had arrived, and all had to be met, fed and found overnight accommodation. At Mary's insistence, Tom's home had become the centre of goings-on, adamant that there should be no commotion at the farmhouse to disturb Erin. Her older brother, Paddy Kelly, along with his wife Orla, and their children Mary Jo and Anne Marie had arrived from Letterkenny. Similarly, Mary's younger sister Agnes, and her husband James Randal, had travelled from Donegal Town in the west, along with their four children Joseph, Michael, Teresa and the baby, wee Kevin. Eileen's own sister, Ann Kelly, known to the family as 'Grandma Kelly', had also made the journey from Donegal, where she now lived with her youngest daughter Agnes.

Tom's small house, crowded and noisy at the best of times, was in uproar. With seemingly innumerable small children screaming and running around, and adults shouting to be heard over the din, Tom was ironically glad to be sent out on one task or another. Whether it was to enquire into availability of rooms at Dooley's Bar or simply to buy more milk from Mrs Brennan's store, he took his time returning. He even volunteered to go with Joe Kearney and Derek McDonagh to Dunkeeny, to bring back provisions for tomorrow's wake, but such an escape plan was ruined when Eileen caught them all leaving the house together.

Walking slowly along the meandering river-bank towards his favourite fishing spot, Tom could hear voices ahead, their owners as yet hidden by the interspersed gorse bushes. But even before he reached the Big Pool, it was clear that none of the voices belonged to Dónal O'Connor. Hidden behind a particularly large shrub, Tom watched as two older boys tried to cast their lines into the pool. He did not recognise either boy, and as he watched one caught his line in the overhanging willow branches, cursing loudly in frustration. His companion only laughed unsympathetically. Smiling, Tom judged with all the noise they were making, any fish in the pool would be long gone, even if they did finally manage to retrieve the line. Amateurs!, he thought uncharitably.

Retreating quietly, he skirted around the Big Pool and continued downstream. After a short distance the channel began to widen and the river bed became increasingly shallow. Following the river as it flowed parallel to the range of low, marram covered dunes prior to reaching the sea, Tom wondered where his friend was.

Behind the dunes he could hear the roar of the surf

and it was not long before Tom came to the Binnion Bridge. Spanning the Finan, the simple wooden footbridge formally marked the end of the Binnion Road, and beyond it, a natural break in the dunes gave direct access to the sea. Whilst not exactly derelict, the Binnion Bridge had, over the years, certainly fallen into disrepair. Many of its wooden foot slats had long since disappeared, whether into the river or stolen for firewood was anyone's guess. Studying the bridge for a moment, Tom's peripheral vision caught movement on the opposite bank. From beneath the structure and half hidden in shadow, a figure emerged and waved. It was Dónal.

With a grin Tom ran to the bridge and gingerly crossed over.

"I didn't think you were coming," Dónal said as he arrived.

"Sorry, but it's been mad at home and I've only just managed to get away."

"What's going on?"

"Nothing very interesting...just my relations arriving, you know, for Da's service tomorrow. Gran's had me running round like a blue-arse fly doing one job after another."

Dónal grunted but did not say anything else.

"Any luck?" Tom added, seeing his friend's fishing pole on the ground and cast line for the first time.

Dónal indicated behind him. "Just a few wee brownies and that eel back there. Stupid bugger swallowed the hook...I had to cut his head off to retrieve it."

Glancing over, Tom saw the dark body of the headless fish slowly writhe and twist upon itself on the grass. "Funny the way they always keep moving like that, once they're dead."

Shrugging, Dónal bent down and picked up the fishing pole.

"Did you see those two by the Big Pool?" Tom continued. "I didn't recognise them but I don't think they're very good."

"Aye," Dónal scowled. "They've been here since this morning…and made enough bloody noise to scare every fish for miles!"

Tom simply smiled. "Worms look grand," he remarked, peering into a rusty tin on the bank, a number of fat black-headed earthworms intertwined inside.

"Hmm," Dónal agreed, fingering the line slightly. After a short pause, he reeled in, checked the baited hook and recast slightly upstream. Watching intently as the line was slowly carried towards the shadowy area beneath Binnion Bridge he said quietly, "So, how are things?"

At first Tom didn't answer.

"Mam said she thought she saw your Aunt Keira yesterday," he added. "Getting off the bus."

"Aye, she did. She's home with her husband."

"What's he like?"

Tom shrugged. "Okay, I suppose. He seems nice enough."

Reeling in a few turns, Dónal adjusted the tension on the line. "I bet your Gran's happy to have your aunt back, to help out at home I mean."

Tom nodded. "Aye, I think so. They're staying at Granny's cottage but came over really early this morning. They were already in the kitchen talking when I came down for breakfast." For a second Tom's face clouded, as he recalled the strange looks he had received when he had appeared in the room that morning. They all seemed surprised and, if he had to describe it, a little embarrassed by his presence. Dismissing such ideas as paranoia, he watched as his friend again reeled in and repeated the upstream cast, trolling the line back with the current.

"I went to see Mammy earlier," he said quietly. "Before Gran had me running all over the place." For the first time Dónal turned from the river to regard him.

"And...how is she?"

Tom shook his head. "Mary Kearney would only let me in for a minute. Mam seemed half-asleep, but I think she knew I was there. She was breathing really strangely though."

"How do you mean?"

"Well, really quick, in short, wee gasps, and when I held her hand, it felt all clammy. Mary said the doctor was coming again later...to do some more tests."

Unsure what to say next, Dónal was spared any potential awkwardness as his pole suddenly bent over. "I'm in!" he cried, all thoughts of Tom's family gone. At his side, Tom watched as he played the fish expertly for a couple of minutes, before finally landing it on the bank. "Ah, another bloody eel!" he cursed in disgust, lifting the squirming fish high into the air.

Tom grinned.

"And it's swallowed the hook." That earned him a wry look.

*

Standing outside the front door to the Kearney's farmhouse, Tom surveyed the grey, overcast sky. It was the morning of Sean Devlin's memorial service and, as if sensing the sombre nature of the day, the changeable weather had again hidden the sun with low, threatening clouds. Beside him, various members of the family and close friends, all dressed in black, waited silently for Mary and Keira to emerge from the house. Catching his eye Cathleen smiled lightly but Tom could do little in return other than nod an acknowledgement. Understandably, he could think of little else other than the forthcoming service. With the start of the day, the realisation that his father was gone forever had finally sunk in. It was also something of a shock to discover that he was genuinely upset by this. Confusingly, such acceptance also aggrieved him.

All eyes turned as first Keira, then Mary stepped into the yard. Unlike everyone else, Mary was not wearing mourning black but dressed in her normal, wraparound apron and working clothes.

"Well?" Eileen said.

Mary nodded. "She's agreed to stay."

Tom's grandmother breathed a heavy sigh of relief.

"Thank the Lord. And thank you Mary, and Keira. You're sure you don't want me to stay instead? I don't mind."

Mary shook her head. "No, Eileen, I'm fine and besides you need to be there." Turning to Tom and startling him slightly she added, "Your mother wants to see you before you go. Please be quick mind; everyone's waiting."

Tom raced through the house and scaled the stairs, two at a time. He knew his mother had argued strongly all morning that she was well enough to attend the service. Even as the extended family had begun to gather at the Kearneys', her raised voice, interspersed with fits of hacking coughing, had resounded from the bedroom making everyone uncomfortable.

In the doorway, Tom knocked quietly and looked into the small room. Lying under the covers but with her arms free, his mother had her eyes closed and seemed asleep. "Mammy. You wanted to see me?"

Turning her head slightly, Erin opened her eyes and smiled weakly. "Aye, love. Come in." Slowly she held out her arm and Tom, kneeling beside the bed, took her hand. Her palm felt hot and sweaty but despite this her whole body was shivering slightly.

"I wanted to be there with you today," she wheezed, fighting for breath.

"I know, Mam."

"You must be strong...for your sisters and ...the baby."

"I will." Biting his lip, Tom was resolved not to cry.

Struggling to sit up Erin's expression became pained.

"Your father was a good man, Tommy...it was the drink that...made him change." Beads of sweat appeared on her forehead as she endeavoured to speak. "He needs all our prayers now...you must pray for – " Without warning Erin collapsed into a violent fit of coughing. Raising her free hand to her lips Tom saw a balled, blood stained handkerchief in her fist. Aghast, he watched in mounting panic as she held it to her mouth until the convulsion past. As the attacked subsided, Erin sank back into the pillows, her face ashen.

"Mam...Mam are you alright?" Unable to speak, Erin could only nod. "Shall I get Aunt Mary? Or Gran?"

"No...just water," she managed to gasp. Looking wildly around the room he spied a small, half-full tumbler on the bedside table. Retrieving the glass, he placed it in her hand and helped her drink.

"Thank you," Erin whispered gratefully. "I'm fine now."

"Is everything okay up there?" Mary Kearney called from downstairs.

Tom regarded his mother intently. Receiving a slight, reassuring nod he sighed, unconvinced. "Aye," he shouted back, but continued to frown with concern.

Caressing his cheek, a ghost of a smile flickered across Erin's pale, drawn face. "You had better go...they're all waiting for you, and you mustn't be late."

"Can't I stay with you, please?"

"No, love. You know you can't – " Again, another painful, coughing seizure gripped her, although thankfully not as vicious as before. When she removed the handkerchief from her lips this time Tom was sure he saw it flecked with red. Before he had a chance to query this, Erin waved feebly towards the door. "Go...please Tom."

Hesitating, he stared at her with pleading eyes.

"Come on now, Tom," Mary said gently from behind. "It's time to leave." Neither of them had heard her quiet approach. Resigned, he bent and kissed his mother's fevered brow.

"Goodbye," he breathed. "I'll come back soon."

With a tired smile Erin replied, "Remember what I said...promise me you'll pray for your Da."

And for you Tom thought, but simply said, "Aye Mam."

Nodding in satisfaction she closed her eyes. In seconds she once again seemed to be asleep.

At the bedroom door, Mary stopped him with a soft touch on his arm. "I will care for her Tom."

For a moment her eyes held his. "Aye, I know." Continuing on alone he reluctantly joined his family outside, just as the rain began to fall once again.

13

REVELATIONS

St Mary's Church was full as Tom nervously entered, holding tightly onto his grandmother's hand. Common with many other small, rural communities, the local parish priest generally expected that every effort be made by all to attend funeral services. Father Aidan was no exception to this rule, and more to avoid his displeasure rather than out of any sense of duty, a sizeable proportion of Ballyfinan's population had turned out to pay their last respects to Sean Devlin, despite Sean's evident unpopularity within the village.

Walking slowly down the central aisle Tom was very conscious of the many faces watching him solemnly from the adjacent pews. Taking his seat in the front row, next to Cianán Devlin, the big man tried to smile reassuringly at him; it was obvious from his red-rimmed eyes that Cianán had been crying already that morning.

Throughout the service, Tom sat impassively, staring straight ahead. He listened attentively as Father Aidan led the congregation in prayer, and to his uncle as he spoke emotionally of his brother's life and hopes. Towards the end of the service, the twins broke down dramatically. Their crying upset wee Cianán, and Eileen and Siobhan were forced to take all three outside. But for Tom, the tears would not come. As his mother had asked he prayed for his father…but could not cry for him.

Although the rain had stopped, it was still depressingly dull as Tom and Cianán Devlin led the procession of mourners from the church. A fresh, biting breeze added to the uninviting atmosphere. Tom stood close to his grandmother as the exiting congregation filed past. Enduring innumerable handshakes and expressions of condolence, he inwardly wished the whole day would end. At one point, as he glanced around circumspectly, his eyes unexpectedly met those of Séamus Quigley. The farmer's face was unreadable, but his persistent stare unnerved Tom and he quickly looked away.

"Are you okay?" a voice enquired behind him. Turning, Tom saw Cathleen regarding him anxiously.

Nodding, he said, "I suppose. I just caught Mr Quigley looking at me; he still makes me feel uneasy."

"Did you know he was in the church?"

Tom shook his head.

"Why do you think he came? I mean, it's not like he likes your family very much."

Shrugging, Tom replied, "Who knows. Perhaps he's turning over a new leaf?" His friend's sceptical look was the only answer necessary.

The traditional 'wake' for Sean Devlin was held in the function room of Joe Kearney's Bar. To the immense gratitude of Eileen O'Brien, the Kearneys had taken it upon themselves to organise the event and an impressive selection of sandwiches, cold meats, cheeses and pickles had been laid out along the back wall. Over forty family members and close friends had been invited, along with some special individuals, such as Father Aidan and Dr Kerrigan and his wife. After a short, initially reserved period, all the guests began to relax and, helping themselves to food, chatted sociably with one another. A free bar, courtesy of Joe Kearney, helped considerably to lighten the atmosphere.

Tom managed to avoid most of his distant relations, feeling not in the mood to enter into 'polite conversation.' He had been cornered by his 'Aunt' Orla (Mary Kearney's sister-in-law), until rescued by Cathleen on some ruse that his help was required elsewhere. Sitting quietly together in a dimly lit corner, they watched the revelry ebb and flow before them.

"I wish my Mam was here," Tom said softly, absently picking at a plate of shared food in front of them.

Cathleen smiled sympathetically but said nothing.

"I'm really worried about her Cathleen," he continued, still toying with the food. "I know she's not well, but I wish someone would tell me exactly what's wrong. Dr Kerrigan visits Mam every day, but I'm not allowed in the bedroom when he sees her. He always talks to your Mam afterwards but she won't say anything to me." The frustration in his eyes was clear. Cathleen studied him for a few moments.

"Do you *really* want to know?" she finally asked quietly.

Tom nodded.

"Fine then, let's go." Standing up, she straightened her black dress and strode determinedly across the room.

"Hey! Where're you going?" he called after her, suddenly worried.

"To see Dr Kerrigan, stupid. He's only over there. Come on, we'll ask him about your Mam."

"Ah, Cathleen..." Tom replied apprehensively, but she did not look back and continued to walk purposefully towards the village doctor. Scrambling to his feet, Tom caught her up just as, smiling sweetly, she interrupted his conversation with Paddy and Orla Kelly.

"Dr Kerrigan," Tom heard, "I'm sorry to trouble you but I was wondering if we could have a quick word?" Behind her, Tom fidgeted nervously.

Glancing down at her he smiled and said, "Of course, what can I do for you?"

"It's a bit noisy in here, perhaps we could go

outside?"

The doctor's eyes narrowed slightly but he did not object. "Please excuse me for a moment," he said to the Kellys. "I'll be straight back."

Following them out into the High Street, Dr Kerrigan fished a cigarette and matches from his pocket and lit up.

"Isn't that unethical?" Cathleen murmured.

"None of your cheek, young lady! Now, what's all this nonsense about?"

Cathleen looked towards Tom. For a moment he hesitated. Then, steeling himself he said, "I want you to tell me what's wrong with my Mam. I'm not stupid, Dr Kerrigan, I know she's sick, but no one will tell me anything."

Regarding him closely, the doctor drew deeply on his cigarette before exhaling slowly. "I can't divulge my conversations with your mother Thomas. They are private, and as I'm sure you know, I'm bound by certain rules and standards of behaviour."

"Aye, but you've obviously said things to Cathleen's Mam about what's wrong. I'm not a child...well, what I mean is, I don't want to be treated like I'm a wee kid. Please, Dr Kerrigan, I want to know what's happened to my Mam?"

On the High Street the Lough Swilly Leyland Lion rumbled slowly past. *Late again* Tom thought absently, continuing to stare at the tall, grey-haired doctor. Debating inwardly, Dr Kerrigan finally nodded. "Very well, if that's what you want, I'll tell you what I've said to Mrs Kearney."

Tom nodded, his heart pounding.

Taking a final, long inhale of his cigarette, he dropped the butt and stamped it out on the wet pavement. "I'm sorry Thomas, but your mother *is* very ill. I'm afraid there's no easy way to say this, but I believe she has contracted pneumonia."

"Pneumonia?

"Do you know what that is?"

"I, ah, think so. My Grandfather had it." The sudden realisation that Eileen's husband had died from pneumonia sent a shiver through his body. "Are you sure?"

"Aye, I am. I've treated enough patients with pneumonia in my time, and your Mam has all the classic symptoms: shortness of breath, sharp chest pains and a high temperature accompanied by severe chills. You've obviously heard her terrible cough which, and I'm sorry to be graphic, is causing her to bring up heavy sputum."

Tom's eyes were watering. "I saw blood on her hanky today," he whispered.

Dr Kerrigan nodded in understanding. "Aye, I know, Son. And that's another indication, along with your mother's general loss of appetite and fatigue."

"Is she...I mean will she..." Tom could not make the words come out but his meaning was obvious. Cathleen glanced between them, but remained silent.

Looking at him gravely, Dr Kerrigan said, "I won't lie to you Tom, I am very worried for your Mam. Pneumonia is a serious, life threatening illness and she is very poorly, but, nothing is ever certain." Seeing the boy's forlorn expression he continued gently, "We must never give up hope, because your mother won't, will she?"

Tom shook his head slightly.

"Exactly. Erin's a very strong lady, and you and I, and all your family and friends, must help her fight this. Do you understand?"

"Aye," Tom replied quietly.

"Now, I think it's about time we all went back inside. We don't want them sending out a search party to look for us." Placing his hands on Tom's shoulders, the doctor steered him towards the door. Re-entering the function room, he smiled kindly in parting and walked away, leaving Tom and Cathleen to stare silently after him.

It was nearly two hours before the guests finally began to leave. Tom had wanted to go himself but Eileen had refused, insisting he stay to the end. He had a 'responsibility' to ensure he thanked everyone personally for coming. As he stood beside Cianán Devlin at the room's exit, shaking hands with the departing men, and enduring kisses and sympathetic hugs from the women, he listened half-heartedly to the various contrite words and wished fervently that he was somewhere else. When all but a handful of guests remained, and most of these helping to tidy up, Tom slipped away from his uncle to find Cathleen. Joining her by the main buffet table, he made pretence of assisting to clear the dirty plates.

"Are you alright?" she said by way of greeting.

"Aye, I just want this all to be over with."

"I know." Regarding his token efforts she added briskly, "Are you going to help with those plates or what?"

"Oh, sorry. Here, take them." Handing them across, Tom stared around the room, his eyes finally resting on the far corner. Seated at a table were his grandmother and Aunt Keira. Derek McDonagh stood beside his wife, an uneasy expression clearly evident upon his face. Tom could not hear what was being said but it was obvious that Keira was talking animatedly to her mother, who herself sat unsmiling and serious.

Following his gaze, Cathleen said, "They've been like that for ages, heads together, arguing about something. I went over there a few minutes ago, to collect glasses, and your Gran just looked at me really strangely. None of them said anything and just waited for me to leave."

Tom nodded. "Something's definitely going on, I've seen Aunt Keira and Gran talking a few times now, but they always stop if they think I'm around."

"Well, your uncle doesn't seem too pleased, whatever it is."

He's not my real uncle, Tom thought, but instead answered, "Aye...I wonder why." Again, an unexplained feeling of foreboding began to creep upon him.

By mid afternoon the morning's dreary weather had started to lift. As the oppressive cloud cover finally broke up, periodic but increasingly longer spells of sunshine developed. The fresh wind did not abate, but at least in the warming sun it was tolerable.

After first returning home to change, Tom had hurried back to the Kearneys' farmhouse to visit his mother. Surprisingly Mary was not in, and on entering, Tom had discovered Declan Kennedy keeping vigil at her bedside. Erin was again asleep. The School Master quietly explained that his grandmother and aunt had called round a few minutes earlier and that Mary had left with them to discuss something or other. Declan assured Tom that they would be due back shortly, if he wanted to wait. His suspicions growing and not feeling inclined to talk, Tom made his excuses and left.

Leaving the Kearneys' farmhouse, he had wandered through the village and the adjacent countryside for over an hour, his thoughts repeatedly going over the day's events. Distracted and distant, Tom had thankfully been generally ignored by all he met; any sympathetic smiles or curt nods of greeting quickly forgotten. Not even encountering his friends Brendan Harkin and James Dooley, with several others, en route to the Park with a football could sway him from his desire to be by himself.

Leaning over the low wall of the Finan Bridge, Tom idly tossed small stones, one after another, into the clear, swirling waters below. On the grassy bank, twenty yards downstream, a grey heron stood perfectly still, watching him warily. After a few minutes, realising that he was probably disturbing the fish, he stopped and turned to leave. It was only then that he saw Séamus Quigley striding determinedly towards him. Too shocked to move, he stood transfixed, frozen to the spot, his stomach contracting alarmingly.

"Well, now," Quigley sneered, standing very close and looming over him. "This is a grand surprise. I've been meaning to be having a wee word with you." Tom said nothing but slowly started to back away. Stepping forward, Quigley matched him pace for pace.

"Not so fast now, lad," he continued with a twisted smile. Striking, quick as a snake, he grabbed Tom's arm, seizing him in a vice-like grip.

"Hey! Let go of me!" Tom cried, finally finding his voice.

Séamus Quigley's smile vanished. "You *owe* me boy," he hissed. Leaning into his face, Tom nearly gagged at his foul breath. "Your stupid prank cost me over twenty sheep to that bastard McGonagle – "

"Let go," Tom repeated, interrupting him. "You're hurting me."

"Hurting you?" Quigley blinked in surprise. "Damn your eyes, Devlin, I'll do more than that! Do you think you can cross me and get away with it?" He was virtually shouting and a thin line of spittle drooled unheeded down his chin.

Tom shook his head vigorously. "I've done nothing, Mr Quigley."

"Don't lie to me! You think I'm some kind of fool? I know you and McGonagle and that eejit Geraghty were all in it together. I'll deal with them in my own way, but you..." his eyes grew unfocused as he looked into space, obviously considering some private thought.

"Please Mr Quigley," Tom said humbly, "I really don't know what you mean."

Glancing back at him, Séamus Quigley smiled again, wickedly. "I shall have your *land* boy, mark my words. With your Da dead and your Mam sick, *you* won't be able to stop me."

Tom started to struggle again but Quigley held him fast and sniggered. "I'll teach you to make a laughing stock out of me."

"Quigley!" A deep voice called forcibly. "Let him go." Turning, they both saw Declan Kennedy walking quickly towards them.

"Sir!" Tom exclaimed, his relief clear.

"This doesn't concern you, Kennedy." Quigley warned.

"It does when I see you abusing a pupil from my school. Let Thomas go, now! Whatever he's supposed to have done, you don't treat a child like that. God, man, don't you know what day it is? The boy's been through enough today as it is."

Quigley's eyes narrowed dangerously but he nonetheless released Tom's arm. "Well, he's not in school *today*, so piss off and keep your bloody nose out of my business."

Tom edged away, subconsciously rubbing his arm. Seeing him sidling off, Quigley made a grab for Tom again. Declan leapt forward and in a blur of motion laid the stocky farmer out cold. Tom's mouth opened and closed like a landed fish.

"Damn, that hurt," Declan said, sucking his bruised knuckles. At his feet, Quigley groaned, clearly semi-conscious.

"I can't believe you just did that!"

Declan grinned. "Neither can I. But he did have it coming. Come on, let's go before someone sees us, although I dare say some curtains are twitching already."

Tom smiled back. "What about..." he indicated, looking down at the prone figure.

Shrugging, Declan replied, "He'll wake up soon enough. Besides, I don't think I want to be around here when he does." Leading Tom back along the bridge towards the Square, he continued, "So, what was all that about back there?"

"Ah, just a misunderstanding," Tom evaded.

"Hmm...sounded more than that to me." When Tom did not offer anything further, Declan added, "If you don't want to talk to me about it, that's fine, but I heard Quigley threatening you. He's an angry man and by all accounts a vengeful one. I think you should talk to Pat Doherty...I'll come with you if you like?"

Tom shook his head. "No, I don't want to."

Declan regarded him gravely, "Tom, whatever's going on between you and Séamus Quigley is your affair, but he's not a person you want to provoke. By all accounts he has a violent temper and I don't trust him. I understand if you can't speak to the Garda, but at least do so with someone else, Mary Kearney perhaps, or even Father Aidan? Just be sensible...your family's got enough to worry about at the moment without you adding to it."

Tom nodded in apparent agreement but said nothing.

Walking in silence they crossed the Square. As Tom made to part company towards Cairn Lane, Declan unexpectantly stopped him with an outstretched arm. "I'm sorry, I should have said, your Granny asked me to find you. She's waiting for you at the Kearney's place."

"Why?"

"I honestly don't know, but when she Mary returned, she made it plain that she wants to see you."

Tom eyed him apprehensively. "Is there something wrong...with Mam I mean?"

Declan continued to walk and indicated that he should follow. "Your Gran didn't say Tom, but if it's any help, I don't think so...she seemed, well, distracted if anything."

Tom ran to catch up. "What do you mean, Sir?" he asked questioningly, but lost in his own thoughts the School Master did not reply.

"Oh Tom, there you are!" Keira McDonagh exclaimed as he entered, somewhat reluctantly, into the Kearneys' large kitchen. Standing, she hurried over to embrace him. "Are you hungry? Thirsty? Can I get you anything?"

Tom shook his head. "I'm fine, thanks."

"Well, come and sit with us then." A number of

chairs had been set facing the open hearth, and seated, silently waiting, Eileen and Mary warmed themselves, studiously avoiding his gaze. Across the room Derek McDonagh was pretending badly to read the newspaper and ignore them.

"Gran, what's going on?" Tom asked quietly, accepting a proffered chair. Looking up, Eileen stared past him, seeming to see Declan for the first time, hanging back by the front door.

"Mr Kennedy," she said, ignoring Tom. "Thank you for fetching Tommy. I'm very grateful."

"You're welcome, Eileen, it was no trouble." Smiling, Tom's grandmother continued to regard him. For a moment he smiled back, before the meaning of her unspoken dismissal became plain.

"Ah, well, I'll be going then" he stammered, a little embarrassed.

"If you're sure now?"

"Aye, it's getting late…and there are a few things I should be seeing to. Good evening everyone."

After Declan had left, an uncomfortable silence developed in the room. Only the cracking of the turf flames and seemingly hypnotic, rhythmic ticking of the mantelpiece clock disturbed the subdued ambience. Occasionally, a weakened cough filtered down from upstairs, an awkward reminder to the adults of what was to come.

For Tom, surprisingly, it was his Aunt Keira that initiated the conversation. "I think you know, Tom, that your Gran, Mary and I have been talking. We all need to work together, as a family, to find a way through these difficult times, all of us doing what we can to help. Our priority, however, must be to make things as easy as possible, in order for your Mam to recover. You know your Mam's very ill, and God willing she will get better, but..." pausing for a moment she glanced briefly at Eileen before continuing, "that's not likely to be soon. Even then, it will take a long time before your Mam will be fully fit and can provide for you all again."

"I don't understand what you're saying," Tom said, depressingly. "Gran, what does she mean?"

Eileen, who had been staring at her hands tightly clasped on her lap, looked up. Before she could reply Keira carried on. "What I mean, Tom, is that to really help your Mam, unfortunately, this will mean all of us having to make some hard decisions."

"Like what?" he asked suspiciously. The familiar knot in his stomach was growing again.

"Keira, perhaps I should explain," Eileen offered gently. When her daughter did not object she said slowly, "What your auntie is trying to say, love, is that with your Mam staying here, with Mary, someone has to look after the four of you."

"Aye, but why can't you do it?"

Eileen smiled sadly. "I'm getting too old, Tom. Having you all for a few days was wonderful, but I'm exhausted."

"Your Mam's going to have to stay with me for weeks, Tom," Mary said, entering the conversation for the first time. "And we've agreed that it's only fair that wee Cianán stays here too. He's only a baby and needs to be near his mother. Your Gran's said that she could probably just manage the twins, at least for a while. But if that becomes too much, we'll have to rethink that as well."

Tom glanced back to Eileen, who again was looking down. He knew instinctively that they were waiting for him to ask the obvious question. Feeling sick with mounting fear his thoughts raced through possibilities, none of which were particularly appealing. Finally he ventured the inevitable, "And what about me?"

For a second time Keira took the lead. Leaning closer she smiled kindly and answered, "We all think it's best, Tom, if you came and stayed with me for a while."

Tom just stared at her, stunned. Convinced he must have misheard, his mind refused to accept what had just been said. They could not seriously mean that –

"I know this may come as a bit of a shock, but think of it as an adventure. We'll have great fun and Derek and I will take you to no end of interesting places. London is truly an amazing place and there's so much to –"

"London?" he interrupted, his voice hardly above a whisper.

"Aye, London."

"No."

"Tom," Keira continued, slightly firmer. "Please listen to me…it's for the best, for everyone. Don't you think we've considered every possible alternative?"

"Gran, please let me stay with you? I won't be any

bother, I promise."

"I'm sorry, Tom, but I've already explained why that's not feasible." Keira replied before Eileen could. "Gran's going to find it difficult enough, as it is, with the girls."

"I'm not an invalid yet Keira," Eileen reminded her daughter, a slight edge to her voice.

"Sorry Mam, I didn't mean to imply you were. I just want Tom to – "

"I know what you are trying to say…and so does Tom." Sighing, she turned back to her grandson. "The truth is that your auntie's right. I'm sorry, really I am…but I can't cope with all three of you. It's just too much for me."

Tom looked desperately towards Mary Kearney. "Why can't I stay with you?"

Forlornly she shook her head. "There's no room Tom…not with your Mam and wee brother here."

Blinking back tears his eyes met Eileen's again, pleading. "Don't send me away Granny…please."

Taking a handkerchief from her sleeve, Eileen dabbed her own eyes. "Oh Tommy, don't make this any harder than it already is."

"It won't be for long," Keira added, trying to sound cheerful. "Hopefully just a few weeks, perhaps a month or so."

"A month!" he cried in alarm. Sniffing, Tom wiped his hand across his nose. For once, no one chastised him. Feelings of concern and self-pity were rapidly being replaced by anger. *It wasn't fair*. There *must* be another option.

"I'm going to tell Mam!" he announced suddenly. "She won't let you do this." Eileen reached out to touch his hand. Recoiling, Tom just glared at her.

"I'm sorry Tom, but your Mam's already agreed."

"No?" he breathed. "I don't believe you! She wouldn't." Standing he pushed passed them and ran towards the front door.

"Tom!" Eileen shouted after him.

"Let the boy go." All three women turned to regard Derek McDonagh, forgotten on the far side of the room, calmly folding his newspaper. "He needs some time to himself...Tom's an intelligent lad and will see sense, but it's a surprise. He'll come round...eventually."

"Well," his wife replied lightly, glancing at her nails. "He'd better not take too long...we're leaving Saturday morning."

*

Tom, Cathleen and Dónal watched dejectedly as the peat stained waters of the Finan River flowed relentlessly beneath their feet. For what seemed like hours they had sat on the dilapidated Binnion Bridge, legs swinging freely, and debated Tom's predicament. It was already nearly lunchtime the next day, Friday, and still they had not thought of a solution. Most of Dónal's ideas, such as running away or hiding in the Den until Tom's aunt had left, were unrealistic or too far-fetched. And besides, none of his or Cathleen's suggestions, or his own for that matter, could resolve the fundamental problem of who was going to care for him, long term, assuming the McDonagh's left without him. Whilst he would not openly admit it, Tom had already conceded inwardly that he was leaving the next morning, but it was reassuring to think that his friends were as upset as he was.

The night before, back at his own house, Tom had deliberately avoided speaking with his grandmother. Sensing his simmering anger, Eileen had heeded Derek McDonagh's advice and left him be. Over breakfast, following a surprisingly untroubled sleep, Tom had, however, relented and calmly they had talked about the decision and the future. Although no longer angry, he was still far from happy and, if truth were told, a little scared. After breakfast, Eileen, Tom and the twins had together left the house in Cairn Lane to call upon Erin. Tom's mother had had another poor night and Mary Kearney would only allow the children to see her briefly. Frustrated at not being able to speak privately and for any length with her, Tom had soon departed, accompanied by Cathleen. His friend had obviously already heard the news, but nonetheless listened patiently as Tom relayed his fears and concerns. They had met Dónal shortly after, leaving Mrs Brennan's store, and from there they had wandered aimlessly, eventually walking the length of the Binnion Road, towards the river, finally ending up at the bridge.

"Tom, I'm going to have to head back soon," Cathleen said after another long period of silence. "Mam wants me home for lunch...you know what she's like." After a moment she added, "You're welcome to join us if you like?"

Continuing to stare at the current Tom shook his head. "Thanks, but I'm not that hungry." Looking up, he continued with a half smile, "Besides, given the mood I'm in I don't suppose I'll be much company." After a few seconds his smile faded. "I'll call round later though, you know, to say goodbye and all."

"So, you're resigned then…to going?" Dónal said sharply, almost accusingly.

Tom shrugged. "I can't see I've got much choice. Can you?" Dónal scowled but looked away.

"What about speaking to Mr Kennedy?" Cathleen exclaimed, hopefully. "You and he are pretty close."

"No we're not."

"Aye, you are. Thick as thieves most of the time…everyone knows that. Perhaps he can help?"

Again Tom shook his head. "I can't stay with him, he lives with his sister and her family. There'll be no room for me there."

"No, I didn't mean that. I meant how he would feel about you missing school. I'm sure he'd have something to say about that. If we could persuade him that – why are you smiling like that?"

"My Aunt Keira's already thought of that," he said ruefully. "She works at some local school and has already arranged for me to go there."

"That was bloody quick," Dónal muttered. "How did she manage that?"

Tom looked across at him and smiled to himself; despite all his faults Dónal was a loyal friend. "Gran said she used the telephone, the one at the Post Office. Presumably she spoke to the Head there and he's agreed that I can go."

Cursing, Dónal continued to grumble darkly.

14
NEW HORIZONS

It was still dark, early on Saturday morning, when Eileen reluctantly opened Tom's bedroom door. Holding an oil lamp before her she slowly approached the bed. "Tommy," she said gently. "It's time to get up."

Yawning, he rolled over and nodded. "What time is it?"

"Half past four," she replied, kissing his forehead. "Joe'll be here soon. I've let you sleep on as long as I dared, but you'll have to hurry now. Your clothes are on the end of the bed. Come down when you're dressed, and I'll have some toast and milk waiting in the kitchen."

Descending the stairs five minutes later Tom looked accusingly at the brown, battered suitcase in the hallway. Following a request from Eileen, Declan Kennedy had brought it round for him the night before. Unknown to his grandmother, when Tom had opened it later, there had been an envelope inside addressed to him. The envelope had contained a note from Declan, wishing him good luck, and a crisp, white, Bank of England five-pound note; a fortune by Tom's standard.

Joe Kearney dutifully arrived a little after five. With the girls still asleep upstairs, Eileen said her tearful farewells from the front door. Hugging him fiercely, she promised to write every week. Emotional himself, Tom could do little more than nod in reply. From the front seat of Joe's truck, he looked behind miserably as his house receded from view, his grandmother waving frantically from the garden gate. Even Séamus Quigley's dogs seemed to respect the melancholy air, refusing to chase and bite at the truck's tyres as they trundled through his yard. In the darkened cab, Joe glanced at Tom once, but wisely decided against trying to start a conversation.

In the Kearneys' kitchen, Keira and Derek McDonagh were already waiting, sitting at the table and quietly sipping tea, their bags neatly placed by the front door. Hovering around them, Mary Kearney busied herself preparing sandwiches and drinks for the journey. Cathleen watched sullenly from the fireplace, wrapped in a towelling dressing gown and ignoring all attempts to enter into conversation. As Joe held the door open for him, Tom immediately sensed the prevailing depressing mood.

"Hello Tom," Mary said by way of greeting. Tom nodded slightly but did not feel inclined to speak.

"Have you eaten?" Again a nod.

"Well, why don't you warm yourself by the fire, it looks chilly out there."

"Aye, you're right enough about that Mary," Joe Kearney agreed, rubbing his thick hands together. "There's a fair nip in the air this morning."

Tom walked slowly towards the hearth, avoiding eye contact with Keira and Derek as he passed.

"Autumn's not far off now, I reckon," he heard Joe continue behind him. When no one answered, Mary's brother-in-law fell silent, and made to study an old news sheet on the table.

Cathleen offered a small smile as Tom stood beside her. "Okay?" she asked softly.

"Not really, but what can I say?"

"I can't believe you're going away." When Tom did not reply she added, "I'll write every day!"

Tom smirked half-heartedly and bumped his shoulder against hers. "Once a week'll be fine."

Cathleen grinned weakly back at him. After a few seconds she continued, "Mam said I can also telephone you, every now and then, from the Post Office. Apparently your aunt's got one in her house. She must be rich to actually have her own telephone."

Whilst Tom hadn't known this, and as impressive as

it sounded, he didn't feel inclined to show any outward sign of surprise. For a while they stood in silence, simply enjoying the warmth of the fire and the closeness of each other's company. At the kitchen table the adults talked in hushed voices, Mary hurrying around them with final preparations.

Turning to face Cathleen, Tom finally said, "I'm going to miss you, you know. I really am."

"I'll miss you too," she whispered back, forcing herself to smile. In mock anger she brushed away tears that were suddenly threatening to spill over her cheeks. "I can't believe I'm getting soppy over you!"

Staring at her, lost for words, he was unaware of Cathleen's mother coming to stand before them.

"Tom," Mary said quietly. "I'm sorry, but it's time now. Joe's going to run you all to the station at Dunkeeny, but if you're going to catch your train, you need to go and say goodbye to your Mam now."

Nodding in resignation and with a final glance to Cathleen, Tom followed Mary out of the kitchen and up the stairs.

*

Through the small, dirt encrusted windows of the railway café, Tom stared gloomily out at Dun Laoghaire harbour. Stifling a yawn, he knew, without turning, that sitting beside him his aunt was watching surreptitiously; as she had for their entire journey. It was only late afternoon and despite having sat down for the majority of the day, the early start and emotional trauma of leaving was beginning to catch up with him. At any other time Tom would freely have admitted that the trek across country from Dunkeeny to Dun Laoghaire was exciting. Until today, he had never ridden on a train before, or travelled in his entire life further than Letterkenny. Even the relatively small locomotives that had pulled their cramped carriages should have been viewed with awe, despite Derek McDonagh's assurances that these were nothing compared to the engines that would greet them in England. But not today; today, he didn't care. Neither, unlike his aunt and her husband, was he concerned by the numerous enforced train changes and inevitable delays they had encountered at Letterkenny, Strabane, Dundalk and, finally, Dublin. As he had watched the lush, green countryside roll past and gazed upon towns and settlements that, until then, had only been names in some school textbook or atlas, Tom could take no pleasure in the experience. The painful, harrowing separation from his mother haunted him, and in all likelihood, would continue to do so for a considerable time to come.

The door to the café opened, its tiny bell ringing shrilly as Derek re-entered.

"Tom, Derek's back," Keira said, waving to attract her husbands' attention. Deliberately, Tom ignored her and refused to look round, continuing to stare out over the grey waters. The scrape of the metal chair and a heavy sigh announced Derek's arrival at the table.

"Everything alright?" Keira asked a little hesitantly.

"Yes. We're all booked on the Hibernia. I told you

there wouldn't be a problem on the evening crossing. She's due in at Holyhead just before midnight and from there we catch the twelve thirteen express to Euston."

"Oh Wonderful, that's great news." Tentatively touching Tom's shoulder Keira added, "That saves us having to spend the night here, doesn't it Tom?"

Turning from the window, Tom just looked at her impassively. He knew he was being rude, but still felt angry at the situation and, as such, not disposed to talk.

"What time do we have to board?" Keira enquired hastily, when Tom didn't reply.

Removing his pocket watch, Derek opened the protective lid, staring for a moment at the ornate face. Snapping it shut he said, "Not until six thirty. That still gives us over an hour. Shall we have dinner here, or wait until we're on board? Saying that, you never know what ship food's like. What do you think, Tom?" he added subtly, trying to bring the boy into the conversation.

Tom's first thought was to shrug indifferently but he was, actually, getting quite hungry. Also, and if he was really honest with himself, he knew both his aunt and Derek had his, and more importantly his mother's, best interests at heart. They were also making sacrifices in terms of their lifestyle in caring for him. Perhaps it was time, he admitted inwardly, to soften his distant stance towards them.

"Well," he ventured quietly, "If it's alright with you, perhaps we could eat now. I am a bit hungry."

"Of course that's alright." Keira replied eagerly.

"Derek, go and ask for the menu." After he had left, she smiled at him kindly. Tom smiled shyly back. Nothing more needed to be said.

"Well Tom," Derek said admiringly, leaning casually over the iron safety rail running the length of Dun Laoghaire's departure quay, "What do you think of her? Isn't she magnificent?" Immediately before them, less than ten yards distant, the chiselled bow of the steamship *SS Hibernia* towered thirty feet above the waterline. One of three modern Irish Mail vessels owned by the London Midland Scottish (LMS) Railway Company, the *SS Hibernia* regularly ferried passengers and mail between the Irish mainland and Holyhead, on the Isle of Anglesey. Following a recent refit, her fresh white superstructure gleamed brightly in the waning evening sunlight, contrasting elegantly with her long, sleek black hull. Smoke from the ship's twin, black rimmed, orange funnels rose gently into the air, dispersing rapidly in the moderate wind, but nonetheless indicating her readiness for sea. On the forward deck, midway between the bow and the raised bridge, an enormous single mast rose skyward, securely fastened by a series of stays, shrouds and other rigging. A second, equally impressive mast was located aft, near the stern, and from each a number of coloured pennants snapped briskly in the stiff breeze.

Tom stood virtually speechless. Never in his life had he seen a ship to match the beauty and majesty of the *Hibernia*. "Aye," he finally managed to whisper. "She's incredible. I can't believe we're going to sail in her."

Derek grinned. Pushing himself off the rail he stretched and unconsciously adjusted his tweed cap. "Well, you'd better believe it because we need to board soon." Already on the steamer's deck increasing numbers of passengers could be seen interspersed amongst the crew, wandering aimlessly around, and generally getting in the way. "I've a bit of a passion for the sea, Tom," Derek added, continuing to look appreciatively towards the ship. I suppose it started during the Great War. Being an engineer, I volunteered for the Navy and served on a couple of ships, but mainly on a Sloop, and I have to say –"

"What's a Sloop?" Tom interrupted. "I've not heard of them before."

"A Sloop? Well, she's a type of small warship, Acacia Class actually, not as big as a Frigate or Destroyer, but for her size still quite powerful. My ship was *HMS Foxglove*, and we were mainly deployed on minesweeping or convoy escort duties. Anyway, I loved being at sea, in spite of some pretty hairy moments..." grinning, Derek added, "But that's another story." Behind them Keira sighed audibly. She obviously had heard all this before. Undaunted, Derek ignored her and continued, "I think there's something very humbling about being at sea, Tom. When you're hundreds of miles from land and a storm's blowing, and there's waves crashing over the decks... well, there's nothing between you and the Good Lord other than the skill of your shipmates, and your little island home in the middle of the ocean."

Unlike his aunt, Tom listened attentively. Despite his relative inexperience with regard to the sea and boats, he could nonetheless understand the attraction its calling had to Derek McDonagh. The tantalising glimpses into his life were fascinating, and as Tom learned more, his opinion and attitude towards Derek were rapidly changing.

"Anyway, the *Hibernia* here has twin screws, propellers I mean," he continued happily, "Which makes her extremely fast. I read in the LMS literature that she can reach speeds up to twenty-five knots, making her one of the fastest merchant ships anywhere in the world."

"This is all very interesting, darling," Keira cut in from behind, "But I really think we should get on board now."

Turning to face her, Derek grinned, but directed his comments towards Tom. "I'm afraid your aunt doesn't share my nautical enthusiasm. But, that aside" he added, learning forward to kiss her on the cheek, "she's right...we'd better go." As if to emphasis the point, a sudden sharp blast from the *Hibernia's* whistle (which made everyone jump) signalled the ship's imminent departure. Walking along the quay they joined the end of a small queue of passengers waiting to embark via the mid-section gangway. At the foot of the steps, a smartly dressed uniformed officer was checking tickets. As the queue filed steadily forward, Derek handed Tom their passes. Standing in front of the officer, Tom smiled and obediently held up their tickets. Ignoring him, the officer gave the tickets a cursory glance and impassively waved them through, obviously impatient to get everyone on board. Hurrying up the steep, narrow walkway, his suitcase repeatedly bashing against the sides, Tom led them on to the main deck just as another deafening ship's blast reverberated through the air.

From a whitewashed wooden bench overlooking the stern, Tom gazed thoughtfully towards the western horizon. The visible coastline of his homeland had long since disappeared from view, its location marked, like an arrow, by the steamer's powerful wake and the trail of dissipating black smoke, expelled from her huge funnels. For two hours since boarding, Tom had eagerly explored the ship. Sometimes accompanied by Derek but more often by himself, he had ventured into every unrestricted room or accessible catwalk. Somewhat disappointed that he could not gain entrance to the bridge or engine room, he nonetheless took great delight in discovering the *Hibernia's* layout. Keira had retired to the central passenger seating area shortly after departure to read, and although Derek kept her company for much of the time, he did pay attention to Tom, sending him off on one investigative task or another. Tom had quickly discovered, for example, that there were twelve main lifeboats on board, five on either side (port and starboard as Derek had corrected him) and two aft. But as the voyage wore on and the setting sun dipped towards the sea, Tom's interest also began to wane.

Lost in thought, he had no idea how long he had sat watching the sunset before Derek had come looking for him.

"May I join you?" the older man asked quietly, standing before him and waiting patiently.

Slightly startled, Tom looked up. "Aye...sure."

Taking the vacant seat, Derek remained silent for a couple of minutes, also staring out to sea. Finally he said, "Your aunt wanted to know if you're alright?"

Tom shrugged. "I'm fine. Just a wee bit tired is all."

"Hmm...well, it has been a long day...and we've still got a long way to go. If you want to get your head down for a couple of hours, we could go inside?"

Tom shook his head. "No, I'd prefer to stay here." He paused for a moment before adding, "It's a lovely night."

Glancing around at the night sky Derek nodded. Already the first of the brightest stars were becoming visible towards the darker east, and with only a few wispy clouds discernible, it was likely to be a very clear night. "It is," he agreed, still gazing at the heavens. "I overheard a couple of the crew earlier. Apparently there's no moon tonight and with this little cloud cover we'll be in for a treat...albeit with a chilly breeze!"

"What do you mean?"

Looking back at him, Derek smiled knowingly. "A moonless, cloudless night at sea is truly beautiful. Somehow it's not quite the same as on land. I may even have to prise your Aunt Keira out from her book to see."

Tom grinned back. "Well, you can try."

Good as his word, the star-strewn night sky was spectacular. Once again Tom was impressed by Derek's knowledge, particularly in an area that he had never really considered. Whilst Tom prided himself in that he could identify the 'Plough', Derek showed him that it was only part of the large constellation of Ursa Major, or the 'Great Bear.' As his interest increased, Derek identified for Tom numerous other constellations, including Pegasus, Taurus and Gemini, as well as pointing out the 'line' of the Milky Way. Tom listened patiently as he explained how to find the North Star, and how sailors, in times past, used this pole star to navigate.

Keira, much to her husband's consternation, stayed in the passengers' lounge.

The lights from Holyhead harbour were visible for many miles, before buildings and structures along the dark shoreline became clearly distinct. As the *Hibernia* slowed in her approach Keira joined Tom and Derek, now at the bow, to watch. A few other passengers, some finely dressed but most much less well attired, stood with them, braving the chill to gaze silently at the looming port and sprawling rail depot. It was nearly midnight and having not slept during the crossing, Tom was beginning to flag. Yawning excessively, he did not protest when Keira placed a comforting arm around his shoulders and pulled him in close.

In a graceful arch, the *Hibernia* turned into the outer harbour, cruising parallel with a long breakwater on her starboard side. "That's Admiralty Pier," Derek pointed out as they passed. A number of small boats and merchant vessels were moored alongside, and even at this hour there was much activity. When no one commented, he continued, "Many years ago, Tom, a famous ship called the *Great Eastern*, built by Isambard Kingdom Brunel, docked there. At the time she was the largest steamship in the world and Queen Victoria, Prince Albert and many others came to visit."

Unable to stop himself, Tom yawned widely once again.

"Derek," Keira said firmly, "That's enough history lessons for now." Somewhat sullenly, Derek fell silent.

At the end of Admiralty Pier, the steamer reduced speed further and turned sharply to port, entering Holyhead's inner harbour. Shaped like an inverted triangle, the inner harbour grew progressively narrower as the ship steered towards its apex. An extensive quayside formed each side of the harbour, alongside which several large merchant vessels lay tied up. Over the ship's loudspeaker, a deep voice informed the crew to prepare for mooring, fore and aft at the East Quay. As the *Hibernia* manoeuvred further to port, angling towards her dockside berth, Tom stared beyond the East Quay at the labyrinth of rail tracks and sidings, clearly visible now under the bright harbour lights. Despite the time a number of small locomotives were obviously still working, busily shunting trucks and goods carriages back and forth to some predetermined plan. Glancing round, Tom looked across the narrowing channel towards the West Quay. Past the moored ships the quay expanded into countless warehouses, good facilities and huge open-air animal holding pens. Tom wrinkled his nose as the smell of innumerable cattle, pigs and sheep drifted across the dark water.

Seeing the gesture, Derek smiled. "There are more animals than people that pass through this port, Tom."

"Obviously," Keira agreed, a little tersely and holding a lace handkerchief to her face.

Gradually the *Hibernia's* forward motion slowed to the point that it was almost imperceptible. On deck, her crew worked hurriedly around the milling passengers, skilfully tossing the heavy mooring ropes ashore, and generally preparing the ship for arrival. Tom listened half-heartedly as orders and directions were called between the vessel and the quay.

"Come on," Derek said quietly stooping to pick up their cases. "We should make our way to the disembarkation point." Nodding, Keira gently steered Tom away from the bow and, following her husband, joined a steady stream of passengers heading aft towards the exit gangways.

Stepping off the *Hibernia* onto the congested quayside, Tom glanced around uncertainly. Keira grasped his hand tightly and with Derek leading, they quickly joined a queue of fellow travellers hurriedly being ushered along by uniformed officers. At the end of the East Quay, the procession filed past an ornately carved stone clock tower on the right, making the head of the inner harbour, before crossing under a canopied iron framed roof directly onto the East Rail Platform. The platform itself was enormous, stretching for hundreds of yards into the distance and was brightly lit by innumerable glass lamps hanging from the rafters. Passengers, many accompanied by porters carrying baggage, meandered everywhere. Some formed small islands around uniformed LMS staff seeking advice; others strode purposefully towards what was to Tom's mind the largest collection of rail coaches he had ever seen.

"Do you know where we are going?" Keira asked, shouting to be heard above the ensuing noise.

"Yes," Derek replied over his shoulder, unnecessarily checking their tickets again. "We're near the front, Coach E. This way!"

Again they manoeuvred through the crowds, walking quickly along the platform, passing rapidly filling carriages. Finally Derek stopped and with a backward glance, climbed aboard an open coach door. "Mind the step up," he called to no one in particular, manhandling the cases through the narrow entrance.

Inside, Tom followed him down the narrow aisle, stopping frequently as Derek peered into individual compartments, checking for their seat numbers. Eventually he slid open the appropriate door. "Here we are," he said entering the small six-seat area. Despite being empty, the compartment was cramped and Tom tried to keep out of the way, taking a seat besides the window, as Derek stowed their baggage on racks above their heads. Keira slumped wearily next to him. Joining them a few moments later, Derek glanced briefly at his pocket watch. "Not bad eh? In our seats, and it's only just after twelve! Amazing really."

Keira closed her eyes, too tired to reply.

"Can I see the engine?" Tom asked impulsively.

His aunt shook her head, eyes still closed. "No love, we'll be leaving soon; just sit still now."

Tom's face fell. Seeing his expression, Derek leant across the compartment, touching Keira's knee to draw her attention. "We've still got ten minutes. Let him go, I'll take him."

Sighing heavily, she opened her eyes and, after a moment's consideration, conceded. "Oh, go on with you then, but be quick...and God help you both if you miss the train." Grinning, Derek stood and led Tom back out of the carriage onto the platform.

"Let's go," he said once they were outside. "Your aunt's right, we'd better hurry." Holding hands they ran past the next four coaches to the front of the train. Steam from the locomotive's huge boiler rolled over the platform like sea mist, its moist, metallic smell strangely appealing. Even idling, the noise from the massive engine was immense and Derek had to shout close to Tom's ear, in order to make himself understood. "So, what do you think?"

Tom could only nod in reply, truly awed by the size and apparent power of the massive locomotive.

"She's called the '*Kings Own*'" Derek added, pointing to a small decorative name plate on the engine's side. "They all have their own names."

"Why?" Tom yelled back.

Shrugging, Derek simply answered, "To identify them, I suppose?"

They stood together admiring the impressive engine for perhaps another minute or so before a series of shrill whistles resounded back along the platform.

"We'd best head back, Tom" Derek said, grasping his arm and steering him round. Hurrying, they walked briskly along the platform, dodging through the embarking passengers, station porters and increasingly frustrated official guards, eager to be away. Twice they passed station staff, their booming voices hollering 'all aboard', before reaching their carriage. More whistles sounded as they made their way along the central aisle, back to the compartment. Keira looked up as they entered, her disapproving expression plainly evident. Wisely, Derek chose to remain silent, but nevertheless as they took their seats, gave Tom a conspirational wink out of sight of his wife.

With a sudden jolt, the Kings Own slowly moved off. Tom, nose pressed up against the glass, gazed out as, with increasing speed, first the sprawling depot, and then the darkened town of Holyhead swept by. Once out in the Welsh countryside the night closed in, and his view was significantly reduced. With little of interest to see, Tom turned away from the window and looked around the compartment. Derek had already closed his eyes, apparently asleep, but judging by his erect posture, Tom suspected he was simply resting. Catching his eye, Keira smiled kindly. "I think you should try and get some sleep," she said quietly. And, as if reading his thoughts, added a second later, "There won't be much to see now, and it'll be hours before we reach London."

Tom nodded. He was tired, more so than he cared to admit. Putting an arm around his shoulder, Keira pulled him in towards her. "Close your eyes now, love," she whispered, gently caressing his hair. Too weary to protest, he did as she asked, instinctively snuggling closer. Heavy-eyed he relaxed and tried to recall the day's events, but his fatigued mind made concentrating difficult. The rhythmic, almost hypnotic sound of the locomotive's iron wheels over the tracks and points further distracted his already fleeting thoughts. In moments, Tom was asleep.

It was some time later that Tom awoke and sleepily glanced around the darkened compartment. Keira and Derek were obviously sleeping, his aunt in particular snoring softly. Cupping his hands against the window, he tried to peer out, but in the pitch night could see next to nothing. Sighing, Tom relaxed back in his seat and with nothing better to do, he simply closed his eyes. Within minutes he had drifted back off to sleep.

Perversely it was the lack of movement that caused Tom to next stir. Blinking slowly as the bright lights shone through the carriage window, he yawned and sat up. Keira was still asleep but Derek, awake and attentive was staring at him.

"Are we there yet?" Tom murmured drowsily.

"No lad, this is Rugby. We're about half way I think – careful you don't wake your aunt," he added quickly, seeing Tom stretch his arms dramatically.

"Sorry." Tom replied, settling back down.

"Do you need to use the toilet? Or want anything to eat or drink? I think there are still a few sandwiches and some apples left from what Mary packed for us earlier."

Tom shook his head. "No, thanks, I'm fine."

"Okay, well try and get some more rest, if you can." Derek said, closing his own eyes.

"I will," he answered, but instead turned to look out at the unfamiliar station.

Within five minutes the *Kings Own* was once more steaming majestically through the dark English Countryside. Five minutes after that, Tom was again dreaming contentedly.

Semiconscious, Tom's mind gradually registered the gentle shaking and a soft voice calling his name. Slowly he opened his eyes. With his head resting comfortably in Keira's lap, he looked up into her smiling face. "I'm sorry to wake you Tommy," she said, caressing his hair, "But we've arrived. We're at Euston Station."

Struggling to rise, Keira offered to help him sit up. Rubbing the sleep from eyes, Tom turned to look out of the window. The *Kings Own* was rapidly slowing as it pulled into a massive, brightly lit, covered station. Dozens of converging lines led to a series of parallel platforms, alongside many of which were equally huge locomotives with extensive trains of carriages. Despite the early hour, Euston was a hive of activity.

"We must've had a delay on the way." Tom heard

Derek say behind. "It's already after six, we should've been here nearly an hour ago." When no one answered, Derek fell silent.

As the locomotive finally slowed to a juddering halt, Tom tried to stifle another yawn. Seeing him, Keira indicated with a look that Derek should retrieve the cases. "It won't be long now Tom," she said quietly as her husband reached up to the storage racks. "We'll be home soon and then you can go to bed and have a proper rest." Turning back to Derek she continued, "I think we should catch a cab from here. I don't want to wait around for an early trolleybus, and I doubt the underground is running yet." Tom had no idea what she was talking about.

"Ah, I think it is, love," Derek replied, depositing their baggage on the seats.

"Well, be that as it may, Tom's exhausted and it's not fair to drag him halfway across the city, not today." From her tone it was plain that she wasn't going to be argued with. Derek suspected that it was his wife who, in reality, didn't want the hassle of using public transport. He considered raising the issue of cost, but knew that, in the long run and judging by her defiant look, it wouldn't make any difference. Resigned to the inevitable, Derek simply nodded.

For the final time that day, Tom and his family joined a stream of passengers, shepherded by uniformed staff, towards the station's exits. Within minutes they had passed into the 'Grand Hall.' At over one hundred and twenty five feet long and sixty high, its size and grandeur had Tom spellbound. Rooted to the spot he stared in awe at the beautiful, Roman Ionic architecture; the deeply coffered ceiling panels and massive, though elegantly crafted, supporting consoles. At the northern end an elaborate staircase led to a gallery running the length of the hall's perimeter, and at the head of the stairs, four magnificent stone pillars, painted dark red, rose majestically to the vaulted roof. Repeatedly nudged from behind, Keira almost had to push Tom from the Grand Hall, such was his wonder. Eventually reaching the outer vestibule, itself stunning with a striking mosaic pavement, Derek led them towards one of Euston's five main exits. Stepping outside, Tom beheld arguably the station's grandest feature, its monumental Doric Arch. The Greek inspired structure marked the formal entrance to Euston, and walking slowly beneath the huge pillars Tom shook his head in disbelief. Gazing out over a crystal clear London morning, the first hints of autumn crispness clearly evident in the air, he sighed deeply and grinned despite himself. *London!* He was actually *in* London! Tired beyond reason, he still could not quite believe it. The tearful, agonising departure from Ballyfinan, twenty-four hours previously, seemed like a lifetime ago.

15
ANTIPATHY

Eyes closed, but nonetheless wide awake, Tom lay perfectly still on the narrow camp bed. Absently he listened to the sound of birdsong filtering through the bedroom's tiny, single window. Ironically, he could almost imagine he was back in his own bedroom in Ireland, except that the regular, heavy rumble of passing trains and the constant, background drone of distant automobile traffic, were a constant reminder to where he was. *How do people ever get used to this?* Tom wondered, trying to concentrate.

The strange euphoria he'd experienced on seeing London for the first time had quickly faded during the long, slow taxi journey from Euston to the McDonagh's home in the East End of the capital. The tortuous drive with its innumerable twists and turns through darkened, dirty back streets had revealed none of the great sights, such as St Paul's or Buckingham Palace, that he'd expected. That, plus the surly nature of the cabby at having to drive across the city at such an early hour hadn't helped to lighten the atmosphere in the cramped taxi. Despondent, Tom had dozed most of the way, barely registering their eventual arrival. Half asleep, Keira had led him through the front door of an unremarkable looking terraced house, and immediately taken him upstairs. Following a brief visit to the bathroom, she had settled Tom into the tiny bedroom at the back of the house, closing the door quietly on departing. He'd fallen asleep within moments of his head hitting the pillow.

From somewhere outside a woman's raised voice, followed by a child crying, resounded. First one, then another dog barked vigorously at the disturbance. Sighing, Tom opened his eyes and, glancing around the small room, considered getting up. Hunger was also beginning to be a motivating factor. Without a visible clock, Tom could only speculate how long he'd slept, considering, correctly, that it had been quite a while.

His stomach grumbling in protest, Tom resignedly swung his legs off the bed as a gentle knock came from behind the door.

"Tom? Are you awake?" his aunt's spoke softly from outside.

"Aye, come in," he replied, standing.

Entering, Keira smiled. "Well, I'm glad to see you're up...I've been up to check on you three times already. How're you feeling?"

"Okay, thanks."

"Grand. Now, do you fancy a wee bit of lunch? Derek's been to the shops...I thought we'd have sausages, eggs and bacon. What do you think?"

Tom nodded enthusiastically.

"Well, that's settled then. I've put your case at the foot of the bed. Get changed now, you know where the bathroom is, then put the rest of your things in that cupboard." Tom glanced across quickly as she continued, "I've cleared out the top two drawers for you. Come down when you're done." It was clear from her pleasant, but firm tone, that while he was staying here, Keira had no intention of waiting upon him. Making a mental note, Tom nodded again and headed for the toilet.

Following lunch, Tom spent the much of the remainder of the afternoon exploring. The McDonagh's house was a fairly new, standard three bedroom terrace. Its design common to many of the newer types of housing being built throughout the East End as a consequence of earlier slum clearances. From the front door, a central hallway ran the length of the property, with a number of doors to either side. A large, immaculately kept 'front room' faced the road to the right of the hallway, furnished with Keira and Derek's prized possessions, including an obviously expensive looking three-piece suite, and a light mahogany 'Broadwood' piano. Keira had told Tom in no uncertain words that, as the 'entertainment room', unaccompanied access by him was strictly not allowed.

A smaller, more modestly set 'living room' containing an oval dining table, four plain wooden chairs and a couple of rather battered looking armchairs, was situated at the end of the hallway, and beyond that a tiny kitchen and pantry. For Tom, however, the most fascinating aspect of the house was the cellar. He had discovered it unexpectantly, when furtively opening one of the doorways leading from the hall. For a few minutes he had simply stood at the entrance, staring at the flight of wooden stairs descending into the darkness below. Finally steeling himself, he had taken a few tentative steps into the blackness, hands held outstretched and body tense, imagining huge spiders or other creepy-crawlies pouncing on him at any moment. A sudden explosion of light, instantly illuminating the entire cellar, had made him gasp and cry out in surprise. Chuckling from behind, Derek McDonagh tapped an electric light switch on the cellar wall and grinned. Electricity! Another marvel of the modern world that he would have to get used to. Derek, still smiling, had beckoned for Tom to return, and sheepishly he had obeyed, vowing inwardly though to come back when no one was around.

By late afternoon, however, Tom was growing bored. Upstairs held scant interest; the main bedroom at the front of the house was again off limits, and his own box room at the back was so small that it contained little in any case. The 'spare room' in between initially seemed promising, packed as it was with cardboard boxes and being used as an obvious store. But despite a careful and extensive search, the contents proved disappointingly uninspiring, being for the most part full of clothing, books and other unremarkable odds and ends.

Seeing his restlessness, Keira had finally suggested that they should all go for a brief walk before supper.

Holding Keira's hand on the narrow pavement, Tom waited patiently as Derek firmly closed the front door behind them. His aunt's house, number 174, was the penultimate property at end of the street, which to the right, ended almost immediately at a T-junction, joining another road running perpendicular.

"Elseen...Elsen..." Tom murmured, struggling to pronounce the street name displayed on a sign on the opposite side of the road.

"*Elsenham* Road," Keira said with a slight smile. "*Elsenham*. Took me a wee while to say it properly too."

"What does it mean?"

Keira paused slightly before replying. "I think it's the name of a nearby village? Is that right Derek?"

"Yes," Derek answered, joining them and offering his arm. "But I think it's somewhere in Hertfordshire...or Essex, so it's not that close. Anyway, which way shall we go? Towards the park or the common?"

"Let's save the Park for another day," Keira said after

a moment. "It's getting a bit late now in any case. Let's go this way." Heading off, she steered them to the left and up the street.

"You'll like it here Tom," Keira said conversationally as they walked past the rows of neat, terraced houses. "It's quite quiet and peaceful, compared to most of the city that is."

Tom glanced between her, the houses, and to his mind the surprising numbers of parked automobiles. In Ballyfinan, car ownership was almost unheard of, but here it appeared as if *everyone* owned one.

"Do you have to be very rich to live in London, Aunt Keira?" he asked absently, still regarding the ranks of almost universally black Austins, Morris and small Ford's, parked either side of the street.

Keira laughed. "Dear Lord, no Tom...why do you ask that?"

"The cars...I've never seen so many in one place before. You must be rich to own one."

"Ah, I see. Well, I grant you we live in a nice area, not like some other parts of East London I'm sure, but Tom, lots of people own automobiles nowadays. We have one, don't we Derek...and we're certainly *not* rich I can assure you!"

"Absolutely," Derek added, trying not to smile at the look of astonishment of Tom's face. "You passed my little black beauty outside the house back there...a four seater Austin 7. Cost me one hundred and twenty pounds and ten shillings last year, and worth every penny."

Tom blinked. How anyone could justify spending such an enormous sum on a car was beyond him.

Passing a couple of middle-aged women chatting amiably on a doorstep, Keira nodded a greeting but didn't stop. A small child, grasping to one of the women's aprons, poked his tongue out as Tom passed, to which, unseen, Tom replied in kind.

It was soon clear to Tom the reason for Elsenham Road's quiet nature; there was no through traffic. At the top of the street, the tarmac abruptly ended in an open building site. No one was working, it being a Sunday evening, but a number of half-built houses, many covered in scaffolding, together with various cement mixers and other scattered building paraphernalia were testament to the activity on site during the week. Beyond the building area, Tom could see a small orchard, and after that another road, again running perpendicular to the line of partially constructed housing.

As they picked their way carefully through the site, Derek said, "Apparently a few years ago, this whole street was part of that orchard. When we bought our house they still hadn't started building up here. It's a shame really, to lose the orchard, but I suppose that's progress. No one at the Council will confirm it, but I suspect they intend to dig up the entire orchard eventually – "

"They won't do that, surely?" Keira cut in, slightly aghast. "Elsenham will just become a rat run then between Dersingham Avenue and Browning Road." Tom assumed these were the roads either end of the street, but wisely didn't interrupt with such a trivial question.

"Of course it will," Derek answered, knowingly. "That's precisely why I think they'll do it."

"But...that's outrageous!"

"No, as I said, that's progress."

They walked on in silence, Keira obviously considering the implications of her husband's words. Leaving the building site, they crossed into the small orchard. Tom wasn't good on trees, especially fruit trees, but even he knew the small dark purple fruits weren't apples. Noticing his interest Derek said, "They're plums, Tom, though I'm surprised to see any of them still on the trees. The local kids raid the orchard most days once they're ripe."

"You mean, they steal them?"

"Well, I suppose strictly speaking, yes, but I'm not sure who owns the orchard. There's an old boy who sometimes comes around every now and again and prunes the braches back, but I've never seen him ever doing any harvesting."

"Perhaps he doesn't like them?"

Derek shrugged. "Perhaps he's too old now to climb trees?"

At the edge of the orchard, the road Tom had seen earlier cut across their path. A much busier road, they had to wait nearly a minute before it was safe to cross. On the opposite side a large expanse of open grassland extended before them. In the distance Tom could see several walkers exercising their dogs, a number of children playing ball games and even a few tethered horses grazing sedately.

"We call it 'the Common'" Keira said quietly, clearly still disturbed by Derek's observations.

Tom nodded but didn't reply. Housing bordered the Common on all sides, and despite its green openness, its featureless visage was not particularly appealing. Tom lingered on the Common for a while, but as Keira's mood darkened, their walk soon drew to a timely end. Turning for home, Tom tactfully decided to walk a little in front, allowing them to talk privately.

"I suppose you're going to tell me that they're building on the Common next!" he heard her say tetchily.

Wisely, he lengthened his stride.

It was mid-morning by the time Tom finally descended from his bedroom, hunger the primary motivating force. Keira had long since left for work, and with no one chasing him, Tom had simply lain in bed, dozing comfortably. He knew things would change from tomorrow when he started his new school, but for now, he felt no qualms giving in to his indulgence. Derek McDonagh had offered a few half-hearted pleasantries as he'd entered, but engrossed in his paper, had effectively left Tom to fend for himself.

Eating his breakfast in silence, Tom cast frequent, furtive glances across the kitchen table, secretly studying Derek as he read the morning paper. If he was aware of the boy's clandestine interest, Derek gave no sign. In the background, the steady, monotonous ticking of the wall clock resounded noticeably. A sparrow, landing on the outside window ledge, chirped briefly for a few seconds, before disappearing again in an instant.

Finishing his cereal, Tom took the bowl to the sink. Staring out at the short, narrow garden he considered striking up a conversation when, coincidentally, Derek folded his newspaper and looked up at him.

"So," he began, simultaneously reaching for his tea. "What do you fancy doing today?"

Tom shrugged and returned to the table. He hadn't expected that question.

"Well, I need to do a few jobs around the house first, but after that, how about we go for a drive? Can you entertain yourself until then?"

"Aye, sure."

"Good lad. I shouldn't be more than an hour or so."

"Aunt Keira mentioned last night about a nearby park. Can I go and find it?"

Derek hesitated for a moment before answering. "I'm not sure you should go off on your own, Tom. Not yet, at least."

Tom frowned. "Why? I'm nearly eleven...and I promise not to do anything silly."

"It's not that, it's just that...it's your first day here and I don't want you getting lost. I'm supposed to be looking after you and, well, you can image what your aunt would say if she found out."

Tom was tempted to reply, *so don't tell her then*, but thought better of it. Derek was probably right, and besides he didn't want to get into any arguments just yet.

"In any case," Derek continued, "why don't you write that letter to your Mum; you said you wanted to last night. It'll be easier to do it today, you know, before school starts." Unable to think quickly of a plausible counter, Tom unenthusiastically mumbled his agreement.

In the end, it was lunchtime before Derek was finally ready. Given the time, they ate a hurried sandwich and headed out. In the warm, autumn sunshine, Tom waited patiently for Derek to start the Austin. In spite of not being used for over a week, the engine fired first time with a single, sharp turn of the starting handle.

"Okay, in you jump," Derek said, opening the single passenger door. Walking round, he climbed in from the other side. "All set?"

"Aye."

"Well, let's go then!"

At the bottom of Elsenham Road, Derek turned right. Passing a small garage on the corner they drove for perhaps fifty yards before stopping at another T-junction. Waiting for a lumbering goods truck to pass, Derek pointed to the right. "That's Chesterfield Road; it runs parallel to our road and if you go that way you end up at Browning Road, you know, where we were last night."

"By the Common."

"Yes, that's it."

With the way now clear, Derek turned left, and followed the road steadily as it swept in lazy, looping meanders, past rows of identical, red-bricked terrace houses.

"This is Barrington Road, Tom," Derek continued. "It's a bit of a rat-run, you know, like a back way...takes you all the way to East Ham."

Tom nodded but didn't reply. He had no idea where 'East Ham' was, but it didn't seem important to ask. After a minute the road disappeared into a wide, low tunnel.

"We call this 'the Arches', Tom, and right above us is the District Line. It's part of the Underground, and if you stand here when a train goes over it can be quite noisy."

"Why's it called the 'Underground' if the trains are on top?"

Emerging from the tunnel, Derek laughed. "Good question. We'll have to take you on it sometime soon, and then you can see for yourself."

As the journey continued, Tom soon became disorientated, as Derek took one turn after another. Street names began to blur as did the almost endless lines of uniform housing, interspersed with the occasional corner shop, or public house.

"So, what do you think?" Derek asked after a while, and grinning expectantly.

"About what?"

"My Austin 7, of course! Isn't she great?"

"Er...aye," Tom replied hesitantly. "How – "

"She's got a four cylinder, side valve engine,

producing nearly eleven BHP," Derek interrupted, heedless to Tom's apparent question. "I admit a 7 can be a bit slow, but I've had her up to forty miles per hour on the flat. Mind you," he added with a laugh, "it nearly shook me to pieces doing it."

Climbing a small hill, they turned left onto a much larger road, which Derek announced as East Ham High Street. For Tom, it was difficult to believe the volume and diversity of traffic before him. Automobiles, trucks of varying sizes and trolleybuses stretched into the distance, and soon their progress was reduced to a virtual crawl.

"Here's another new experience for you Tom," Derek grumped. "Traffic jams. I swear it gets worse each year."

Tom nodded, quite awed by the spectacle. "I've never seen so many motorcars in one place before. Is it always like this?"

"Sometimes."

On both side of the High Street scores of other Austin 7s, Morris 'Bullnose' Cowleys plus larger Bean 12s and Standard Big 9s, slowly navigated the crowded roadway. At one point Derek became quite animated, indicating to Tom a passing brand new Ford Model Y.

"They've only just come out," he explained, gazing longingly at the sleek, dark green two-door 'Tudor' saloon. "Ford designed them in the States, but they're built over here at their new factory in Dagenham." Despite its distinctive short radiator grill and obvious American inspired styling, to Tom, it looked just like any other motorcar.

Derek's continued recounting of the virtues of Ford's new offering to the British automobile market faded into the background as Tom's attention began to wander. Glancing around, he found himself drawn to the passing shops and bustling crowds lining the pavement. As they slowly passed successive intersections, groups of poorly dressed men, lounging idly at the street corners, often returned his stare. Suddenly a shabby, unshaven individual shouted something unintelligible. His aggressive manner was, however, clear and, unnerved, Tom turned quickly away.

At the end of East Ham High Street, another main road intersected their route. Turning left, Derek was able to increase speed, the traffic having eased somewhat in this direction.

"Where are we going?" Tom asked quietly. Something in his tone made Derek glance across. Frowning slightly, he considered for a moment. "Barking Park's not too far ahead. How about we stop there and stretch our legs? Okay?"

Shrugging slightly, Tom nodded. The journey continued without further conversation.

Sitting on a bench overlooking a small boating lake, Tom ate his ice cream in silence. In front of him, a mother and toddler were feeding bread to a group of ducks and noisy, hovering, black-headed gulls. Out on the water, half a dozen couples rowed back and forth across the circular lake, with slow, lazy sweeps.

"Do you fancy going out on a boat?" Derek asked, watching him closely.

Tom shook his head. "No, thanks. I'm fine."

"How about a stroll round the gardens, they're very nice, especially this time of year. I don't suppose you have many parks like this back home?"

Again, Tom repeated the gesture. "No...perhaps later. I'm really quite happy here for the minute."

Derek shifted in his seat, but for the moment let the matter drop. They continued to sit together in silence for a few more minutes before Derek, finally, had had enough.

"Listen Tom," he began a little firmly, "I'm not one to beat around the bush, as it were. What's the problem?"

"What do you mean? I'm alright," he lied, trying and failing to look surprised.

"No you're not. You've hardly said a word for the last half-hour. Are you feeling sick?"

"No."

"Well, what is it then? Have I annoyed you somehow?"

"No, it's not you...it's just..." looking down and feeling miserable, his voice trailed off.

"Come on, Son," Derek said kindly, trying to reassure him. "Tell me what's troubling you."

A well dressed, elderly woman, leading a small terrier, looked across at them. Waiting for her to pass, Tom sighed heavily. "A man shouted at me."

Derek frowned. "Sorry? What man? When was this, I

didn't hear anything."

"You were driving. It was when we passed all those shops, in the High Street. There was a group of men on the corner and one of them stared at me, and then started shouting."

"What did he say?" Derek asked, obviously concerned.

"I didn't hear, to be honest, but he seemed very angry; he scared me and I looked away. Why did he do that? I hadn't said anything to him."

Silent for a moment, Derek considered his reply. With a nod he indicated that Tom should continue to eat his ice cream which, unnoticed, was beginning to drip down his hand. "What you need to understand, Tom," he began, "is that times are hard for many people at the moment. A lot of men are out of work, and there are very few new jobs to be found."

"Why?"

This time Derek sighed before answering. "It's quite complicated, but essentially the country's in depression, the 'Great Depression' some are calling it, but what that means is that many people are suffering and struggling to make ends meet. I'm not defending what that man said, but he was probably just envious of you, is all."

Puzzled, Tom shook his head. "I don't see why; I've got nothing he would want?"

Derek smiled. "Haven't you? He saw you driving in an expensive motorcar, and probably assumed, correctly, that you were well cared for, live in a nice house and have a hot meal waiting for you every night."

Tom opened his mouth to reply, but closed it almost immediately. He couldn't think of anything further to say.

"I think, Tom," Derek added seriously after another moment, "this has probably been a valuable lesson." Tom said nothing, waiting expectantly, the ice cream all but forgotten. "Whilst you're here, you will meet some that will resent what you have, and if I'm honest, who you are."

*

Tom stood nervously beside Keira McDonagh's desk trying, though failing badly, not to fidget. The secretary's office of Manor School was tiny, and with only one small window to the outside, dark and claustrophobic. The bell, signalling the start of the new school day, had already sounded twenty minutes earlier and in all that time Tom had waited anxiously before the foreboding door of the school's Headmaster, Mr A H Montgomery.

As he and Keira had walked to school together that morning, his aunt had explained at length the arrangements at Manor School, and what he could expect. It was soon clear that Manor School was far larger than his own school at Ballyfinan. With nearly three hundred pupils up to the age of fourteen, many of whom were from very poor backgrounds, Tom was feeling distinctly apprehensive. That, coupled with Keira's repeated emphasis towards discipline and obedience to school rules, did little to calm his nerves.

The door to Keira's office opened unexpectedly and

a tall, gaunt looking middle-aged man entered. His pale eyes flicked briefly over Tom before fixing on Keira. "Mrs McDonagh," he said, in a rasping, unfriendly voice. "I need a word with the Headmaster. Is anyone with him?"

"Ah, no Mr Dawson, but – "

"Good. See to it we aren't disturbed." Without waiting for a reply, Dawson marched purposefully to the Headmaster's door, knocked once and immediately entered. As the door closed behind him, Keira swore under her breath in Irish. Suddenly realising Tom was still there, she blushed slightly and smiled apologetically.

"Who was that?" he asked quietly.

Keira frowned and made pretence of rearranging the papers on her desk. "That's Mr Dawson. He's the Deputy Headteacher and Principal of the Upper School...and a more miserable individual you're never likely to meet!"

Tom laughed, in spite of his uneasiness.

It was another fifteen minutes before Dawson finally emerged. His face unreadable, he strode passed them. "Mr Montgomery will see the boy now," he said curtly, without a backward glance. Keira pushed her chair back, scraping the floor and half rose. "Just the boy, thank you, Mrs McDonagh" he added sharply. Hesitating for a moment, she glanced across at Tom, before slowly sinking back into her seat.

As Dawson closed the office door behind him she smiled weakly at Tom and said, "Best you go, Tom. You don't want to keep the Headmaster waiting." Nodding, Tom walked up to Mr Montgomery's office, and steeling himself, knocked tentatively.

"Come."

Opening the door, he stepped inside, hanging back uncertainly.

"Close the door, please."

Turning he did as asked, reluctantly taking a few steps into the room. Dressed in a dark suit, Mr Montgomery sat ominously behind a large, ornate wooden desk. Head bowed, studiously reading the pages of a report, he ignored Tom completely. Despite a vacant chair in front of the desk, Tom didn't dare ask to sit down. Seconds became minutes. Biting his lip, Tom squirmed uncomfortably, unconsciously staring silently at the Headmaster's bald, shiny head and fervently wishing he was somewhere, anywhere, else.

"So, Mr Devlin," Montgomery said suddenly, but still not looking up from the report. "I understand you are to be with us, for a while."

"Aye, Sir." Tom replied, his voice unusually shrill.

The Headmaster's head slowly rose. Behind round, wire-rimmed spectacles he fixed Tom with an icy glare. "Yes Sir...not Aye Sir. I'll have none of your damned Irish talk here. Understand?"

"Sor...Sorry, Sir." Tom stammered, shocked and intimidated.

"Can you read, Mr Devlin?" he continued smoothly, as if nothing had happened.

Tom swallowed, his throat suddenly dry. "Yes, Sir."

"And your tables?"

"Well enough, Sir." Tom decided short, concise answers were probably safest.

"Hmm." Removing his spectacles and a handkerchief from his pocket, Montgomery slowly began to methodically polish them.

"What are seven eights?"

"Fifty six, Sir." Tom answered instinctively.

"And nine sevens?"

"Sixty three."

The Headmaster grunted, in seeming approval. Standing, he turned and limped slowly towards a large window on the far side of the office. Curious, for a second Tom considered asking what the problem was, but wisely thought better of it. For over a minute Montgomery stared silently out over the now deserted playground. Tom waited anxiously, waves of growing anxiety beginning to rise within him.

"Your aunt tells me you recently lost your father?" Montgomery asked finally over his shoulders, his back still to Tom.

"Aye Sir, I mean yes Sir. Sorry Sir." Tom stumbled over the unexpected question. The Headmaster turned to regard him.

"Hmm," he repeated again, but made no further comment. Returning to his desk, Montgomery sat and once more took up the report. Without looking up he said, "You'll be in Mr Blackwell's class...he's expecting you. Go and ask Mrs...your aunt, to come in." Dismissed, Tom gratefully fled the office to fetch Keira.

"Headmaster?" she said, entering a few seconds later. Tom tried to remain as inconspicuous as possible behind her.

"Please escort your nephew to Mr Blackwell's classroom."

"Certainly, Headmaster."

Turning to leave, Keira reached for the door when Montgomery looked up and said quietly, "And Mr Devlin – "

"Sir?"

"I never expect to see you in my office again, unless I send for you. Do I make myself clear?"

"Yes, Sir."

"Very well, close the door on your way out."

"What did he mean by that?" Tom asked as Keira led him through a virtual rabbit warren of corridors and short staircases.

"We'll talk later," she replied over her shoulder, without slowing in her hurried march. "Come on now." Scowling, Tom could do little but follow.

Without warning, Keira stopped adjacent to a solid, frosted-glass fronted door. Turning to him she smiled gently. "Ready?"

Tom nodded. "Aye...I think so."

"Good boy." Glancing up and down the corridor, Keira quickly leaned forward and lightly kissed his cheek. "You'll be fine, Tom. Trust me." Knocking softly, they only had to wait a moment before a dark figure loomed through the opaque glass, and the door firmly pulled open. A tall, painfully thin man with sandy, grey flecked hair and hazel eyes, glared irritably from one to the other.

"Yes?" he said sharply, clearly unhappy about being interrupted.

"Mr Blackwell," Keira began, "this is Thomas Devlin...I understand the Headmaster has spoken to you about him?"

"He has not, Madam." Blackwell replied briskly.

Keira blinked, suddenly unsure of herself. Hesitating for a second to collect her thoughts, she finally said, "Ah, well Thomas has joined the school today, and Mr Montgomery wishes him to be placed in your class."

"Indeed."

Keira breathed in deeply. Even Tom could see that his haughty manner was clearly annoying her.

"I'm sorry, Mr Blackwell," sighing somewhat dramatically. "Obviously there's been a mix up in communication. Would you like me to fetch the Headmaster...I'm sure he would be delighted to come down here and clarify the situation."

From within the classroom a cry rang out and, turning, Blackwell growled threateningly at the unseen miscreant. Regarding Keira once more, he stared thoughtfully at her whilst she, waiting patiently, simply smiled pleasantly. The gesture wasn't lost on him.

"Thank you Mrs McDonagh," Blackwell said eventually. "I don't think that will be necessary."

"Are you sure now...it wouldn't be any trouble?"

"No, you may leave the boy with me."

Nodding in satisfaction, and without a backward glance to Tom, Keira departed. Watching her retreating back, Blackwell's face was unreadable.

Closing the door behind them, Blackwell indicated Tom should stand in front of the dusty blackboard and face the class. Forty pairs of eyes stared at him guardedly from behind neat rows of wooden, flip top desks. Feeling his cheeks burning, Tom instinctively looked down.

"Head up, boy!" Blackwell barked, walking across the room to lean casually against the far wall. "Let's have a good look at you then." From the watching class, a few sniggers resounded.

"Quiet!" the teacher snapped loudly. "So, the Headmaster says you're to join our merry band."

"Yes, Sir." Tom murmured diffidently.

"Speak up lad!"

"Yes Sir. Sorry Sir."

"Very well, so tell us a bit about yourself then."

"Sir?"

"Where you come from for starters, since with that accent you're obviously not from around here? Have you any family, Thomas? What do you like doing?"

Tom licked his lips and swallowed, moistening his suddenly dry throat. "I prefer Tom to Thomas, Sir."

"Uh-huh."

"And I, er...I come from a wee...small...village, Sir, called Ballyfinan."

"Never heard of it...though I assume it's in Ireland somewhere?"

Tom nodded. "Yes, Sir. It's in Donegal, on the North West coast. I've got two sisters and a little baby – "

"Not another bloody Paddy," a low voice murmured from the back of the classroom.

The sudden reaction from Blackwell made Tom jump. Launching himself from the wall, he stormed across the classroom and physically dragged a thick set, unkempt looking boy with brown hair from his seat. Struggling, the boy kicked over his chair but couldn't shake off the teacher's firm grip.

"You're an arrogant, small-minded bigot, Harris!" Blackwell snarled angrily. "I've warned you more than once about your prejudice...this time we'll see what Mr Montgomery has to say on the matter."

Stunned, Tom watched open-mouthed as Blackwell shoved Harris before him, forcing the boy to walk reluctantly in front. As he drew level Harris glared venomously at Tom muttering unintelligibly under his breath.

Blackwell had already turned to face the class so the gesture went unseen. "And if I hear so much as a whisper when I get back," he warned menacingly. "Or if anyone is out of their seats, they'll follow Harris to the Headmaster's Office. Is that understood?"

Universal nods followed.

"Good."

Prodding the unwilling Harris, Blackwell followed the boy from the room. Unsure what to do, Tom stood still and glanced round the class. The majority of children appeared to be his own age or a little older. Most ignored him and began talking quietly with their neighbours. Some however continued to regard him curiously, whilst a few, mainly boys, stared with open hostility.

Avoiding unfriendly eye contact, Tom's gaze fell on a small black boy in the far corner, his head turned, looking out of the window. He had never seen a black person before and after a few seconds realised he himself was staring. Conscious of being caught, he was about to turn away when the boy unexpectedly looked up and across at him. His dark eyes held Tom's for a second. Embarrassed, Tom looked down and as such didn't see the conker thrown at him from across the classroom. Striking him a glancing blow to the head, Tom cried out, more in surprise than actual pain.

The class erupted with laughter. At that moment the door flew open and Mr Blackwell reappeared, on his own. "What's going on!" he roared. Everyone began studiously regarding their own reading books at once.

Scowling angrily, Blackwell walked to a nearby shelf and retrieved a well thumbed, worn book. Handing it to Tom, he indicated he should take a vacant seat near the front of the class.

"Right then, Mr Devlin...let's hear you read."

16
CONFLICT

Resting with his back to the playground wall, Tom let the warm lunchtime sun bathe over him. Eyes closed and relaxed, his thoughts wandered, content that his first morning had gone, if not wonderfully, then at least reasonably well. To be fair Mr Blackwell had been impressed with his reading, and what's more had openly said so. Feeling rather pleased with himself, Tom had only one slight worry; none of his new classmates had spoken or attempted to make friends with him yet. However, even in this regard his natural optimism put that down simply to a matter of time. He couldn't have been more wrong.

The bell for the end of lunchtime resounded sharply. Opening his eyes, Tom watched as the chaotic, swarming mass of children quickly transformed into a series of generally straight, parallel, class lines. Recognising a few individuals, Tom rose and walked calmly towards the back of that which he assumed was

Mr Blackwell's class. Caught completely unawares, he almost cried when a sudden and forceful grip swung him savagely round. Glaring angrily, Harris leant forward until his face was mere inches from Tom's own. Behind him three other boys hovered menacingly.

"I just got caned 'cause of you, Paddy." Harris snarled revealing discoloured, yellowing teeth. His breath almost made Tom gag.

"I'm...I'm sorry," he answered weakly, trying to back away. "I didn't – "

"You're *dead* later." Harris interrupted, pulling him back. "After school, see. *Dead*."

"Yeah, you're dead!" One of the boys behind him echoed. "You tell 'im, Bert."

"Shut up!" Harris snapped. The offending boy quickly fell silent. "Remember, after school, Paddy," his eyes never leaving Tom's. "And if you don't show, everyone'll know you're chicken!"

Pushing Tom away, Harris laughed and turned to join the rest of the class, his three companions in tow. Shocked and intimidated, Tom stood still, too stunned to move.

"Hey, you...yes you, new boy." An unknown teacher supervising the class line-ups shouted. "Do you know what class you're in?"

Tom nodded, vaguely.

"Well move then! We haven't got all day." Still shaken, Tom shuffled obediently to the end of the line. Harris and most of the class watched his every move.

As the afternoon progressed, Tom found it increasingly difficult to concentrate. Frequent knowing looks from around the class, coupled with hungry, expectant grins from Harris and his friends, severely unnerved him. At one point, distracted and inattentive, Mr Blackwell had to slap his hand down hard on Tom's desk, to gain his attention. Mumbling an apology, Tom tried to focus, and to a degree succeeded, until he was surreptitiously passed a folded note from a girl sitting behind him. Waiting until Blackwell was occupied with another pupil, Tom quickly opened the paper and read the scrawled contents: *'school gates, 10 minutes after the bell. Be there.'* The note was unsigned but Tom had no doubts as to its author…or its meaning.

As the end of school bell sounded Tom's stomach churned, fear gripping him. Harris and a number of other boys sprinted out of the room, earning an unheeded remonstration from Mr Blackwell. There was going to be no escape. As the first feelings of panic rose, Tom considered speaking to the imposing teacher.

"Come on you lot, hurry up." Blackwell urged, disturbing Tom's thoughts. Obviously impatient to leave, Blackwell was actively driving the last of the stragglers out of the classroom.

"Please, Sir?" Tom said quietly, standing at his side by the doorway.

"What is it?"

"Ah, can I go to the staff room…to wait for my aunt there?"

"Your aunt?"

"Aye..yes, Sir, I mean, Mrs McDonagh."

Blackwell frowned and scanned the classroom behind him. Satisfied no one was left inside, he closed and locked the door. Placing the key in his pocket, Blackwell turned to face Tom, shaking his head. "No, boy! The staff room is for *staff*, not children. Wait in the playground like everyone else." Without waiting for a reply he briskly walked away, leaving Tom anxiously contemplating the future.

Standing on the entrance steps outside the main school building, Tom gazed out over the playground. From the numbers of children milling around, unwilling to go home, it was obvious word had spread that trouble was brewing. At the far end, close to the playground gates, a larger gathering was waiting, ominously. Tom had previously agreed to meet Keira at the end of school by the main gates. Unsure whether she was already there, reluctantly he had no choice other than to walk towards them.

Head bowed, he tried to remain inconspicuous; it was never going to work. Barely halfway across the playground a cry went up, and in moments a jostling, heaving crowd surrounded him. Grinning, shouting faces were everywhere. Pushed and shoved, Tom was virtually swept along towards the gates. Confused and frightened, he cried out to be left alone but was universally ignored.

A ritual-like chant developed. "*Fight! Fight! Fight!*" Over and over; louder and louder. Disorientated, Tom felt his head spinning.

Suddenly the shouting stopped and without warning the crowd of expectant faces drew back, forming a rough circle. Directly before him stood Bert Harris. Unsmiling, fists balled at his sides, Harris stared at Tom for several seconds before purposefully stepping forward. Instantly the chanting restarted. Violently pushed from behind, Tom staggered, head bowed, into the larger boy. Immediately Harris began raining down punches; around him the massed children screamed in frenzied excitement. Keeping his head down, Tom forced most of the blows to land on his shoulders and back, doing little real harm. Harris kept up his pummelling for nearly a minute before realising what Tom was doing. As comprehension dawned, he tried to pull away and give himself more room, but was hemmed in by the swarming mob.

"Stand up and fight!" he hissed angrily, leaning close to Tom's ear and breathing heavily. Despite the surrounding noise, Tom registered Harris' voice inches above him, and instantly thrust his own head backwards, butting him hard in the face. Crying out, Harris lurched from the force of the blow, clutching his nose with both hands. Blood coursed through his fingers and down his cheeks, dripping uncontrolled onto his shirt.

"You've broken me bleeding nose, you bastard!" he groaned nasally. The irony was not lost on Tom and he smiled in spite of himself.

Suddenly incandescent with rage, Harris roared and charged. Taking Tom by surprise they collided violently,

Harris' momentum knocking them both to the ground. The crowd howled in glee. Rolling over and over, fists and elbows flying wildly, they traded blow for blow. Abruptly, Tom received a savage strike to the head and stars exploded before his eyes. Slightly stunned, he found himself lying on his back, the larger boy sitting astride his chest. More punches fell and Tom's vision swam...feeling himself beginning to lose consciousness he tried to call out when, unexpectantly, Harris' weight lifted. Peripherally, he registered a blur of motion as the crowd rapidly dispersed.

"Leg it!" Someone shouted

Roughly and none too gently, he felt himself hauled to his feet. Shaking his head slightly, Tom's eyes finally focussed on a gaunt, stern looking grey-haired woman.

"You wicked boy!" she snapped. "Fighting like an animal, *and* on school premises! Have you no shame?" The woman's bony fingers gripped his shoulders like a vice.

Glancing around, Tom discovered they were alone; Harris and the throng of onlookers had fled the playground completely. Misreading his gesture as an attempt to escape, her grip tightened.

"Stay where you are, young man. It'll only be worse if you try and run."

"I wasn't going to." Tom protested.

From the withering look it was clear she didn't believe him. "Who are you anyway? I don't recalling seeing you before. I hope for your sake you're not from Langdon or St Winifred's, coming here looking for trouble?"

"No, I'm not! It's my first day...my name's Thomas Devlin. I'm Mrs McDon –"

"Well, Thomas Devlin, and assuming you're not lying, which remains to be seen, it's not a very good start then, is it?"

Tom looked down, genuinely dismayed. "No Miss."

"*Mrs*, not Miss...Mrs Phelps. Now, come with me."

"Why? Where too? I'm supposed to meet – "

"The only person you're going to meet, Devlin, is the Headmaster. We'll soon see if Mr Montgomery has heard of you."

Still keeping a firm hold of his arm, Mrs Phelps led Tom back across the playground towards the main building. The double entrance doors still stood wide open, and as they approached three adults and a couple of older children emerged. To Tom's horror, the last person in the group was Keira McDonagh, blinking rapidly as her eyes adjusted to the bright sunshine.

"Tom?" Keira questioned, suddenly recognising him. Looking down he tried, unsuccessfully, to hide his bruised and dishevelled appearance. "My God, what's happened? Are you alright?"

"You know this boy, Mrs McDonagh?" Phelps asked somewhat haughtily.

"Of course. He's my nephew. What's going on?"

Tom opened his mouth to reply but Phelps answered first. "*Fighting*, Mrs McDonagh. Fighting, if you can believe it. That's what *your* nephew has been doing. I'm taking him to Mr Montgomery...he can decide what's to be done with the boy." Without waiting for a reply, she swept passed, dragging Tom along.

At first, too shocked to speak, Keira could only gaze after them. As they entered the school she finally called out for them to wait. Turning, Phelps regarded her coldly, an eyebrow half raised enquiringly.

"Mrs Phelps," Keira began, "it's Tom's first day, surely we can address this ourselves? Is there really a need to involve the Headmaster?"

Phelps smiled derisively. "You know the rules concerning fighting at school, Mrs McDonagh...we can't be seen to have favourites can we? Besides, what kind of message would that then send to trouble-makers, eh?"

"I hope you're not insinuating that Tom is a trouble-maker, Mrs Phelps." Keira answered, frostily.

"Well, I only have your word on that, and from recent evidence I should say the jury's still out, wouldn't you? I hope for your sake your confidence in the boy hasn't been misplaced. I should hate for someone in your position to be labelled with introducing a disruptive influence to the school." Before Keira could reply further, Phelps turned and marched Tom back inside.

Seething, Keira had no option but to follow.

"Hello, I'm home," Derek McDonagh called, closing the front door behind him. When no one answered he shrugged and removing his coat, threw it over the bottom of the banister. "I've had a hell of a first day back, Love," he continued out loud. "You wouldn't believe it, the day after we left for Edinburgh, the office secretary went off sick, and no one bothered to keep tabs on my in tray for over a week! I've spent most of the day on the telephone to clients, trying to explain why…" Derek trailed off. Something didn't seem quite right. Keira and Tom were obviously both in, given the bags and coats dumped carelessly at the bottom of the stairs. Walking cautiously down the hallway, Derek paused for a moment listening, before entering the small living room. Tom sat at the dining table, picking uninterestedly at a half eaten bowl of stew.

"Tom?" Derek asked quietly. "Everything alright, you're awfully quiet?"

Ignoring him, Tom continued to play with his meal.

"And where's your aunt?"

A shrug.

"Dear Lord, what's happened to your face? You look like you've been in a fight?"

"That's because he has," Keira said tersely, striding in from the kitchen. "He's been fighting at school…and on his first day, God help us."

"Is that right, Tom?" Derek asked, frowning slightly.

Another shrug.

"Jesus, Mary and Joseph!" Keira virtually exploded. "The shame of it! Having to stand in front of the Headmaster…like…like, well, I can't think but, I've never been so humiliated in my life."

"Calm down Keira, I want to hear what Tom has to say."

"Don't tell me to calm down! I nearly lost my job today...and would've too if that witch Marion Phelps had her way. She may only be the Head of Year but she exerts a big influence over Mr Montgomery...and he listens to her."

"I didn't know she was Head of Year," Tom murmured without thinking. Keira rounded on him.

"Well, there's a lot you don't know, my lad," she snapped. "Especially about fitting in...you can't go around throwing your weight about here."

"I didn't, and I told you it wasn't my fault!" Tom retorted, growing angry in his turn. "He called me names...I didn't start it – "

"Listen to me, Tom," Derek interceded. "Just because somebody says hurtful things, doesn't mean...doesn't give you the *right* to pick a fight with them."

"It wasn't like that! I didn't do *anything*. He picked on me!"

"There's no need to shout. Who did...picked on you I mean?"

"What? Bert Harris I think he's called. He's in my class...he said he was going to get even with me after school."

Derek frown deepened. "Well, you must've done something to upset him. No one seeks a fight unless –"

"God!" Tom swore angrily. "I don't believe this! You're not listening either, you're just like her!"

Face flushing, Derek took a step closer. "Don't you *ever* speak of your aunt in that tone again. Do you hear me?"

"Or what? Are you going to hit me too?"

"Tom!" Keira exclaimed, suddenly concerned at the escalation. At that moment a shrill ring resounded through the tense atmosphere. Instinctively Tom turned towards the door and the origin of the sound, the hall telephone. After a second he looked back, still glowering, at Derek. The ring repeated.

"Damn." Derek swore and stamped off to answer it. It was Eileen O'Brien.

To his immense relief, and many others in the class Tom secretly suspected, Robert Harris did not turn up for school the next day. There seemed to be an almost tangible lightening of the mood within the room. Although he admitted inwardly this could be a complete coincidence, Tom judged Harris' absence as being the key contributory factor. He wasn't wrong.

Stifling a yawn Tom tried to concentrate on Mr Blackwell's lesson. Geography had never been his favourite subject, and try as he might, his thoughts stubbornly continued to wander. Images of the conversation he'd had with his grandmother the previous evening haunted him. Eileen was no fool, and despite his clumsy attempts to sound cheerful, had quickly realised something was wrong. Hoping he'd managed to convince her he was simply homesick, Tom was grateful she hadn't questioned him too much. The fact that Eileen had subsequently interrogated Keira ruthlessly until she had admitted the truth, Tom remained blissfully unaware.

Eager for news of home, Tom had pressed Eileen about his Mother's condition. Ironically, Eileen couldn't hide her own feelings from him. Erin Devlin was still gravely ill, albeit slightly more stable since the weekend. Whilst the generally pessimistic Dr Kerrigan had been cautiously more hopeful, Tom's grandmother couldn't help qualifying the *actual* extent of the doctor's optimism.

"Psst! Watch it," a hushed voice said from behind. Attentive once more, Tom risked a glance backwards. Two desks back, the small black boy that he had first seen yesterday was staring directly at him. With a slight nod of his head, the boy indicated towards the front of the class. Turning swiftly round, Tom saw Blackwell bearing down the row en route to him.

"Eyes front, Devlin," the teacher warned, stopping to examine the notebook of a boy in front. Tutting, Blackwell grimaced in disgust. "The Falkland Islands are in the South Atlantic, Jennings, not off the north coast of Scotland. And since when has Colombo been the capital of India! It's Ceylon, you stupid boy." Slapping Jennings sharply across the back of the head, he tossed the notebook back onto the desk. "Haven't you been listening to a word I've said this morning? You'll stay behind for an hour tonight, and we'll see if that improves your concentration."

"But Sir, I've got – "

Another slap silenced any further protest.

Tom stared down at his own scribbled notes,

suddenly thankful for the warning; what punishment he would have received for being caught daydreaming didn't bear thinking about.

"And what about you, Devlin? Is your knowledge of the world's demographic centres of excellence going to eclipse the pinnacle of wisdom displayed by young Jennings here?"

"Sir?"

Blackwell sighed. "Nevermind...just tell me what's the Capital of Austria?

"Vienna, Sir."

"And Norway?"

"Ah, Stockholm...No Oslo! Sir."

Blackwell nodded appreciably. "Very good, Devlin. Nice to see someone at least is paying attention." As he moved on, Tom breathed a silent prayer of thanks, unaware that others glared resentfully at his back.

At the mid-morning break, Tom again found himself wandering alone through the crowded, noisy playground. Mrs Phelps was on duty, and meandered constantly though the heaving mêlée chastising one pupil after another for some minor misdemeanour. Tom kept a careful watch on her; at all costs he wanted to avoid any confrontation today. Although she had calmed somewhat, Keira had remained irate during their walk to school that morning. At one point Mrs Phelps had come up in conversation, and although circumspect, Keira had confirmed she and the teacher didn't get on well. For some reason, which Keira wouldn't elaborate on, Phelps had apparently tried to block her appointment at the school. Tom had vowed silently never to give Phelps reason again to cause trouble for his aunt.

Lost in thought, Tom gasped in surprise as an unexpected voice behind made him start. "Be careful, man, they're following you."

"What?" Beside him, the small black boy from his class returned his gaze expressionlessly.

"Behind you; Harris' gang." Tom turned and saw two of Harris' mean-spirited friends slowly stalking him. Spotted, they froze for a second before continuing to advance, but now much more quickly. "This way, let me show you something," the boy urged, grasping Tom's arm and dragging him away. Dodging through the mass of children, Tom was led to an area of the playground marked out with a faded 'hopscotch' figure painted on the ground. Three girls were playing as they approached, but other than a casual glance, they were otherwise ignored.

"You're safe here," the boy said, his accent strange and lilting. "They won't dare touch you now."

"I don't understand," Tom replied, worried and unconvinced. "We can't even see Mrs Phelps now...I think we should go inside."

"Nah, man, there's no need. Look where you are." Sure enough the following boys had stopped, but continued to glare at them angrily. Tom shook his head, puzzled. He couldn't see any reason why, though clearly vexed, they refused to come nearer. After a few moments, one of the two elbowed his companion, and muttering irritably, they both slouched away.

"I still don't understand why they did that," Tom repeated.

For the first time a fleeting smile forced its way across the boy's face. "See that there?" he said, pointing to a large window behind them. "That's Montgomery's office. He's always staring out over the playground at break times. If you stand here, he can see you easily...and no one will bother you."

Tom nodded, impressed. "Thanks for telling me." On impulse he held out his hand. The boy hesitated for a second before accepting it. "Tom Devlin," he said by way of introduction.

"I know, man...you made quite a start yesterday."

Tom grinned. "Aye, not that I was looking for trouble. So what's your name?"

Again the boy seemed slightly reluctant. "Jerome Wilson," he said after a slight pause. "But you can call me JP."

At that moment the bell rang for the end of break. Walking together they joined the horde of children funnelling towards the main entrance. Tom asked the obvious question. "Why JP?"

"Huh?"

"Why call yourself JP and not Jerome. Don't you like your name?"

"No, Jerome's fine, but my middle name starts with a 'P'. My Nan in Barbados always called me JP, since I was a baby. I kinda like it, you know?" Pushed and shoved they eventually squeezed inside through the doors.

Shouting to be heard above the noise, Tom said, "So what's the 'P' stand for then?"

JP smiled, flashing perfect, white teeth. "Not on your life, man. Not on your life."

"So, you had a better day at school today, Tom?" Derek asked as they sat down to dinner that evening, the row from the previous evening seemingly long since forgotten.

"Aye," he replied, his mouth half full.

"Manners Tom," Keira reproached lightly. "Finish what's in your mouth first."

A pause. "Sorry. Blackwell...Mr Blackwell I mean," he added hastily seeing her eyes narrow alarmingly. "Anyway, he seemed happy enough with me...can you pass the salt please? Thanks. We had Geography and then writing practice in the morning and arithmetic in the afternoon. I think I answered all his questions well enough. Well enough that is," he continued with a smile, simultaneously shovelling more food into his mouth, "that he didn't throw the blackboard duster at me!"

"Tom. Slow down, and don't – "

"Do teachers still do that?" Derek interrupted. "I thought throwing dusters stopped when I was a lad."

"Oh no, Mr Blackwell still does. If he catches you not paying attention or talking he'll often throw it. He's not done it to me yet," he added quickly, seeing Keira's suspicious frown.

They continued eating in silence for a minute before Tom ventured quietly, "I think I made a new friend today."

"Oh?" Keira said, genuinely interested. "Who's that?"

"Jerome Wilson...but he likes to be called JP."

"Is that the little black boy in your class?"

"Aye."

Keira nodded knowingly in reply, then said, "He's not been at the school for long; joined us a couple of weeks before the summer break. A clever lad from what I've heard...and well behaved. I think his family come from the West Indies, Jamaica – "

"Barbados," Tom corrected. "His grandparents are still there."

"Oh, right. And has he any brothers or sisters?" Keira asked. Tom shrugged, unsure.

"Presumably they came over looking for work?" Derek offered.

Keira glanced at her husband. "Aye, presumably."

*

"Watson?"

"Sir."

"Wilson?"

"Sir."

"And Young. Young!" Blackwell growled, not bothering to look up from marking the register. "I know you're here boy, I saw you earlier."

"Yes Sir! Sorry Sir."

"Hmm." Closing the book, Blackwell stood and walked round to face the class. Leaning causally against his desk, he signalled to a slim, fair-haired girl in the front row to stand. "Miss Aldridge, take the register to the Office please...and mind you come straight back."

"Yes Sir."

Waiting for the door to close, Blackwell regarded the silent, expectant faces closely. Tom felt a slight paranoia surfacing, as the teacher's gaze seemed to linger unduly over him.

"Right then, before we start today I've something to say. Even the least observant amongst you will notice that Robert Harris is again absent from class. This absence, I can now tell you, is due to Harris having being suspended for two weeks for a catalogue of unacceptable behaviour, culminating in him being observed fighting on the school premises last Tuesday."

Tom swallowed nervously; Blackwell had been looking directly at him as he'd spoken.

"Furthermore, the Headmaster has said that fighting will no longer be tolerated. A letter to this effect will be going out to all your parents this afternoon. From today, should any pupil be caught fighting at school, they will be permanently expelled. Is that clear?" There were collective nods from around the classroom. "Good. Right then, get your notebooks out. This morning I want to move on from our discussions yesterday and look at some of the reasons why these cities have developed the way they have." Tom felt another yawn developing.

By lunchtime a stiff breeze had developed, and a noticeable chill descended over the playground. Wrapped in their coats, Tom and JP sat with their backs to a wall, watching brown, windswept leaves race wildly across the open space, often pursued eagerly by shrieking, younger children.

Finishing a sandwich, Tom shivered and rubbed his hands together. "I can't believe how cold it's got today."

JP grunted an obvious agreement. "My Dad says it gets really cold here in the winter. And it snows...I don't t'ink I'll like snow."

Tom looked at him. "You've never seen snow before?"

JP smiled slightly. "No, man. Don't get snow in Barbados...far too hot!"

Tom returned the smile. "What's it like there?"

"Ah, it's beautiful...there's no place like it in the world." Gazing into space, JP's face became strangely animated. "You want to look out, Tom, high up from Cherry Tree Hill, over the green, rolling hills and listen to the branches on the tall palms rustling gently in the breeze. Or walk along the coral sandy beaches on our West Coast, and feel the warm waters of the Caribbean wash lightly over your feet." Turning back to face Tom, he continued, "But on the East Coast it's different; the waves are huge there, man. They come in straight off the Atlantic, and they crash along the shore, or on the ragged cliffs further North, throwing mist and foam high into the air!"

Captivated, Tom nodded, imagining the wonders of such a tropical paradise. "It sounds fantastic. I bet you miss it?"

JP's smile faded slowly. "Yeh. I didn't want to leave, but me Dad lost his job and couldn't get another back home. That's how come we ended up here, you know, looking for work." He fell silent again and Tom tactfully steered the conversation elsewhere.

"What do you think about what Mr Blackwell said this morning?"

"About what?"

"About Harris being suspended...and being expelled if caught fighting."

JP shaded his eyes as a shaft of dazzling sunlight broke through the patchwork of fast moving clouds. "I t'ink he's going to be as mad as hell when he gets back. Best you keep out of his way."

"What do you mean?" Tom answered, suddenly concerned.

"Well, t'ink about it. He's probably in big trouble at home for being suspended in the first place, and he'll have two weeks to dwell on it."

"So?"

"So, Harris is a stupid, vindictive git, Tom...and who do *you* t'ink he's gonna blame for getting him sent home in the first place?"

The penny dropped. "But I didn't do anything! You were there, he called me a 'Paddy' and – "

"I know, man" JP interrupted, spreading his hands out wide. "But do you really t'ink he'll care about that?"

Downcast, Tom regarded with little interest the half-eaten contents of his lunchbox. "It's so unfair," he protested dejectedly. "What've I ever done to him?"

Nodding in sympathy, JP agreed. "If it makes you feel any better, you're not alone. Harris and his gang pick on virtually everyone. They bully Ernie Jones 'cause he's small; Liz Joyce 'cause she's got a lisp and, well, he hates me, and now you, 'cause we're different."

"Different?"

"Yeh, different. We don't come from around here. I'm black and you're Irish...what chance have we got?"

Struck by the revelation, Tom was silent for a while, thoughtfully considering his friend's words. JP closed his eyes and tried to relax.

"Has Harris ever hit you?" he asked finally. JP opened his eyes and glanced at him briefly.

"No...but he and some others have chased me often enough." Laughing unexpectedly he added, "But they're never caught me yet, man...I'm far *too fast!*" Tom couldn't help laughing too, but after a few moments they became sober once more. "Mainly they just call me names, you know, black stuff, or throw things across the classroom. I can handle that, but sooner or later Harris is gonna get me."

Tom shook his head. "Can't we tell someone? Mr Blackwell, or what about Mr Montgomery, even?"

JP pursed his lips. "You t'ink they'll listen? Nah, man, nobody cares."

A shadow fell across them. Looking up Tom recognised another boy from his class. With a pronounced overbite and large, prominent ears, he had an almost comical appearance; not that Tom would've ever dared comment. The boy's name was Eddie Barron, and whilst Tom had never spoken to him, he knew that Eddie was someone Harris and his companions avoided.

"Charlie Reynolds wants to see you, Wilson," he said ignoring Tom.

"Why?"

Barron shrugged uninterestedly. "Dunno. But he's waiting by the drinking fountain."

"Who's Charlie Reynolds?" Tom asked after the boy had wandered off. "I've not heard of him."

JP stood and brushed breadcrumbs from his coat. He regarded Tom strangely for a moment. "I'll tell you later; I'd better go." Without waiting for a reply he ran off across the playground, leaving Tom slightly confused and alone once again.

17
ADJUSTING

Standing on the open platform of East Ham Station, Tom looked eagerly up and down the twin, parallel tracks, determined to be the first to spot the anticipated Metropolitan District Railway Company train. Unseen behind him Keira and Derek exchanged a knowing look.

"It'll be coming from the left, Tom," Derek said with a slight smile.

Concentrating intently in that direction, Tom stared into the distance, impatient for the day's excursion to begin.

It was Saturday morning, and at breakfast Derek had unexpectedly announced that, seeing as it was Tom's first full weekend in London, they should all go on an adventure. Despite Tom's repeated pleadings, and to a lesser extent Keira's amused interest, Derek would say little of his plans. All he did reveal was that they were going to travel on the Underground.

"I think I can see it!" Tom said excitedly, pointing enthusiastically up the track.

Theatrically shading his eyes, Derek nodded in agreement. "I do believe you're right, my boy." In the far distance, the vaguely square shaped outline of an approaching 'District Line' train began to appear. Derek watched Tom closely as the front of the train rapidly became more clearly defined. With a sideways wink to his wife he said, "Notice anything different, Tom?"

"Huh?" Tom replied, distracted.

"The train. Is there anything unusual about it?"

Tom shook his head. "No...I don't think so."

Derek smiled. "Are you sure?"

Frowning, Tom concentrated on the approaching train. He was about to shake his head again when suddenly it struck him. "Wait! There's no steam...but, I don't understand, where's the engine?"

Derek chuckled, "Well done, lad. The first time I saw one of those, it took me ages to figure out what it was that was bothering me."

Tom did shake his head again, but this time in confusion. "But, how can it run without steam?" By now the front of the train, its driver clearly evident within the glass fronted cabin, was nearing the station. Tom absently registered a strange clicking sound emanating along the tracks.

"Don't tease him, Derek," Keira warned quietly. Derek made to reply but seeing her stern expression, thought better of it. Instead sighing, he turned back to Tom.

"It's an *electric* train, Tom. It doesn't need an engine since the power comes directly to it along the rails. It's quite impressive really, don't you think?

"Aye," Tom breathed, in obvious awe. *Electric trains!* The wonders of London seemed without end.

As the multiple carriages slowed to an orderly stop,

Derek indicated they should move forward. Already a number of the awaiting passengers were surging ahead, queuing at either end of the nearest carriage.

"On these trains," Derek explained, "there's a sliding mesh gate at the end of each carriage where we get on or off. But on some of the more modern ones, there are sliding doors in the middle, and some even have air-operated automatic ones. Clever, eh?" Not entirely understanding what he meant, Tom nonetheless nodded. Keira rolled her eyes heavenwards.

Stepping eagerly onto the carriage platform, Tom quickly disappeared inside. Already many of the seats were occupied, but leading the way between the adjacent, neat longitudinal seating, he soon spotted three vacant spaces at the far end. Sitting between his aunt and Derek, Tom couldn't help grinning, staring happily around at his fellow passengers and the overhead advertisement posters and route maps.

For nearly half an hour the 'District' train continued its journey over ground, stopping regularly every few minutes at a number of similar looking stations. From Upton Park through to the approach to Bow, Tom, much of the time nose pressed hard up against the window, gazed at the grim mixed industrial and residential heartland that was the East End of London. Gas holders, chemical works and innumerable factory buildings swept by. But for Tom, used to the open, clear countryside of Donegal, it was the view of so many streets, crammed with closely spaced, often squalid terrace housing that was most depressing. Many houses were literally built back-to-back, so the side walls were shared, with only a narrow courtyard, invariable filthy and filled with rubbish, between them. Some of the poorest looking housing shared back walls, so there was no space even for a yard. Stained, begrimed washing was strewn across narrow streets or shared yards, and over everything a low, dark haze of soot hung in the air, testament to the countless domestic coal fires and industrial chimneys. Everywhere he looked, dirt and grime, it seemed, clung to everything.

As they neared Bow, the train suddenly plunged into a tunnel and the world outside turned black. In moments it emerged into the light of the enclosed, underground station and slowed to a halt.

"From now on Tom, we'll be travelling beneath the City," Derek explained. "Hence why we call it the 'Underground.'" Tom nodded vaguely, distracted by a group of elderly Jewish men, dressed completely in black, entering the carriage.

"Don't stare, Tom." Keira admonished quietly, leaning forward.

Looking quickly away, he said after a moment, "Are there many tunnels like this?"

Satisfied, she answered, "Yes, there are. They connect all across London and many of the lines are expanding into the suburbs, obviously above ground though."

Within a minute the doors had been manually closed and the train began accelerating out of the station. In seconds the outside was once again enveloped in darkness.

Emerging from Regent's Park Station and blinking momentarily in the dazzling sunlight, Tom glanced around, amazed. Everywhere he looked there were people. Many hurried along the crowded pavements, weaving skilfully amongst their fellows, impatient to be about their business. Others, particularly well dressed couples, strolled sedately through the throng, casually gazing about them as if emphasising their station. On the Marylebone Road opposite, huge six wheeled trolleybuses, their distinctive red and white roofed livery interspaced by prominent advertising posters, cruised by. Seeing his interest, Derek said, "Another modern marvel, Tom, trolleybuses. They're new and, if you believe the papers, are going to completely replace the tram networks someday...not that I'd moan their loss, mind you. You see those strange looking metal rods extending from the roof?"

"Uh huh."

"Well that's the collecting gear; it's how they get their power. If you look carefully you'll see it connects directly to those overhead lines running up and down the street. Quite inspired really, since it means trolleybuses aren't restricted like trams to fixed tracks in the road. Anyway," he added with sideways look towards Keira, "we'd best get on...your aunt's got that impatient look brewing."

Holding his hand, Derek led Tom, with Keira a step behind, to the kerbside and concentrating upon crossing, repeatedly looked back and forth across the busy road. Before them delivery trucks, taxis and numerous other mainly dark coloured automobiles competed with the trolleybuses for the crowded road space. As Tom watched, the occasional motorcyclist sped past, taking his life in his hands, weaving dangerously in and out of the heavy traffic. Preoccupied with the riders, a sharp tug on his arm and stern look this time from Derek, reminded him to pay attention.

It was only after they had negotiated the Marylebone Road and walked north a further hundred yards, that Tom registered the huge swath of open parkland before him. Stopping at the edge of the Outer Circle, he stared open mouthed at the flourishing green expanse of Regent's Park. Faint, sweet smelling scents of flowers and cut grass drifted over him on the cool autumnal breeze. Breathing deeply, Tom closed his eyes as memories of flowering gorse and the heather landscapes of home threatened to overwhelm him.

"This is Regent's Park, Tom," Derek said, unknowingly distracting him from his inward distress and bringing him back to the present. "I bet you've never seen anything like this, eh? It's absolutely huge and full of beautiful flower gardens, all wonderfully arranged and cared for, plus woodland areas, lakes and elegant walkways. Apparently it was once the hunting ground for Henry VIII – have you learned about him in school yet?"

Tom shook his head.

"Ah, well, never mind that then, let's go and explore.

Do you like gardens?"

Tom shrugged, indifferently.

Derek glanced at Keira and winked. "Well, I'm sure there'll be something here that will interest you."

Following the Outer Circle for a few minutes, Derek soon led them onto Broad Walk, a pedestrianised pathway that ran, straight as an arrow into the distance, dissecting the park in two. It was a bright morning and, despite the fresh September air, Tom felt the pleasant warmth of the sun on his back as they strolled serenely along. Both Derek and Keira nodded and exchanged polite greetings with passers by. Tom couldn't help notice how relaxed everyone seemed compared to the frantic turmoil outside the Underground station minutes earlier.

He was about to comment on this when Keira pointed to the left and said, "Tommy, you see that circular pathway over there?" Waiting for him to nod first, she then continued, "Well, that's called the Inner Circle, and within it are the Royal Botanic Gardens; they're absolutely fascinating. There're plants growing in there that you wouldn't believe. Do you think we'll have time to go round later Derek?"

"If you want to, but let's see how it goes." Grinning, he added, "There's a lot more we need to see first here, though." Inclining her head in agreement, Keira returned the smile. She had already guessed where they were going, but for Tom, this still remained a mystery. "Incidentally, Darling," Derek continued conversationally, "I read in the paper the other day that the Botanic Gardens are moving, apparently they're going to Kew."

"Really, why in the Lord's name to they want to do that. They're perfectly lovely here."

"Not sure really, but there was something about their lease expiring."

Keira frowned. "Well, if they *do* move them, they'd jolly well better replace them with something nice, that's all I can say."

Derek laughed. "I'm sure they will, I don't suppose the King would be happy with any old rubbish being put up in *Regent's* Park, would you?"

As they passed St Catherine's Lodge on the right, Tom began to hear strange calls and howls resounding from ahead. Around them, increasing numbers of pedestrians were becoming apparent, the majority all travelling in their same direction. Similarly, growing numbers of children, many in family groups, were appearing, chatting excitedly or running ahead only to be called back by irate parents. As the unmistakable animal cries became louder, Tom turned and looked curiously towards Derek and Keira.

In answer to the unspoken question, Derek simply nodded and smiled. "Yes, Tom. We're going to the Zoo."

A gentle tap on the shoulder stirred Tom from his reverie. "We're here," Derek said, standing and offering his hand to help Keira. As the slowing train approached East Ham Station, Tom, tired but happy, sighed and rose to join his aunt and her husband by the exit gates.

Inwardly he still couldn't quite believe what had happened; quite simply, today had been the most remarkable day of his life. From first entering London Zoo, he'd been astounded by the array and diversity of animals on view. Many he'd never even heard of before, and of those he was familiar with, albeit from books or pictures, to actually see them up close and in the flesh, was indescribable. To file past the uniform, enclosed cages in the old Lion House and watch the 'big cats' feeding, was a memory that would stay with him forever. More than anything Tom had been surprised at how large the lions and tigers actually were. Amused and standing behind him, Keira and Derek had grinned and whispered closely together as he had watched mesmerised. For perhaps twenty minutes he'd stared through the open bars as the lions devoured their meal, snarling and fighting for its possession in equal measure.

As they stepped off the train, Tom remembered fondly feeding currant buns to the elephants and watching the grey wolves trot excitedly back and forth within their enclosure as their keeper tossed scraps of meat inside. The pungent smell of the gorillas in the uniquely designed, semi-circular Gorilla House had been completely unexpected, as had the incensed shrieks of the Rhesus monkeys and other small primates as they scampered and chased each other around the Monkey House. But for Tom, the one recollection that still made him smile outwardly was the chimps' tea party. Put simply, today had been fantastic!

Alone in his room, Tom sighed heavily and continued staring absently at the ceiling. On the bed beside him lay the opened letter from Cathleen Kearney, discarded for the present, but each line virtually memorised. Cathleen's letter had been waiting for him on the hallway floor when they had arrived home. Racing up the stairs, delighted and desperate to read it, it had seemed then to be the perfect end of a perfect day. For a few minutes, he neither moved nor spoke, simply considered inwardly the letter's content.

Sighing again, Tom glanced down and reached for it once more. Holding the single page above his head, he re-read it for perhaps the sixth time.

"Dearest Tom,

I hope you are well and enjoying life in London — I can't imagine how exciting it must be for you. You must write and tell me all about it.

I walked home with Dónal from school today and he said to say Hello. He did say he would write soon, but you know what he's like. Since you've been gone he seems to be friendlier to me. I think he's a bit lonely and misses you; not that he would ever admit that!

Dr Kerrigan came round and visited your Mam again this morning. He spent a long time with my Mam afterwards, but I managed to listen at the door for a while (before getting caught!). Your Mam's still poorly but at least doesn't seem to be getting any worse. Dr Kerrigan said he was fairly pleased with this. I sneaked in to see your Mam afterwards and told her I was writing to you. She told me to tell you she thinks about you every day, and loves you very much.

Séamus Quigley is still trying to cause trouble. Apparently he reported Mr Kennedy for hitting him in the street. Mr Kennedy denied it, of course, and no one believes Quigley even though he does have an impressive black eye. Mam reckons he got it in a fight in one of the bars, and is just trying to stir up ill feeling against Mr Kennedy for some reason.

Anyway, I had best say goodbye for now. I'll write again next week but it would be great to hear from you before then.

Much love
Cathleen, xx"

Unheeded, a single tear spilled down Tom's cheek, trickling unnoticed onto the bed covers. Cathleen's letter was a bitter - sweet irony. Absorbing the craved for news from home only served to fuel his feelings of loss and longing. Suddenly the homesickness, the anxiety for his mother's health and the strains of adapting to his new life all became too much. Turning onto his front, Tom buried his head between his arms and sobbed.

Outside the door, Keira stood silently listening, a glass of milk and a biscuit forgotten in her hands. For a minute she remained motionless, poised to enter but racked with indecision. Finally, she turned and quietly retreated, retracing her steps down the stairs, her mind troubled.

Scowling, Tom swore inwardly. For nearly two hours he had sat in the McDonagh's front room, listening quietly to the interplay between his aunt, Derek and their two guests, but still could fathom little of their complex card game. The adults were playing 'Bridge,' a game that, until today, he'd never heard of. Aside from being warned to be on his best behaviour, not touch anything in the room or interrupt the game, Keira had tried to explain the rules before their visitors had arrived. Despite this, once play had started Tom had soon become lost with the strange sounding terms and monosyllabic language. With only short breaks between 'rubbers' when they discussed previous hands and considered strategy, he'd managed to discern little of what was going on.

The McDonaghs' friends, an older couple called Ted and Rose Burrows, were regular 'Bridge evenings' company. Ted Burrows, a stocky man with a balding pate and a neatly trimmed grey beard, was a retired policeman. Solemn and intimidating, he rarely spoke and on first being introduced had fixed Tom with a discomforting, baleful stare. Rose Burrows, by contrast, was open, friendly and genuinely welcoming. Short and plump, her round face was heavily made up for the evening. She had brown eyes and dark, wavy hair, and Tom had taken an instant liking to her. Nonetheless, despite her pleasant, affable manner, once play started Tom was soon under no illusions that both the Burrows and the McDonaghs took the game very seriously.

Around the small card table, Keira sat opposite Derek, her partner for the evening. Similarly, the Burrows sat facing each other, Ted to Keira's left and Rose to Derek's. Despite his frustration, Tom lay on the settee watching closely. He knew enough now that with Rose having dealt, the focus of attention was now on his aunt, to 'open the bidding.' Heads bowed, the adults studied their own cards expressionlessly; the three initially non-bidding players waiting patiently.

After several moments Keira looked up and said firmly, "One Diamond."

Almost immediately Ted replied, "One No Trumps," and stared directly across the table at his wife. From observing previous hands, Tom was aware that this bidding process was the means by which players conveyed information to their partners about the quality and strength of their cards. Not that he really understood the details, but it was clear that each couple strove to win the bidding 'contract', and thereby dictate the ultimate goals of an individual round.

Derek had paused after Ted's counter bid, thoughtfully considering the implications. "Two Spades," he finally said, indicating his strength in spades and preference over diamonds. A two spades bid had also raised any potential contract to the second level. Rose to his left subsequently passed, effectively signally to all her poor hand. The bidding round now passed back to Keira to consider her husband's intentions. Forgotten in the corner, Tom could almost feel the tension in the room.

With four medium Spades to the Queen and Derek's obvious strength in that suit, it took her only a moment to raise the bid again, and 'play in game.'

"Three Spades," she announced confidently.

Ted shook his head, passing and effectively confirming the contract would indeed be Three Spades. Sighing contentedly, Keira relaxed noticeably; with her partner having originated the Spade bid, Derek was now required to play both her hand and his own. As 'dummy', Keira's cards would be laid out, face up, on the table for all to see. Using both hands it was Derek's responsibility to play against Ted and Rose to try and secure at least nine of the possible thirteen tricks, given a Three Spade contract, and thereby win the round. Tom understood that points were awarded for making the contract, winning 'over tricks' but conversely 'lost' to the other side if less than nine tricks were made. How that worked out the actual points still remained a mystery.

With the contract established, Rose began, laying the Six of Hearts on the table. All but Tom realised this was the standard 'fourth down longest suit' opening play. Keira placed all her cards down, in suit columns, and sat back, her participation in the ensuing hands now over. Studying the exposed pack for a while, Derek reached across and selected the Jack of Hearts, the highest visible in that suit. Ted played the Four and Derek himself threw away with the Seven. With the hand won in dummy, Derek considered his next move, clear in his own mind at least as far as Hearts were concerned, Ted had neither the Queen, King nor Ace.

As Tom watched, Derek soon won trick after trick, testament to his skill in playing the cards. As he won the penultimate hand, he threw his final card, the Six of Spades, into the middle pronouncing the last trick his. With no other trumps in either hand, the Burrows conceded.

"And that's game and rubber," he commented, unnecessarily glancing at the points tally on a small note pad beside him.

"Well played," Ted acknowledged, holding out his hand. "I thought we might've had you earlier, when I finessed that Queen, but you recovered well.

"Thanks," Derek answered, nodding slightly at the proffered praise. Pushing his chair back he rose and crossed to an adjacent mahogany cabinet. Removing four small glasses and a half full bottle of sherry, he returned to the table and poured drinks. "I have to say though, Ted," he continued, passing the glasses round in turn. "I was surprised you waited so long to lead the King of Clubs, once you'd won the fifth trick!" For the next few minutes, Tom listened to the virtually incomprehensible discussion as they reviewed each hand played in minute detail. If watching Bridge was trying, having to endure the seemingly endless debate on the subject stretched even Tom's forbearance. Unwittingly, he yawned excessively.

"Oh, for shame, Keira," Rose exclaimed, reacting instantly to the gesture. "The poor love's done in." All eyes turned to face him. Suddenly conscious of the interest, Tom flushed and looked away. "And such a good boy, staying quiet like that. I'd almost forgotten he was there." Glancing at her husband, she added with a smile. "A true gent in the making, don't you think Ted?" Without waiting for a reply, Rose pressed on. "Not like our Alice, eh? She wouldn't have kept to herself for five minutes, let alone a couple of hours."

Embarrassed, Tom didn't know what to say.

Thankfully Keira interceded. "I'm not sure that's entirely true, Rose. Alice has always been well behaved whenever we've been over. Derek, pass the sherry round again please."

Allowing his glass to be refilled, Ted made an inarticulate 'Humph' sound. "You've no idea how much that's cost me afterwards."

The adults laughed easily, though for Tom the comment didn't seem particularly funny.

"Perhaps Tom, you'd like to come over one afternoon and meet Alice," Rose said quietly. "She's about your age, and I'm sure she'd like to play with you." Ted shifted noticeably in his seat, and unseen by Tom, gave his wife a sceptical look.

"Why Rose, I think that's a lovely idea," Keira replied earnestly. "Thank you."

Rose beamed. "Well that's settled. How about this Sunday – "

"Can't this weekend," Ted interrupted. "You've got your sister coming."

"Oh, yes! Sorry, I forgot. What about next weekend

then, if that suits everybody?" Keira and Derek exchanged glances. When neither objected, Rose added, excitedly. "Excellent, Sunday week it is then! You can all come round for lunch. I'm looking forward to it already!"

No one bothered to ask Tom his opinion on the matter.

Days passed, and the end of Tom's second week at Manor School drew near. Deliberately trying to keep a low profile, he had successfully managed not to alienate Mr Blackwell or any other teacher, as well as avoiding any fracas with his fellow pupils. The majority of his classmates either ignored him, or for those generally less well disposed, seemed content to watch from a distance. Nonetheless, Tom was under no illusions that things were likely to soon change. The impending and unwelcome return of Bert Harris was progressively beginning to play on Tom's mind.

Only Jerome Wilson exhibited any semblance of friendship, although even this was peppered by occasional periods of awkwardness, particularly when they were in the presence of some other boys. Why JP now and then became cool with him, Tom had no idea. The fact that as far as Tom was concerned there seemed to be no obvious reason, only served to fuel his anxiety. Friday morning had been such a time.

After the morning register, Blackwell had tasked Tom with returning the register to the main office. It was the first time he'd been asked to do so, and in a sudden moment of inspiration, had glanced inside. Despite his disappointment at seeing his friend's entry in the book as 'Jerome P Wilson', Tom nevertheless looked forward to telling him of his latest attempt to discover his middle name.

As the class filed out for the morning break, Tom fell into step beside JP and eagerly started to recount his latest scheme. Jostled by their rowdy classmates streaming towards the main exit, Tom had to shout to be heard above the noise. Despite his initial excitement, Tom's enthusiasm soon waned as it became obvious JP was only half-heartedly listening.

Venturing a few yards into the playground, JP turned left and began slowly walking around the perimeter, head bowed and clearly distracted. Following dejectedly behind, Tom trailed off into silence, troubled and unsure what to do. Something was obviously worrying his friend, but he'd no idea what it was or how to find out.

After a few minutes, JP stopped and leaned casually against the far wall. A few feet in front two younger boys were playing marbles over a drain cover. Watching with interest, Tom took a step nearer, observing closely as they took turns flicking a marble onto the open groves between the iron grills. When a marble landed on the same grove as an opponents, both were claimed gleefully by the victor. Suddenly conscious of their audience, both boys looked up, regarding Tom in particular with unconcealed suspicion.

"We call this 'drainsies' back home," Tom said

pleasantly, trying to appear friendly. "Do you call it that here?"

Neither spoke, but as one collected their own marbles hurriedly, stood and ran off. Amazed, Tom stared after them.

"What did I do?" He asked incredulously, watching them sprint away.

"*You* didn't do anything," a voice said behind him.

Startled, Tom span round to see three figures standing directly behind him, all grinning openly. One he recognised as Danny Blake, a skinny black-haired boy from his own class. The others were noticeably older, and unknown. One had fair, almost blonde hair with a thin, rangy look; the other was bigger built with a thick thatch of dark brown, unruly hair. All three were dirty and poorly dressed in old, stained clothing, much of it showing evidence of repair. The dark haired youth in particular was filthy, his face cover in prominent spots, and Tom couldn't help wrinkling his nose as a powerful unwashed smell wafted over him.

"Do you know who I am?" the fair-haired boy asked, still smiling and directing his attention to Tom.

Tom shook his head but said nothing.

Casting a quick glance at JP, the boy paused for a second before addressing Tom once more. "Has Wilson 'ere, told you anything?"

Again Tom indicated no. "I don't understand, told me what?"

"You said not to." JP said quietly, coming to stand next to Tom.

"You're right, I did. And I'm glad to see you can take orders."

Orders? Tom considered inwardly. *What is this?* He was about to protest further when the boy held out his hand.

"I'm Reynolds, Charlie Reynolds. And this is Alan Osborne," he continued with a nod towards the large, grubby boy next to him. "But we just call 'im Lugsie for obvious reasons." Again, Tom said nothing, trying not to stare at Osborne's prominent ears. "And I assume you know Blakey, since he's in your class."

"Aye, I mean yes," Tom replied, warily shaking the proffered hand. "But —"

"Jolly good. I'll let Wilson explain everything then. Must dash, we'll get together next week and sort out your initiation test." Still smiling, Reynolds turned to leave. "Cheerio," he added, waving over his shoulder. Blake and Osborne traipsed after, following closely like a pair of obedient dogs.

Utterly confused, Tom simply stared after them. "What was that all about?" he finally asked, still watching their retreating backs.

JP didn't reply. Only after Tom turned to regard him did he sigh deeply and say, "Charlie Reynolds wants us to join his gang."

"His gang? What gang...never mind, but why should we want to do that?"

JP looked directly into Tom's eyes. "Because if we do, man, he said he'll protect us from Harris."

18
FALSE HOPES

For almost a week a dense, virtual impenetrable blanket of fog had greeted Tom's daily walk to school. Despite taking to wearing a thick woollen scarf wrapped around his face, the chilly, soot contaminated air still infiltrated, leaving his throat sore and irritated well before reaching the school gates. Damp, cold and miserable, Tom felt little inclination to converse with his aunt as they walked together, and as the days progressed, their journeys began to take on a familiar, virtually silent drudgery. Each afternoon the lingering fog would lift slightly, allowing thin watery sunshine to break through, only to thicken and descend rapidly once more as evening approached. The depressing weather had noticeably dampened Tom's usually buoyant spirits...as had the inevitable return to school earlier in the week of Bert Harris.

To Tom's surprise, however, Harris had completely ignored him, ostensibly settling calmly back into the school routine. Even Harris' associates, whilst outwardly loud and boisterous around their returned leader, had made no overt approaches, and Tom had begun to wonder whether Harris had actually forgotten about him. Unfortunately, he was sadly mistaken.

Filing into class on Thursday morning, Tom looked quickly around the room for JP. It took only a few moments to confirm that his friend was once again not present. Stripping off his damp coat and scarf, Tom tried not to let his disappointment show as he joined the shoving queue of pupils in the narrow, adjacent cloakroom. JP had been off all week, presumably with some illness, and Tom had invariably found himself sitting alone everyday at their paired desks. Sighing privately at what promised to be another lonely day, Tom headed for his seat. In the confusing melee of children entering, hanging up their coats and getting settled, it took him a moment to register that someone was already sitting at JP's desk. For a second Tom just stared at the occupant, Ben Parker, a notorious member of Harris' gang. Big and imposing with short closely cropped hair, Parker, like Harris, was someone Tom tried his best to avoid. Seemingly indifferent, Parker stared straight ahead, deliberately ignoring him, though a barely concealed smirk threatened to betray the unsettling effect he was undoubtedly trying to achieve.

"Right you lot, hurry up and sit down," Mr Blackwell's voice boomed from the doorway. Startled into action, Tom cautiously took his seat, his eyes watching the larger boy closely.

The morning lessons passed without incident, as did the mid-morning and lunchtime breaks. In the afternoon, Mrs Phelps took over the class for writing practice, and again Tom concentrated intently; Parker sitting silently at his side.

Tom glanced at the clock. Only thirty minutes until home time he thought happily, glad that the school day was coming to an end. Trying to stifle a yawn, he fearfully looked back towards Mrs Phelps but quickly relaxed, seeing her back to him chalking on the blackboard. Suddenly Parker screamed and clutched his face with both hands. Shocked, Tom watched incredulously as he writhed from side to side, moaning loudly.

In an instant Phelps was standing before their desks, towering menacing over them. "What on Earth's going on here?" she demanded angrily. Tom looked up at her in astonishment, mouth open but with nothing to say.

"Devlin *hit me*, Miss," Parker half sobbed, reluctantly dropping his hands and staring accusingly at Tom. "I only wanted his rubber; I thought he'd said yes...I'd reached for it and he just punched me in the face."

Phelps turned to fiercely glare at Tom. "Well," her

voice dangerously quiet. "Did you hit him, Devlin?"

Speechless and completely at a loss to what was happening, Tom could only gaze stupidly back up at her. Phelps read his silence as damning evidence of guilt.

"You *wicked* boy. Stand up!" When Tom didn't move, she yanked him roughly to his feet.

Staggering to regain his balance, Tom finally found his voice. "I didn't, Miss. I swear!"

"Don't lie to me Devlin, you're in enough trouble as it is. Go and stand in that corner until I decide what's to be done with you."

Taking a few steps as indicated, Tom stopped and turned back, shaking his head. "It wasn't me, he's lying, I didn't do anything!" Tears were being to well up. Ignoring his protests, Phelps advanced threateningly and pushed him forwards. Behind her back Parker was grinning openly and waving, as were Harris and several others.

"I told you not to lie to me!" Phelps roared, inches from his face. "Now get in that corner. No, face the wall, not me, I don't want to see you. You'll have an hour's detention tonight, and mark my words, young man, I'll be reporting this disgraceful behaviour to Mr Montgomery."

Turning back to face the class, Parker's smile vanished an instant before her gaze fell upon him. Adopting a contrite, pained expression he nodded to her obvious, but unasked, question that he was alright. His ears burning in anger and embarrassment, Tom fumed impotently.

"And let that be a lesson to you, Devlin," Phelps said, sitting behind her desk and inspecting his work. Tom stood before her, hands behind his back and head bowed. This was the second set of one hundred lines he had produced stating: "*I shall not disrupt Mrs Phelps' lessons or hit my classmates. I am sorry for the trouble I have caused.*" The first a consequence of his punishment for "hitting" Ben Parker; the second for continuing to "lie" to her in claiming his innocence. Tom had learnt quickly that protesting further would only serve to prolong the misery. His anger at being tricked had long since waned, and like the coalescing, gloomy fog outside, despondency was beginning to set in. Staring absently at his scuffed shoes he wondered whether his aunt wouldn't believe him either. Distantly he was aware that Mrs Phelps was talking again.

"Devlin! Pay attention. I said you can go." His thoughts scattered, Tom forced himself to focus on her voice, loud and clearly irritated. "Do I have to repeat myself a third time?"

"No, Miss. Sorry."

"Well, go on then."

Without replying or looking up Tom turned and, crossing the room, retrieved his coat.

"And Devlin?" Phelps said quietly, as he headed for the door.

"Miss?"

"Make sure you tell your aunt why you were kept back tonight. I'm sure the Headmaster will want to speak to her tomorrow."

Again Tom said nothing. Phelps' smug, supercilious smile was almost too much to bear.

Turning his coat collar up, Tom stepped out onto the chill, fog-bound playground and headed for the gates. Despite the poor visibility and lateness of the hour, a dozen or so hazy figures were still evident, kicking a football and calling loudly to one another.

It was cold, and stuffing his hands into his pockets, Tom walked briskly, head down, eager to be home. Still smarting over the unfairness of the day, and worrying how he was going to explain what had happened to his aunt, Tom absently avoided the footballers, his thoughts distracted. He had barely passed through the school exit gates, when a harsh cry to his right made him turn instinctively.

"There 'e is!" Twenty yards away, leaning casually against the iron railings were three partly obscured figures. One he didn't recognise was pointing at him excitedly; the others were all too familiar. A shiver, but not from the damp, foggy air, ran down Tom's back as he stared into the grinning faces of Bert Harris and Ben Parker.

"You ain't in school now, *Paddy*." Harris said menacingly. "Get 'im!"

Tom fled.

Running as fast as he could in the opposite direction, Tom heedlessly sped across the road and ducked down a narrow street, opening on his right. Behind him the constant jeering and taunts from Harris and his friends were ever present. Heart pounding, Tom desperately tried to think of a way out. Pedestrians appeared unexpectedly out of the gloom, only to just as quickly disappear as he tore recklessly down the pavement, angry cries of protest ignored. Adrenaline surged through his veins and as Tom ran on, all rational thought was driven from his mind as he strove to escape.

From behind, the calls gradually lessened and finally stopped. Hoping he had outrun his pursuers, Tom risked a quick glance over his shoulder. Aghast, he cried out in near panic at seeing Parker only a few yards behind, mouth set in a harsh grimace, arms pumping at his sides. Somewhere in the distance he heard Harris' voice calling out to Parker to catch him quickly.

His rhythm thrown, Tom turned back but only managed two more strides before colliding violently with a large, dark figure stepping out from a gateway. In a tangled heap they both crashed to the floor, pain shooting through Tom's elbow as he landed heavily. Desperate to get to his feet, Tom slipped on the damp pavement and fell forward again, fear threatening to overwhelm him. Cursing loudly, the figure, a heavy set man in a black overcoat, made a grab for Tom just as Parker skidded to a halt, narrowly avoiding crashing into him also. Catching sight of the larger boy from the corner of his eye, he struck out, grasping Parker by the collar. Struggling but nonetheless firmly held, Parker kicked and screamed to be released. Chest heaving,

Tom finally scrambled up and ran on, nursing his bruised arm. Within seconds he had disappeared into the fog, Parker's continued protests and Harris' angry shouts rapidly fading into the distance.

Tom stared miserably out of the McDonaghs' kitchen window, uninterestedly picking at his cereal. Derek had already left for work and Keira, seemingly ignoring him, made pretence of clearing up the breakfast things. The events of the previous day had already been discussed at length, and in spite of his aunt having accepted Tom's version, neither he nor Keira were looking forward to the impending school day. Both knew Mrs Phelps would have enthusiastically carried out her threat to inform the Headmaster. At best Mr Montgomery would believe Tom, but not before subjecting him to an intensive and thoroughly nerve racking interrogation. Notwithstanding, the Headmaster would still be immensely annoyed at having his time wasted. Tom did not even want to consider the consequences of a worst case scenario.

Leaving the house together, Keira made a passing comment in light of the fog having finally lifted. Tom said nothing. Its dispersal to reveal slate-grey storm clouds and replacement by persistent, heavy drizzle did little to lighten his mood.

As usual, the journey to school passed with little conversation, each content to dwell on their own thoughts.

"So, he believed you then?" JP said, trying to sound positive.

Tom shrugged nonchalantly. "I suppose."

"Hey, man, he must've done...otherwise you'd be in a heap more trouble."

Tom merely shrugged once more.

It was lunchtime and although it still remained dark and overcast, the rain had at least stopped, allowing all the classes to be let outside into the playground. Mr Blackwell was on duty and Tom and JP deliberately hovered nearby. Tom's day had brightened considerably on seeing his friend back that morning. With little chance to talk before the morning register, JP had regarded Tom curiously when the inevitable summons to Montgomery's office had arrived, a little after ten o'clock. With the poor weather preventing the class from going outside for the mid-morning break, Tom had found speaking privately to JP difficult in the cramped, noisy room. Conscious of not wanting to be overheard, he had only managed a few whispered comments prior to being called back to their desks, when the lesson resumed. Tom had to wait until lunchtime for a more appropriate opportunity to explain the previous day's events.

A flight of pigeons swooped low across the playground, momentarily capturing the boys' attention. Watching the birds bank sharply to rise and disappear over the adjacent roof tops, JP said, "So, what did Montgomery say about Parker and Harris chasing you? Presumably they'll be for it now?"

Tom glanced guiltily at his feet. "I didn't tell him about that."

"What? Why not? Didn't your aunt say anything?"

Tom shook his head. "She doesn't know either."

JP pursed his lips. "Jesus, man, what's wrong with you? Don't you want to…" Unexpectedly, he trailed off and fell silent. Looking up, Tom saw the reason – walking calmly towards them were Bert Harris and Ben Parker. Tom's stomach contracted involuntarily as a sick feeling of fear welled up within. His mind screamed to run, but somehow his legs wouldn't move. Stopping a few feet before them, Harris spread his hands expansively and grinned, showing yellowed, crooked teeth.

"If I'd known you were such a fast runner, Paddy, I'd 'ave thought up a better plan to catch yeh. Damn nearly gave me a heart attack chasing you."

Parker laughed, but neither Tom nor JP replied. Harris' smile gradually faded as he eyed them menacingly. "Next time," he added in a quieter voice, "You won't be so lucky."

Tom looked momentarily over Harris' shoulder towards Blackwell, standing a few yards behind them. Seeing the gesture, Harris glanced behind also, whilst Parker continued to watch them intently. The teacher's back was turned to them and was engaged in conversation with a couple of other boys.

Looking back to Tom, Harris grinned again. " 'e ain't gonna help you, Paddy. 'e's too busy talking to Jennings…convenient, huh?" Taking a step forward,

Harris advanced threateningly, Parker a stride behind. Reaching for JP's hand, Tom backed away, his eyes darting left and right, seeking escape. Seeing the rising panic in his eyes, Harris laughed out loud.

"What's so funny?" an unexpected voice said at Tom's shoulder. Startled, he turned to see Charlie Reynolds, along with Alan Osborne and Eddie Barron standing beside him. Ignoring Tom, Reynolds stared straight ahead, whilst Osborne and Barron moved subtly to stand either side of Harris and Parker.

"Piss off, Reynolds," Harris snarled. "This ain't got nothing to do with you."

"Oh, but it has, old chap, since these are me mates...and I can't have a Neanderthal like you ruffing 'em up." For a moment Harris simply glared at him, unsure what to say. Smiling serenely, Reynolds pressed on. "I'd push off, if I was you."

"Bollocks!"

Shrugging, Reynolds sighed. "Suit yourself." Taking a quick step forward he reached out and, to Tom's mind, rather gently pushed both Harris and Parker simultaneously in the chest. Unbeknown to any of them, two smaller boys had quietly crouched behind the legs of Harris and Parker, and so even Reynolds' small shove was enough to topple them over. Landing heavily on their backs both cried out in shock and pain as the wind was knocked from them. Reynolds' two accomplices, well practiced in such a manoeuvre, were up and running within seconds, long before either Harris or Parker comprehended what had happened.

As Reynolds and his gang laughed heartily, Tom and JP stared dumbfounded at the floundering bullies. The commotion finally attracted Blackwell's attention.

"Everything alright back there?" the teacher enquired as the two boys finally scrambled to their feet.

"Yes Sir," Reynolds shouted back. "Harris just fell over, Sir."

"And Parker?"

Reynolds just smiled and shrugged once more. Seeing no obvious trouble, Blackwell didn't reply, but nonetheless continued to glance frequently in their general direction.

Fists clenched at his sides, Harris was near beside himself with rage. "You're *dead*, Reynolds, you and your –"

"Oh change the record," the taller boy interrupted with an air of apparent apathy. "Can't you come up with anything more original than *"you're dead Reynolds"*. I know you're stupid, Harris, but even I'd given you more credit than that."

Harris pulled his arm back to strike but Parker grabbed him before any blow fell.

Smiling, Reynolds thrust his own face to within inches of Harris'. "Remember, fat boy, *I'm* not the one who'll be expelled for stepping out of line again. You wanna take me on, well just try it, or are ya just scared?"

For a second, Tom thought Reynolds' taunting had worked. Seemingly blinded by anger, Harris struggled in Parker's grip desperate to attack the older boy, who stood calmly waiting.

"Harris!" Blackwell's voice boomed out. "Move away. Now!"

Hesitating for only a second, Harris suddenly regained control and stopped struggling. Shrugging Parker off, he stepped back a couple of feet. Reynolds continued to smile smugly at him, their eyes never leaving each other.

"You too Reynolds," Blackwell continued firmly. "I don't want to see you two near each other for the rest of the break. Clear?"

"Yes Sir," Reynolds replied calmly, walking away. With a slight nod he indicated Tom and JP should follow him.

Strolling casually towards a shabby wooden bench in the far corner of the playground, Reynolds sent Barron on ahead to clear off the current occupants. Taking the now vacated seat, he motioned for Tom to sit beside him. Osborne, Barron and JP stood a little way off, watching.

"So then, Devlin," Reynolds began pleasantly. "Are you going to join my gang then?"

Slightly taken aback, Tom at first didn't reply. Seeing his hesitation, Reynolds ran his hand through his sandy hair and directed his gaze at JP.

"Wilson's already signed up, haven't you?" Looking up, Tom caught his friends stare; his replying slight nod, obvious confirmation. Still unsure, Tom remained silent...*things were going too fast.*

"Now listen, old bean," Reynolds said, throwing a

companionable arm across Tom's shoulders. "I saved you from Harris just now, didn't I?"

"Aye," Tom allowed guardedly.

"Well then? That's what mates are for, eh? You become one of us and you'll never 'ave to worry about that fat git again. As it was the stupid bugger nearly got himself kicked out of school today...if it hadn't been for Parker stopping him. I wouldn't 'ave retaliated if he'd hit me, and with all those witnesses, Harris' *unprovoked* attack would've been the end of him."

"Oh."

"You see? So, you help me and I'll help you...between us we can come up with a plan to get rid of Harris for good, but you've got to be in me gang first. What do you say?"

Scared of what he was potentially letting himself in for, but nonetheless conscious he didn't really seem to have a choice, Tom finally nodded. "Okay."

Reynolds beamed. "Good man. Harris won't touch you now; that's one of our rules. Lugsie and Eddie will spread the word that you're in, won't ya?"

Both boys nodded. "Sure."

JP said nothing but continued to look apprehensive.

In the distance the end of lunch break bell was sounding. Instantly the screaming, chaotic mass of school children began to disintegrate and orderly lines of year classes started to form up. Teachers similarly began to emerge from the main building, chatting together and heading for their respective classes.

"Come on, we'd better go." Reynolds said, standing.

Tom stood too, and as a group they ambled towards the coalescing lines. "We'll see you tomorrow then, to sort out your initiation test," he added as Tom and JP joined the end of their class. "Can't be in the gang unless you pass the test."

Tom frowned. "Tomorrow? But it's Saturday?"

"So?"

Slightly confused, the meaning of Reynolds' words suddenly registered. "What do you mean by a test?"

Grinning, Reynolds tapped the side of his nose knowingly. "You'll see. And also, you need to tell me a secret; a good one mind or again you can't be in."

"Why?"

"Insurance. If you ever cross us, I'll grass you up." His tone was still pleasant and friendly, but Tom nevertheless detected the clear threat underlying the remark.

"Reynolds!" a man's voice shouted from across the playground. "You and those others get to your own classes immediately, or you'll be standing outside the Headmaster's Office for the rest of the afternoon."

Muttering something unintelligible, Reynolds cuffed Eddie Barron lightly about the head and ran in the direction of his class line up. "See ya," he called without looking back. Barron and Osborne followed closely without giving Tom or JP a second glance.

Before Tom had a chance to say anything to JP, Mr Blackwell appeared striding purposefully down the line, firmly chastising anyone not facing front, or out of place.

"Jesus, what have we done?" Tom whispered, more to himself than anyone else, when the teacher had passed.

JP shrugged. "Whatever it takes man, whatever it takes."

Tom nodded soberly. As their class began to file in towards the main building, Tom glanced at his friend and smiled dryly. "I bet I know what your secret's going to be?"

Half smiling, JP said nothing, and continued to stare straight ahead.

"Tom," Keira said re-entering the kitchen, a slightly amused expression upon her face. "You've got some visitors. Looking up from his unfinished letter to Cathleen Kearney, Tom was still surprised, despite everything that had happened the day before, to see JP and Charlie Reynolds follow his aunt into the small room. "You should have said your friends were coming over," Keira continued. "I'd have gotten some cakes in."

"Ah, I forgot." Tom lied. "Sorry."

"Well, never mind, but do tell me next time." Turning to regard her guests she added, "Do come in boys. Would you like a drink, or something to eat? It'll have to be a biscuit I'm afraid since *someone* didn't tell me you were coming."

JP smiled shyly at the weak joke and simply shook his head.

"Nah, that's alright, Mrs McDonagh," Reynolds replied confidently. "We just wanted to see if Dev –

Tom wanted to come out?"

Glancing at her nephew, Keira was a little surprised when he didn't respond immediately and looked away, seemingly uncomfortable. Regarding him quizzically, a slight suspicion began to surface. "Tom?"

"Huh? Oh, aye," he stammered, still refusing to meet her gaze. "If that's okay?"

For a moment she hesitated.

"Of course it is," Derek McDonagh interjected, folding the newspaper he had been reading and looking up. "But where're you boys going?"

"Just to the park, you know, for a kick about." Reynolds answered quickly. "We're going to meet some mates there."

For some inexplicable reason Keira suspected that the smiling, fair-haired youth was lying.

"Well, sounds like a great idea to me," Derek continued, reaching for the teapot. "Do you good to get some air, Tom. Just make sure you're back for lunch, mind. Your aunt wants to go to Greenwich this afternoon and we don't want to be late. It's getting darker earlier in the evenings now."

Keira looked across at her husband as Tom stood, scraping his chair loudly on the tiled, kitchen floor.

"I won't." Heading for the hallway, JP and Reynolds turned and followed.

"I'd better see them out," Keira said, also standing.

"Oh, leave the boy be," Derek answered, sipping his tea and gesturing for her to sit down. "You don't have to mother him, Keira. Tom's big enough to shut the front door by himself."

"I wasn't *mothering* him," she retorted crossly, clearly offended by the accusation. "And how dare you —"

"Seems like they're 'aving a bit of a barney?" Reynolds observed as Tom shut the door and joined them outside the house. Before he had a chance to reply, Reynolds had turned right and started to saunter towards the end of Elsenham Road. "Come on, the others are waiting."

Walking beside JP, Tom looked across to his friend and said, "How did you know where I lived?"

"I didn't. But Charlie did."

Overhearing their exchange, Reynolds looked back over his shoulder. "Nothing to it really. There's a big cabinet in your aunt's office at school and inside they've got a folder for each of us. Lots of really interesting dirt, you know reports from the teachers, plus the usual stuff like addresses and such. I was in there on my own the other day, waiting to see Monty. 'e was busy on the phone, so seeing as your aunt wasn't about, I had a good look inside." The final sentence was said with a wicked grin.

Shocked, Tom couldn't believe anyone would have the audacity to rummage through school files, but wisely kept his opinions to himself.

At the corner, Osborne and Barron were lounging indifferently against the end of terrace retaining wall. With only a cursory acknowledgement towards Tom and JP, they fell into step behind Reynolds, who, turning left led them into Dersingham Avenue. Quickly crossing to the opposite side, they passed a series of small, local shops including a butcher's, several grocers' and a hardware store. The final shop in the line was an old shoe repairer's, and Tom always found the sweet, pungent smell of glue, resin and leather from within strangely alluring. Next to the cobbler's, a narrow road branched off to the right, leading steeply downhill and directly to the local park.

When Reynolds ignored the turning and carried straight on, Tom held back and called out. "Ah, Charlie...I thought we're going to the park?" Pointing towards the turn off, he added unnecessarily, "It's that way."

Reynolds glanced at Osborne and Barron, raising his eyes expressively before addressing Tom. "Listen, Devlin" he began slowly. "We ain't going to the park...I said that just to get you out of the house."

"Okay, so where are we going then?"

"Ilford."

"Ilford? But why? What's the point – "

"Look. You and Wilson said you wanna be in the gang, right?" After both had nodded in reply, Reynolds added, "Then we're going to Ilford, for your initiation test, see. Now come on." Without waiting for a reply he marched off. Resigned to the inevitable, Tom reluctantly followed.

After about ten minutes, Reynolds unexpectedly stopped. Before them Dersingham Avenue continued on, stretching into the distance straight and long for perhaps a further half mile. "Who fancies a game of 'Knock Down Ginger' then?" he asked offhandedly.

"Yeah, great idea," Barron replied enthusiastically. "You up for it Lugsie?"

"Sure…what about you Devlin?" Osborne was looking directly at Tom, who frowned visibly, unsure what he meant.

Reynolds laughed. "Blimey, I don't reckon he knows what you're on about. Go on, Lugsie, show 'im."

Sneering in obvious contempt, Osborne glanced around quickly before calmly walking up the short, front garden path of the nearest house. Grinning, Reynolds nudged Barron and still watching Tom and JP, began to slowly sidle away. Tom was about to ask JP if he knew what was happening when a loud banging on the door resounded. A second later Osborne reappeared, sprinting towards them.

"Leg it!" he shouted, speeding past. Instantly Reynolds and Barron followed, whooping with delight. Bewildered, Tom stood routed to the spot.

"Come on, man," JP encouraged, forcefully tugging his arm.

From the house a clearly irate, heavily set woman of middle years emerged. "Oi! Come 'ere you little sods," she shouted, catching sight of the boys and lurching angrily towards them.

Tom ran.

"Should 'ave seen his face," Osborne said a few

minutes later, hands on hips and breathing hard. "Like a littl' frightened rabbit 'e was…it was well funny." Tom scowled, looking down and refusing to be drawn.

As a group they had run on a couple of hundred yards before stopping to rest and catch their breath. Behind them, the offended housewife was still gesticulating angrily, although her words were drowned out by the distance and passing traffic.

"That was a good one, Lugsie…well done." Reynolds said with a strained smile. Motioning them to carry on, he walked next to Tom and JP. "Sometimes," he began conversationally, "we 'ave a real laugh and tie some string to the door knockers of two houses. Then when you bang on the doors, at the same time mind, they can't open them at all!"

For Tom, this sounded truly distasteful; not for the first time did he wonder what he was doing here. Uncomfortable with the conversation, he tried to change the subject.

"Charlie, you know you said I had to tell you a secret, well, I'm not sure – "

"Oh, don't worry about that now, old man." Reynolds interrupted. "You can tell me on Monday at school. You've got to get through the test first."

"So, what do we have to do for that then?"

Reynolds simply turned to him and smiled. "All in good time…you'll find out soon enough."

Passing a horse drawn milk float parked at the side of the road, Reynolds unexpectedly cast about furtively. The driver was no where to be seen. In an instant he had helped himself to a couple of pints, and unconcerned handed them around as they continued to walk calmly along the pavement. Despite his inward reluctance, Tom felt compelled to accept his share, and it was only after Barron and Osborne had deliberately thrown the empty glass bottles against a wall that panic took hold, and he was the first to flight. Behind, the sounds of his companions' laughter rang loudly in his ears.

"Well, there it is." Reynolds said pointing. "Your initiation test." Tom shook his head, not understanding.

Leaning casually against the kerbside safety railings, Reynolds, Barron and Osborne all were smiling knowingly. Behind them along the busy Ilford Lane thoroughfare, a number 693 Trolleybus rumbled slowly passed, followed by numerous trucks and other automobile traffic.

"There...look." Reynolds reiterated, his arm still outstretched and seemly exasperated.

Together Tom and JP turned to follow his direction. Before them a wide pavement continued in either direction, crowded with Saturday shoppers hurrying about their business under leaden, overcast skies. Directly opposite and through the shoppers, was a large open frontage building, above which in large red letters over a white background, were the words 'Pioneer Market.' Pointing towards to the market entrance, Reynolds' meaning became clear.

"We call it the 'lucky dip', he explained cordially. "On

account of it being so easy. You should thank me really, Eddie's test was ten times worse than this, wasn't it mate?"

"Yeah...I real – "

"What do we have to do?" JP interrupted cautiously.

Reynolds smiled. "Simple. Go into the market and nick me something that I'd like."

"Nick? You mean steal?" Tom voiced, taken aback. "No way! We're not doing that...what if we get caught, or someone – "

Without warning Reynolds sprang from the railing and grabbed Tom by the collar. "Listen Devlin," he began, his eyes flashing dangerously. "You'll do it if you wanna be in my gang. You gotta prove yourself...if you can't, then sod off!" Shocked by the suddenness and intensity of his anger, Tom unconsciously took a step back, only to collide with a passing woman pushing a pram. Momentarily distracted by the woman's protests, Tom at first didn't register that Reynolds was speaking again, unnervingly calm once more.

"... and besides, you don't want everyone at school to know you're chicken!"

An uncomfortable silence developed. Tom felt his ears burning as emotions stirred within him.

"I'll go," JP finally said quietly. "What do you want me to get, Charlie?"

"Ah, that's part of the test. It's gotta be something I'd want. Nothing stupid, or too easy like an apple...something useful. And remember, if you get caught, you've failed. Understand?"

Nodding, JP turned to go, his eyes briefly connecting with Tom's. Neither had anything further to say.

"Look, 'ere 'e comes." Eddie Barron said pointing. For ten minutes they had waited outside the Ilford's Pioneer Market, Reynolds and his two friends chatting and larking around, whilst Tom had stood to one side, moodily silent. Glancing up, Tom saw JP walking slowly towards them, head bowed and hands in pockets.

"Well?" Reynolds asked as the smaller boy came to stand before them. "How did you get on?" For a second JP didn't react and simply continued to stare expressionlessly at him. Then, with deliberate slowness he removed his right hand, and opening his palm, revealed a finely crafted, wooden hilted pen-knife. "Wow!" Reynolds exclaimed snatching the knife as Barron and Osborne crowded round. "It looks like one of them army ones, you know with all the different blades and gadgets."

"It is," JP answered, again almost imperceptibly. "There's a hardware stall inside, and it had lots of army stuff on it as well."

Tom had not moved, but nonetheless continued to watch closely.

Grinning, Reynolds pocketed the pen-knife and slapped JP on the shoulder. "Well done, Wilson. That's excellent. You've passed the initiation test and are in. Right lads?" Barron and Osborne both nodded their agreement. Despite his earlier discomfort, JP couldn't help but smile in return. All eyes turned to Tom.

"Go on then," Reynolds said, suddenly serious. "Get us something good too."

Stepping cautiously through the large, open-fronted entrance, Tom was at once struck by the noise and variety of smells emanating from the indoor market. The building itself was huge, and everywhere Tom looked traders' stalls were packed tightly together in neat, orderly lines. The aisles formed between the parallel stalls heaved with shoppers, many laden with heavy bags, which only added to the overcrowding.

Selecting an aisle at random, Tom meandered slowly through the crowds, endeavouring to study each passing stall whilst trying to avoid being crushed in the process. To his disappointment, the majority of traders were selling fruit and vegetables, or textiles and clothes; with little to hold his interest, Tom didn't linger long. At the end of the aisle, he turned the corner and began walking back up the next one, passing first a fish monger's and then a toy stall. Despite its potential appeal, Tom quickly moved on, intimidated by the intense, watchful stare of the stall owner.

Continuing to explore the market, Tom soon found the hardware stall JP had referred to. For a few moments he paused to gaze at the knives, drills and other tools on display. Without warning he was unceremoniously shoved aside by a broad-shouldered man, impatient to inspect the market trader's goods. Staggering slightly, Tom inadvertently bumped into the stall's owner who had eagerly come over to converse with his potential customer.

"Hey, watch it!" the trader growled, pushing Tom away. Wide-eyed with fright, Tom fled into the crowd, his heart racing.

After his second circuit, the first feelings of panic began to surface in Tom's mind. There were too many people; too many watchful eyes. He knew he'd been inside the market for sometime now, and began to fear that Reynolds and the others would soon come in looking for him. But inwardly, Tom knew also that the heaving crowds were only an excuse; he just couldn't bring himself to steal. Desperately, he tried to think of some way out.

Wandering aimlessly, Tom slowly retraced his steps, deep in thought and oblivious to the swirling maelstrom around him. After a few minutes he found himself once more in the central area, where a small, open-air café was situated. Standing by the entrance, he allowed the delicious smells of fried bacon and onions to wash over him. Closing his eyes, Tom breathed deeply, savouring the intoxicating aroma...and in an instant the answer came. He didn't need to steal anything! With the money that Declan Kennedy had given him, all he had to do was buy something Reynolds would like, and simply say he'd stolen it. Reynolds would be none the wiser and in any case, could never prove otherwise. Tom grinned. It was perfect.

"What'll it be, Son?" the portly café owner asked as Tom, standing on tiptoe, tried to peer over the high serving counter.

"Ah...how much are the bacon rolls?"

"Sixpence."

"And the sausages, the big ones?"

Without turning the man thumbed over his shoulder.

"All the prices are on the chalk board, lad. Now 'urry up, I ain't got all day."

"Oh, right...sorry." For a minute Tom made a pretence of studying the board. "Can I have five large sausage sandwiches please...no, ah sorry make that three, and two bacon rolls.

The café owner eyed Tom shrewdly. "You sure?"

Tom nodded.

"And you got the money?"

"Aye," Tom said patting the outside of his coat pocket. "My Mam give it to me to buy lunch."

Apparently satisfied the man turned to deal with Tom's order. For some reason the lie had come too readily, and Tom felt a stab of guilt as he again wrestled with his conscience.

"You want sauce and onions with this lot?" the owner called out, disturbing his thoughts.

"Please." Smiling inwardly, Tom couldn't help but congratulate himself. The plan was brilliant.

After another minute the owner returned, a large white paper bag in his hands. "There you go, Son" he said, placing the bag on the counter. That'll be four shillings."

Tom reached inside his coat...and felt his stomach contract. The envelop with Declan Kennedy's five pound note was not there. Frantically he searched the other pocket and then, in growing desperation, his trousers. His mind racing, Tom knew the envelope had been in his inside coat pocket that morning...

"Don't mess me 'bout, lad." The café owner growled ominously, suspecting some ruse. "You owe me four shillings."

"I'm not!" Tom said, his voice sounding suddenly shrill. "I can't find my money. It's gone."

Inhaling deeply the owner frowned cynically, clearly not believing a word. "Gone or not, I can't put 'em back, not with the onions and all added."

"But – "

"No 'buts'...you'll come with me and we'll go see your Mum...she can then pay up what you owe."

Tom panicked. Without thinking he snatched the bag from the counter and ran.

"Oi! Stop!" the man hollered behind him. "Someone stop that boy!"

Weaving left and right, Tom evaded several attempts from other customers to apprehend him. But the disturbance was attracting attention, and at the café entrance a huge man in a grocer's apron appeared, blocking his path. Unable to stop, Tom careered into him and was held firm.

"Thanks Norm," the owner said approaching and grasping Tom's arm, none too gently.

"No problem. I heard the ruckus and thought some 'ittle toe rag was trying to do a bunk again."

"Yeah. Could you watch the place for a minute? I'm gonna to take 'im to the Station."

"Sure, but I've just seen a copper walking through the market...if you hurry you'll save yourself a job."

As the two men talked, Tom tried to squirm free but was held firmly in a vice-like grip.

"Stop fidgeting, you!" he was warned crossly, with a savage shake. "Now, c'mon before I lose my temper."

Half dragged, Tom was led through the crowded market, his face flushed with embarrassment from so many watching eyes. He felt his throat constricting as tears began to fall.

"Mister, I'm sorry," he said sobbed quietly, looking up at the angry trader. "I really have lost my money...I don't know why – "

"Shut up. You save your hard luck story for...ah, Officer, may I have a word?"

Glancing round Tom's face fell. Standing before them, tall and grim faced was a policeman.

19
DELIVERANCE

Weeks passed.

October came and went, and as if mirroring the progressive shortening of days, as November dragged on Tom's mood grew increasingly despondent. At first Keira and Derek put this down to their enforced punishment, following the incident in Ilford's Pioneer Market. Only the fortuitous intervention of the McDonagh's friend, Ted Burrows, had resulted in him receiving just a warning, rather than a more severe punishment. As it was, the price of Burrows' intercession with his ex-colleagues was banning Tom from ever entering his house in the future. As such, and in one swift stroke, the friendship Keira had hoped to encourage between Tom and their daughter, Alice, died before it began.

Despite her relief in the police's leniency, Keira McDonagh was nonetheless incensed by Tom's behaviour and had strictly curtailed his freedom. She didn't accept his argument that he had owned five pounds, let alone subsequently lost it. Although, as Tom later did admit to himself, that wasn't really the point. He had taken (he couldn't quite bring himself to use the word 'steal') the bag himself, and with, albeit in a moment of panic, no intention of paying for it.

Throughout October, Tom had been confined to the house in the evenings, and prohibited from having anyone over. Similarly, at weekends he wasn't allowed to go out on his own, and at the end of each school day, had to report immediately to Keira's office, and wait there until she was ready to escort him home. Tom kept to himself the fact that he didn't have any friends, and was secretly glad to walk home with his aunt every day, thereby avoiding the likes of Harris and his gang. However, no punishment the McDonagh's could impose would ever match the direst consequence of being caught that day; the loss of his only true friend, JP.

Having failed the 'initiation test', Reynolds had effectively shunned Tom. Whilst not openly hostile, the older boy had nonetheless made it clear that neither he, nor any of his gang would have anything more to do with him. JP, torn between his friendship for Tom, and his desire to be accepted (and thereby protected) by a faction within the school's social makeup, had reluctantly chosen the latter. Tom was, to all intents and purposes, on his own. He spent most days sitting by himself in class, and at break times stayed close to the duty teacher, or within view of Mr Montgomery's window, anxious to avoid encountering Harris, Parker and the others. On rare occasions, he did manage to snatch fleeting conversations with JP, when they believed no one else was watching, but aside from that, Tom was desperately unhappy. Mr Blackwell, and indeed every other teacher at Manor School, seemed oblivious to his plight.

The only positive aspect of Tom's life throughout those dark, cold, pre-Christmas months, was the news from home. The weekly letters from his Gran, and occasional ones from Cathleen, became increasingly optimistic. His mother's health was improving, and Erin's illness was no longer a cause for grave concern. She was growing stronger day by day, and by the third week in October, Tom received his first, short, sketchily written letter from Erin herself. From then on, her letters arrived with increasing frequency and length. For the first time Tom dared entertain the hope that his enforced separation may be coming to an end.

*

In the first week of December, the weather turned bitter. Biting easterly winds swept inland from Northern Europe. Temperatures plummeted virtually overnight to well below freezing, and driving, icy rain made travel on foot almost unbearable. At the same time, Keira became ill with a severe cold, and was forced by her husband to stay at home to recover. Consequently, for the first time in weeks Tom found himself having to walk to and from school on his own each day. As he feared, it wasn't long before Harris again realised he was once again vulnerable, and twice during the week he had been chased, but thankfully not caught, on the way home. Lying in bed awake each night, Tom became resigned to the inevitable...another encounter with Harris was simply just a matter of time.

By Thursday the stress of avoiding Harris and his gang, coupled with his mounting loneliness at school, became too much to bear. Feigning illness, Tom tried to persuade Keira he was too unwell to go in. Despite initially appearing sympathetic, his aunt's suspicions were soon aroused. Never comfortable with lying, Tom eventually conceded that his sudden 'illness' probably wasn't as bad as he had first thought.

Despondent, Tom trudged slowly through the familiar, terraced streets towards Manor Park School. He knew he was already late (it was already after nine) following his illness ploy earlier, and as such felt no inclination to hurry. Inwardly he scoffed at the thought of getting a 'black mark' in the register; that was the least of his worries.

Head bowed and wrapped up tightly against the cold, Tom was virtually at the school gates before he realised something was amiss. For a moment he simply stopped and stared; across the street the playground was still full of children, running and playing noisily. Frowning, he wondered way the bell hadn't rung; even conservatively he considered it must be at least half past nine by now.

Smiling ironically at his apparent good fortune, Tom crossed the road and entered the playground via the main gate; at least he wouldn't get that black mark now. Continuing to keep his head down, he made his way through the congested playground, manoeuvring skilfully around the various ball or chase games going on. Here and there small knots of parents remained, in spite of the cold, chatting in close huddles and equally curious at the morning's unusual events. Similarly avoiding these groups, Tom headed towards the main building entrance, keen to seek shelter from the raw wind.

"Tom!"

Turning at the sound of his name, Tom saw JP running and waving towards him. Glancing nervously around, Tom waited.

"I've been calling you for ages, didn't you hear me?" JP's laboured breathing steamed vividly in the cold air.

Tom shook his head, distracted and continuing to look fleetingly about.

As if reading his mind, JP continued, "Don't worry, man, there's no one around. I've not seen..." unexpectedly the boy paused, closed his eyes, and a second later sneezed heavily.

"Bless you." Tom said instinctively, and regarding him closely for the first time.

"Thanks."

"You look awful." He added, trying not to stare at his friend's red-rimmed eyes and slightly pale complexion. "Are you feeling alright?"

JP smiled and sniffed loudly. "Felt better, man....not that me Mum would let us stay off school though."

Tom smiled back. "Aye, I know what you mean."

Before JP could ask what he meant, the doors to the main school entrance opened and Mrs Phelps, stern and unsmiling, marched out, followed by a number of other grim faced teachers. No bell had rung, but pupils and parents alike stopped what they were doing to watch the grave procession.

JP nudged Tom. "Something's up." Tom only nodded slightly in reply, his eyes fixed on the thin, severe looking Head of Year.

Standing in the centre of the playground, Mrs Phelps dramatically swept her intimidating gaze across the assembled, expectant faces. A cowed silence descended, broken only by the incessant howl of the wind. A few seconds ticked by.

"All classes are to report to the main hall immediately!" she finally shouted, her voice booming and making Tom jump slightly. "The first lesson this morning has been cancelled for all classes. The Headmaster has an important announcement to make, and will address you in the hall shortly."

For a moment nobody moved; like hundreds of his fellow pupils Tom was intrigued as to what was going on.

"Do you think I'm standing out here for the fun of it!" Phelps roared angrily. "The main hall. Now!"

Suddenly spurred into action, the entire school, en-masse, ran for the main entrance. The ensuing scramble for the doors was predictably chaotic, despite the best efforts of the accompanying staff to salvage a degree of order.

Hands on hips, her iron-grey hair flaring uncontrollably in the wind, Mrs Phelps looked on irritably, ignoring all attempts from interested parents to engage her in conversation.

From a side entrance to the hall, Mr Montgomery appeared, grim faced and clearly unhappy. Approaching the stage, he climbed the short flight of steps and quickly took his seat behind a table, previously placed there for his use.

Tom, along with the rest of the school, had been in the hall for at least twenty minutes and the noise from the speculating chatter was almost deafening. Shouting to make himself heard, JP leant across to him and asked, for what was probably the third time, what he thought had happened. Shaking his head, Tom shrugged and indicated that they should watch the Headmaster.

Momentarily removing his glasses, Montgomery began meticulously polishing them on a handkerchief, staring at the table as if deep in thought. Tom watched as Mrs Phelps also emerged from the side entrance and went to join him on the stage. Sitting beside the Headmaster she inclined her head, apparently trying to say something, but was unceremoniously waved away. Finally replacing his glasses, Montgomery looked meaningfully across the stage towards Mr Blackwell and the other hovering teachers, and nodded once.

Standing up straight, Blackwell returned the gesture and turned to face the assembled classes. "Right you lot," he shouted loudly. "Settle down, now. The Headmaster has something to say to you all."

Within seconds silence descended over the hall.

"Last night," Montgomery began without preamble, "a serious incident occurred at this school. An incident, the like of which has never occurred in our entire history." Pausing for effect, he let the words sink in. Tom swallowed involuntarily; all around him there was a heightened, almost tangible, nervous excitement in the air.

"At 9 pm, the police called to my house and reported that the school had been broken into. Apparently a passer by had called the Police after hearing breaking glass, and seeing lights being switched on and off in the main building. To my shock, when I arrived, I found my office, as well as Mrs McDonagh's ransacked. But – " and again the Headmaster paused briefly, "the culprits to this scandalous and shameful act had, thankfully, also been apprehended."

Unexpectedly, Montgomery stood and came to stand in front of the table. "It is with great sorrow that I must inform you that those same individuals who so blatantly placed their own selfish needs above all others...were pupils at this school."

An audible gasp resounded throughout the hall. JP nudged Tom. "Who do you – "

"By their wilful disregard and rejection of the principles we cherish and strive to achieve here at Manor Park, they have not only disgraced themselves, but betrayed you all also." Returning to his seat, he glanced briefly at Mrs Phelps before continuing to address the assembly. "This morning, I have summoned and discussed the actions of these pupils with their respective parents. Why they broke into the school is not your concern, but, and I'm sure each and every one of you would agree, their actions can not be tolerated. I am, therefore, informing you that, and with immediate effect, the following pupils have been permanently expelled from our school: Edward Barron, Robert Harris, Richard Jennings, Alan Osborne, Ben Parker and Charles Reynolds. Furthermore, I am assured that the police intend to prosecute these boys, following their despicable act, and I would advise any of you with outside school relationships with them to end such associations."

Leaning back in his chair, Mr Montgomery seemed to relax slightly. "That is all. Please follow your form teachers back to class...and in an orderly fashion!"

Predictably, everybody stood and starting talking at once.

"Quietly, if you please!" Phelps shouted and was universally ignored.

It took Tom nearly ten minutes to finally make it back to the classroom. The buzz of conversation around him was unsurprisingly dominated by disbelief, speculation, and in the way children often behave when someone else is in trouble, unashamed glee. Sitting at his usual desk near the front, Tom was secretly heartened when, unasked for, JP naturally appeared to join him.

"Alright now, the fun's over." Mr Blackwell said, entering last and closing the door behind him. "Hurry up and sit down, we've lost half the morning already."

As the class settled, Blackwell sat behind his desk and opened the register. Tom looked across at JP. "I think I'm still dreaming."

JP smiled. "Yeah, I know what you mean, man...it seems too good to be true."

"Austin?" Blackwell's voice resounded in the background, along with the customary 'Sir' reply a second later.

"But it is true." Tom persisted. "You realise what this means? We're free, JP. Harris, Reynolds, all of them...they're gone – "

"Cooper?"

"Sir."

JP nodded but didn't reply, staring off into space, lost in thought.

"God only knows why they were all together, seeing as they hated each other." Tom said, thoughtfully.

"Davis?"

"Sir."

"Probably some sort of dare?" he added, theorising.

"Devlin? Devlin! Pay attention boy."

"Sorry Sir."

"Well?" Blackwell added, an eyebrow raised.

"Well what, Sir?"

"Are you here?"

Tom grinned. "Yes Sir!"

"Good." As he looked back to the register, Tom noticed a slight smile hovering upon the teacher's lips. "Foster?"

"Sir."

Tom smiled inwardly. It seemed the expulsion in one fell stroke of so many trouble makers from the school had lifted not only the pupils' spirits.

Not for the first time that week, Tom ran home as fast as he could, but unlike the fearful anxiety of before, now he was filled with thrilled optimism. A great, oppressive weight had been lifted. Harris and his fellow bullies were finally gone. With Reynolds' expulsion, JP was no longer under his sway, and they were both free to resume their friendship. Those few, minor members of each gang that still remained at school were, to Tom's mind, irrelevant. All were weak minded individuals that without the coercive influence and intimidation of Harris and Reynolds would, likely as not, simply fade away into the background. No longer would he have to constantly watch over his shoulder, or pry into darkened shadows, fearful of reprisals.

Desperate to tell Keira the news, Tom sped down terraced street after terraced street, oblivious to both the cold and the numerous looks he received from passers by. Only when he reached the junction of Browning Road and Elsenham Road, did he finally slow to a walk, gasping for breath. Chest aching as the frigid air coursed through his lungs, Tom entered the small plum orchard and strolled happily along the narrow gravel trackway towards the opposite end. On either side neat rows of fruit trees stood like solitary sentries, their leafless branches thrashing violently in the strong breeze.

From the orchard he passed quickly through the new building works, waving pleasantly at several workmen, themselves closely wrapped against the icy chill. Breaking into a jog once again, within minutes he was home. Knocking loudly on the front door, an uncontrolled grin spread across his face as heavy footsteps approached from within.

"Ah Tom," Derek McDonagh said opening the door, a strange knowing look upon his face. "I'm glad you're back…your aunt wants a quick word."

"Thanks." Tom replied, eagerly pushing past him, and sprinting down the hallway.

"She's in the living room," he heard Derek call out unnecessarily from behind.

"Aunt Keira!" Tom cried bursting into the small room. "You won't believe what's – "

Stunned, Tom stopped dead and stared.

"Hello Tom," a familiar figure said smiling and rising from his seat. Holding an outstretched hand before him, Declan Kennedy added, "It's good to see you again."

Tomorrow. Tom thought silently, staring at his half eaten cereal and still not quite believing it. *I'm finally going home tomorrow.*

"Tom," Keira said briskly, looking over his shoulder as she busied herself about the small kitchen. "*Will* you hurry up? I told you earlier we mustn't be late this morning."

Alone at the breakfast table, Tom was stirred into renewed interest towards the bowl's contents. As usual Derek had already left for work, and Declan, apparently, was still in bed, having stayed up late into the night talking with the McDonaghs. Despite still feeling unwell, Keira had insisted on going into school today. Her argument, following Tom's news of the expulsions, that urgent administrative issues had to be addressed in addition to those now resulting from this being his last day, even Derek found hard to counter.

Smiling to himself, Tom's mind began to wander…he couldn't wait to tell JP his news. His joy however was quickly tinged with a sudden sadness at the prospect of having to leave his one and only true friend.

"I mean it young man. Get a move on!" Keira growled.

With a jolt, any such melancholy feelings evaporated. Wolfing down the last of his breakfast, Tom twisted round in his chair, passing the empty bowl back to his aunt. A curt nod was the only thanks received. Subduing a belch, Tom stood and headed for the hallway to fetch his coat, his spirits once again high with expectation.

"So, I understand you'll be leaving us after today?" Mr Montgomery said from behind his desk fixing Tom with an intimidating stare.

Tom nodded nervously, but declined to speak.

Standing beside Keira in the Headmaster's office, and trying desperately not to fidget, Tom wished for the ordeal to be over. Morning lessons had already started, but at Keira's insistence, they had gone to see Mr Montgomery immediately upon arriving at school. For twenty minutes Tom had waited alone in her office as they had met privately; the inevitable summons hanging over his head like the Sword of Damocles.

"Your aunt tells me that your Mother's health is much improved."

Again Tom nodded. "Yes Sir."

"And you're leaving tomorrow morning...quite a story you'll have to tell when you get back home!"

Unsure how to reply, Tom once more decided to say nothing. For a moment an uncomfortable silence developed in the room.

"Hmm. Well, brief as it's been, Devlin, I hope your time here has taught you something," Montgomery still regarded Tom intently, clearly implying more than he was actually saying.

"It has Sir," Tom answered carefully.

"Good." Apparently satisfied, the Headmaster cleared his throat. "Return to class now, and ask Mr Blackwell if he could spare a moment. Mrs McDonagh, if you would be so kind, could you wait a while longer please?"

Grateful to be dismissed and escape the scrutiny, Tom walked quickly back to Mr Blackwell's classroom. Entering, he apologised for being late and informed the willowy, fair-haired teacher of Mr Montgomery's request. Without hesitation, Blackwell departed, pausing only to issue dire warnings of retribution for any misdemeanours in his absence. It was only after he had closed the door, and Tom sought his seat, that the awful truth registered...Jerome Wilson was not in the room.

"Why the long face, Tom?" Derek asked later that evening. Unusually, they were sitting together in the McDonaghs' front room; Keira and Declan were still in the kitchen, clearing up after the evening meal. From Derek's new Phillips wireless, the soothing melody of a chamber music recital by the Catterall Quartet played softly in the background.

Relaxing in an armchair, Derek ran his finger slowly round the rim of a part filled tumbler of whiskey, watching Tom closely. "I thought you'd be looking forward to going home?" he added quietly.

On the carpet, Tom seemingly continued to concentrate on his game of stacking playing cards. "I am," he replied, head still bowed.

"Well, if you don't mind me saying, you don't look it." When Tom didn't answer, Derek sipped his drink thoughtfully. For a few minutes neither spoke. Outside the room faint traces of conversation drifted along the hallway from the kitchen.

"Tom," Derek began again, his tone serious enough for Tom to look up. "What's wrong? Has something happened at school again today?"

Sighing, Tom paused for a moment before nodding. "Aye, but it doesn't matter now..." his voice trailing off sadly. Derek said nothing, but continued regarding him closely. As the silence lengthened, Tom finally felt obliged to explain himself. "My friend wasn't in."

"Your friend?"

Again a nod. "Aye, my best friend, Jerome Wilson."

"Oh, well I'm sorry to – "

"Don't you see?" Tom interrupted, now slightly animated. "He doesn't know I'm leaving...I didn't get to say goodbye."

Tom's last morning in London dawned bright and clear. Sunlight, so long absent from the capital, streamed in through the partially opened curtains, illuminating the small bedroom with a golden glow. Lying on his side, facing the wall, Tom was in no hurry to get up. Sleep had been a long time coming the night before; too many memories and conflicting feelings had plagued him. Unsure as to when he had eventually fallen asleep, Tom knew nonetheless that it must have been late.

Yawning, he pulled the warm, comfortable blankets more tightly around himself and considered trying to go back to sleep; hunger finally drove him downstairs ten minutes later.

"Ah, it lives," Declan said with a smile as Tom, slightly jaded, entered the kitchen. Standing, he beckoned for him to take his chair at the table. "I'm glad you're up. Your aunt left strict instructions, and I was just coming to get you."

Registering that they were actually alone in the kitchen, Tom asked, "Where's everyone?"

Crossing to the fridge Declan retrieved the milk. "Derek's taken Keira into school for something or – "

"But it's Saturday?"

Declan shrugged. "I know, but that's how it is sometimes. Anyway, they won't be long, and *I'm* under orders to ensure you're dressed and ready to go when they get back. Now, what do you want for breakfast?"

Cramped in the back seat of Derek McDonagh's Austin 7, Tom tried not to fidget. Gazing out at the now familiar streets and passing landmarks, he felt a strange sense of loss to be finally leaving. Beside him Declan sat silently studying their train tickets, whilst in the front Keira was chatting quietly with her husband. They were heading for Euston Station and the first stage of Tom's homeward journey.

"There, that's it! No wait, sorry the next one." He heard Keira exclaim suddenly. Looking up he saw her pointing to a road off to the left.

"You sure?" Derek answered, slowing the Austin noticeably.

Keira hesitated for a moment. "Aye, Ruskin Road...that's it." Following her directions, Derek turned left. Tom looked at Declan questioningly who, infuriatingly, only raised an eyebrow and smiled.

Studying the uniform, terraced housing, Keira again pointed and said, "Pull over by that lamppost, Derek." As they slowed to a halt, she turned round to face Tom. "Tommy dear, do me a wee favour and knock on number forty three please, there's something there waiting for us."

"Sure." Stepping out onto the pavement, Tom obediently walked towards the front door. He had barely got half way before it was wrenched open and a grinning Jerome Wilson ran out to greet him. Dumbfounded, Tom just stared, speechless.

"Tom, I'm sorry but we really do need to go now." Keira repeated her request from a minute previously.

Still somewhat amazed, Tom continued to shake his head slightly in disbelief. Captivated, he had listened to JP's account of how his aunt, an hour or so before, had arrived and fleetingly explained his imminent departure. Apparently, having heard last night of his distress at not being able to say goodbye, Keira had gone into school earlier that morning to get JP's address. Although saddened at Tom's leaving, they were both pleased that they had had an opportunity to part properly.

"Tom, please now," Keira called more firmly from the waiting automobile.

Glancing back, Tom raised a hand in acknowledgement. "I'd better go," he said quietly.

JP nodded soberly. "Yeah, I know." Sighing, he added, "I'm gonna miss you, man."

Tom tried to smile but failed. "Aye, you too – but listen, we can write, and remember what your Dad just said about potentially coming over to visit next summer. You'll really love Ireland." As usual, Tom's natural optimism was striving to come to the fore.

JP nodded again, but remained sad looking. Unexpectedly he took a stride forward and hugged Tom fiercely. "Take care, man," he whispered close to Tom's ear. Caught off guard, Tom stiffened for a moment but quickly returned the gesture, albeit a little embarrassed. Stepping back, JP reached for something in his pocket. "Here, take this," he said handing Tom a folded piece of paper. "It's got my address on it."

Staring at it Tom kept his head bowed, not wanting to go but unable to think of anything meaningful to say.

"Jerome honey," a voice called softly from behind. Glancing round, Tom saw a black, slightly overweight woman in her early thirties smiling sympathetically from the doorway, but gesturing nonetheless for his friend to return.

"Your Mam?"

"Yeah. Listen, I'd better go...I'll see you around, Tom...take care." Without waiting for a reply, JP turned and walked slowly away towards his mother, his eyes watering. Unseen, Tom could only nod silently – nothing further needed to be said.

Staring miserably out of the Austin's window, Tom toyed absently with the paper, his thoughts wandering. From the front seat, Derek manoeuvred skilfully through the busy traffic on the Euston Road, heading for the main station entrance.

"What's on the note?" Declan asked gently, tapping his shoulder to attract Tom's attention.

"Huh?"

"In your hand...the piece of paper you're been playing with for ages. I assume it's a note of some kind?"

For a second Tom just stared at him. "Oh, aye. It's just my friend's address." Unfolding it for the first time, Tom silently studied the contents...and then unexpectedly laughed out loud.

"What's so funny?" Declan asked as Tom continued to chuckle. Handing over the note, Tom nodded appreciatively in fond memory.

Looking up, Declan shook his head, still puzzled.

"The name," Tom said still smiling. "Look at the name."

Declan glanced once more at the note and then handed it back at Tom. "I admit it's unusual, Tom," he said misreading the boy's meaning. "But that's no reason to make fun of him. Your friend can't help it if his parents called him Jerome Primrose Wilson, can he?"

*

Venturing a tentative smile, Tom closed his eyes

momentarily and allowed feelings of immense relief to flow over him. He was home.

"No sleeping now?" Declan teased, sitting beside him as the antiquated Lough Swilly bus swept by the Ballyfinan village sign. "We're nearly there."

Tom smiled broadly but kept his eyes closed. "I'm not...just relaxing."

It was Sunday, and the late afternoon sun, waning beyond Reachtain Mhór and the western Urris Hills, sent lengthening shadows across the main village street. Looking out once more through the grimy, mud splattered window, Tom's exhilaration soared. Familiar landmarks passed one after another: St Mary's Church; the narrow turning to the Kearneys' farmhouse; Dooley's Bar; Mrs Brennan's store. He really was home!

As the bus slowed noticeably, Tom eagerly scanned a small group of people waiting close to the single petrol pump in the Square; the traditional stopping point for the journey from Dunkeeny.

"Ballyfinan," the driver announced unnecessarily, steering the bus to a juddering halt adjacent to the garage. Tom was out of his seat and heading for the exit in seconds. Stepping onto the rutted tarmac, glistening and slick from recent rain, he looked around, suddenly and unexpectedly uncertain.

No one was there to meet him. Around him, other disembarking passengers pushed past, mingling in a confused mass with those waiting to board the bus, keen to get out of the cold. Across the street a few familiar figures walked uninterestedly by, but none sparing more than a cursory glance in his general direction.

Joining him, Declan rested a hand lightly on Tom's shoulder. "Come on," he said, sensing the boy's disappointment. "Let's get you home."

Collecting their cases, Declan led Tom across the Square, angling towards Cairn Lane. Behind them the departing bus made its slow, deliberate U-turn, and headed back up the High Street for the return journey to Dunkeeny.

At the bottom of the lane they paused, allowing a small group of Friesian cows to be driven into the Square. Acknowledging the nod of thanks from the young labourer at the rear, Declan nudged Tom, who had turned away and was staring into the distance, his arms folded across his chest.

"I bet you didn't see many of those in London?"

Tom smiled half-heartedly. "No, but I did see a tiger."

Declan raised an enquiring eyebrow and indicated that they should keep going. "Well you did now? You'll have to tell me about it sometime."

Side by side they entered Cairn Lane and began the steep ascent, Declan continuing to make light conversation. As they neared Quigley's Farm, Tom grew increasingly reserved and troubled. Attempts to draw him out failed, and eventually Declan was forced to accept his brooding silence. Even their brief, and unavoidable, trudge through the muddy, dishevelled farmyard did little to distract Tom from his reverie. The dogs, as usual lounging by the porch and bathing in the fading, watery sunshine, watched their passage intently.

Twenty yards from his home, but still hidden from the house by the tall bankside hedgerows and overhanging trees, Declan finally laid a hand on the boy's arm, stopping him.

"Tom," he began, regarding him closely, "Are you alright? You've been quiet for ages and seem, if you don't mind me saying, a wee bit distracted." Overhead a small gathering of rooks cawed raucously, settling within the bare tree branches for the evening roost. Gazing up at the restless birds, Tom said nothing.

Inhaling deeply, Declan was about to repeat his question when Tom turned to face him. "Do you...do you think Mam will be pleased to see me?"

"Of course she will. Why wouldn't she be?"

Tom looked at the ground, unwilling to meet the School Master's eye. "Well...she's probably heard stuff, you know, from Aunt Keira – "

"What 'stuff' would that be?"

Tom squirmed uncomfortably. "Things that, uh, happened in London."

"Do you mean things like trouble?"

Nodding, but still not looking up, Tom added, "And she wasn't there to meet us at the bus stop."

Sighing, Declan smiled reassuringly and knelt to face him. "Now listen, young man, your Mam has missed you terribly since you've been gone. A day hasn't passed when she hasn't spoken of you. The only reason she didn't come to London herself to collect you was that I, and to be fair now, your Grandmother, insisted that she stay at home. Your Mother may have got over her illness, but she's still not that strong...despite what she may say otherwise. Whatever she may or may not have heard about your time in London is irrelevant – all that matters to Erin, to your Mam, is that you are home now."

Smiling, Tom felt a surge of assurance welling up from within.

"And as for not meeting us," Declan continued, "you know there was no way of letting anyone know what time we – "

"Tom!" a piercing scream suddenly resounded from further up the lane. Startled, Tom and Declan turned to see his sister Niamh, her dark hair hanging loosely about her face, staring at him from over the low garden wall. "Mammy! Mammy!" they heard excitedly as she vanished, running back into the house. "Tom's here!"

Standing, Declan straightened his coat and smiled down at Tom. "Come on."

They managed only a few more yards before Erin appeared, bursting from the garden gate and racing towards them. In seconds, Tom was in her arms.

The turf fire crackled and spat gently, imparting a warm, welcoming radiance throughout the small living room. Cuddling next to Erin on their worn, threadbare settee, Tom had for the last hour, simply taken pleasure from her closeness. After the initial emotional and inevitably tearful reunion, they sat together, frequently talking but, more often than not, lost in their own thoughts. Sprawled on the floor, Tom's sisters played quietly together, an unusual enough occurrence in itself for him to notice. Only wee Cianán seemed indifferent to his return and constantly sought to escape to other parts of the house. Strangely to Tom's mind, it was Declan who invariably followed, watching over him or fetching him back. The knowing looks and grateful smiles Erin bestowed on Declan similarly didn't go unnoticed. Something had changed since he'd been away.

"Mam?" Tom said softly, when Declan was once more out of the room pursuing Cianán.

"Aye love?"

"Everything's going to be alright now, isn't it? I mean, you're not going to send me away again are you?"

Sitting up, Erin took Tom's hand in her own and smiled lovingly, staring into his eyes. She was thinner and paler than he remembered, but still beautiful.

"Do you trust me, Tommy?"

Tom nodded, albeit apprehensively.

"Then believe me when I say nothing will ever make me send you away again. It was only the thought of seeing you again that gave me the strength, the purpose, to get well. I love you more than I can ever say in words, and that will never change."

Tom felt his eyes growing moist and blinking rapidly, nestled into her again. For a while they remained silent, Erin slowly stroking his hair. From the kitchen came sounds of Declan playing some chase game with Cianán, and his brother's corresponding squeals of delight.

"They seem happy enough," Tom ventured, wondering at the change that seemed to have happened.

"Aye," Erin replied, in almost a whisper. "That they do."

Tom turned to face her. Opening his mouth, he hesitated for a moment before looking away.

"Say what's on your mind, Tom" she asked carefully.

"It's just...just that everyone seems happy."

"And shouldn't we be?"

"No, I didn't mean it like that. You seem happy...much more than I can ever remember. And somehow, it doesn't seem to feel like it's just due to me coming home. Or am I being daft?"

Erin smiled. "No Tom, you're not daft. I've always said you are a very astute – "

"What does that mean?"

"Clever...very perceptive." Sighing, she continued, "The truth is that I am happy...and yes, it's more than just you that's – "

"Is it Mr Kennedy? Are you going to marry him?" Tom asked suddenly.

Erin blushed visibly. "Stop interrupting," she scolded laxly, momentarily thrown. "And who's said anything about marriage?"

Undeterred, Tom pressed on. "Well, are you?"

Pausing for a moment, Erin then said, "There's much you need to know Tom, but now's not the time. Suffice to say, I'm very fond of Declan...as he is of me. We've become very close over the last few months...but whatever my feelings are on the matter, it's you and the girls, and wee Cianán, who are most important to me. You're 'Man of the House' now, Tom, and I'll not do anything that you'll disapprove of. Do you understand?"

Tom nodded gravely. "Aye Mam, I do. And I do like Mr Ken – Declan too."

Erin smiled, seemingly relieved. "And if, someday, we were to be married...how would you feel about that?"

At that moment Declan re-entered the living room, a squirming Cianán in his arms. Grinning, he gently lowered Tom's younger brother to the ground, who instantly ran, arms outstretched towards his mother.

"I don't know where your wee man gets his energy from, Erin." Declan said, still smiling. "He's fairly worn me out...what?"

Both Tom and Erin were beaming unreservedly at him.

"That would be fine, Mam," Tom said meaningfully, and genuinely happy.

"What's fine?" Declan asked carefully, slightly unnerved by their reactions.

"Declan, Tommy knows." Erin said quietly.

For a moment, Tom thought the School Master was going to faint; his face drained of colour and a look of panic seized him.

"Knows about...?"

"Just about us, sweetheart, nothing else." Erin said,

staring at him directly. "There's plenty of time for the rest later."

"Oh...Well, ah, right you are...that's grand then."

Tom was about to ask what she meant by the last comment when a strange voice said, "You're back then." A grinning Dónal O'Connor was leaning casually against the open living room door.

"Dónal!" Erin exclaimed. "Don't you ever knock!" As an afterthought she added suspiciously, "How long have you been there, listening?"

"Never a moment, Mrs Devlin. Your front door wasn't locked, and well, I didn't want to disturb, you know in case wee Cianán was in bed and all?"

"At quarter past five?"

"Is that all it is? It seems much later." Despite the obvious feigned innocence, Erin couldn't find it within herself to be cross with him...not today.

"I suppose you want to see Tommy?"

"If that's alright, now?"

Erin didn't need to look at her son to know he was fidgeting excitedly. Sighing, she surrendered to the inevitable. "Just for a while then, and no further than the bridge...it's getting dark already and it's school for you both tomorrow." In seconds the boys had fled the house.

"So," Dónal began causally, as they sauntered down the twilight lane, "your Mam's going to marry Mr Kennedy then?"

Stunned, Tom looked at him aghast. "But you said you didn't hear anything?"

"Well, I may've heard a little."

"Dónal," Tom said seriously, "you mustn't say anything. Mam'll go mad."

Grinning, Dónal laid a companionable arm around Tom's shoulders. "Now, would I do such a thing?"

EPILOGUE

"Shut that bloody door!" a grizzled shipyard labourer growled from his seat near to the canteen's entrance. A few yards away a powerfully built man stood in the open doorway. Dressed in dark, oil stained working clothes and black overcoat, he scanned intently the room's occupants. A raw, cutting wind whipped in behind him, causing many other patrons to similarly curse angrily. Scowling, he ignored them, and let his gaze sweep coolly from one seated man to the next. You didn't get to become a Harland and Wolff dockyard foreman by being popular. Having already searched unsuccessfully the two other canteens within the shipyard's huge red-brick, three storey office building, the foreman's mood was as frosty as the weather.

The canteen was extensive and being a lunchtime, as usual, very busy and noisy. From behind he felt a none too gentle shove, as more men sought to enter. Time was precious and work hard at the massive shipyard on Belfast's Queen's Island, and no one wanted to waste a moment of what scant breaks they were allowed. Stepping inside, a stream of new yard labourers entered, the last closing the door, cutting out both the bitter cold and the continual, almost deafening noise of riveting hammers, striking relentlessly in the distance.

Slowly meandering between the numerous tables and seated workers, the foreman finally spotted the target of his anger.

"Oi!" he roared, striding across the room to stand before a large, dark haired man, sitting alone at a corner table. "What the bloody 'ell are you playing at? You were due back twenty minutes ago."

The man turned his head to slowly regard the irate foreman, pale blue eyes focussing on him expressionlessly. A veteran yard employee of twenty years, and not easily intimidated, the intensity of the stare, nonetheless, began to make the foreman uncomfortable.

"Just get back to the joiners shop, will you," he said gruffly, forcing himself to look away. "I'll not cover for you again."

Inhaling deeply, the seated man said nothing.

"And if you're not there in five minutes, you can sling your hook," the foreman added irritably. "There's plenty others that'd like your job." Without waiting for a reply, he turned on his heels and headed for the exit.

With a half-smile, the silent worker turned back to the table, an untouched cheese roll and cold mug of tea still lying where a serving girl had placed them. His gaze fell once more on a sealed, white envelope held loosely in his left hand. The smile faded.

For over a minute he continued to stare intently at the envelope, its hand written address clearly visible. Outwardly he remained calm and composed, but from within intense feelings of remorse raged, threatening to overwhelm him. With deliberate slowness his large, calloused hand closed over the envelope, crushing it into a ball. Almost immediately he seemed to regret the action, laying the envelope on the table and smoothing it out, cursing inwardly as grease and grime from his hands smeared the address. Although still legible, the address was now decidedly grubby, and angrily the man stood, tossing the envelope on the floor. He was half way to the door when a shrill voice called for him to stop. Instinctively he turned round. A young waitress was standing beside his table, holding the letter aloft and gesturing.

"Sir, you dropped this," she shouted, trying to make herself heard.

Glaring at her angrily above the heads of his fellow workers, he hesitated, uncertain what to say.

"Bin it," Sean Devlin growled finally and, without looking back, stomped out of the building.

Staring after him, the girl faltered; the dim of the canteen had drowned out his softly spoken words.

What was it he'd said? Anxiously, she glanced at the envelope; it was stamped and addressed, clearly readable despite the obvious smudges:

'Mrs Erin Devlin
Gaddy Duff House
Cairn Lane
Ballyfinan
Donegal'

Unsure, she wavered, wondering what to do.

"Can we 'ave some service 'ere, love?" a gruff voice called from a few feet away. At an adjacent table, a group of middle-aged men were motioning meaningfully with empty mugs.

"Aye, what'd you like?" she replied, smiling sweetly and stepping up to them. Distracted, she inadvertently slipped the envelope into her apron pocket...she'd decide what to do about it later...

PAUL DOHERTY

CANDLE IN THE WINDOW

DEVLIN FAMILY TREE (C. 1932)

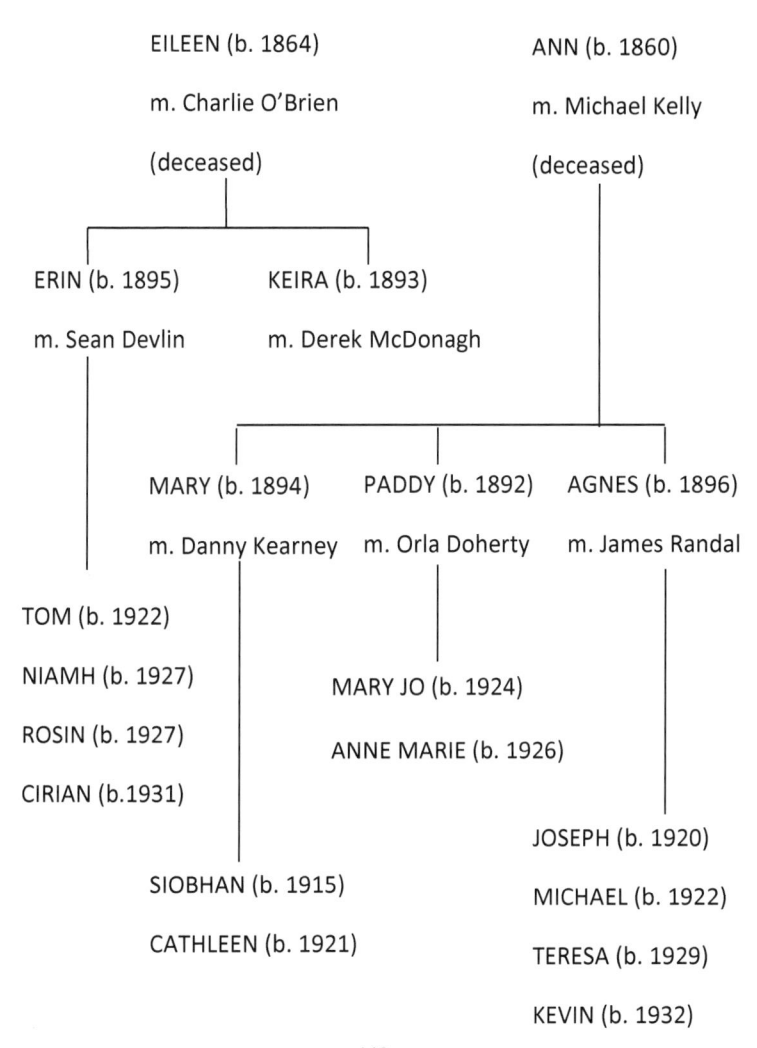

EILEEN (b. 1864)
m. Charlie O'Brien
(deceased)

ANN (b. 1860)
m. Michael Kelly
(deceased)

ERIN (b. 1895)
m. Sean Devlin

KEIRA (b. 1893)
m. Derek McDonagh

MARY (b. 1894)
m. Danny Kearney

PADDY (b. 1892)
m. Orla Doherty

AGNES (b. 1896)
m. James Randal

TOM (b. 1922)

NIAMH (b. 1927)

ROSIN (b. 1927)

CIRIAN (b.1931)

MARY JO (b. 1924)

ANNE MARIE (b. 1926)

JOSEPH (b. 1920)

MICHAEL (b. 1922)

SIOBHAN (b. 1915)

CATHLEEN (b. 1921)

TERESA (b. 1929)

KEVIN (b. 1932)

Printed in Great Britain
by Amazon.co.uk, Ltd.,
Marston Gate.